request the honour of your presence
as

Cleo Slade & Jude Mescal

and

Kate Hardie & Aidan Crawford
enter a new life together.

Please share in their joy as they discover
the wonders and surprises of marriage.

Diana Hamilton is a true romantic and fell in love with her husband at first sight. They still live in the fairy-tale Tudor house where they raised their three children. Now the idyll is shared with eight rescued cats and a puppy. But, despite an often chaotic lifestyle, ever since she learned to read and write Diana has had her nose in a book - either reading or writing one - and plans to go on doing that for a very long time to come.

Amanda Browning still lives in the Essex house where she was born. The third of four children - her sister being her twin - she enjoyed the rough and tumble of life with two brothers as much as she did reading books. Writing came naturally as an outlet for a fertile imagination. The love of books led her to a career in libraries, and being single allowed her to leap into writing for a living. Success is still something of a wonder, but allows her to indulge in hobbies as varied as embroidery and bird-watching.

SOLUTION: MARRIAGE

A SECURE MARRIAGE
by
Diana Hamilton

A PROMISE TO REPAY
by
Amanda Browning

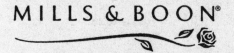

MILLS & BOON®

MILLS & BOON and MILLS & BOON with the Rose Device are registered trademarks of the publisher.
Harlequin Mills & Boon Limited,
Eton House, 18-24 Paradise Road, Richmond, Surrey, TW9 1SR

A SECURE MARRIAGE and *A PROMISE TO REPAY* were first published in separate single volumes by Mills & Boon Limited.
A SECURE MARRIAGE in 1989 and *A PROMISE TO REPAY* in 1991.

This edition printed 1997

A SECURE MARRIAGE © Diana Hamilton 1989
A PROMISE TO REPAY © Amanda Browning 1991

ISBN 0 263 80022 9

*Set in Times Roman 10 on 11.5 pt
05-9611-115427 C*

*Printed and bound in Great Britain by
Mackays of Chatham PLC, Chatham, Kent*

A SECURE MARRIAGE
Diana Hamilton

CHAPTER ONE

JUDE MESCAL walked through the office and Cleo thought, as she had thought so many times before: he moves like a cat, a mean, moody, magnificent cat.

She had heard other adjectives ascribed to the chief executive of Mescal Slade—cold, remote, terrifying. But one of the many advantages of being the personal assistant to the most powerful man in one of the City's most prestigious merchant banks was a certain degree of invulnerability. Jude Mescal didn't frighten her; nannies were rarely afraid of their charges, they knew them too well. And that was how Cleo sometimes regarded him—as a difficult but gifted charge.

He appeared to be in one of his thankfully rare irascible moods this morning, she decided with a serene half-smile as she noted the way his secretary, Dawn Goodall, cringed at her desk. The way the sedate middle-aged woman was lowering her head, hunching her shoulders and trying to look invisible made Cleo forget her own problems just for a moment.

Jude paused at the heavy, highly polished door to that inner sanctum, his office. He had failed to issue his customary cool good mornings, and the black bar produced by the frowning clench of brows that thundered down above the almost startling azure of his eyes and the forceful line of his nose attested to his ill temper even before the words, 'I'm seeing no one today, Cleo. Cancel all appointments. Understood?' were barked out in that husky, slightly gravelly voice that had the power to make even the chairman of the board look as though he felt like a five-year-old on his first day at school.

'Certainly, Mr Mescal.' Cleo dipped her smooth silver-blonde head, feeling the expertly cut wings of her hair brush against the perfect ivory of her pointed face, hiding the amused smile that hovered around the full, curved contours of her mouth. It was obviously going to be one of those days.

'And bring in the Research file on Chemical Holdings.' He slewed round quickly on the balls of his feet, the blue steel of his eyes turning Dawn Goodall to stone at her desk. 'And if anyone from First Union calls, I'm unavailable until the lunch appointment we arranged for tomorrow. Got that, Mrs Goodall?'

An agonised squawk was the nearest Dawn could get to an acknowledgement, but Cleo chimed in, ultra-sweet and smooth as silk, 'As rumour has it, First Union have been shopping around. Could tomorrow's lunch be the preliminary to a hostile bid?'

She hadn't been able to resist that dig, and for a moment the muscles of his wide shoulders tensed beneath the dark silk and mohair suiting, then his mouth quirked acidly. 'No one makes a bid, hostile or otherwise, for an efficient house. And Mescal Slade's one of the top rankers. Your job is safe, Miss Slade. For the moment. Bring that file through.'

In the silence following the thud as heavy mahogany closed on its frame Dawn let out a pent-up breath,

'The file's right here. I had it brought up from Research first thing. And rather you than me. I'd ask for a transfer to washroom attendant if I didn't need the money I get sitting here.' She scowled at a typing error and Cleo picked up the file, shaking her head,

'You're a damn good secretary, otherwise you wouldn't *be* sitting there,' she told the older woman.

'You've only been working for him for three months, you'll soon learn to ignore the iceberg image. He's a sweetie underneath.'

'If you say so.' Dawn didn't look convinced and Cleo turned away, going into her own small office to collect her notebook, the file from the Equity and Research department tucked under her arm.

Jude Mescal had a reputation for being an iceberg, a well-oiled automaton plugged into his work; remote as a god on top of Olympus, occasionally breathing fire and thunder down on the heads of lesser beings, but not often enough for it to become cause for justifiable complaint.

When she had been appointed as his personal assistant a year ago, with her degree in economics safely in her pocket and her inbred fascination with the world of merchant banking, she had known she could handle the Frozen Asset—as Jude Mescal was popularly and irreverently known. She had countered cool cynicism with a disregard that was in no way negated by her slightly amused smile, met his rare temper outbursts with total equanimity, did her job faultlessly and enjoyed the keen working of his incisive brain, even, latterly, anticipating the way his mind would jump. They made a good team and she was, quite possibly, the only one of Mescal Slade's employees who wasn't openly or secretly afraid of him.

He was standing at one of the windows, looking out, when she walked through. An undeniably attractive hunk, she thought inconsequentially as the cool, smoky grey of her eyes appraised the breadth of shoulder and back, the supple leanness of hip and length of leg. Wealthy, worldly, with a brain as quick and sharp as a rapier, he was one of the City's most eligible bachelors, never without a beautiful woman at his side when the occasion demanded such a decoration, and never—Cleo had noted with wry humour and a somewhat incomprehensible feeling of satisfaction—looking other than politely bored by the adoring postures and antics of the woman in question.

Rumour had it that Jude Mescal was wary, saw all women as mercenary gold-diggers, that he merely used them before they could use him. Idly, she wondered what it would feel like to be dated socially by Jude. Sheer hell, she decided, if boredom was the only emotion that looked out of those remarkable eyes. But if those eyes were to warm into sexual awareness, to intimacy...

'Sit down, Miss Slade.' The command was abrupt and he didn't turn. So Cleo sat, taking the chair angled across the huge leather-topped desk, smoothing the silver grey fabric of her designer suit over her knees. There it was again, 'Miss Slade' for the second time this morning. Annoyed by her dig about the prospect of a hostile takeover bid from the American bankers, First Union? Possibly. Cleo sucked in her breath. So the biter didn't relish the prospect of being bitten!

As if the intensity of her gaze had penetrated his mood of absorption at last, he turned, his eyes briefly flicking over her, moving from the top of her groomed silver-blonde head to the tips of her expensively shod toes.

'Right. To work. Let's see if the findings from Research coincide with my gut reaction about CH.'

He kept her hard at it for over an hour, probing for her reaction to the report, the complicated balance sheets spread out before them, until Dawn came through with the coffee-tray, putting it down on the desk and sidling out apprehensively when Jude eyed the offering as if it were an intrusion of an unspeakably vulgar kind. Although Cleo had tried to reassure the older woman, Dawn didn't appreciate that when he was engrossed in his work he was on another plane entirely; it was nothing personal.

And Cleo, pouring from the chased silver pot, said, 'It stinks,' not meaning the coffee, of course. 'I wouldn't advise a cat to buy into that little lot, let alone our valued Trade Union clients. Can't think why they showed interest in the first place.'

Jude grinned, his whole body appearing to relax as he took the cup she gave him, stirring the brew reflectively although he took neither sugar nor cream.

'Absolutely right.' He looked pleased with her, almost as if he were about to pat her on the head, as if he had been testing her in some way, finding out if her judgement of market trends was sound.

He needn't have gone to the trouble, she thought, her cool, liquid eyes betraying not the slightest hint of her inner amusement as she sipped her coffee. The idea of a literal pat on the head was funny enough in itself; Jude Mescal never descended to personal levels. He was too remote, too cool. And she made it her business to know her chosen profession backwards and inside out. She wasn't big-headed about it, it was simply in her, bred in the bone, so the idea that he might have been testing her had to be amusing. He shouldn't need to be told that a Slade, as well as a Mescal, had banking in the blood.

Although he now seemed marginally more relaxed, the bite was back in the deep husky voice as, his coffee-cup empty and the offer of a refill waved aside, he asked, 'How is John Slade?'

The question didn't surprise her too much; there had been close business connections for decades between the Slades and the Mescals. Since her parents' deaths ten years ago her Uncle John had run the largely family-owned finance house, Slade Securities, until a couple of years ago when he had been forced to retire after a near-fatal heart-attack.

'Not too good,' she replied sadly. Her uncle had become her guardian after the deaths of her parents, the only person to offer her any comfort at all during those earlier, lonely years. 'He has to take things very quietly. We've been warned he mustn't get excited or upset.'

'And your cousin Luke?' Jude's eyes, over steepled fingers, were cool, astute.

Cleo hunched one shoulder, 'Coping in his father's stead, as far as I know. Keeping his nose clean, I hope.'

It was fairly common knowledge that a spiteful piece in a gossip column concerning a brawl Luke had been involved in at some notorious West End nightclub had been responsible for his father's latest and most serious attack, and Cleo could sense the condemnation in Jude's eyes. Luke was brilliant in his way, but emotionally immature, and his father wasn't the only person who thought it was high time he faced up to the responsibilities he now carried. Running a successful finance house demanded more than a clever mind and financial bravado.

Thankfully, Jude let the subject drop, instructing, 'Have a word with Chef. I want tomorrow's lunch arrangements to be perfect. Nothing ostentatious, just the best. You know the drill. And have everything you can lay your hands on pertaining to First Union on my desk in half an hour. And make sure I'm not disturbed. Oh—and Cleo——' this as she was already on her way, file and notepad neatly gathered, thinking with a touch of satisfaction that he *did* have the jitters about the Americans 'have lunch with me. One-thirty?'

Her heart dropped to the soles of her feet and squirmed back up again because the mention of lunch, today, gave her a very sick feeling indeed. But her answering smile was tinged with polite regret, exactly right, as she told him, 'I'm sorry, Mr Mescal. But I've a prior appointment. I would break it if I could, but it's not possible.'

If he was disappointed, he didn't show it. But she was. If she had been free to lunch with him it would have meant that she didn't have that prior date with Robert Fenton.

Robert was the last man she wanted to see, but his telephoned invitation—more of a command, really—late last night had been dark with a threat she didn't want to speculate about too deeply. Not until all the cards were down. She couldn't understand why he wanted to see her and, knowing him, she had been worrying about it all morning. They had parted far from amicably, so why was he insisting they met?

She signed the routine letters and memos Dawn had left on her desk, made a couple of brief inter-office phone calls regarding the details of First Union which were to be sent up, pronto, then took the lift to the executive dining-suite, the back of her mind ticking over the list of precise instructions for Chef, the front of it occupied with regret over the missed opportunity to have lunch with Jude.

They lunched together fairly frequently, sometimes dined at his home in Belgravia, and she always enjoyed the occasions. He used them to put his mind in neutral, allowing it to digest some problem or other, a decision that had to be quickly and correctly reached—no margin for error. She used them to get to know him better, an exercise she found increasingly fascinating. It was essential, she told herself, to know what made one's boss tick. And during those quiet interludes she had gained a rare and, she firmly believed, unique insight, catching glimpses of his droll sense of humour, the underlying deep humanity of the man. And she found that liking for the man himself had been added to respect for his remarkable brain.

Latterly—although there was nothing personal in it, she always assured herself—she had found herself wondering why, at the age of thirty-six, he had never married, never come close to it as far as subtle probings had allowed her to gather. Because, subtle as they were, the steel shutters had always come down decisively whenever he had sensed he was in any danger at all of giving away more of himself than he intended to do.

And Cleo pushed through the swing door into the immaculate kitchens, feeling fraught because she knew full well that lunch with Robert Fenton would be no pleasure at all.

The restaurant Robert had suggested they use was pricey, exclusive and secluded, and she looked at him across the beige linen-covered table and wondered what she had ever seen in him.

At twenty-seven, three years her senior, he was superficially good-looking. His mid-brown hair was a little overlong but superbly cut, his clothes of good quality but a little on the flamboyant side. Compared with Jude Mescal he was a shadow, lacking the other man's strength and sheer presence. Cleo wondered why such a comparison should have come to her mind, and unwillingly remembered how when her cousin Luke had introduced her to Robert Fenton at a party two years ago she had thought he was the cat's whiskers.

Coming to the end of her final year at the LSE she had had little time for dates. But what time she'd had had been spent with Robert, his seemingly effortless charm helping her to relax.

With her Finals behind her at last and her sights fixed on joining Mescal Slade in whatever capacity offered, she had seen more of Robert. Until, her brief infatuation dying an inevitable death on her emergence from those long years of dedicated hard slog, she had at last begun to realise that Robert Fenton was not quite what he seemed. The image he chose to project was at variance with the man inside the skin. And with her eyes wide open at last she had discovered that she rather despised him.

Nothing was said until their order had been taken and then he told her, his hazel eyes sly, 'You're looking more beautiful than ever, Cleo, my love. Work obviously agrees with you. I must try it some time.'

Cleo didn't deign to reply; she was in no mood for facile flattery and she was no longer amused by the way Robert seemed able to afford the best things in life, even though he had no visible means of support. She was no longer the naïve, emotionally backward student who rarely lifted her nose from her books for long enough to look around and find out what people were like.

'Why was it so vitally important that we meet?' she demanded, echoing the words he had uttered over the phone last night, the tone he had used very different from her own cool, almost disinterested one.

He leaned back in his chair, looking at her with lazy eyes.

'You haven't acquired any finesse since I saw you last—when was it? About ten months ago?'

She ignored that. She hadn't needed finesse to tell him to go and take a running jump. And yes, it would have been about ten months ago. She had been Jude's PA for just over two months, still hardly able to believe her good fortune in hearing through the grapevine that the chief executive's then personal assistant would be leaving to

have the baby she and her husband had been longing
for. That she had landed the job out of a formidable
list of applicants had still been responsible for the warm
glow of achievement that had totally negated the blow
of discovering exactly how perfidious Robert Fenton was.
Not that she had still imagined herself in love with him
at that time; she had simply been annoyed by her own
lack of judgement.

Cleo drank a little of her dry martini, smiled as a waiter
placed her order of smoked prawns in front of her, then
raised an impatient eyebrow in Fenton's direction. She
was in no mood for games.

'It's brass tacks time, is it?' He read her mood. 'I
need money, my love. Rather a large amount of the stuff.
And you are going to have to divvi up.'

She might have known! His primary interest in her,
she had discovered, had always been financial. But the
wealthy were always prey to the avarice of others—Aunt
Grace had drilled that into her often enough!

'Like hell I am! And if that's all you wanted to say
to me, I'm leaving,' she said softly, a distant smile hovering around her mouth because she wasn't worried, not
then. She reached for her bag, not willing to waste one
more second on this importuning louse.

But he caught her wrist across the table, his fingers
hurting. To force him to release her would cause the type
of public scene she abhorred, so she subsided, fury
tightening her mouth.

'Very wise.' Fenton's voice was suave as he gradually
released his hold on her. 'Eat your nice prawns, duckie—
this might take some time. You see, it concerns that pillar
of respectable society, your good Uncle John. Though
he's not so good, healthwise, I hear.'

He tossed back his whisky and soda and clicked his
fingers at the hovering wine-waiter. Cleo felt ill, and she

was worried now, but there was no emotion in her voice as she interrupted his conversation with the waiter.

'There's no way my uncle can be any concern of yours.'

'No?' He tipped his head as he finished ordering. 'But I am concerned. And he will be concerned about you—about the state of your morals, in particular. Such a highly moral man, your guardian, I hear. And your Aunt Grace is also a pious lady, very concerned with the family image, with some justification. A twenty-room mansion in Herts and a bank account that must be touching the two million mark is an image even I would try to live up to.'

'Will you get to the point?' Cleo snapped, thrown off balance, thrusting aside her untouched starter as her main course of sole appeared.

'The point? Ah—yes.' He cut into his veal, smiling. 'Adverse reports on your morals would not faze Aunt Grace. Annoy her, of course, but it would be something she could handle—especially if the dirt could be swept under the Aubusson. But dear old Uncle John—now there's an entirely different ball game. Two massive heart-attacks already——' He shook his head in a parody of sorrow. 'If he heard what I could tell him—through the gutter press—then the shock could very well finish the old boy off. Especially when we consider that the second attack followed right on the heels of that naughty little piece about his son Luke which appeared in the Dezzi Phipps column. And we wouldn't want that, would we, my love?'

She wanted to hit him. Sitting at the same table with him made her insides heave. His tactics were blackmail, but he had no leverage, and that puzzled her even more than it worried her.

But that state of affairs didn't last long after she hissed, her eyes darkening with disgust, 'You're spouting hot air and garbage! You can have nothing to say about my morals, either way. We dated a few times——'

'Rather more than a few.' The look he gave her made her skin crawl. 'And I think my version of the events that led to our break-up might make more titillating hearing than yours. I'd put it about like so: a poor but honest young man—me——' he dipped his head as she snorted violently, 'falling in love with a beautiful young student. You. A touch promiscuous, but our hero overlooked that—being head over heels, you understand. And then the problems—beautiful student had such expensive tastes, having been brought up in the lap of luxury. This forces our hero to take risks with the small amount he does have—it being common knowledge that no one gets to first base with the lady without vast expenditure. But she has promised to marry him, so he believes the risks he's taking worth it. So he gets deeper into debt: gambling, loan sharks, you name it. All to keep the lady happy. He has to give her a good time because if he doesn't she will find someone who will.'

Cleo's eyes narrowed and she sucked in a deep breath. The man was a lunatic. 'If anyone who knew me, least of all Uncle John, would believe that trash, they'd believe day was night.' She had listened to enough verbal slime to sever her connection with her inbred cool caution, but he quelled the imminent storm with five well chosen words.

'The Red Lion Hotel, Goldingstan.'

Then he relaxed back in his chair, his meal finished, raising an eyebrow at the congealing, untouched food on her plate.

'Not hungry? Pity. However, my dislike of waste is tempered by the knowledge that you are going to pay the bill. You can afford it. I can't. Now, where were we?'

'You were trying to blackmail me,' she clipped, her voice controlled. But she was shaking inside and there was no way she could disguise the disgust on her face, the loathing in her huge dark eyes. 'You make me sick!'

'Now that *is* sad.' His voice was heavy with sarcasm and the smile that curved his lips as he refilled his wine-glass made her shudder. 'But I think I'm going to be able to live with that, especially as you are going to settle my debts and get a couple of rather threatening heavies off my back. Oh, and by the way,' his voice was almost a purr as she opened her mouth to categorically deny her intention of doing any such thing, 'I kept the hotel receipt. Mr and Mrs Robert Fenton, room four, on the night of the eleventh of June last year. And in case there's any doubt, I'm sure Mrs Galway—you remember her— the hotelier's wife who was so obliging and told us she never forgot a guest, will be able and willing to identify you as the said Mrs Robert Fenton. She might even be able to recall that we couldn't drag ourselves out of that room until half-eleven the following morning!'

Still smiling his odious smile, he lit a cigarette and blew a cloud of smoke across the table. 'Not that it will come to asking Mrs Galway to identify you. You've no intention of being awkward about this, have you, my love?'

'Don't call me that!' she rasped, her voice hoarse, as though her throat had turned to sandpaper. She was more disgusted by his repeated use of the endearment than anything else. It was a crazy reaction, but that was the way it was, and she wanted to get away from him, get the whole distasteful episode over, so she asked stonily, 'How much?'

'Twenty-five thousand.'

She didn't believe it at first. But she saw from his face that he was serious, deadly serious, and she laughed, without humour.

'You're mad! Where would I get that kind of money? And even if I could, do you honestly think I'd believe keeping the Red Lion incident secret worth that amount?'

Leaning forward across the table he called her bluff, 'I think you'd consider it worth it at twice the price. Can you imagine dear old John's face if he read a headline that might go something like: *"Slade Securities Chief's Niece Involved in Debt Scandal"* With an opening paragraph that could say something like: *"Slade heiress's lover threatened with knee-capping by loan shark's heavy mob. 'I'm in real trouble. I only got in debt for her sake,' explained Robert Fenton, Cleo Slade's former lover. 'She's used to the best and she said she loved me. But she won't lift a finger to help now I'm in this mess. I'm devastated,' added the distraught Mr Fenton."* Or something similar.' He stubbed his cigarette out and Cleo felt the trap close more tightly around her, squeezing until she thought she would die of it.

Yes, she could just imagine what that kind of publicity could do to Uncle John—the piece about Luke had been mild in comparison and that, as almost everyone believed, had brought on that second, near fatal heart-attack. And it wouldn't exactly ease her career along, either, but that was a minor consideration beside the damage it could do to her uncle.

Fenton added, 'What's a mere twenty-five thousand to a girl who will inherit her father's share of the Slade Millions in—what will it be? Around a year's time? A drop in the proverbial ocean!'

Her mouth tightened. 'Can the heavy mob—in which, incidentally, I don't believe—wait a year? I don't inherit until I'm twenty-five, as you very well know.'

'Or until you marry,' he put in slyly. 'I did my homework.'

'And are you going to suggest I marry you to get my hands on the money?' She wouldn't put it past him, and there was an edge of hysteria in her voice and it sharpened his eyes.

'I'm not that stupid. Should you marry before you reach your twenty-fifth birthday, then, in order to obtain an early release of your considerable inheritance, your guardians, your so upright and proper uncle and aunt, would have to unreservedly approve your choice of husband. And they wouldn't have to dig very deep to realise that no way could they approve of yours truly. No,' he smiled oilily, 'I've always known that wasn't on the cards, although at one time I had hopes of keeping you sweet until you were twenty-five and free, not only to inherit, but to marry whomsoever you pleased. But the Fenton charm didn't blind you for long enough. I did ask you to marry me, though, remember? I was beginning to realise you weren't as starry-eyed as you had been, so I suggested we marry and, in true romantic tradition, keep it a secret from those stuffy relatives of yours. I thought that might have set the little female heart pounding away again. However,' he sighed theatrically, 'that wasn't to be, so I've given the matter much thought and decided to cut my losses and settle for twenty-five thou. You can raise it somehow—with your collateral.'

He beckoned for the bill and stood up, pushing the folded slip of paper between the fingers of her clenched hand.

'See you, my love. And thanks for the lunch. I'll keep in touch. Oh, and by the way, I'll want my little pressie in four weeks' time. Cash, if you please.'

Cleo was in her office early the following morning. The thickly carpeted corridors had been silent as she'd walked through the hushed building with the uniformed commissionaire's cheery words echoing hollowly in her head. 'Good morning, Miss Slade. A real touch of spring in the air today!'

The early morning City streets might be awash with warm April sunlight, but winter was in her heart; icy, steel-edged winter.

Her features taut and expressionless, she hung her coat in her cupboard and smoothed the long, narrow lapels of the deep mulberry-coloured Escada suit she was wearing. Expertly applied make-up went some way to hide the pallor induced by a sleepless night and the eyes that met her in the mirror on the back of the cupboard door were sharp with determination.

She had no way of knowing if Robert Fenton was in debt, was being hounded for repayment. It didn't really signify. His threat to her uncle, via herself, was real enough. That kind of heavy blackmail, the threat of the worst kind of publicity in one of the seamier tabloids, would finish the already frail old man. She had no doubt that Fenton could get the slimiest publicity possible. He knew some very dubious characters in the newspaper world, men who didn't care what was printed, or whose lives were shattered, so long as it sold papers.

There was no way she could raise that kind of money without approaching the trustees. And they would, quite rightly, want to know details. And that kind of detail she couldn't give.

She sat at her desk, her spine upright, staring at the polished surface. For the first time ever she regretted the restrictions her father had placed on her massive inheritance.

Throughout her life she had never wanted for material things. Her allowance had been on the generous side, but sensible, and her life with her parents and, later, with her uncle and aunt, had been discreetly luxurious—until, needing to be in London while she was studying, she had persuaded the trustees to buy the small terraced house in Bow where she still lived. She had nothing personal to sell that would raise anything like the amount Fenton was demanding. But unless she was able to raise it, in four weeks' time, Fenton would see those vile lies printed. They had all seen the damage such malicious tittle-tattle had done when Luke's exploits had been snidely publicised and the specialist had warned that the frail old man be treated with kid gloves, that upsets and worry had to be avoided at all costs. So she had to raise that money! She couldn't have his death on her conscience!

Hearing the snick of the outer office door as it opened, she held her breath. It was Jude, as she had hoped, early, well before Dawn was due to arrive. And now had to be the best time to speak to him.

Her breath caught flutteringly in her throat and her stomach wriggled about uncomfortably as she watched him walk past her partly open door to his own office, the inevitable briefcase in his hand. The immaculately cut dark suit he wore clothed his body with easy elegance, and the crisp whiteness of his shirt contrasted sharply with his dark blue tie, with the natural darkness of his skin tones. He always looked as if he had a tan.

Quelling an unwanted spasm of nerves—apprehension had been talked out of her plans during the long, lonely hours of last night, hadn't it?—she rose to her feet and squared her slim shoulders. She had wrestled with the problem Fenton had presented her with and as far as she could see there was only one viable solution— and she had looked long and hard for alternatives. So there was no point in giving way to the jitters now.

The man could always say no. He had said no to business deals before now. But only ever after giving the matter full consideration, after a careful weighing of the pros and cons. He surely wouldn't turn her business proposition down out of hand.

Drawing in a long breath, she tapped lightly on his door and walked in, her features severe, cool, her heart not picking up speed by the smallest fraction. She had learned the trick of unemotionalism in a hard school. She met the vivid azure of his eyes, the small, courteously pleasant smile as he acknowledged her brief greeting. And before he could launch into plans for the day's work, or return his attention to the papers he had already extricated from the black leather briefcase, Cleo dragged a quick breath in through her nostrils and asked, 'Mr Mescal—will you marry me?'

CHAPTER TWO

FOR an agonisingly drawn-out moment Cleo thought he was going to refuse her without giving the matter any consideration at all. His body grew still, very still, before a ghost of a smile flickered briefly around the hard male mouth and was then erased, as if it had never been, as if she had dreamed it.

And then, as he still remained silent, her spine stiffened with impatience beneath the smooth, expensive fabric of her suit. Was he going to say nothing, nothing at all? What if he, like the gentleman he was, ignored her question? What if he treated her startling proposal of marriage as a regrettable mental aberration on her part, deeming it kinder, more polite, to pretend the words had never been said?

Well, in that case, she would just have to repeat her offer, she decided with grim stoicism. Against all her expectations she felt perspiration slick the palms of her hands and, slowly, she ran the tip of her tongue over lips gone suddenly dry. At that, as if her physical unease had recalled him, made some impact on his mind, he gestured her to a chair with an almost imperceptible movement of his hand. And Cleo sat, glad to, because for some reason her knees felt as if they were about to give way.

Silently, her eyes too big for her face, she willed him to answer, to say he'd give it some thought, at least. His agreement was the only solution she could see to a grotesque problem, and she needed it. For her uncle's sake she needed it.

But now, without knowing how or why it should have crept in, there was an indefinable something going on inside her head that warned her that his acquiescence was important on an entirely different plane. Whatever it was, she couldn't understand it, although she felt she should, and, whatever it was, it made her feel light-headed, breathless.

'And?' he said at last, his tone prompting, his eyes holding hers from beneath thick, dark lashes.

Thrown off balance by the softly put question, the probing she hadn't expected, not in that nebulous form, her smoky eyes widened again, filling her face, while a faint flush of colour stole into her pale skin. 'And?' she repeated, parrot-fashion, her mouth dry.

'And why the unexpected interest?' Jude supplied. 'We've worked together for twelve months, very amicably, I do agree, but I've yet to see signs of a deathless passion from you. Neither,' his voice continued, polite in inflexion, perfectly level, 'do you strike me as being the type of woman who would be desperate for the married status—at any price.'

He was wrong there, she was desperate, but not for the reasons he imagined. Marriage, for the sake of it, had never appealed. She had learned how to be sufficient unto herself, not to need emotional props. But marriage to someone as undeniably suitable as Jude Mescal would be in the eyes of her guardians was the only answer to her awful problem.

But now, at least, he was asking her to give logical answers to her own seemingly illogical question, and she could handle that. For a moment back there she had felt herself to be losing her grip on the tangible, admitting the intangible—that nebulous thread—into her mind so that a union with this man had, for a strange, disjointed moment, seemed important on an entirely unexpected level.

And that particular reaction, she told herself firmly, was due to the momentary panic of nerves. She hadn't expected to feel nervous—so nervous, at least.

She began to relax, feeling the tension drain out of the tautly held muscles of her back and neck. She was completely at home with the unequivocal logic of facts, and she was fully prepared to present him with those facts—as far as she deemed entirely necessary.

She clasped her hands loosely together in her lap and her eyes were cool and frank as she told him, 'Under the terms of my father's will I don't come into my inheritance for another year, and I need a rather large amount now. However, if I marry before then, provided my uncle and aunt approve my choice, my father's money automatically passes to me. They would approve of you, and if we married within, say, three weeks, I could control my inheritance, use the money I need. It wouldn't be a great deal,' she assured him, in case he thought she would spend the lot and then expect him to keep her in luxury. 'Not when seen in context. My future inheritance is popularly known as the Slade Millions.'

He dipped his head in brief acknowledgement of the facts that were, after all, common knowledge in City circles, and she knew the facts had been concisely put, the reason for her proposal made clear enough. She was devastated when he chuckled, a rare occurrence indeed for the Frozen Asset!

His incredible azure eyes were irradiated with amusement and Cleo, looking at him, felt her skin crawl with hot colour. To ask him to marry her had been humiliating enough in itself, without him adding to her discomfort by treating the whole thing as a joke!

'Wouldn't it have been simpler to arrange a loan?'
The amusement lingered for a while, sparkling in his
eyes, then faded, leaving his face as it ever was—remote,
cool, intelligent. 'Embarking on the commitment of
marriage seems rather drastic. Couldn't you approach
the trustees of your late father's estate? Come to that,'
his wide shoulders lifted fractionally, 'I could lend you
what you need. Your credit rating is excellent,' he added
drily.

He sat down then, taking his chair on the opposite
side of the huge desk, his clever eyes narrowed over
steepled fingers as he watched her. 'How much? And
what for?'

But Cleo shook her head decisively, the shimmering
silver fall of her hair swinging across her face. 'I'd prefer
not to borrow.' She didn't want anyone to know why
she needed the money, and anyone prepared to lend that
amount would certainly demand to know where the
money was going! And her eyes met his in unconscious,
mute appeal and he asked her softly, 'Are you in some
kind of trouble?'

Again the sharp negating swing of her head; the mess
she was in was of her own making, she would extricate
herself from it in her own way, without involving anyone
else in the sordid details. She had made a mistake, a bad
one, when she had allowed herself to be infatuated by
Robert Fenton's silver tongue, his easy charm. But she
had learned her lesson and was about to pay dearly for
it. And sitting here, mutely supplicant under the remote
eyes of the man who was known never to suffer involvement—except with his work—suddenly became
unbearable.

She should never have dreamed up the idea, and clearly
she was getting nowhere. The slow burn of anger started
inside her, making her hate herself for the foolishness

that had brought her to this totally humiliating position, hate Robert Fenton for the slimy, blackmailing creep he was, hate Jude Mescal for taking her vulnerability and examining it like something curious on the end of a pin.

She started to scramble to her feet, wanting nothing more than to get away from those coolly analytical eyes, but his voice stopped her.

'I can gather, roughly, what you would stand to gain from marriage. But it involves two. So can you tell me what I would get out of a situation I've spent my adult life steering well clear of?'

The slightly sardonic lift of heavy black brows, the look of superiority and distance the gesture imparted to his unforgettably strong features boosted the slow fuse of her anger, creating an explosion that errupted in scalding words.

'Rumour has it that you've never committed yourself to a woman because you're afraid of tying yourself to a gold-digger,' she snapped insultingly. 'If you married me you'd know I hadn't married you for your money. I've more than enough of my own—or will have! And I inherit a sizeable block of Slade Securities shares, which I could be persuaded to turn over to you—and I'd have thought that might interest you more than somewhat! And if that isn't enough——'

'Enough to be going along with,' he interrupted, and she was glad of that, because she'd run out of reasons, and all she had left was hot air and bluster.

The shares had been her best card; if he married her and she gave him her voting rights he would have the majority shareholding, and that, surely, would be tempting to a man such as he.

She held her breath, her heart pumping, sensing she had his interest now, and he commented, rising to his feet, almost smiling,

'May I have time to give your——' he hesitated, but only fractionally '——your delightful offer the consideration it merits?' And, taking the carefully blank expression on her face for acquiescence, he glanced at his watch and returned his attention to the papers strewn on his desk.

'I shall be away over the weekend and in Brussels on Monday. So shall we have dinner on Monday evening?' His eyes drifted over her slender height as she pushed herself to her feet, making her feel uncharacteristically gauche, dry-mouthed and tongue-tied. 'I'll send Thornwood to pick you up at seven-thirty.'

Cleo left her car on the sweep of gravel at the front of Slade House and carried her overnight grip towards the impressive Edwardian building. She rarely visited now, but she needed to see her uncle and aunt, to reassure herself that she was doing the right thing in not allowing herself to follow her instincts and tell Fenton to go ahead and do his worst because she wouldn't give him one of her nail parings!

She hadn't phoned to let them know to expect her; her mind had been edgy, jumpily occupied with trying to work out how Jude's 'considerations' would take him, which way he would jump. She had learned to anticipate the way his mind worked when it came to complicated dealings in his capacity of chief executive of one of the most successful merchant banks in the City. But this was different, very different. And the more she had tried to extend her own mind, to tune it in to his, the more confused and uncertain she had become. She couldn't get him out of her mind.

When the butler opened the door she wiped the frown from her brow, her voice level and cool,

'Good afternoon, Simmons. Is my aunt in?' then walked past him into the huge hall. 'They're not expecting me, I'm afraid.' She surrendered her camel trenchcoat, her cream kid gloves, the overnight grip, and the butler's expressionless mask gave nothing away; not surprise, certainly not pleasure. No one, not even the servants in this huge luxurious house, was spendthrift when it came to displaying emotions, or in having emotions, quite probably.

'Mrs Slade is in the drawing-room, miss. I'll see your things are taken to your room.'

'Thank you, Simmons.' She turned away, her graceful stride taking her over the polished parquet to find her aunt.

Ten years ago she had been fourteen years old, and she had come to this house because her parents had been drowned when their yacht had capsized in a freak storm off the Cornish coast. She had looked, then, for affection, warmth—for mere interest, even—but had found nothing save a cool concern for her material well-being. She had been luxuriously housed, fed the right food, sent to the right schools, but that was as far as the caring had gone. She had never found the warmth of affection she had so desperately craved in those first terrible years of bereavement. And as she had grown older she had learned to do without it.

Only her uncle had ever taken any interest in her. He had seen her as a person, with needs of her own, fears and hopes of her own, rather than just another responsibility. He was fond of her, she knew, in his own abstracted way. But he had been more often in his office than at home and she had seen little of him. And when he had gone into semi-retirement, due to illness, she, of course, had been living and studying in London, visiting rarely.

Grace Slade was in the drawing-room, a tea-tray on a low table beside her. She was a spare, formidably handsome woman and it was a beautiful room, perfect. But then the Slades demanded perfection in everything, even in people. It was hard to live up to such standards.

'This is a surprise.' Her aunt's voice was coloured with asperity, just a tinge of it, and Cleo sighed. She should have phoned, would have done, but her mind had been in a tangle.

She sank down on a Regency sofa which was upholstered in oyster brocade and said, 'I'd like to stay overnight, drive back tomorrow after lunch.' She was stating her right to be here, using cool dignity. This house was her home, her aunt one of her guardians, for another year. Inhibiting, but a fact. And Grace had taught her by example how to stand on her dignity. Yes, her aunt had taught her well. But sometimes Cleo wondered if the sterility of dignity, of the austere self-command she had learned to wear like a cloak, made her lacking as a human being. Wondered if the suppression of deep emotion was a loss, turning her into a machine, programmed to display good manners, breeding and dedication to the duty which was the good standing of the family.

But now, looking at her aunt—poised, elegant, in perfect control—Cleo decided that she had probably chosen the right path when she had sought to please by emulation, all those years ago, when gaining the approval of her aunt, and possibly her affection, had been something she had striven for. And her single foray into the realm of emotion had been a disaster, landing her in her present sordid predicament. It would never happen again.

'Shall I ring for fresh tea?' Grace wanted to know, her eyes dispassionate. 'You look tired after your drive.'

As well she might, Cleo thought drily, but it had nothing to do with the drive. Two sleepless nights in a row, the image of Jude Mescal tormenting her mind, would hardly make her look sparkling. But she said, 'No tea for me, thank you, Aunt. How is Uncle?'

'As well as can be expected. He frets about the business, which doesn't help. As I've repeatedly told him, it's in Luke's hands now.'

They talked for a while, their conversation polite but wary, until Cleo excused herself and went to find her uncle. He was in the library, the most comfortable room in the house in Cleo's opinion, sitting on the leather chesterfield, a photograph album open on his knees.

'The older I get the more I tend to peer into the past,' was his greeting. Cleo wasn't surprised; Uncle John often came out with such statements, seemingly apropos of nothing, it was one of the humanising things about him that had made her fonder of him than she was of either her aunt or her cousin Luke. 'No one told me you were coming.' His mild eyes questioned her and she sat down beside him, sinking into the squashy leather.

'No one knew. I just arrived—it was a spur of the moment decision.'

'Ah.' He looked vaguely puzzled, as if he couldn't comprehend a decision being taken, just like that. Years of living with Aunt Grace had made him very careful, very precise, leaving nothing to chance.

'And how are you?' Her smoky eyes searched his face. He looked older, much more frail than when she'd seen him last a couple of months ago.

'I'm as well as can be expected, so they tell me.' A fleeting look of terror, so brief it almost wasn't there— because the occupants of Slade House didn't betray emotion, even fear of dying—flickered over his gaunt features, and Cleo, understanding, changed the subject.

'Is Luke expected home this weekend?' She hoped not. Her cousin was pompous and stiff, he always had been, even when he'd been seventeen to her fourteen and she'd tried to make friends with the only young person in a household that had seemed to consist of elderly, rigid machines. But he had been pompous even then, stand-offish, making it clear he didn't like her, considered her addition to the household an invasion of privacy. Luke's attitude had been primarily responsible for her decision to seek work elsewhere, rather than join the family firm of Slade Securities.

'No, he's tied up with some meetings. Look——' a finger stabbed at the open album on his knee, as if he found the subject of Luke too difficult to talk about, and Cleo wondered if she'd touched a sore spot, re-minding John Slade of the spiteful piece in that gossip column that had pointed out the other side of his son's character—the reckless, belligerent, hidden side. 'That's your father and me. A village cricket match well over fifty years ago. I was sixteen, your father almost eighteen.'

Cleo peered at the faded print; two youths in white flannels, holding bats, looking impossibly solemn. She grinned, recognising the jut of her father's jaw, an early indication of the stubborn, determined character he would develop in later life. And John Slade, mistaking the reason for her amusement, shook his head,

'It's probably impossible for you to imagine us as ever being young men, or children. But we were, my goodness we were! We were both high-spirited, a little arrogant, and we knew where we were going—or thought we did.' His shoulders slumped a little, his eyes looking into the distant past. 'I'm afraid we both left it late to marry, to get a family, your father even later than I—so you young things must think we were born old! But I can assure you, that wasn't the case!'

'You must still miss him,' Cleo probed gently. At times she still keenly felt the loss of both her parents, and perhaps that was something that might draw her closer to her uncle. For the first time in her adult life she felt she needed to be close to someone, and her uncle touched her hand, just briefly, as if such a demonstration of affection embarrassed him. But it was enough, and his fingers still touched the surface of the photograph, as if he could recapture lost days, lost youth, through the sense of touch—as if he were holding on to a past that was precious because it had held promises, promises which had never been truly fulfilled, she now divined with sudden insight.

And then, in that moment, sitting beside the man whose years were all behind him, she knew she couldn't bring the bitterness of family shame to darken his declining years or, maybe and quite possibly, deprive him of those few remaining years.

Her decision to pay Fenton what he demanded had been the right one. And the only way she could gain access to her inheritance straight away was through marriage. So her proposal to Jude had been the only way out.

And then, out of nowhere, the appalled thought came: What *have* I done? She had asked for the Frozen Asset's hand in marriage, that was what she had done! And, the right, the only thing to do, suddenly became terrifying. What his final decision would be, heaven only knew. He'd probably fire her and suggest she spend the next six months in a rest home!

She wanted to give way to the unprecedented feeling of hysteria she could feel building up inside her—to shriek and scream and hurl things around the room to relieve the pressure inside her head. Instead, she asked her uncle if he'd like her to go with him for a short walk in the garden—the weather was remarkably good for the time of year, wasn't it?

She had been jittery all day, Jude on her mind making her unable to concentrate. She kept thinking of the enormity of what she had done in asking him to marry her, and she wanted to buy a plane ticket to the other side of the world.

She had thought that marriage to such a suitable man would be the answer to her problems. Her intellect had assured her that she would not enter such a business arrangement—which was basically what the marriage would be—empty-handed, far from it, and she was presentable, she wouldn't be a wife he need be ashamed of. And as far as she knew there wasn't a lovely lady in the background—not one he had considered marrying, at least. He was reputedly wary where the state of matrimony was concerned.

There would probably be women for him in the future; she didn't doubt that he possessed his full measure of male sexuality. But provided he was discreet she would be tolerant, understanding. And the hot little pain that made itself felt at the direction her thoughts were taking was solely due to her state of apprehension over the outcome of his 'considerations'—surely it was?

However, what had seemed such a neatly feasible idea began to look like a crass, idiotic blunder. Crasser and more idiotic as the minutes ticked away, their growing total an insupportable weight as Monday morning turned into Monday afternoon...

Unable to bear the suddenly stifling confines of her office a moment longer, she left early, taking the tube back to Bow and entering her own small terraced house, looking for the relief it always gave her.

Her home was her sanctuary, inviolate, the furnishings, the décor, echoing her own cool yet gentle character. It had provided a haven during her years of study and, later, a place to unwind in, to potter around wearing old jeans and shirts after the concentrated mind-stretching that being at Jude Mescal's beck and call all day often entailed.

But this afternoon tranquillity had been forced through the walls as her thoughts, despite all her best efforts, centred on the outcome of her dinner engagement with him later this evening.

Catching sight of herself in the mirror in the hallway, she stopped in her tracks. It was like looking at a crazy woman! Her grey eyes looked haunted, half wild with worry, and far too large for her pale, pointed face.

One look at such a distraught creature, she decided, would be enough to put any man off the idea of marriage—let alone Jude Mescal, who was definitely choosier than most.

And if she were to arrive at his house looking even half-way normal then it was time to take herself firmly in hand, she decided grimly. Deliberately assuming the cloak of self-command, of dignity, that her years with the austere Grace Slade had taught her to wear with ease, she ran a bath, pouring in expensive essence, then relaxed in the perfumed water, planning what she would wear, wondering if she could make time to give herself a facial. She didn't look further ahead than that. She dared not—not if she was to remain in control of herself.

At seven-thirty precisely she was stepping into the Rolls, her voice light and pleasant as she replied to a remark Thornwood had made about the mildness of the weather.

Thornwood was a dear, one of a dying breed, Jude often said. Cleo had met him and his wife, Meg, on several occasions and had marvelled at how well they ran Jude's house between them. They made it a home.

As the luxurious car whispered through the streets towards the quiet square in Belgravia where Jude lived, Cleo took stock. The discipline she had at last been able to bring to her preparations for this evening had transformed her from near nervous wreck into a composed, sophisticated young woman—the sort who would never get the jitters over anything—the sort of creature she had been until she had decided to propose to Jude Mescal, she admitted with a wry half-smile.

He could only say no, and if he did she would have to think of some other way out of the mess she was in. And if he did say no, it wouldn't be because she looked like a crazy woman!

Her black silk dress, falling in wide pleats from a high square yoke and supported by two narrow ribbon straps, was vaguely twenties in style, rather expensive, and the perfect foil for her slender height, for the pale silver gilt of her hair which hung in a shimmering, newly washed curve to her jawline.

No, her image wouldn't let her down tonight, and as long as she could control her nerves—and her temper if he should turn scathing or flippant—then she would be able to manage perfectly. That he might actually agree to marry her, and solve the problem of Fenton, was something she thought it wiser not to consider just now. It was, on the whole, rather too much to hope for, and if she didn't allow herself to hope then she wouldn't be too disappointed when he replied in the negative, as any right-minded man would do.

Even thinking along those lines brought a sudden return of the hated stomach-churning apprehension—to come out of this evening's encounter with her job intact was the most she could hope for—but her inner disturbance wasn't allowed to show as Thornwood held the car door open for her.

She slid the elegant length of her silk-clad legs to the pavement and walked with all her customary grace up the steps towards the panelled front door which Meg already held open in welcome.

CHAPTER THREE

JUDE turned as Meg ushered Cleo into the drawing-room. He held a glass in his hand and had been apparently lost in contemplation of a misty seascape which hung above the Adam fireplace. Strange—the thought brushed Cleo's mind fleetingly—why the intent scrutiny when he must know the painting brush-stroke by brush-stroke? And he had once told her that he didn't much like it but hadn't the heart to throw it out since he had inherited it from his uncle, along with this house.

Her knees shook a little; he looked so improbably handsome in the formal elegance of his dinner-jacket, and now she was looking at him with different eyes. She was accustomed to reacting to him on a business level, regarding him as a much-liked, respected boss, and the way he looked just didn't come into it. But it was coming into it now, and it shouldn't because what she had suggested had, after all, been a business arrangement.

Giving herself a mental shake, she endured the appraising drift of his eyes. His assessment of the way she looked was gentle, like a caress, and she returned his slight smile.

'How was Brussels?'

'Smooth. No problems. There's no danger now of an American takeover, you'll be pleased to know. But you didn't come here to talk about Brussels.'

His smile was tight and gave no impression of warmth and Cleo sank on to a chair and thought, my God! What have I let myself in for? Then she let her eyes laze around the room because it was peaceful, an anodyne for fraying nerve-ends, an harmonious mix of fine antiques, good fabrics, nothing showy. She had been here before on one or two occasions, enjoyed herself. She didn't think she was going to find this evening enjoyable.

He had been pouring the white wine he knew she preferred and she took the glass from him, careful that their fingers should not touch. And one corner of his mouth quirked in a smile, as if he knew just how careful she had been.

Something caught in Cleo's throat; either he was enjoying this, creating a tension calculated to shred the staunchest nerves, or he was waiting for her to make the opening gambit. And she would have done, simply to get it over, behind her, but she didn't know what to say.

Suddenly, the enormity of what she had put in motion when she had proposed to him hit her again, right in the gut. He couldn't have seriously considered her crazy offer—so why was he spinning the agony out? She wished she could shrivel away, become invisible. She didn't know what was happening to her—one minute she was in control, quite calm, the next she was on the verge of hysterics. It wasn't in character for the woman she knew herself to be. And she could stand no more of it!

'Have you reached a decision?' she blurted, her voice thick. She put her glass down on the small round table at the side of her chair, her fingers clumsy, fumbling, and she looked up in time to catch his expression of surprise at her unpolished question and could have bitten her tongue out. Where was the poised image now? she groaned inwardly, resisting the impulse to wring her hands.

But the fleeting look of surprise was gone, his impressive features displaying little more than polite interest as he stood with his back to the crackling wood fire, his whisky glass held loosely in one hand. His eyes were veiled, thrown into shadow so that she couldn't read what was going on inside his head. She probably wouldn't have liked it if she could.

He nodded briefly, 'I have, but we'll talk about it over dinner.' And that told her nothing, nothing at all. If he was trying to test her nerve, her ability to keep cool in the face of mental pressure, he was doing an excellent job!

Lifting her glass again, she recalled how he'd often probed for her reactions to balance sheets, research reports. She had never failed herself on that score—but this probing, if such was his intention, was something else, something more closely allied to emotion than to hard, indisputable fact.

Trouble was, she was unused to handling emotion, and she hadn't, until now, equated it with that proposal of marriage.

So she searched for something to say, something light but not inane, and kept talking, with the occasional interjection from him, until Meg came in with a heated trolley and Cleo realised that the palms of her hands were hot, slippery with sweat, that her insides had turned to jelly with the sheer nerve-shredding effort of trying to look and sound in control of herself.

Meg and her trolley broke the tension, just a little, and Jude said, 'You don't mind if we eat in here?'

She rose fluidly, noting the oblong linen-covered table in the window alcove for the first time.

Long velvet curtains were drawn, closing out the blue April twilight, and candles were lit, creating an atmosphere of intimacy, drawing glittery lights from silver and crystal, casting a softening, warming glow over the cool features of the man opposite, making them enigmatic but not fearsomely so.

The food was delicious, Meg's unobtrusive service effortless. The wine was friendly, relaxing, as was Jude's attitude, his conversation. But Cleo didn't relax, not for a moment, and Meg's superbly cooked food tasted like nothing. However, only when Meg had gone, leaving them with the silver coffee-pot, did she allow a little of all that pent-up anxiety to show through.

'I don't want coffee.' Her voice came out as a snap as his hand hovered over the bone handle of the Queen Anne pot. Then, 'Thanks,' she added, mumbling now. The man was inhuman. Didn't he know how this suspense was pulling her apart?

He hesitated, then poured a cup for himself, and Cleo thought, it's crunch time, and cursed for the fiery colour she felt creeping over her skin.

'Well——' They both started to speak at once and he dipped his head, waving her on, and Cleo wished she'd kept her mouth shut. The onus was on her again, and he knew how to turn the screw.

But enough was enough, she decided savagely, and producing the courage, the composure, from somewhere she remarked levelly, 'You said you'd reached a decision.' A lift of one silky eyebrow gave emphasis to her question. 'May I know what it is?'

'Of course you may.'

So smooth, so suave, so damnably cool. She could have hit him! She couldn't imagine now why she had ever thought she liked him, believed that an expedient marriage to a man such as him would be no intolerable thing.

He lit a slim cigar, taking his time, and the flame of his lighter threw his features into harsh relief, sharpening every slashing angle, every plane. And his eyes, darkened to midnight, dealt her a glancing blow, knocking the breath clear out of her lungs because he'd looked at her before, of course he had, but never like that, never as if he owned her.

'I have decided,' he regarded the glowing tip of his cigar with lazy interest, 'to agree to your suggestion of an alliance—a marriage of convenience. Successful marriages have been based on less,' he told her, his magnificent eyes lifting from their inscrutable contemplation of the glowing tip, meeting the hazy smoke-grey of hers. A smile flickered briefly over the long, masculine mouth. 'That is to say, I agree in principle—however, there would be one stipulation.'

Cleo stared, her eyes wide, hardly able to take it in as the breath she hadn't known she'd been holding was expelled silently from her burning lungs. If Jude Mescal had accepted her proposal of marriage then the idea couldn't have been as demented as she'd come to believe it was. And she need no longer lie awake at nights worrying about the likelihood of failing to pay the money Fenton demanded. She would have control of her inheritance once she was married, and the whole dreadful business could be kept quiet. Everything was going to be all right!

A sudden smile of utter relief made her face radiant, and Jude raised one black eyebrow. 'Don't look so delighted. You haven't heard my stipulation yet.'

'No. No, I haven't.' She felt light-headed. Her conscience wouldn't have to bear the burden of knowing she had been instrumental in darkening her uncle's declining months with shame and misery or, even worse, being the cause of another and almost certainly fatal heart-attack. And Jude's stipulation, whatever it was, couldn't be too daunting.

She tilted her head in easy enquiry, the movement elegant, eloquent, and saw the way his eyes narrowed on her pointed face, on the warm curve of her lips as he said, 'It would have to be a full marriage. I want children.'

The long, square-ended fingers of one hand flexed round the handle of the coffee-pot and, watching them, letting the words he'd said sink in, Cleo felt her insides clench. Fool that she was, she hadn't viewed marriage to him from that angle, merely from the academic side. Two compatible adults merging their lives, their assets, for mutual benefit—that was the way she'd seen it. A marriage of convenience, a business arrangement, made tolerable by their mutual respect.

A full marriage, having children, meant sleeping together, having sex. It put an entirely complexion on the whole idea. Sex without love seemed unconscionably squalid in her view. But not in his, obviously. And why, oh, why hadn't she at least considered the possibility that he might demand a full, physical marriage? Because her head had been too full of the need to take control of her inheritance, she answered herself drily, to think about what Jude Mescal might want!

She stared at the tablecloth, as if the fine fabric held a weird fascination, quite unable to meet his eyes as the beginnings of a slow, deep flush made itself felt. She knew those clever azure eyes were on her, analysing her reaction, and she strove to keep calm.

She had seen the outcome of his acceptance only from her narrow viewpoint, as a means of enabling her to pay off Fenton, shield Uncle John. She had looked no further than that, believing that Jude would view the union as a business arrangement, too, that the offer of the Slade Securities shares and the addition of her own considerable fortune to his might be enough.

However, he was not a eunuch and naturally enough he wanted children, and as a male he was biologically different and could enjoy sex without love; his emotions would not have to be involved. And if he wanted children then it would be her duty, as his wife, to produce them. But could she go through with such a marriage—to a man she did not love?

She would have to, the answer came starkly. She was no twittery, starry-eyed teenager, and if she accepted the benefits of his acquiescence then she must accept the other. The alternative, Fenton's foul threat to go to the seamier tabloids, was impossible to contemplate.

Having rationalised the situation, accepted it with the logic that was such an intrinsic part of her way of thinking, she was able to meet his eyes squarely, unconsciously lifting her chin and setting her shoulders.

'I accept your stipulation. I can understand that a man in your position needs an heir.'

She thought she had countered him with suitable dignity, admitting no hint of the carnal which his deliberate introduction of the subject of children, and the getting of them, could very well have produced.

But her tongue ran away with her then, panicking, betraying the intimate nature of the thoughts she'd hoped to hide from him.

'But I would like to make one stipulation of my own— that we don't—we don't actually sleep together for, well, a couple of weeks or so after we're married.' She met the cool questioning of his eyes, the slight upward tilt of one strongly defined black brow, and blundered heedlessly on, her gaucheness totally out of character. 'I'd like time to adjust, to get to know you better—as a husband, I mean—before we actually, er——' Words failed her then and he supplied,

'Make love.'

His eyes moved with lazy boldness over her lips, her throat, the sweet, curving line of her shoulders and breasts.

'It's a bargain, Cleo. Two weeks to the day.' And she hung her head, her fingers twisting mindlessly in her lap. It sounded less like a bargain than an awful threat!

They were married quietly three weeks later, and the only people at the sort civil ceremony were Aunt Grace, Luke and Jude's sister Fiona.

It was fitting in a way, Cleo thought as she left the registrar's office on Jude's arm, that there weren't vast throngs of people waiting to celebrate a wedding that had been arranged, on her part through dark necessity, and on his a need, at last, to begin a family to carry on his name, to inherit his vast wealth.

But Grace had been delighted when she'd heard the news, Cleo recalled as she watched her aunt and Fiona climb into Luke's BMW for the drive back to Slade House.

'An excellent match!' That lady had come as near to open enthusiasm as it was possible for her to do. 'It will be good to have the Mescal name so closely allied with the Slades' again.'

And later, Uncle John had told her, 'I'm glad. Glad. You couldn't have made a better choice. I have great faith in young Mescal's judgement—I only wish your father and I had had as much in his uncle's.' He had taken her hand, holding it in an unprecedented display of affection, 'But when your father and I were young we thought we knew it all, so we took the bit between our feet, pulled out of Mescal Slade and founded Slade Securities. We took risks, we had to, and it paid off. Though Grace always thought secondary banking to be socially inferior, I'm afraid. But we made up for that in superior living in every degree—Grace saw to that.' He had sighed then, as if he regretted the breakaway still. 'Yes, it's good to know the two families will be allied again, that "Slade" won't just be a redundant name on a letter heading.'

So everyone was pleased, Cleo thought; even Jude had behaved like a devoted bridegroom-to-be when they'd accepted a dinner invitation at Slade House. Not that she'd seen much of him during the past three weeks. She'd spent most of her time booking him on flights to Zurich, Bonn, New York, arranging his hotel accommodation, fixing meetings with foreign bankers and clients.

'I rather think we should have gone first.' Jude placed a hand on the small of her back, only lightly, but it made her shudder. Today just did not feel like her wedding day. She stared unseeingly at the grey façades of the buildings on the opposite side of the street as if she didn't know where she was, what she was doing. She couldn't bring herself to look at him and Jude enquired softly, feeling that betraying shudder, 'Cold, darling?'

'Yes. Yes, I am, a little.' Cleo grasped at the excuse gratefully. It wouldn't do his ego much good to know that his bride of ten minutes had shuddered like a startled mare because he had touched her! And the weather had changed, feeling more like November than May, and there was little warmth in the cream silk suit she was wearing, little warmth in her heart, but he wasn't to know that.

'Shall we go, then?' The arm he put round her shoulder as he hurried her over the pavement to where the Rolls, minus Thornwood today, was parked was protective, but Cleo felt her whole body go stiff, rejecting even that small intimacy.

But the tug of the wind on her small hat, cream straw decked with apricot roses, came to her rescue, gave her yet another useful excuse in the automatic way both hands fled up, securing the nonsensical headgear, because that instinctive movement effectively knocked his arm away.

He looked down at her as she struggled to secure her hat, tipping it further down over her eyes in the process, and his eyes were light with laughter.

'That scrap of silliness suits you. Makes you look ultra-feminine and in need of protection. It's a side of you that's never on display in the office. I like it!' There was warm appreciation in the way he smiled and Cleo scrambled into the car as he held the passenger door open for her.

She felt a fraud, and she said over her shoulder, trying not to sound stiff, 'You'd think I'd flipped if I turned up for work wearing this!'

She heard his deep chuckle as he walked round the car, and she gritted her teeth. She was as she was, there was nothing more. The coolly sophisticated woman he knew as his PA was all there was to her. She had no frivolous, ultra-feminine side. Would he be disappointed when he realised that?

He slid in beside her and the engine purred aristocratically to life at the start of the journey to Slade House where Grace had arranged a small celebration lunch party for them. Uncle John hadn't been well enough to attend the ceremony, but she'd see him at the house. She wondered, her face white and set, what his reaction would be if he knew exactly why she had married Jude Mescal. But he would never know; that had been the whole point of the exercise.

'You're very quiet, Cleo.' Calm, azure eyes left the road for a split second, probing hers. 'Second thoughts?'

'No, not at all,' Cleo lied. During the past three weeks she'd been having second through to tenth thoughts, but they'd all led to the same inevitable conclusion. She was doing the only thing she could, given cold circumstance.

She would be in a far worse position had Jude refused to marry her, or if she'd got really cold feet and had called the whole thing off. She would just have to make the best of the situation, and she had far too much respect for Jude to allow him to know that his stipulation about a full marriage had her running scared.

'Good,' he said softly, his strong profile relaxed as he returned his full attention to the road. There was even a smile in his voice, and Cleo marvelled that he should appear so much in control, so easy in his mind. He, for one, could have no doubts about their future.

'I've some news for you,' he told her. 'Interested?'

'Of course. Tell me.' Cleo jerked herself out of the dangerous and all too often recurring mood of introspection, and Jude grinned.

'I've managed to fix us a honeymoon on a Greek island. Only a week, I'm afraid, that's all the time I can spare right now. But we'll have time to relax together.' He braked for traffic lights, his hands light on the wheel, and turned to her, his eyes enigmatic, 'It might help you to adjust.'

'It sounds delightful.' She carefully kept her tone neutral, not letting him know she had recognised the specific words she'd used when making her own stipulation. 'But a long way to go for just one week.'

'I suppose so,' he concurred absently. If he was disappointed by her lack of enthusiasm he wasn't showing it. 'But when a colleague offered me the use of his villa, the thought of all that sun, sea and solitude was too tempting to turn down. I'd been thinking along the lines of asking Fiona if we could borrow her cottage in Sussex, but I think we'd enjoy the island better. Besides,' his eyes slanted a totally unreadable message, 'we could both use a break in the sun. We'll leave in three days' time—

give you some breathing space to settle into your new home.'

He was arranging everything with no recourse to her. Was his private persona to be as dominant as his public one? She didn't know whether she liked that idea. But the tiny frown between her eyes was eased away as rapid calculations informed her that they would be back in London before her fortnight's period of grace was up. And then, as if he knew every nuance of her thoughts, every twist and turn of her brain, he added drily, 'To the world at large it will appear as a brief and romantic honeymoon. You can regard it simply as a lazy week in the sun.'

'You've picked yourself a great guy, and I should know! And I just know you're going to be happy.' Fiona was the first to greet them when they reached Slade House. 'Welcome to the family, poppet!'

Cleo was roundly kissed on both cheeks, and her hat slid further down over her nose. Laughing, she took it off and tossed it on a nearby chair, instinctively liking Jude's sister.

After retirement his parents had settled in New Zealand, so Jude had told her, leaving Fiona as his only effective family. Cleo hadn't missed the pride in his voice as he'd talked of his sister. She was lovely to look at, strong-minded, and at thirty years of age she was still unmarried because she preferred the uncomplicated single state, putting all her energies into her nationwide string of boutiques.

'The Mescals don't take lightly to the state of matrimony,' Jude had commented after giving Fiona's potted biography, and that had left Cleo wondering why the Slade Securities shares had been important enough to make him finally plunge into the married state—something he had carefully avoided before.

The shares would be useful to him, but important? Well, fairly. That important? Very unlikely—unless there was something she had missed. Later, she had come to the conclusion that she must have missed something. Jude's brain was clever, quick, and, astute in City matters as she liked to think she was, she knew that his grasp of financial affairs left her as far behind as a snail trailing in the wake of a comet.

Granted, he had decided that the time had come to start a family, but he could have had his pick of women only too eager to have his ring on their wedding fingers. So those shares had to be far more important than she had imagined.

Looking at him across her aunt's beautifully arranged lunch-table, Cleo's heart performed a series of totally disconcerting acrobatics. Fear, she supposed, sipping Dom Perignon to steady herself, fear of the consequences of the chain of events which had led to this day, this moment of sitting opposite a brand new husband—a man whose mind she had grown to know well, to respect and admire, but whose body was a stranger, a stranger she was going to force herself to learn to know.

Oh, dear heaven! She dabbed at her mouth with her white linen napkin, not allowing for one moment that the flip and flop of her heart might have anything whatsoever to do with the sheer masculine charisma of the man whose lithely muscled body was covered with such easy and understated elegance by the fine, dark grey fabric of a formal suit, impeccably white shirt and pearl-grey tie.

Dragging her eyes away from him, she slid a sideways smile to Simmons who, impassive as ever, replaced the plate a housemaid had moved with an oval platter

bearing a thick, succulent steak of sea-trout. And while
the performance was repeated around the table she
caught Jude's eyes, swallowed her breath at the cool di-
rectness in those azure depths and turned quickly away,
fastening her attention on Grace, who was unusually
animated, chatting between Luke, Fiona and John. And
Cleo wondered if what her uncle had said regarding her
aunt's disapproval of the way the break between them
and Mescal Slade had come about had any bearing on
her coldness towards herself.

People were complicated creatures, present actions and
attitudes often stemming from the effects of the past—
even if they didn't realise it themselves. It made them
incapable of acting differently. Cleo could no more blame
her aunt for her cool rigidity towards the daughter of
the man who had, in her opinion, enticed her husband
away from the more socially acceptable world of merchant banking than she could blame a hedgehog for
having prickles.

'I think we ought to attempt a little light conversation, don't you?' Jude's cool, soft voice splintered her
solitary thoughts as he laid a hand over hers, imprison-
ing her fingers as she absently played with the stem of
her wineglass. The sensation of skin on skin, of the
tensile strength of those long, square-ended fingers, made
her catch her breath. Her teeth sank into her lower lip
and Jude said, 'Don't scream, you're safe for another
two weeks, my dear,' then commanded, a trace of acid
in his voice, 'Smile for me. Or is that too much to ask?'

And because she sensed the others were watching, their
conversation broken while they turned their attention to
the newly weds, who surely should be looking ecstatic,
Cleo pinned a brilliant smile on her face, then felt like
crying because she could see by the sudden bleakness in
his eyes that he knew just how false it was.

*   *   *

'There's a gentleman to see you, madam.' Meg stood in the doorway of the study where Cleo had just finished a phone call to an estate agent about the marketing of her home in Bow. She frowned, wishing Meg wouldn't insist on that formal, ageing mode of address. 'Call me Cleo, or Mrs Mescal, if you can't manage that,' she had instructed when she had arrived here as Jude's bride two days ago. But Meg, friendly and co-operative as she was, wasn't having that. Meg was of the old school, and that was that!

'Oh—put him in the drawing-room.' Cleo closed her notepad and pushed her fingers through her hair, asking belatedly, 'Who is it?'

'A Mr Robert Fenton, madam. He said it was urgent.' Meg sniffed, her expression showing that in her opinion nothing could be urgent enough to keep the new mistress of the house from what she should be doing—getting ready for her honeymoon! 'Shall I tell him you're too busy? Ask him to leave a message? There's all the packing still to be done for tomorrow.'

'No, I'll see him.' Cleo turned, able now to smile briefly at the housekeeper. At the mention of that hated name she had gone icy cold, averting her head and pretending to search through a drawer in the desk for something. Now, her scrabbling fingers were stilled, her features composed, or reasonably so, she hoped. She had to see the creature some time, she knew that, but had hoped that their next contact would be by letter or telephone.

But she could be thankful for small mercies because at least Jude was out, enmeshed in paperwork back at the office, she told herself as she walked through the hall as steadily as she could on disgracefully trembly legs. She could thank heaven, too, that Jude had insisted she use the day or two before they left for that Greek island to get better acquainted with her new home and begin the disposal of her old one. Had he not, then that snake Fenton might have tracked her down to the office, and that would have taken some explaining away.

Suddenly, though, and with a depth that shook her, she longed for the reassuring presence of the man she had married; longed for his strength, for the gentleness that had been the hallmark of the sensitive way he had handled their ambiguous relationship ever since they had arrived here after the wedding lunch at Slade House.

Jude, I need you! The words took wing in her mind, echoing, and she bit her lips in exasperation for the maudlin, weakly character those silent words conjured up.

She needed him here, at this precise moment, like she needed a sledgehammer to drop on her head from a great height! What he would have to say if he discovered she was being blackmailed, and why, would make a Colossus quake! And she wasn't weak, not weak at all!

Squaring her shoulders, she opened the drawing-room door and walked quickly through and Robert Fenton drawled, 'May I offer my congratulations on your marriage, Mrs Mescal?'

Cleo ignored that, although she felt her face, her whole body, go hot. The mere sight of him made her blood boil.

'Don't come here again, under any circumstances,' she told him, her eyes letting him know how much he disgusted her. To think she had once found him charming company! To think—— But no, her brain shifted gear, moving swiftly, decisively; she must not think of the past. It was done with, over. Or almost. This creep meant less than nothing to her now. She loathed and despised him, and the act of handing over a sum of money would rid herself of the poison that was Robert Fenton finally and for ever.

'I won't—if I don't have to.' His eyes were nasty, his mouth curved in a sneer. He had helped himself to a large measure of Jude's brandy, she noted savagely. And to see him here, lounging on Jude's sofa and drinking his brandy, turned her stomach. But she had her rage under control, because to rant and rail at him might give her temporary relief but it would accomplish nothing useful.

So she said tonelessly, 'There was no need for you to come here today. A telephone call would have done.'

'Would it, now?' He mocked her careful dignity. Swirling the contents of his glass, he leaned back, his smile deadly. 'I'd like to see you try to feed twenty-five thousand smackers down a telephone line.'

'I haven't got it yet.' Cleo's hands balled into tight fists. But she trod warily, guessing how nasty he would become if he weren't reassured that the money he demanded would be forthcoming. 'I have been married for two days. Things can't move that quickly. As soon as I can, I'll let you have it. I don't want this sordid business hanging over my head any longer than necessary.'

'How soon? Next week?' he asked, his eyes sharp, and Cleo dragged in a deep breath, feeling the wetness of sweat on her forehead, the palms of her hands, her back.

'No. The week after. We're leaving tomorrow on our honeymoon.' Sharing any details of her life with him made her feel ill and the words were stiff, difficult to push past her teeth. 'Leave me a phone number. I'll contact you when I have it.'

'Just see you do.' He had pushed himself to his feet, moving to stand close, and Cleo was too frozen with loathing to move away, her feet rooted to the silky oriental carpet. 'Because, quite apart from poor old Uncle John, you have someone else to consider now, don't you, my love?' An eyebrow arched with hateful mockery. 'The sort of stuff I could dish out about you would make that new husband of yours look something of a laughing-stock in the City, wouldn't it? A bit of a fool, wouldn't you say? And he wouldn't be one bit pleased, would he?'

She couldn't speak; there was nothing to say. But she longed to lash out at him, to hit, kick and batter, but the moment of temper, of hot temptation, passed. And Fenton drawled, 'Yes, we must consider your husband's feelings in all this, mustn't we, my love—my clever, clever love? And you are clever, damably so. I admire you for it! To get your pretty little hands on a large fortune, you marry an even larger one! Nice thinking! Go right to the top of the class!'

And behind them, in a voice that would have frozen a molten lava flow, Jude said, 'Won't you introduce me to your friend, darling?'

And Cleo, her eyes darkening with panic, watched with horrified fascination as Robert Fenton gave her a leering wink over the rim of the brandy glass he was lifting to his lips.

CHAPTER FOUR

AFTERWARDS, Cleo had been unable to remember precisely how she'd coped. Her heart had been slamming, her stomach clenched in a sickening knot, but she'd managed to perform the introductions gracefully although she'd been agonisingly aware of Jude's eyes on her as she'd watched, as though mesmerised, as his brandy had slid down Fenton's throat.

'Can't stay, I'm afraid,' Fenton had handed the empty glass to Cleo, his eyes flickering to Jude as he swaggered to the door. 'Just dropped in to offer my congratulations. Lovely lady you have, Mescal. Quite lovely.'

'I'll see you out.'

Jude's voice had been toneless as he'd followed the other man out through the door, ignoring Fenton's airy, 'No need, I can find my way.'

And Cleo had sagged against the wall, still clutching the empty glass, her hands shaking. How much had Jude heard? Panicking, she tried to force her mind to remember exactly what Fenton had been saying. Something about how clever she'd been to marry Jude's fortune in order to get her hands on her own! He would think she'd been bragging about it—and to Fenton, of all people—and plying him with the best brandy to add insult to injury!

Quickly, she put the glass on a table, drawing in deep breaths and trying to compose herself as she heard Jude's approaching steps along the hall.

'Known him long?'

The enquiry was almost polite and she said, 'About two years,' searching his eyes for a clue to his mood. But there was nothing, just a blank careful coolness, only a hint of a question in the gravelly voice.

'Just called to offer his congratulations?'

'Yes, that's right.' She was sure he must hear the lie in her voice, see it in her eyes, and she had turned away, rearranging an already perfectly balanced bowl of tulips, feeling the cool, waxy petals beneath her shaking fingers, waiting for the accusation that must come if he had indeed overheard the remark Fenton had made.

But there had been nothing, and, when she'd steeled herself to look around, the room had been empty.

And now the sun beat down from a paintbox-blue sky, shimmering on the fine golden sand, bouncing off the cluster of angular white buildings of the fishing village further down the coast.

Cleo stirred, stretching her long legs, revelling in the heat of the sun, and Jude said, so very casually, 'Turn over. You've had as much sun on your back as your skin can stand.'

Her heart picking up speed, Cleo's body went rigid and wary, very still. She hadn't heard him come over the sand. But then she wouldn't, would she? The sand was very soft and she'd been drowsing, and the hypnotic suck and drag of the waves as they lapped the shore and retreated again would have drowned out any sound he might have made.

Then he spoke again, repeating his directive, his voice sharper this time.

Recognising the sense of his command, Cleo turned, feeling the beach towel rumple beneath her, wishing she'd been more prepared. She still trod carefully through the minefield of uncertainties, unspoken anxieties, that was her week-old marriage to this man.

She fumbled for her sunglasses and put them on, something to hide behind. There was little else. Her tiny black bikini revealed most of what there was to reveal, and she wouldn't have worn it if she'd known he would be back from that fishing trip so soon. She had imagined she had the best part of the day to herself.

'You're back early.' So light her voice, so carefully neutral. Cleo was proud of the way she was containing those creeping, unnerving anxieties, the doubts, the dread. He was looming over her and she snapped her eyes away. Dressed in only a pair of brief black denim shorts—faded and ragged—the dark golden body which was dusted with crisp black hair seemed impossibly male, superbly athletic and very, very threatening. The sight of him made something inside her shudder, tremble with a sensation she couldn't identify. It was fear, she told herself, primitive fear. But there was something more, something nameless.

'I didn't want to be accused of neglecting my wife.' There was a bite to his tone that she hadn't heard during the week of their marriage, and she sensed a difference in his attitude. A subtle difference that made her feel tense, more wary than ever.

It had been as much as she could do to adequately cope with the way he had been since their wedding: cool, polite, but pleasant with it. And the four days they'd been on the island hadn't been quite the ordeal she'd anticipated. He had been courteous, making sure she was content, had all she needed. And what the maid, who apparently came with the villa, thought about the arrangement of separate bedrooms, the way they spent most of their days following separate pursuits, Cleo didn't know, or care.

She clung gratefully to that separate room, her own private space, like a child counting and re-counting those last few precious days of a school holiday, because she had seen the way he looked at her from time to time, seen it and instinctively known what that look meant. He was a normal, virile male, after all, and she was his wife.

But if he was going to be tetchy because there was another week to go before he could, with honour, claim his conjugal rights—the very phrase made her squirm— then she didn't know how she could bear it. And she didn't know how she would bear it when she would be expected to share his bed. Close her eyes and think of England, she supposed! And——

'Eeek!' she yelped, her dreary thoughts sharply interrupted by a sensation of cold squelchiness, then of warmth and strength as Jude's hand began to massage sun-cream into the soft, heated skin of her naked midriff.

'I can do that!' she gabbled, galvanised into action and struggling to sit up. A mistake, she realised; his hand was now trapped between her updrawn thighs and her breasts.

Smoky grey eyes, wide behind dark lenses, winged sideways apprehensively, met his, and held. His ebony-fringed eyes were as blue as the improbably blue sea that sucked at the shore and, like the sea, contained small depths of clear emerald, brilliant flecks of light. The glinting lights of laughter, damn it!

He was laughing at her, not openly, but inside—which made it worse. Laughing at her foolishly coy and virginal behaviour, making her feel foolish, clumsy and gauche.

'I know you can do it.' His husky voice came close to her ear, his breath fanning her skin as he leaned forward, prising his hand from its softly sensual trap and laying her prone on the towel again. 'But so can I, so why not just stop twittering, and lie back and enjoy?' he added, his words pricking her mind on different levels.

Other than lashing at him with hands and feet, there was nothing she could do. And fighting him physically would achieve exactly nothing. He could, if he wished, flatten her with one hand, the muscled strength of his naked torso left her in no doubt about that at all! Besides, it would be undignified, and it would make him think he had a hell-cat for a wife. He didn't deserve that.

And so she gritted her teeth and endured, and closed her eyes and tartly reminded herself that she had to get used to such liberties, liberties that in exactly one week's time would sharply escalate up the scale of intimacy!

They had made a bargain and she had too much respect for him, and for herself, not to keep her side of it, and she wondered whether to try self-hypnosis. Not very hopeful as to the outcome, especially when the self-prescribed treatment was instigated in a moment of panic, but willing to try anything, she silently repeated, 'I will be a good wife. I will. I will.' And eventually the silent exhortation assumed the soothing rhythm of the sea, of the gentle pressure of his hands as he massaged the cream on to her long, slender legs.

A pulse began to flutter in her throat as his fingers feathered the soft skin of her inner thigh, accelerating as his plundering fingers took more than was honest when they slid a little way beneath the fabric of the tiny triangle which made the bottom half of her bikini. Agonisingly, she felt every muscle and sinew of her body clench in a spasm of purely instinctive rejection, but the thieving fingers moved onwards, towards more legitimate areas, covering the flat plane of her stomach, the soft flare of her hips, the arch of her ribcage.

And to Cleo it suddenly began to feel like nothing she had ever experienced before. Frightening—but obviously not frightening enough! Her mind told her to defend herself against the marauder, but her body had definite ideas of its own, was acquiescent, limpid. And she was drowning in something warm and deep, and not really painlessly because her lungs felt tight, as if she should be gasping for air, and her heart was pattering wildly... And any self-defensive thoughts she might have had were being subdued by his lean, knowing hands, and she knew that if she allowed herself to relax, by just that necessary fraction, she would be completely and utterly subjugated...

When his fingers found the front fastening of her bra top, moving aside the two small halves to expose the twin rounded peaks to the sun, to his eyes, to his hands, she made an effort to protest, to tell him, acidly, that she was unlikely to get sunburned just there, especially if he could refrain from interfering with her clothing! But the words just wouldn't come out coherently. They emerged thickly, like a moan, a moan of pleasure. And as she felt her nipples harden as a tug of something sweet yet achingly fierce flared to life deep inside her, she knew that the fraction of relaxation had been achieved, that the erotic, wordless lovemaking of his hands had dissolved the very last barrier... He was her man, her mate, and she wanted him as she had never wanted anything before. And without conscious design her body arched sensually beneath his hands, a blatant invitation, and he said, 'That should do it.'

The clipped, disinterested tones came as if from a very great distance and it was several seconds before Cleo realised that the sweet ache inside her, the sensual and unstoppable need he had aroused, was to remain an ache. A sour ache.

He was standing up now, his lithe body taut, a glistening bronze masterpiece in the bright Greek sunlight, totally imperious and quite unmoved by what had happened to her because, quite obviously, nothing had happened to him.

He began to unzip his shorts and Cleo closed her eyes, her throat tightening as he told her blandly, 'I'm going for a swim. See you.' And when she opened her eyes again he had gone.

She searched the water and found him, cleaving through the deep blue depths in a powerful crawl, and she scrambled to her feet, her fingers shaking as she re-fastened her bra top then gathered her things together, pushing them in her beach bag.

Her face was burning, and it wasn't from the effects of the sun. It was shame. Shame and humiliation both. He, no doubt bored by this empty charade of a marriage, but bound by his agreement to her stipulation, and irritated to the point of exasperation by the way she had previously skittered nervously away from the slightest physical contact, had taken the opportunity to demonstrate just how he could, if he wished, subdue her.

And he had done so, and to add the final telling insult had walked away, showing her how completely unmoved he was by her obvious arousal. He could take her or leave her—that was the message his actions had transmitted, loud and clear.

She didn't think she would ever forgive him for that. Ever. And the ease with which he had physically dominated her would make her shy away from him in the future more than ever before!

Back at the white one-storey villa Cleo helped herself to a tall glass of fresh lemon juice from the jug in the fridge, gulping it down thirstily, her stormy eyes darting around the cool gleaming kitchen as if she expected someone to leap out of the shadows and attack her.

Someone? Jude, of course! His hands on her body had been a form of attack—insidious, almost unbearably erotic, but an attack all the same!

But gradually she relaxed, her eyes calmer, her hands almost steady as she rinsed her glass. Jude would be back on the beach, or still swimming. Either way, she had again put distance between them. However, a nasty little voice intoned maliciously, deep in her brain, she wouldn't always be able to keep her distance. And he wouldn't always draw back at the moment of capitulation, not if he wanted children, he wouldn't.

And beginning a family had been the reason he had decided to marry, and the Slade Securities shares had meant that she had been the woman he had chosen to bear his children. Suddenly, the idea was mortifying. She had thought she was doing the right and sensible thing when she'd suggested they marry, but now she wasn't so sure. She seemed to be pulling herself out of one mess, only to find herself entangled in one which was worse!

She had always admired Jude for his ability to remain aloof, cool, and for the way he was always in total control. But as she flounced from the kitchen and down a cool corridor to her room she could see the other side of that ability of his—the darker, cruel side.

The way he had shown her how he could bring her to the point of begging for his lovemaking—despite the absence of the love she had always believed to be essential—had left her shaking with unfulfilled need and self-disgust. A potent mixture, poisonous. And that very ability of his, which she had once so admired, now sickened and frightened her.

Stripping off her bikini, she hurled it into a corner of the spacious, traditionally furnished bedroom she was using and padded to the en suite bathroom to stand under the shower, sluicing away every last trace of the sun-cream, as if his fingerprints still lingered in the oily substance. She hoped that their children, when they arrived, would look like her—grey-eyed blondes—with not one trace of their father's dark, cruel beauty. They would be her children, not his! Hers! She would make them so, and that would be the final irony. She hated him at this moment, she really did, she didn't want to give him one damned thing—not even children that resembled him in the slightest!

Cleo heard the maid arrive in time to prepare the evening meal, bringing the fresh fish, fruit and vegetables she bought in the village each day.

Edgy, she put aside the book she'd been trying to read and walked from the terrace through the arched doorway that led to her room, pushing the silvery tumble of silky hair back from her face.

Jude was late. It only ever took the middle-aged Greek woman an hour to make their meal, sometimes less. So where was Jude?

Catching sight of the frown-line between her huge grey-eyes, she turned away from the revealing mirror reflection. She couldn't actually be worried about him, could she? A few hours earlier she hadn't cared if she never saw him again!

But she was calmer now and knew she had over-reacted. He had made her want him. So? He was her husband, wasn't he? That she was fastidious and had always believed she would have to love a man before she could be sexually aroused was something she had taken for granted. But he had aroused her, revealing a depth of sexuality she hadn't known she possessed. She was learning things about her character that alarmed her, but that didn't mean she had to go over the top.

And she was learning things about Jude, too. That he was male enough, arrogant enough, to need to lay claim to his ownership, to let her know that he could make her want him whenever he felt like doing so.

Restless now—where was the man?—she riffled through the few garments she'd brought with her and eventually selected a silky amethyst calf-length dress and laid it on the bed, then paced back to the terrace to stare out along the deserted beach.

Since they had been here they had always met on the terrace at this time in the evening. Usually they had spent the daytime hours at separate ends of the island, because he seemed no more anxious for her undiluted company than she was for his. But they always began their evenings here, having a drink or two before dinner, making light, impersonal conversation. And now his absence was making her nervous.

But that in itself was nothing new. He had been making her nervous ever since he had agreed to marry her! And it had grown progressively worse, aggravated by the way he'd said not a word about Robert Fenton's presence in his home, about what he might have overheard when he'd walked in and found them together. This afternoon's episode on the beach had been the final straw!

She paced the terrace, her feet making rapid patterns of sound on the terracotta tiles, the edges of her lacy robe fluttering in a soundless echo of her own agitation as she thought back to the days—now seeming totally unreal—when she had confidently believed herself to be the only person Jude Mescal couldn't make nervous!

And then he was there, in the archway leading from her room, his body relaxed, like the mean and magnificent cat she had always thought he resembled.

He was already dressed for dinner, his narrow black trousers and formal white lightweight jacket fitting him to perfection, making him look suave yet deadly.

'Good book?' His eyes drifted to her discarded novel as he walked, soft-footed, to where she had been sitting earlier, placing the two dry martinis he had brought with him on the low marble-topped table, and Cleo shook with anger, shrugging aside his question with a tight shrug of her shoulders.

It was no use his asking her if the book was a good one; she couldn't remember a word of the few she had read. Mostly she hadn't been reading at all, just sitting here, wondering why he was late, when he would come home. And all the time he had been here, showering, changing, fixing drinks, not bothering to let her know he was in the house. Dammit, she'd actually been worried about the insouciant swine because the last time she'd seen him he'd been swimming out to sea as if the hounds of hell were following him! The man was intolerable!

And she didn't know why he had this power to make her angry because, as his PA, she had always been able to handle him. And he had gained the terrace by coming through her room. He hadn't set foot inside it before now, and that, coming after what had happened this afternoon, made the palms of her hands go slippery with sweat.

Mentally shaking herself for her own foolishness, for the inner agitation she would have to learn to come to terms with, she took the drink he had fixed for her, carrying it over to the stone balustrading of the terrace and staring blindly out to sea.

If she joined him at the table she would have to look at him. She didn't want to meet those clever eyes because she knew she would be able to see in them the mind pictures of the way she must have looked this afternoon when she'd abandoned her practically naked body to the exploration of his hands.

'Cleo——' Her name on his lips sounded, suddenly, quite unbearably intimate, and she reluctantly made a half-turn towards him, hoping he wouldn't notice the way the hand that held her drink was shaking. 'Come and sit down, I want to talk to you.'

'What about?' A rapid but ostentatious glance at her wristwatch. 'It's time I went to change.' So cool her voice, the small half-smile she angled at nothing in particular. She should be winning Oscars! The last thing she needed right now was to have to sit with him and listen to whatever it was he had to say. The memory of the way she'd felt when his hands had stroked and teased her willing body was still much too close.

'You look fantastic as you are.' A slow drift of long azure eyes over her flushed face, the filmy gown, the length of bare, tanned leg, said it all: sexual interest but overlaid with slight amusement because, after all, he'd seen it all before, and more. He'd touched, and could have taken her had he been so inclined. He hadn't, neither then nor now, it seemed, and for Cleo the sexual embarrassment which the drift of his knowing eyes had engendered became the deeper misery of sheer humiliation as he consulted his own watch. It was as if he had taken stock and mentally dismissed her.

'You've got over half an hour before we need go in to eat.' His mouth tilted with heavy irony. 'Do I have to beg for five minutes of my wife's time?'

'I'm sorry.' Flustered, Cleo sat. Put that way, she could hardly refuse, and she sipped her drink, waiting, and he said,

'I think we should consider buying a house in the country. Somewhere close enough to use at weekends. It would be particularly useful after the children arrive.'

His eyes slid over her, making her skin burn. 'What do you think?'

That it was a pity he had to keep harping on about children! That was what she thought! But she could hardly tell him as much. Holding her glass by the stem, twisting it, she stared into the swirling contents unable to meet those knowing, faintly amused eyes.

'There's time for that,' she answered stiffly, 'After all—— ' she made a concession to his mention of all those children she would be expected to bear '—I expect to continue with my job for some time to come. I enjoy it.'

She couldn't imagine him as a family man, making swings in apple trees, playing football or snakes and ladders in front of a log fire while she busied herself darning endless tiny socks in between baking and preserving in some farmhouse-type kitchen. And how many children did he expect her to have, for goodness' sake? And would she be expected to start producing them right away? One litter after another, like a rabbit? Her throat tightened with what she recognised as incipient hysteria, and if she hadn't been so busy trying to control that disgraceful and, up until becoming entangled with him, alien state, she might have taken his ambiguous reply as fair warning.

'The expected sometimes doesn't happen, Cleo——'

She finished her drink in a gulp, her eyes flicking to his and away again because the message contained there was unreadable—or perhaps she wasn't ready to read it. She didn't know. She got to her feet, trying for poise, 'I really must go and change,' she tossed over her shoulder, her smile brittle. 'By all means we can cast our eyes over a few properties, get to know the market for when we seriously want to buy—some time in the future.'

* * *

If he had decided to charm her he was certainly succeeding, Cleo thought, rising from the table where they had lingered in lamplit intimacy over the delicious meal the Greek maid had prepared.

The trouble was, he could so easily disarm her, she realised as he followed her out on to the moonlit terrace, bringing the brandy decanter and two glasses with him.

And to allow herself to be disarmed would be fatal. She didn't want her emotions involved, it would only lead to pain, because he would never become emotionally involved with her, with anyone, as far as she could tell. And she was no masochist. She would keep to the letter of their bargain, but that was as far as it would go.

But as she went to the balustrade to look out over the silvery night, he followed her, placing a hand on her shoulder where the halter neckline of her dress left it bare. And this time she didn't shy away from his touch, even though that touch felt like needles of excitement pricking her skin.

'Cold?' he said. 'Shall I fetch you a wrap?'

She turned, simply to deny any feeling of coldness because for some reason she had never felt warmer in her life. He was close, so close, and even in the shadowy light of the moon she could see he was not quite as implacably cool as he pretended to be.

'No—I'm fine, thanks.' She moved back to the upholstered bamboo loungers, angled around the table, and sat cradling the drink he'd poured for her.

Something was coming to life between them, a vital new growth, but not something known. Not really known, although she could make a fairly accurate guess. But she had to remember, always remember, that this was a marriage of convenience. And then a thought passed through her mind, leaving an annoying footprint, that maybe her motives had been suspect all along the line.

Solving her problem had depended on finding a husband her uncle and aunt, as her guardians, could approve of. But would she have asked Jude to marry her if he'd been fat and bald with a face like a pug and a mind like a geriatric slug? It was a question she wouldn't like to be forced to answer.

The sea was blessedly cool, lapping against her feet as she walked slowly along the water-line, the soft black night hiding her. Not that there would be anyone about at this time of night to see her. The thought comforted her a little, and a small smile tugged at the corners of her mouth as the breeze moulded the almost transparent lawn of her nightdress to the shape of her body.

She hadn't been able to sleep; the night was too hot, her thoughts jumping this way and that, making her mind ache.

That tension between them, that awareness, had been growing throughout the long evening, muddling her. And her 'goodnight' to him had been abrupt, far more terse than usual as she'd left the terrace, making for the solitude of her room.

But if she'd been looking for safe haven she hadn't found it there, and at last she'd slipped down to the beach, noticing the light coming from his room and wondering if he, too, found it impossible to sleep, if he found this marriage, entered into so coolly and objectively, had strange and rather terrifying facets that were only now beginning to reveal themselves.

She had never been drawn to the idea of marriage, the total commitment of love. Love was something she'd learned to do without since she'd lost her parents. Her mind, she supposed, was closed to the concept of it. She had imagined, for a brief span, that she was in love with Robert Fenton—and that had turned out to be an all-time disaster. And she'd emerged from the short period of infatuation recognising that what she'd felt had been a natural reaction to the years of dedicated study, the absence of close family love, the absence of fun and frivolity in her life. It had been a necessary, if unpleasant, part of growing up.

But if she had been looking for love, for a man she could respect, share the rest of her life with, then Jude could have been everything she could want in a man. He had a brilliant mind, was even-tempered—well, mostly—and he was strong, yet capable of tenderness, of deep humanity. He also respected her as an equal, and that counted for much—for more than the sum of his undoubted sex appeal, his wealth and position.

Yes, had she been looking for such a man, for love… A small wave, but higher than the rest, took her unawares, wetting her to her knees, and she stumbled, almost fell, then righted herself and turned and saw him a mere two yards away. Everything inside her seemed to stop, just for a moment, before racing on, the blood thudding through her veins, her heart pattering a demented tattoo.

'Jude——' Her voice was thick, his name dragged from her on a sighing breath that faltered hopelessly, because she had known in that instant when time had stood still for her, when her breath, her very heartbeat, had hung suspended, that she loved this man, had probably been falling in love with him since she'd first set eyes on him. It was almost laughably simple! It had certainly been inevitable.

Moonlight, slow and silver, touched his face, stroked his magnificent body with tender moulding fingers, stopping the breath in her throat.

Naked, save for brief dark swimming shorts, he looked pagan—the dominant male to her feminine fragility—and he said her name, like a question, his shadowed eyes, bereft now of their startlingly vivid colour in this ghostly light, raking her, lingering hungrily on the shape of her, on the aching softness of feminine curves only lightly and tantalisingly concealed beneath gossamer fabric.

'I couldn't sleep.' He moved closer, close enough to touch, and her skin turned to flame with the nearness of his almost naked body as he cupped her face in his hands, his eyes searching hers, revealing the depth of his own wanting.

His body shook with it. She could feel the fine tremors that ran over the taut, glistening skin so near to her own, feel the control as he released her, his fingers feathering lightly down the length of her throat before they fell away, clenched into fists now, revealingly, though she knew she was not supposed to know the effort it had cost him to restrain himself from touching her more intimately.

'I'll walk you back.' His voice was kind, but there was a roughness in it, just below the surface, that told her he wanted her, as she wanted him. 'Perhaps a hot drink might help? Me, too—probably more than the swim I'd decided to take before I saw you along the shore.'

He could have been a father, soothing a wakeful child for all the emotion he allowed himself to show. But Cleo knew better, and she wasn't afraid, not now, because she had at last admitted to herself the fact that she must have unconsciously known for months. She loved him, and that was why her proposal to him had seemed so logical, so right! She had been blind for so long, so convinced that she didn't need or want emotional ties that she hadn't recognised what was happening to her!

But she knew it now, knew that the restrictions she had placed on these early days of marriage must be almost intolerable to a man such as he. And they were intolerable to her, now, quite intolerable.

But, such was his sense of honour, he would make no move towards her until the period of restriction he had agreed to was over. Any move had to come from her.

'Jude——' He was waiting for her, just a step or so ahead now, but he pivoted round as her voice touched him, tense, his skin glistening in the silver light as though drenched with sweat, although the breath from the sea was cooling.

'Make love to me.' The husky ease with which she spoke the words didn't surprise her. They were right, so right, and should have been said so very much sooner. She caught the sound of his sharply indrawn breath and her soul shook with the wonder of this moment, with the simple knowledge of her love for him, with what she read in his eyes as he took the hands she held out to him, folding them inwards against the wall of his chest.

'Are you sure?' His voice was throaty, urgency contained. 'Quite sure?'

And she nodded, too full of love for him to speak, too near to tears, or laughter, because she'd been such a blind fool these last months. She lifted her face to him, and he caught his breath, drawing her closer so that their bodies touched, just; magic was born as after one long and incredibly tense moment their bodies joined, and the softness of her melted into the demanding hardness of him, hands and lips seeking, finding, consuming.

And there on the shore, with the pulse of the sea melding into the rhythm of the blood in their veins, he made love to her with subtlety, with a tender poignancy that made her want to cry.

She loved him so.

CHAPTER FIVE

'YOU were leaving without saying goodbye!' Cleo's voice was a husky accusation as she stood in the breakfast-room doorway, fastening the belt of her fine voile robe around her narrow waist. And Jude looked up from the breakfast-table, his smile lazy, his azure eyes incredibly sexy.

'Not so. I would have come to wake you before I left.' He put his morning paper aside. 'Shall I ring for Meg to bring your breakfast through?'

'No, thanks.' Cleo pushed a hand through her rumpled silvery hair and sat opposite, helping herself to a morsel of crisp bacon from his plate, eating it from her fingers. She didn't want anyone to intrude, not even Meg, who was one of the most unobtrusive people she knew; she wanted Jude to herself. Never again could she affect to be cool and blasé towards this husband of hers. She loved him so much.

Her only regret was that she couldn't tell him so. He had married her because it was convenient to do so, no other reason. That she had proved to be as sexually eager as he, would, to his logical masculine mind have proved a bonus. To admit her love would embarrass him. He wouldn't want the responsibility of it.

He was looking good, very good, his dark hair, still damp from the shower he must have taken earlier, clinging to his skull, his deep tan contrasting dramatically with the stark whiteness of his shirt. Her fingers ached to touch him. Every morning when she had wakened from luxurious sleep she had reached out for him and he had woken, turning to her, nuzzling her hair and then lazily, languorously, they had made love.

Not this morning, though. It was their first back in London because he'd said, 'What the hell!' contacted Mescal Slade and informed Dawn Goodall that they were taking another week, staying on the island. And this morning she had reached for him and he hadn't been there. Just an empty space between cool sheets, and she'd panicked, remembering he'd said he'd be going to the City today.

Stumbling out of bed, she'd grabbed at her robe, struggling into it as she'd run down the stairs, not wanting him to leave before she'd had a chance to see him, simply see him.

Now, relaxed again because she was with him, she reached for his coffee-cup, cradling it in both hands, sipping while he finished his bacon and eggs, and he asked, 'What are you going to do with yourself today?'

Cleo hunched one shoulder, her mouth curving in a warm, slow smile. 'Go shopping?' she hazarded. For some reason Jude had suggested she take a further week off. She would have preferred to be behind her desk again, close to him, working with him. But he had insisted and she wasn't up to arguing with him about it, about anything, not in this mood of euphoria she wasn't. A dark eyebrow lifted and she elaborated, 'I might get a new dress.' She felt in the mood for celebrating, and buying something exciting would serve. That her ever-deepening love for him was just cause for celebrating she couldn't explain, not yet, so she tacked on, 'We're entertaining the Blairs on Thursday, so I need to pull out all the stops!'

She expected him to comment on the planned dinner party. Sir Geoffrey Blair was chairman of Blair and Dowd Developments, a company that was climbing fast and far, and Jude had been angling for their account. Thursday night could well clinch it. But he growled, leaning over the table to take his coffee-cup from her hands, 'Do you intend to consume all my breakfast, woman?' However, the quirk of his mouth belied the black bar of his lowered brows, and he drank the remains, then refilled the cup, took a mouthful then put the steaming cup back between her hands. 'Henpecked already,' he grinned and she nodded sagely, as if she quite agreed, although she knew that henpecked was the last thing this man would ever be. But their developing relationship admitted this type of gentle teasing and she welcomed it, as she welcomed everything about him.

'Do you know how irresistible you look in that thing?' Lazy eyes swept her, the soft movement of his mouth adding erotic emphasis to the drift of his eyes as they roamed from the spun silver disorder of her hair, her flushed cheeks, the slope of her shoulders, to the swelling roundness of her breasts.

The robe she had pulled on was meant to be worn over a matching nightdress. Worn over nothing at all, its pink transparency was little more than a blush, and Cleo's pulses quickened as the sensual curve of his mouth became more pronounced, his voice a growly inspiration as he whispered, 'Irresistible enough to take you back to bed and let Mescal Slade look after itself.'

For a silent, timeless moment their eyes held, the intimacy almost shocking, and she thought he might just do that, but then she saw the change, the assumption of briskness that told her he had moved away from her, on to a separate plane entirely, and she knew—as if she could ever have doubted it—that work would always take first place for him.

She reluctantly respected him for that, she decided, watching as he shot a glance at his watch. The most she could hope for was that in time she would become as necessary to him as he was to her.

And there was a chance of that, she knew there was. The knowledge was like a small, bright flame inside her, warming her, allowing her to see more clearly ahead. He liked and respected her and he took pleasure in her body, and that was as good a basis as any to build on. And she would build on it, brick by patient brick, be as much to him as he would allow, hide the depth of her own emotional involvement, her total commitment, until he was ready to accept it.

He stood up, reaching for the light grey suit jacket which had been hanging over the back of his chair, shrugging into it, his movements, as ever, sheer male elegance. And Cleo got to her feet, too, longing to go to him, to slip her arms beneath the beautifully tailored jacket and feel the warmth of muscle, sinew and bone through the crisp whiteness of his shirt.

But she wouldn't do that, of course. She couldn't give herself that luxury. Their marriage was a compartmented thing and his mind was now geared to the working day ahead; he wouldn't welcome an untimely display of her physical need of him. It might annoy him, and it would certainly reveal the depth of her emotional involvement.

He picked up his briefcase and she lifted her face to receive his goodbye kiss, an unsatisfying brush of his lips over hers, and she expected that to be that, but he stood for a moment, smiling down at her, making her heart tumble about beneath her ribs.

The character lines on either side of his mouth indented wryly as he held her eyes, and it was all Cleo could do to prevent herself from reaching up and fastening her lips over the superbly crafted lines of his mouth. But she knew she had to be circumspect if this unusual but already beautiful marriage of theirs was to work out, to live and grow. Their relationship was too new, too delicately balanced as yet, to give him one inkling of the way she really felt. He could, at this stage, be horrified by the implications.

Then he touched the side of her face with a slow-moving finger and his eyes were soft.

'I'll give you lunch at Glades. One o'clock.'

Cleo had finished dressing and was half-way down the stairs when Meg came out of the kitchen.

'There's a phone call for you, madam. Luke Slade.'

'Thanks, Meg, I'll take it in the study.'

Cleo responded warmly to the housekeeper's smile. Meg's devotion to Jude had lapped over on her, and the older woman asked, 'Shall I bring your breakfast through, madam? How about a nice boiled egg—free-range and fresh?' she tempted.

Cleo shook her head, admitting, 'I finished off the toast Jude couldn't eat, thanks,' and was aware of Meg's cluck of disapproval as she went to take that call, wondering why Luke had bothered to contact her. He certainly wouldn't be enquiring about her health—they had never got on very well together.

'Cleo?' His voice sounded harsh and tinny. 'Thank God you're back. I was afraid you and Jude might have skived off for yet another week. How soon can you get here?'

His urgency worried her and she asked quickly, 'What's wrong? Not Uncle John?'

But Luke snapped, 'He's fine. Just get here. Fenton's been round, making unpleasant demands. We can't discuss it on the phone. Just get here.'

She arrived at the Slade Securities head office in Eastcheap still in a state of shock, but as she dismissed

Thornwood and the Rolls and walked across the pavement her thoughts began to unlock themselves, tumbling out all over her brain.

In the exquisite delight of recognising her love for Jude, in the joy they had discovered together during those long golden days and jewelled nights, Robert Fenton, and her reason for needing a husband in the first place, had been pushed from her mind, because garbage like that had no place in the ecstatic, the delicate, the passionate act of falling in love.

She had told Fenton they would be away for one week. But Jude had taken two. And Fenton hadn't been able to wait. So his greed had taken him to Luke, to spread his poison, make his threats, turn the screw.

Her hands were wet with sweat as she took the lift to Luke's office. His secretary told her to go right in, her eyes puzzled, sensing something was wrong. Luke was pacing the floor and he shot over to her, slammed the door closed behind her and grated, 'What the hell kind of mess do you think you've got us into? His narrow face was flushed and his hand shook as he took a bottle from the hospitality cupboard and sloshed two inches of Scotch into a glass. 'He walked in here on Thursday with his oily threats and I've been going spare ever since.' He took a long gulp of the neat spirit and told her, 'He said you'd promised to hand over twenty-five thousand pounds last week, for withholding certain information. By Thursday he'd decided you were reneging so he came to me.'

'I'm sorry you had to get mixed up in this.' Cleo slumped weakly on to a chair. 'I forgot. We didn't get back to London until late yesterday afternoon.'

'Sorry?' Luke bared his teeth in a mirthless grimace, his eyes incredulous. 'And how the hell can you forget a thing like that? Or do you have so many blackmailing threats hanging over you that this one just slipped your mind? It wouldn't surprise me,' he jeered, 'you always did seem too good to be true!'

She wanted to walk out there and then, but couldn't afford the luxury, so she asked, tight-lipped, 'Is this as far as it's gone? Just trying to get the money out of you?'

'He'd be lucky!' His mouth twisted. 'And isn't it far enough? Can you imagine what the kind of publicity he's threatening to put around would do to the company—stuff like that can affect confidence. I can't afford to have that happen. In the state we're in, it could finish us.' He sat down heavily. 'If the money isn't in his hands by tomorrow he threatened to go to Father for it, and if that failed he's seeing some newspaper creep—as bent as he is, no doubt. I would have kicked him out of the door, but I knew he had to be telling the truth about what happened between you, otherwise you'd never have agreed to pay up in the first place.'

'He told you everything?' Cleo felt sick and she almost asked for a drink when Luke got up to pour himself another Scotch. But she needed a clear head to contact her bank and ask them to have the money ready for her to collect in the morning, to arrange a meeting place with Fenton.

Luke sat down again, disgust on his face. 'About your affair, the debts he ran up trying to give you a good time, your promise to marry him, the night you spent together at some out of the way hotel just before you gave him the boot.'

And Cleo said tiredly, 'It wasn't like that. We did date, but it never got heavy and I soon woke up to the fact that all he wanted from me was a share in the Slade Millions.'

'So why did you agree to pay up?' Luke sneered. 'If your relationship was that innocent he wouldn't have had a thing to hold over you. You've got to be as guilty as hell. Not that it bothers me,' he added spitefully. 'I couldn't care less if you have to pay him to hold his tongue for the rest of your life. But I don't go a bundle on being personally threatened by a creep like Fenton. Anyway,' his eyes glittered triumphantly, 'if your relationship was so pure, what about the night you spent together at that Red Lion place? He said he could prove you'd shared a room as man and wife.'

'And so he could,' Cleo agreed wearily. 'We went for a drive in the country—he'd asked me to marry him, secretly, and I turned him down because by that time I knew he was primarily interested in the money I'd eventually inherit. He seemed to take my refusal well, said he hoped we could still be friends. God, I was green!' Her brows knitted over cloudy grey eyes. 'I'd already realised he was a bit of a con-man, but I didn't know he could be evil. I don't know why I'm explaining all this to you, but he engineered the whole Red Lion episode. He booked us in as man and wife and when I found out it was too late to do anything about it. But I spent the night in an armchair. Fenton and I have never been lovers——'

'Yet you're willing to pay out that kind of money!'

Cleo saw the sneering disbelief in his eyes and she said grittily, 'I can't prove we weren't lovers. He can prove we shared a hotel room for a night. I can't disprove his lies—that I said I'd marry him, made him spend money on me he couldn't afford then walked away when he got into debt. And I've found——' her eyes lashed him scornfully '—that most people prefer to believe the worst of others.'

He didn't even look uncomfortable, she noted bitterly, and she punched her message home,

'Had I been the only person concerned I would have told him to go to hell before I gave him a penny. I've no doubt at all that he could have got the whole pack of lies into some grotty scandal sheet, and it wouldn't have done my career much good, but I would have survived. But your father wouldn't. He's old and he's sick, and that type of publicity would finish him. He couldn't take it, and why should he, if I can prevent it? He's always been good to me and he showed me more affection—more understanding, I should say—than you or your mother ever did.'

She reached for her black alligator-skin handbag, fitting the fine shoestring strap over her arm. 'I'm paying up because I owe it to your father, because he was the only person who cared a rap for me after my parents died. And for no other reason.'

'And you married Jude to get your hands on the wherewithal? I thought the whole thing was a bit sudden.'

Luke got to his feet as she made for the door and she told him icily, barely turning her smooth, silvery head, 'I married Jude because I love him.' And it was the truth. She had been falling in love with Jude for a long time, but love was an emotion she had learned to live without. When it had happened it had taken her a long time to recognise it. But that was no business of Luke's.

'So you'll get in touch with Fenton?' Luke was just behind her as she reached the door, and he sneered, 'If it weren't for the trouble that kind of publicity could give Slade Securities I'd happily pay Fenton to spread the dirt.'

'You'd what?' Cleo went cold. 'I don't believe I'm hearing this!'

'You heard,' he drawled, his mouth curling. Cleo knew he'd always resented her, but she hadn't realised that over the years the resentment had deepened to hate.

'Why?'

'There was enough pious fuss from my father when he'd had his attention drawn to that relatively harmless piece about me,' he said bitterly. 'It was even said that it caused his latest heart-attack. So I'd like him to know that Wonder Girl isn't as perfect as he thought she was. It might just put your nose out of joint. He's always holding you up as an example.'

Cleo's mouth went dry as she stared at the cousin she had thought she knew, realising that she didn't know him at all. His cloak of pompous indifference had hidden his hatred. She half turned, her disgust and anger burning her up, and grated, 'You'd want that, even though you know what it would do to your father? He damn near died when he read about the brawl you got yourself involved in. You can't think anything of him at all—you selfish bastard!'

The feeling of rage and disgust kept her going, but even that evaporated completely as she stood in a call box after contacting her bank, phoning Robert Fenton. She felt slightly sick and trembly as she slid into her seat at the table Jude had reserved for them at Glades.

'You're looking tired,' he said after he'd handed back the menus and given their order. Concern clouded the vivid blue of his eyes. 'Bad morning shopping? Or did your visit with Luke upset you for some reason?'

It had been a bad morning, and how, but she couldn't tell him why so she shrugged, putting on a smile, 'So-so,' then, wondering, 'How did you know I'd gone to see Luke?'

'I telephoned home. Meg told me Thornwood had driven you to Eastcheap. A simple deduction.' He looked amused and he leant his elbows on the small linen-covered table-top, trailing the fingers of one hand softly down the curve of her cheek. 'Pretty—pretty and soft,' he murmured, and her heart lurched over with love for him. And as the feathering caress moved over her mouth she parted her lips, closing them over his fingertip, nipping gently, then drew back, her face hot. Never in a million years would she have imagined herself and the chief executive of Mescal Slade making such a public display of themselves!

'Why did you try to reach me?' she asked then, creditably cool, trying to get things back on a more manageable level because if she didn't, and he kept eating her with his eyes, then she would certainly end up making an even more public display of her love for him! She needed him, needed his tenderness, after the battering she'd taken this morning.

And Jude removed his elbows from the table, leaning back as their first course arrived.

'No particular reason. I just needed to hear your voice.' And that made her feel good, so very good, and it melted away some of the distaste which had been produced by this morning's conversation with Luke.

Then, without knowing why, because she and Jude never talked about the circumstances of their marriage, she asked lightly, toying with a forkful of chicken in a light wine sauce, 'Why did you agree to marry me, Jude?'

'Because, as you pointed out, I would always be in the happy position of knowing you hadn't married me for my money. Call me a cynic if you like, but I've never been able to distinguish between people who liked me for what I am and those who just like the smell of wealth.'

It was a flippant reply but it told her he was probably as far away from loving her as he had been when she'd proposed. And that was daunting, but she wasn't going to let it worry her too much. And at least he'd had the sensitivity not to mention the shares, because although they had probably been his first consideration when agreeing to marry her, she didn't want to hear him say as much. It would put what they did have together down on the level of a purely commercial agreement.

She didn't know why she had asked that question, and she didn't know what she'd expected him to say. She hadn't really hoped he would tell her he'd suddenly realised, over that weekend he'd taken to think it over, that he was madly in love with her, had she?

Of course she hadn't. She didn't believe in miracles, and she knew that if he were ever to grow to love her then the process would take time. So why was she now feeling so empty inside?

And he smiled at her lazily, as if they'd been discussing nothing more important than the state of the weather, and lifted the bottle the waiter had left in the cooler at the side of the table. 'Let me give you some wine. I think you'll like it.'

And she smiled, just slightly, because suddenly smiling was difficult. 'Thank you.' She knew that, for him, although their marriage of convenience was working out well so far, it would remain just that, a marriage of convenience, for some long time to come.

Lifting her eyes to him over the rim of her glass, she smiled again, put more into it this time, making herself sparkle. After all, she was a fighter, a stayer, and one day she'd damn well *make* him fall in love with her!

Because, if he didn't, her life might well become unbearable.

CHAPTER SIX

'So I suppose you'll be buying up Harrods this afternoon, as you spent the morning with Luke?' Jude queried as he escorted her from the restaurant, his hand under her elbow, making her feel safe and protected.

'Just a dress.' Cleo smiled quickly. She'd forgotten she'd said she'd be going shopping this morning, Luke's phone call had driven it out of her mind, and she still went cold when she remembered the hatred she'd later seen in his eyes, his bitter resentment.

'Give Thornwood a ring when you've finished, he can collect you. That's what he's paid for.' His eyes warmed, holding hers briefly before he hailed a cruising taxi. 'I don't want a worn-out wife in my bed tonight.'

Cleo wasn't in the mood for shopping, and as she turned into Bond Street her thoughts were miserably chewing over the interview with her cousin that morning. Perhaps she'd always subconsciously known that his dislike of her went deeper than mere resentment, and perhaps that was why she hadn't even thought about approaching him for advice when Fenton had made his first blackmailing demands.

She stared unseeingly into shop windows until she realised she had to snap herself out of this mood of introspection. She had always known that her aunt and cousin had little time for her, were unwilling and unable to absorb her into the family. But Uncle John cared about her, and she had Jude, and Jude had become everything to her.

Things were looking good, she assured herself, and there was real hope for their marriage. It would succeed, and one day he would love her as she loved him. On that she was quite determined! And tomorrow, after she'd paid Fenton off, she would be able to put the past behind her and concentrate all her energies on the most important thing in her life—her marriage to Jude.

An hour later she walked out of a boutique, mingling with the crowds on the pavement. The dress she had bought was more daring than her usual choice. It was calf-length, with a full, soft skirt, in ice-blue—which made the most of her recently acquired tan. So far, so good, but the front of the bodice dipped lower than anything she had ever worn before and the back was non-existent—except for the band of the halter strap around the neck. The quiver of inner excitement she experienced as she imagined Jude's reaction when he saw her in the dress brought a dreamy smile to her lips. And someone said, just behind her, 'Been buying something super?'

Cleo turned, smiling down into the eyes of Polly Masters. Polly worked in the Equity and Research department at Mescal Slade and Cleo asked, 'Day off?'

'Umm. A couple of days, actually.' Her brown eyes slid to the classy carrier Cleo was holding. 'I want to buy a summer suit, but I couldn't afford the prices they charge in that place. You look great, by the way, a tan suits you—and the whole building's still buzzing over the way you upped and married the Frozen Asset. Ooops!' Polly clapped a hand over her mouth, looking mortified. 'Me and my big mouth!'

'I think I may have thawed him a little,' Cleo grinned, and felt proud, and deliriously happy because it was the truth. And everything was almost perfect, and one day, in the not-too-distant future, she hoped it would be completely, utterly perfect.

'Well, bully for you! No one knew there was a big romance going on under our noses. Ouch!' she winced as a passer by knocked into her, nearly sending her flying. 'Tell you what, why don't we grab a coffee, have a natter? We've been having a collection for a wedding present for you and Jude—I mean, Mr Mescal—and he said you'd drop in one day next week—he'd arrange which day with you—and we could do the presentation bit then. Have you retired, or something?' Her head tilted to one side, 'I wish I could. I fancy myself as a Kept Woman!'

'No such thing!' Cleo was quick to scotch that rumour. Polly was a small fish in Equity and Research but she had a large mouth, and Cleo was going to be behind her desk first thing on Monday morning, if not sooner, because idling around was nice and relaxing—or would be when the vile business with Fenton was over—but she couldn't wait to start working with Jude again. 'OK, we'll have that coffee.' She didn't want one, not after her delicious lunch with Jude, but it would give her the opportunity to make it clear to Polly that retirement was the last thing on the cards. She was still Jude's PA and she had no intention of giving up that coveted position.

At the cramped table in the tiny restaurant, Polly picked up the menu. 'I haven't had lunch yet and my stomach thinks my throat's been cut—do you mind?'

'No, of course not, go ahead,' said Cleo. 'I'll just have tea.'

'Well, I'm glad you're not aiming to be a lady of leisure,' Polly confided when she'd given her order. 'Word had it you were resigning, and when Sheila Bates from Takeovers and Mergers heard she nearly flipped. She fancies her chances as your successor! Oh, she's qualified,' Polly twisted a springy black curl around her index finger, her head on one side. 'But she's a pain in the neck. As your husband's PA she'd be insufferable.'

'There's no question of my resigning,' Cleo denied firmly. But something cold wriggled around inside her all the same. Jude had been adamant about her staying away from the office for the rest of this week, and that could have been consideration on his part, because she did have a lot to attend to—clearing up at the house in Bow, deciding what to do about the furniture. But why had he said she'd be dropping in one day next week when he'd been approached about the presentation of the wedding gift? He had obviously made it sound as though she wouldn't be around on a permanent day-to-day basis.

'And talking about Takeovers and Mergers——' Polly's brown eyes were avid as she looked up from her tuna salad. 'A client phoned me yesterday morning, and this guy said he'd heard a rumour that we're making a takeover bid for your uncle's company, Slade Securities. He wanted to know if he should buy in.' A morsel of tuna disappeared between her glossy red lips and Cleo's heart did a small somersault. Her uncle's firm—the largely family-owned company—to be swallowed up by Mescal Slade? It would break his heart, make all the years he and her father had spent building the business up from scratch seem like a waste of time. And Polly said, 'I thought you'd like to know what was in the wind. Why don't you get on to someone in Takeovers and Mergers, find out what's going on. Know what I mean? You could come up with something interesting.'

It was no secret that Cleo's father and Jude's uncle, direct descendants of Harry Slade and Reuben Mescal who had founded the merchant bank way back in the eighteen hundreds had quarrelled. It had happened a long time ago, almost fifty years ago to be exact, and Cleo's father had sold out his shares to Jude's uncle and had gone into secondary banking, founding Slade Securities with his younger brother, Cleo's Uncle John.

When her father had died ten years ago Uncle John had carried on the by then successful company until the second of his heart-attacks had forced him into retirement. Now Luke was at the helm, and if Mescal Slade were considering a takeover bid...

And why hadn't Jude told her? Surely she had a right to know? He would have the final say in any such decision; the board was like putty in his hands. They respected his judgement too much, and with good reason, to do more than superficially question his decisions— and then only for the look of it...

'Hey!' Polly snapped her fingers under Cleo's nose. 'Come on back here—you looked miles away!'

Cleo glanced at the other girl with a start, her eyes unfocused, then smiled automatically, picking up her cup to finish her tea and Polly, eyeing the slenderly cut suit in fine olive green crêpe Cleo was wearing over a white silk V-necked blouse, asked wistfully, 'I don't suppose you'd help me look for a suit. You've got such fantastic taste.'

'I'm sorry,' Cleo said quickly, perhaps too quickly, she conceded as Polly's face set in a huffy mask. This latest bombshell made her unfit company for anyone, and the last thing she could settle to do was trail round the shops looking for clothes. She had to contact Jude. 'I really don't have time,' she offered, her grey eyes serious.

Polly shrugged. 'That's OK.'

But she looked brighter when Cleo told her sincerely, 'You don't need me to help you choose what to wear. You always look great.'

*   *   *

'I'm sorry, Cleo, your husband is tied up in a meeting all afternoon.' Dawn Goodall sounded perky. 'Your husband! You could have knocked me down with the proverbial when I heard you and Mr Mescal were married! I suppose congratulations are in order!'

'Thanks.' Cleo injected warmth into her voice although she felt like howling with frustration. 'How are you coping?'

'Fine,' Dawn laughed lightly. 'I couldn't believe it at first, but he's actually smiled at me a time or two. Marriage has turned him into a human being.'

'I told you you only needed time to get used to him,' Cleo reminded, hating to have to waste time on chit-chat when all she wanted to do was find out from Jude if there was any truth in the takeover rumour.

But the smile slipped from her face as Dawn told her, 'As a matter of fact I was about to phone you. Mr Mescal asked me to let you know he'd be late home this evening. Something suddenly cropped up and he's got a working dinner with some of the consortium who are handling the bid for a chain of American hotels. Just preliminary discussion, you know the sort of thing.'

Cleo did, and if she'd been in the office, functioning in her normal capacity, it would have been she who had arranged the dinner, sat near him, taking it all in, every word, ready to chew over with him later. She would have been the recipient of his innermost cogitations... Instead, she was to dine alone, biting her nails and waiting for him to come home. She didn't know how she managed to end the phone conversation with any civility at all, but she must have done because Dawn sounded unruffled as she said her goodbyes and hung up.

She couldn't believe that Jude would have told her nothing had Mescal Slade been seriously considering a takeover bid for Slade Securities. And why he had to pick this night, of all nights, to be late coming home, she didn't know! It was enough to drive her distracted.

She had kicked her shoes off the moment she'd walked through the front door this afternoon, and now her silk-clad toes curled into the soft pile of the Persian carpet that partially covered the polished oak boards of the study floor as she stared at the phone. She resisted the temptation to call Takeovers and Mergers to fish for the information she needed; she had to speak to Jude about it first.

And there was no question of warning Uncle John. The rumour might be completely unfounded and there was no point in worrying him unnecessarily. Equally, there was no point in speaking to Luke, not until she had the facts. She didn't particularly want to speak to Luke about anything, not after the way he had been this morning, but he was in charge of the company. Her hand hovered over the phone and she bit her lips in indecision before getting up and leaving the room. She would wait for Jude, see what he had to say before alerting any of the family...

She had fallen asleep in front of the drawing-room fire but she snapped to immediate wakefulness when she heard the snick of the door as Jude walked in. He didn't notice her at first, and watching him loosen his tie and run his fingers through his crisp dark hair she thought he looked tired, but when she said, 'Hi—had a good evening?' and uncurled her long legs, standing up, his face lightened, a slow, warm smile curving his long, masculine mouth.

'You shouldn't have waited up.' He came over to her, reaching for her, pulling her close so that their bodies were touching, breast to thigh, the sharp burn of wanting sparking to quick life between them. He bent his dark head, dark hair mingling with soft silver gilt, and he murmured, his mouth finding the taut, slender column of her throat, 'God, you smell good, taste good.'

In a moment, Cleo knew, there would be no question of her mentioning the rumour of the takeover bid. Already the deep need his nearness invoked was claiming her, turning her blood to flame, her mind to mush. So, her hands against the strong wall of his chest, she pushed him away. 'Can I fix you a drink? You look tired.' Her breath was sucked in through her nostrils, making them flare with the sheer effort of clearing her mind, of holding him at bay when all her instincts dictated that she become mindless, melting, a creature created for his pleasure, for the pleasure only he could give her.

'I don't want a drink.' His voice was thick. 'I want you.' He reached for her again but she was too quick for him, her voice rapid and high as she told him,

'I must ask you something.' The smile she slanted in his direction was shaky, because this wasn't what she wanted, not really. She, too, wanted only the wonderful magic that could only be found in his arms, in the depth and delight of their lovemaking.

'Go ahead.'

He slumped in the chair opposite the one she had sunk into and she noticed the tiredness was back in his face, the marks of a man who drove himself too hard. But she owed it to Uncle John, to herself, to find out, so she asked him, 'Is it true that Mescal Slade are considering a takeover of Slade Securities? I heard a rumour.'

'Ah. I think I will have that drink.' He moved over to the drinks tray and Cleo, her eyes on the long male elegance of his back, knew the rumour had solid foundation. And that hurt, more than she had thought possible. Why hadn't he told her? But his features had assumed the poker player's mask that he always used to hide his true feelings when he turned to face her again, and he went to stand in front of the fire, straddle-legged, his glass held in one loosely curved hand.

'So you've heard about the possible takeover bid. It's the good old Chinese Wall syndrome again!' He smiled thinly, rocking back on his heels, his eyes stony. 'The old fiction that each department keeps itself to itself with no gratuitous overlapping of information is a pretty theory, but it hardly ever works.'

'Why didn't you tell me?'

With an effort she kept her voice level, light; she had too much pride to allow him to see her as a whining child, and a cold smile flickered over his mouth as he told her, 'We don't work like that. You, of all people, should know that. You're an interested party.'

'Of course.' Her expression was carefully blank, but she was hurting inside. How could he have kept such a thing from her? She loved him, she was his wife! But, a cold spiteful voice inside her reminded, he didn't love her. As far as he was concerned theirs was an expedient marriage, nothing more. Beyond the bedroom door she was no more to him than she had ever been—one individual among the many employed by Mescal Slade, slightly closer to him than most because of her position as his PA, but that was all.

All at once she needed a drink, too, and she got up stiffly, her body feeling uncoordinated as she moved across the room. When John Slade found out about this it would finish him. He would see all his work, the decision he'd made with her father to break free of Mescal Slade all those years ago, count for nothing.

Her back to Jude, she poured herself a vodka and tonic, trying to control the tremor of her hand, and Jude said quietly, 'There's something else. I think it's time you knew—I'm going to have to find another PA.'

Quite suddenly, the ticking of the pretty grandmother clock seemed louder, the crackle of the logs on the hearth almost deafening. Or maybe it was the silence, the stillness that flooded her brain as she waited for him to explain, that brought everything into sharper focus. So they'd all been right—Polly, Dawn, Sheila Bates—when they'd picked up undercurrents. Jude wanted her out.

She loved her job, didn't want to lose it. Working with Jude made her feel fully alive, it had done since that very first day. And surely he wasn't one of those ghastly old-fashioned men who, clinging to archaic concepts, believed a woman's place was in the home, preferably in chains!

In any case, her chin jutted mutinously, he could fire her—that was his prerogative—but he couldn't stop her going out and finding another job!

He had waited for her to protest, to comment. That much was evident from the arching of one black brow. But Cleo couldn't trust herself to speak, not just yet. And then, as if he could feel her bewilderment, her quick instinctive mutiny, his eyes softened, understanding making them warm as he watched her go back to her chair with the stiff movements of a tautly held body.

'I shall miss you,' he told her quietly. 'Miss your quick mind, your unfailing tact, the flick of dry humour you produce when you want to put me in my place.'

So he had noticed that! And all the time she had imagined she was quietly and unobtrusively manipulating him into making slightly less than impossible demands on himself, on the rest of the staff! And if he would miss her, why then should he fire her? It didn't make sense!

'There are two reasons why I want you to make a move,' he answered the question posed by the puzzled grey eyes. 'In the first place, I don't think it's a particularly good idea for a husband and wife to work so closely together. And secondly, in view of the board's interest in the possibility of a takeover, you'd be far more useful at Slade Securities.'

She hadn't thought of that, but now her mind reluctantly began to follow his.

'Are they in trouble?' Grace had said that her husband had been fretting about the business. Cleo had put that down to his general ill health, but obviously there was more to it than that. And Mescal Slade had started to take a serious interest. Shaky finance houses did well to keep looking over their shoulders, because there were always rock-solid merchant bankers only too ready to swallow them up.

'Some,' Jude replied evenly, shifting, stretching out long, immaculately clad legs, the dark fabric pulled taut across his thighs. 'Since John had to retire, Luke's been overreaching himself. It's a high-risk-capital game, as we know, but recently he's been risking too much—especially in the entrepreneurial section; high flyers with no real and solid grounds for success. The City is getting to know it by now, but if I could persuade the board to back off, forget we ever contemplated a takeover bid, then the other big fishes would have to rethink. If they find out, which I shall make sure they do, that Mescal Slade's interest in Slade Securities has cooled, then they're going to hold off while they sniff the air. You understand?'

She did. She understood, but could do nothing about the game of financial chess Jude was outlining. He had seen her offer of her block of Slade Securities shares as a means of taking personal control of the finance house Mescal Slade were interested in controlling. With her at the helm of the company, no doubt with strong guidance from him, he could become the major shareholder in a newly prosperous concern. Little wonder he'd decided to take up her offer of marriage after she'd told him she'd give him those shares!

'And if you are there,' he leaned forward in his chair, his eyes holding hers intently, 'with your brain, your grasp of what makes the City tick, your financial common sense, then you should have enough time to get Slade Securities back into a position of strength before anyone realises what is happening. Interested?'

'You don't need to ask that,' Cleo replied, her throat tightening. If it were within her power to rescue Slade Securities then she had no choice but to do her damnedest. And that would be what Jude was counting on. The shares she had brought to this marriage would be worth so much more if the company was sound. He was manipulating her, making sure the assets she had brought with her were worth as much as possible. It hurt, like nothing else had hurt before, because in spite of her earlier optimism about the state of their marriage he was no nearer loving her than he had ever been. He was using her. In bed or out of it, he was simply using her.

'When you told me you were firing me I thought it was because you were the type of man who meant to keep his wife at home, looking after the children.' No way was she going to let him know the way she really felt—betrayed, used, as far as ever from having his love. Her role was to be the amenable, totally sensible wife, pulling with him, never against him, never letting him know by word or action how desperately she craved the commitment of his love.

'But I do.' His soft answer left her gasping, but he amended, 'But not quite in the way you imagine. When the children do arrive we'll turn a room here into an office for you, install a computer link-up with Slade's head office, and you can do most of your work from home. No problem. You'll have a nanny, of course, but we'll both make time to be with the children—that's where the house in the country will come in. A place for holidays, weekends, that sort of thing. Fair?'

She nodded, unable to meet his eyes in case he saw the pain there and wondered... Oh, he was being fair, doing everything possible to make their life together a success, and if she didn't love him she might feel the marriage was perfect. But she did love him, more than life, and his calculated manipulation of their future, of the assets she'd brought to this marriage, made her feel cold, cold and lonely.

But she nodded, 'Very fair,' and finished her drink. 'I hope Uncle John and Luke approve our intentions,' she added drily, flinching when he told her,

'I've already consulted them.'

She had been living in a fool's paradise, the last person to know of his intentions. His brain must have been working overtime ever since she'd mentioned those shares in conjunction with her proposal of marriage.

She hardly heard him when he elaborated, 'Your uncle's firmly behind the idea of your joining Slade. So is Luke—but only, I must warn you, because he can't see any way out of the near shambles he's created.'

'Then there seems nothing further to say,' she told him, surprising herself by the equable tone she achieved, and he countered,

'I've often wondered—why didn't you join Slade when you got your degree?'

'Luke.' She shrugged minimally, containing her misery. 'I couldn't stomach the idea of him treating me like a backward junior clerk. Apart from being pompous, he's the type who thinks that being male automatically makes him superior in every degree to a mere female.' And I've discovered that he hates me, which will make working

with him almost intolerable, she thought. But Jude
wasn't ever going to hear about that, so she added, 'Not
to worry, you now own as many shares as he and his
father between them, and that, if nothing else, makes
me his equal.'

And to her astonishment Jude grinned lazily,
stretching, cat-like, in his chair. 'You have a finer mind
by far, determination and guts, not to mention all that
exquisite packaging. The poor guy's going to have to
resign himself to taking a very inferior back seat indeed!'

Almost, she felt flattered. But he was simply seeing
her as a brain, a means of pulling Slade Securities—in
which, of course, he had a vested interest—together
again. He wasn't seeing her as a wife, a woman to be
loved.

'I think I'll go up, I'm very tired,' she excused herself,
hoping to get out of there before her misery began to
show through, and she had reached the door before his
voice stopped her, and she turned to see him leave his
chair, come over to her.

'You don't mind? It might not seem so from where
you're standing, but I don't want to push you into doing
something you don't want to do.' The character lines on
either side of his mouth indented wryly and he touched
the side of her face with a slowly moving finger, his eyes
sober. She almost flinched away from his touch because
the meaning behind it was shallow. She craved the depths
of emotion, not the shallows. But she smiled, shaking
her head.

'Of course I don't mind. It's the sensible thing to do.'
And she watched his face change, assume the blank poker
player's mask again.

That mask always worked well in his business dealings,
and had always amused her because she knew how the
mind behind the mask was working. But now, when he

said, 'And you always do the sensible thing. Quite right, Cleo,' she didn't know whether to take it as a compliment or not. It was one thing to understand how his mind worked in his dealings in the City, quite another to understand his motives, his feelings, in the arena of their marriage.

And that night, for the first time, she pretended to be deeply asleep when he came to their bedroom.

CHAPTER SEVEN

THE last of the everyday cooking utensils and crockery went into a packing case, ready to be taken to Oxfam, and now Cleo had to start wrapping the things of sentimental value—mostly bits and pieces her student friends had given as housewarming presents when she had first moved into the small house in Bow.

These and most of the furniture would go into store. Jude had said, 'You might like to hang on to your things, put them about when we get a place in the country,' and she had agreed, because she had taken time and trouble when furnishing, and some of the pieces were like old and valued friends.

Getting up from her knees, she decided on coffee to help steady her nerves because Robert Fenton had said he'd be here around lunch time, and that could mean anytime between twelve and two.

She tucked the hem of her blue and green striped Viyella shirt back into the waistband of her sleek green needlecord jeans and filled the kettle, plugging it in with hands that shook a little. She would be thankful when today was over, this whole horrible business behind her.

She spooned coffee granules and powdered milk into a mug and waited for the kettle to boil, chewing on a corner of her lower lip. It had seemed a good idea to suggest Fenton collected the money from here. She hadn't wanted him anywhere near the house in Belgravia, but she could have laid down a definite time, an anonymous meeting place—outside some tube station or other.

101

But she wasn't used to this kind of cloak and dagger stuff, and she hadn't been thinking too clearly when she phoned him yesterday. He would be here anytime during the next two hours. But at least, after then, it would all be over and she could put all her energies into making this marriage work.

But that would be an uphill struggle, she admitted. Those shares had been the primary reason behind his decision to accept her proposal, make her the mother of the children he wanted to have. But she'd always known that, hadn't she? Her conversation with him last night had merely reinforced what she'd already known. Nothing had changed, not really, and besides, she wasn't a quitter and would do everything she could to make this marriage work, and pray that in time love would grow for him, too.

She smiled at this thought, a small, tight smile, and as she poured water into the mug she remembered how she'd sat opposite him at breakfast this morning and he'd asked, 'Are you going to take a look at the Slade Securities books this morning?'

She'd shaken her head, her stomach tying itself in knots because this morning she was collecting the money from the bank, seeing Robert Fenton, and it wasn't a prospect she was over the moon about.

'I'll give him a call and ask him to send all the relevant stuff over in a taxi this afternoon,' she had told him. 'I can work through them in peace here, without him breathing down my neck.'

'Good idea. And don't let him try to put you down.' His mouth quirked humorously. 'Not that I think he could, not in a million years. But just remember, your uncle's on your side all the way, and if you need any help or advice you know you can count on me.'

Jude had finished eating and he'd be leaving for the City soon. Cleo had tried to look on the bright side, because the next time she saw him the nightmare of Robert Fenton would be over and behind her, so she smiled and said, 'Have a good day,'

'Make it a better one?' he'd countered lightly. 'I miss you around the office, so have lunch with me?'

'I'd better not,' she'd said quickly, perhaps too quickly, because she'd caught the slight lift of his brows over cool, enquiring eyes, and she'd just had to explain as she'd followed him to the door, feeling like a worm, 'I thought I'd take myself over to Bow this morning. I need to get things sorted out and packed, and arrange for some of the stuff to go into store. The house agents will be putting the board up next week.'

It had felt like telling lies, although it was part of the truth. And she would phone through and make those arrangements just as soon as Fenton had gone. Until then, she was too edgy to make coherent arrangements with anyone about anything.

It was almost an hour later when the shrill of the doorbell made her drop the pile of books she was moving down from her former bedroom. Her nerves were stretched tight as she stepped over the scattered books, but she took a deep breath and told herself that this would soon be over, and after that she felt calmer, better able to cope.

As she opened the door he was leaning against the frame, smiling unpleasantly; she stepped back and he walked through as if he owned the place.

He was casually dressed and she thought: brown leather trousers, ye gods! and decided they didn't suit him. Neither did the brown silk shirt, open almost to the waist. The outfit marked him as the poseur he was.

Saying nothing, she preceded him to the living-room, untidy now with the bulging cartons and carriers she'd dumped haphazardly because this morning she hadn't been functioning on her normal calm and efficient level. There was a small wall safe behind one of the pictures, installed by a previous owner, and she'd put the package in there as soon as she'd come from the bank. Twenty-five thousand was a lot of money to leave lying around, even for a few hours.

It took a few moments to extract the package, and when she turned he was sprawled out on the sofa, his booted feet on the almond-green upholstery, his eyes avid, following her every movement. He held out his hand wordlessly but she shook her head.

'The hotel receipt first.' She watched coldly as he pulled the scrap of paper from a pocket in his shirt and released it so that it fluttered to the carpet.

'How do you know I haven't had it photocopied?' he asked, his face blank, and she snapped,

'You probably have. But I'd advise you not to try it on again. Just pay off your debts and stay away from me.' She tossed the package at him, disgust on her face. 'Now get out!'

He turned his head, staring at her, his face tightening. 'You weren't always so keen to see the back of me.'

'I didn't know what a creep you were then,' she grated, her control precarious now. She couldn't bear to be reminded that she had once found him remotely likeable. It made her feel ashamed to know that she had ever been so blind, so gullible. And he knew that, he'd have to be a fool not to, and his mouth whitened with temper as he retaliated,

'But *I* knew what a pain *you* were! My God—when I think of the time I put in—all those boring trips to the country, the ghastly picnics, the cosy meals you dished up here and the predictable, prissy "hands off" signals if I did more than kiss you! God, what a bore it all was. And for what? For sweet damn-all!'

He tipped the contents of the package on the sofa, swinging his legs to the floor, his eyes furious. 'I reckon you owe me this! You can't actually imagine I enjoyed sucking up to you, listening to you boring on about your wretched exam results and then your precious career? So, having said that, and put the record straight,' his voice changed, was smooth as oil, 'you don't mind if I count this, I hope. Not being trustworthy myself, I don't trust anyone else. Not even a self-righteous prude like you.'

So she gritted her teeth, not bothering to tell him to be quick about it, because even saying that would waste precious seconds and she wanted him out of here. He tainted the air. And when he had finished he stood up, looking down at the piles of notes—tens and twenties—spread out on the almond-green fabric.

'I should have asked for double,' he said.

'Just take it and go,' she gritted, controlling her voice with difficulty because she felt like screaming.

He raised his head then, tearing his eyes from the small fortune spread out in front of him, and he looked at her, at the taut whiplash lines of her body, and his eyes held something unspeakable.

'You always were a frigid bitch,' he mouthed slowly, and then advanced, putting himself between her and the door. 'But you're a married bitch now, and maybe Mescal's taught you what it's all about.'

He began to circle her and she sidestepped, her heart beginning to race, and she realised when it was too late to do anything about it that he had manoeuvred her into a corner.

'Don't come near me!' Her eyes glittered with a mixture of rage and fear, and he said thickly,

'Why not? I'll show you what you missed that night in Goldingstan.'

He made a single swift movement, lunging for her, but she twisted out of his reach, his hands finding nothing more substantial than the cloth of her shirt, and the buttons ripped as she jerked frenziedly away, the fabric parting to reveal the rounded globes of her breasts, barely covered by the midnight-blue lace of her scantily cut bra.

There was no time to think about making herself decent again, she had to get out of here because Fenton was serious, deadly serious, his hot eyes on her exposed skin. She made a desperate attempt to reach the door, but he was quick—and fitter than he deserved to be, considering his life-style—and he caught her, bringing her down in a fair imitation of a rugby tackle, knocking the breath out of her lungs as his body fell on hers.

Cleo twisted and fought, but he caught her head between his hands, twisting until she thought her hair would come out by the roots, and she began to scream, but he silenced her with his savage mouth and blood thundered in her head, a pounding roar. But she heard, above it, a voice like perma-frost.

'Just what the hell is going on?'

And then there was silence, and stillness, like the eye of a storm. Fenton's body went rigid on top of hers, and the taste of fear was on his lips which were still clamped over her mouth.

Then all was violence, movement and noise as Fenton's body was dragged from her, the sound of ripping fabric, the tearing of brown silk as Jude hauled him to his feet, flinging him against the wall.

Cleo opened her eyes, relief at Jude's timely arrival warring with panic as his glittering eyes swept over her sprawled body, her near-naked breasts, her wildly tangled hair. And his eyes held murder, dark, icy murder.

She tried to tell him it wasn't what it seemed, that she had not been a willing partner in that torrid embrace, that he had saved her from possible rape, but the sounds she made were thickly incoherent and he turned from her as though she sickened him and she saw the lean, strong hands curl into fists as he swung round to tell Fenton, 'Get out before I tear you apart.'

Fenton hauled himself together as Cleo scrambled to her feet, tugging the two halves of her ripped shirt together, her breath coming raggedly. The younger man wasn't leaving without taking what he had come for, but Cleo saw how his hands shook as he tucked his shirt back into his tight leather trousers.

Jude's face was set, the darkly tanned skin pulled tight over jutting bones, danger explicit in every line of his athletically powerful body, so Cleo had to give Fenton a grudging ten marks for courage as he sauntered over to the sofa and began to pick up the piles of notes.

'On my way, mate,' he drawled. 'But I can't leave without taking my little gift, can I? Might hurt the lady's feelings.'

'Did you give him that?' Jude's eyes flicked coldly to her then back to Fenton, and the harsh, incisive tone made her blood run cold.

'Yes.' There was no point in lying, no point at all, and she felt giddy, the room swaying, and she wished she could faint because she'd rather be unconscious, in a coma, than have to try to explain all this away.

She closed her eyes briefly, fighting rising nausea, and she didn't see what happened next but she heard Jude's voice, dark and deadly, 'Get out. Now, before I plaster the wall with you.' And no one who wasn't a suicidal idiot would ignore that kind of menace, because it filled the small room, turning the air sharp with violence, and she dragged her eyes open to see Fenton scurrying out.

He had left the money behind, and Jude grated, 'Pick it up.'

He looked as if he hated her, as if the very sight of her disgusted him, and she stared at him with huge grey frightened eyes, her body shaking, perspiring—although she felt very cold.

The evidence he had walked in on was damning in itself; the money she'd admitted she'd given Robert Fenton made everything worse. She was going to have to tell him the truth about the way she'd been black-mailed, explain that she'd rather part with a slice of her inheritance than bring shame and embarrassment—and possibly something much worse—on to the sick old man who had been the only person she had ever received any-thing remotely like affection from during the past ten years.

Agitation made her voice shake as she took a tentative step towards him, her hands outspread in involuntary supplication.

'Jude—let me explain.'

'Just do as I said,' his voice lashed her. 'Pick that stuff up. And don't say anything, not a word, otherwise I might forget you're a female.'

He wouldn't listen, not now, not in this mood. She dragged herself to the sofa and dropped to her knees, her fingers shaking as she began to push the piled notes together in a bunch. He didn't consider that anything she could say could explain or justify the situation he had walked in on. He couldn't trust her. But then, he didn't love her, so why should he?

From the corner of her eyes she saw him move, bend to pick up a scrap of paper from the floor, and his voice was iced over with contempt as he crumpled the hotel receipt and dropped it to the floor again.

'A souvenir, I take it. Been reliving old times, have you? God, he must have something if the affair's been going on that long!' His mouth curled bitterly and she had never seen his eyes so cold. 'So why didn't you marry him to gain access to the money you obviously intend to pour all over him? And don't bother to answer, let me tell you! Because there was no way your guardians would have approved your marriage to him—and so your considerable financial assets would have been frozen for another year. Tough on him, that. He likes to spend, I take it!' His mouth thinned, displaying a cruelty she hadn't seen before. 'Was he getting restive, threatening to move to greener pastures? Was that why you hatched a plan to marry someone your guardians *would* approve of? And so, as I heard him saying when you'd invited him to my house, two days after becoming my wife, in order to get your hands on one fortune, you married another. Mine. Sweet heaven—did you imagine I'd sit by and let you lavish mine on him once you'd run through yours?'

Things were going from bad to worse, and she couldn't bear it because what he was saying, accusing her of, was nothing like the truth. And now, if ever, was the time to make him see that. She was crazily in love with him and she wanted him to love her, and if she couldn't put the record straight then this morning's débâcle would put the possibility of that ever happening back a hundred years.

She scrambled to her feet, the notes pushed all anyhow back in the package, and he held a hand out, wordlessly, his eyes midnight ice as they swept dismissively over her.

'It isn't what you think,' she began, her courage almost deserting her under that cruelly denigrating look.

'Save your breath,' he cut in tonelessly. 'The scene I walked in on was explicit enough, and the hotel receipt confirms that you had no intention of losing a lover of some long-standing.' His hard eyes impaled her, making her feel ill. 'He must be sensational in bed. So much so that you couldn't stand the deprivation. That's why you asked me to make love to you on the island. Any port in a storm.'

'No!' Appalled, she put a hand to her mouth to stop the words from tumbling out. She had asked him to make love to her because she had just realised how much she loved him. But he wouldn't believe that, not now, and if she tried to make him believe it he would end up despising her even more because he'd think she was trying to wheedle her way round him!

'No?' A black brow arched disbelievingly. 'I can't think of any other reason. And I've no intention of listening to any fairy story you might try to invent.' He tossed the package around in his hands, as if trying to evaluate the exact amount. 'I'll pay this back into your account. You are free to do as you like with your own money,' he commented savagely, 'except to give massive handouts to your lover. Like it or not, you are my wife, and, as my wife, I expect certain standards of behaviour.'

He turned from her dismissively, staring out of the small paned window. 'Get your coat. I'm taking you home. And don't ever think of trying to see that jerk again or I'll keep you under lock and key.'

Staring at the rigid line of his shoulders, the arrogant tilt of his head, a hot tide of pure rage flooded through her, burning her up, and she turned on her heels to fetch her jacket from the kitchen, her voice shaking with anger as she spat over her shoulder,

'Who the hell do you think you are? God? Well, I hope you find the judgement throne comfortable—although it's probably too small for your massive ego!'

She wasn't waiting for any reply, and she wasn't even going to try to tell him the truth! He had sat in judgement, condemning her, without hearing her side of the story, saying things, horrible things, things that cheapened the love she had felt for him, the ecstasy she had found in his arms. And she had her pride; she wouldn't go down on her knees and beg!

But the heated rush of anger fell away, draining her, and her eyes filled with scalding tears as she saw the carton he must have dropped on the table near the door as he'd walked in and found his wife sprawled out on the floor, another man's body covering her, another man's mouth on hers.

The name of the local delicatessen was plainly printed across the carton in bright yellow letters, so the contents were a foregone conclusion. And there was no mistaking the bottle of Moselle for what it was, either. He'd asked her to have lunch with him, to make his day better, and she'd told him she'd be here, working, and so he had come to her, bringing their lunch, because he'd rather picnic with her than eat off the best china in the most exclusive restaurant in town. And if he hadn't walked in and found her with Fenton then she would have been the happiest woman alive because his action, even if he hadn't realised it, meant that she was at last beginning to mean something to him.

But now he thought her to be a two-timing slut, and the hopes she'd had of their marriage developing into a two-way, long-term love-affair were dead as cold ashes. And no sadness could be as great as this.

CHAPTER EIGHT

'CLEO?' Dawn's voice came brightly over the wire. 'I've just had a call from Mr Mescal. He asked me to get you to have Thornwood meet him at the airport at five-thirty, and to remind you the Blairs are expected tonight. OK?'

'Thanks, Dawn. I'll pass the message to Thornwood right away.' She was about to ring off, feeling herself colour as she realised that Dawn just had to be wondering why Jude had phoned her and not his wife, but Dawn chattered on, 'How's the new job going? I must say I miss you here. And couldn't you have persuaded your husband not to promote that Sheila Bates to your old job? Nobody likes her, I'm told, so I'm sure I won't.'

As Dawn seemed set to gossip for hours, Cleo cut in smoothly, advising, 'I'm sure she'll be fine, just get on with your job and leave her to get on with hers. Lovely to talk to you, but I must dash—Jude wants to make an impression on Sir Geoffrey this evening.'

Which was as good an excuse as any to cut the conversation short, even though Meg had everything in hand for this evening and there wasn't a thing Cleo had to do apart from dress herself up and dredge up a smile and a line in relaxed conversation from somewhere. She didn't feel in the mood to talk to anyone, not even Dawn. She was so tense she felt she might explode, disintegrate into a million ragged pieces.

On Tuesday morning, after discovering her with Fenton, Jude had driven her home in a stinging silence and had departed, almost immediately, for Zurich. And late this afternoon he would be back, and before the

112

Blairs arrived for dinner she was going to have to make him listen to her explanations.

He had been too angry to listen to anything she could have said the last time she had seen him, and she could understand that, but today he simply had to hear her side of the story. The sordid business about Fenton's blackmailing threats would have to be exposed and, in a way, it would be a relief because Jude might be able to help.

Her hands shook as she pushed together the pile of papers, the reports and balance sheets she'd been ploughing through, and slid them into an empty drawer in the desk in Jude's study. It hadn't taken her long to realise that Slade Securities was in a mess, and she couldn't begin to see a way out while her mind was in such turmoil. Loving Jude as she did, his disgust with her, the loathing she'd seen in those cold, azure eyes, was a constant and debilitating pain, blinding her to everything else.

And her worries about Fenton's possible next move didn't help any, she acknowledged as she pushed herself listlessly to her feet on her way to find Thornwood and relay Jude's message. Fenton hadn't had the money he'd demanded, so heaven only knew what his next move would be. She didn't know whether to expect a renewed demand or to see, in print, the whole sordid pack of lies. And if that happened she couldn't bear to think what would happen to Uncle John. And Luke, for one, would make sure the old man read every word.

It was like living with a time bomb. But maybe, when Jude knew the truth, he would know what to do.

'You certainly know how to make yourself look sexy, but then you've had plenty of practice, for Fenton, haven't you?'

Cleo twisted round, her heart pumping wildly. Wearing her new dress, she had been putting the finishing touches to her make-up when he'd walked in on her.

She hadn't heard the bedroom door open and now he was leaning against the frame. He looked tired, world-weary, the lines of cynicism deeply scored beside his mouth. Disadvantaged, she looked at him with anguished eyes, the smoke-grey irises deepened to charcoal. She had planned on being ready when he returned, composed, waiting in the drawing-room. But Thornwood must have had a smoother drive from the airport than she had bargained for and her fingers froze, dropping the scent spray she'd been using on to the polished rosewood surface of the dressing-table. The tiny clatter broke the silence of his long, unwavering scrutiny and she said, 'We have to talk,' and tried to get herself together. He had to listen to her. He had to. She would never get through this evening if he didn't.

'Must we?' His tone was bored as he moved slowly into the room, loosening his tie, and her heart jumped, but she resisted the impulse to run. She wasn't a coward, although his patent disgust with her, his terrifying coldness, wasn't making things easy.

'Yes, we must.' She was ashamed of the slight tremor in her voice, of the hunger she was sure must show in her eyes as she watched him remove his suit jacket, his hands moving next to the zip of his trousers. God, but he was superb, almost frighteningly male, and he was her husband, and she loved him, and he loathed her!

But she was about to change all that, wasn't she? Because after she'd explained about Fenton he would go back to being the caring, exciting lover and beloved companion he had been before, surely he would? She knew he had been on the verge of growing more than fond of her. She couldn't believe that wasn't true, and she had to cling on to that.

He was naked now and she closed her eyes against a sudden inrush of pain, of need, that gripped her like a giant steel hand. She had to get him to listen, to understand.

'Jude——'

'Don't you think you ought to go down?' The look he flicked in her direction might have been given to an irritating child. 'Sir Geoffrey and his wife will be here in an hour. You should be checking with Meg.'

He didn't pause in his progress towards the bathroom, and that, and the irritated look, riled her. She wasn't so completely besotted by love that she would allow him to brush her aside like a subnormal hireling!

'This won't take long.' Resolve stiffened her spine as she moved between him and the adjoining bathroom door, her chin lifting defiantly, her eyes unwavering even as she faced the exasperated lowering of his black brows. 'You've judged and condemned me without a hearing, and I deserve better than that!'

'You deserve a thrashing.' His mouth twisted down in a sneer. 'But I'm too much a gentleman to give it to you! But I tell you this——' He moved closer, and his tanned, taut nakedness seared her through the filmy fabric of her dress, making her shudder at the awareness of how easily he could rouse her, even in his hatred. He didn't touch her, he didn't need to, and her words of hot protest at his high-handed refusal even to listen to her side of the story died in her throat, clogging it. 'I know now why you married me. I didn't have to be a genius to work that out,' he flared, controlled anger making his eyes glitter. 'You needed to get your hands on your inheritance and you couldn't afford to wait another twelve months because your lover was getting restive. He wanted to get his hands on that so-called little gift he was practically drooling over. And you couldn't marry him to gain access to your inheritance, no matter how much you might have wanted to, because there's no way your guardians would have approved a jerk like him. So you married me, and, OK——' his breath sucked harshly into his lungs, making the rough satin of his skin quiver with an inner tension she could feel through every fibre of her being, as if he were an extension of herself '—so now I know, and, granted, our marriage was only ever one of expediency—but you're still my wife.'

Suddenly, his hands were at her throat, making her heart flutter in panic as the balls of his thumbs, beneath her chin, forced her head back, forced her to read the dark intent in his eyes.

'You will not be seeing Fenton again, and as that means you'll be deprived of the pleasures of his bed and his body, I've decided to help you.' His voice lowered to the threatening purr of a tiger and she shuddered helplessly, cold with the chill of the hating mockery that was looking at her from those narrowed, glittering eyes. 'You are one hell of a highly sexed lady, as I found out when you begged me to make love to you, when you used me to satisfy your needs in Fenton's absence. So, just to help you,' his mouth curled derisively, 'I'll make love to you until you're reeling. I'll make damned sure you know who you belong to, and you won't have enough strength left to even *think* of Fenton!'

He released her suddenly. And shaken, appalled, by what she was hearing she registered his voice, coming as if from a misty distance.

'Now get downstairs and see if Meg needs any help. Start earning your keep!'

*   *   *

Meeting Jude's sardonic eyes across the table Cleo thought, *I hate him! Hate him!*, then inclined her head to listen to what Sir Geoffrey was saying.

He was a short, round man who loved his food—as evidenced by the way he had relished the saddle of lamb and was now enjoying a second helping of syllabub. No doubt he would make hearty inroads into the cheese-board, Cleo decided, thus prolonging the agony of having to sit opposite Jude with his sardonic eyes and derisive endearments. But at least Sir Geoffrey's appetite made up for her lack of one, although Jude would have noticed, she conceded edgily, picking up her wine-glass and drinking recklessly. He had hardly taken his eyes from her throughout the meal. It was a subtle form of torture.

Whenever she had glanced up at the cold, hard, self-righteous devil, she had found him watching her with those clever, knowing, shaming eyes. And her skin had crawled with hot colour as she'd recalled his threat to make love to her until she reeled—and why. And so she had looked his way as little as possible, putting her mind to conversing with Sir Geoffrey and Hilda, his scrawny, overdressed wife.

Neither of them would know that things were very far from perfect between the handsome, urbanely charming chief executive of Mescal Slade and his new wife. They wouldn't be able to read behind the cynicism of his superficial smiles, those lying words of endearment, to the utter contempt he felt for her.

So much for her stupid belief that she only had to talk rationally to him to make him listen to her because he, more than anyone else she knew, was rational to his fingertips. And how could she have ever believed she could make things right between them again? Her arrogant husband had made up his mind. As far as he was concerned she was devious, sly, unfaithful and greedy, and that was that. No amount of pleading or explaining on her part would make him change his mind.

And so she wouldn't demean herself by pleading for a fair hearing ever again!

Unguardedly, she caught his eyes again, saw the hateful, mocking gleam as he answered a gushing request Lady Blair had just lobbed into the air.

'I'm sure Cleo will let you have the recipe for the syllabub, Hilda. Won't you, my darling?' And, expounding hatefully, his long strong fingers toying idly with his silver fruit knife, his smile holding a savagery only Cleo could detect, 'I'm fortunate in having such a devotedly domesticated wife. She, I'm delighted to say, neglects no area of my—comfort.'

'Such a beautiful wife, too,' Sir Geoffrey chimed in gallantly, and Cleo felt her face burn with rage because domesticated she was not, and Jude knew it, and his reference to 'comfort' had an entirely different connotation.

Hoping the Blairs would attribute her fiery colour to new-bride embarrassment over Jude's seeming compliment, she plastered a smile on her face.

'I'll ask Meg for the recipe, of course. Now, shall we have coffee in the drawing-room, Hilda? Leave the men to what will probably be interminable business talk.'

Thankfully, Hilda was a talkative lady and Cleo only needed to make smiling responses now and again, so she should have been able to relax, but she didn't. Sooner or later their guests would leave. And then what? Would Jude walk away from her with icy contempt, or would he make good his threat to make love to her until she couldn't even think? Both options made her feel physically ill. She didn't want to be alone with him.

Almost hysterically, she wondered what Sir Geoffrey and his wife would say if she begged them to stay for the night—for the rest of the week, for the rest of the month!

Curbing the impulse to stride around the room, pulling her hair out by the handful, she injected what she prayed were the right noises into Hilda's non-stop chatter and almost leapt out of her skin when the door opened and Jude brought Sir Geoffrey through.

The tubby little man looked pleased with life, rubbing his hands together, his smile effusive, and from that, and Jude's look of grim satisfaction, Cleo deduced that Jude had won the Blair and Dowd account, which was what he'd been angling for.

It wasn't long before their guests left and the house was silent, the only sound Cleo was aware of was her own shallow breathing. And she scrambled to her feet as Jude came back into the drawing-room, closing the door behind him, leaning against it as he untied his tie, his eyes never leaving her face.

'How much have you been able to gather from the Slade Securities books? I take it you made a start on them while I was away?'

About to tell him she was on her way to bed—the frosty words on the edge of her tongue—she stared right back at him, her heart jerking. Did he have to be so cold, so unforgiving? Not that there was actually anything to forgive, but he wouldn't believe that in a million years.

If only, a desperate little voice in her mind nudged, if only they could start conversing normally again, together about something in which they shared a common interest, then maybe she could find a way through to him and force him to accept he'd been wrong about her.

'As far as I've been able to tell, it's looking pretty groggy.'

She forced a level tone, forced herself to return to a chair. She had to stay calm. This wasn't personal, this was business, and they were perfectly attuned on that level, she had to remember that. But could she hold her own, given the churning state of her emotions? She doubted even that when he shot, smooth as ice, 'And?'

Her eyes clouded, and her hands felt clammy. He clearly expected her to have some idea of how to remedy the situation, and he was short on patience. But she hadn't been able to bring her usual concentration to the project—how could she, when her equilibrium had been shattered by what had happened? Not to mention her worries about what Robert Fenton might decide to do next!

'I'm waiting to hear your conclusions.' He had removed his tie now, his jacket, and the whiteness of his shirt contrasted starkly with the depth of his tan, his crisp, dark hair, the close-fitting black trousers that skimmed long, lean legs. He was standing, a brandy-glass in his hand, but although he was still there was a restlessness in him she could feel, an intimation of tension in the way he held his head.

'I honestly don't know.' She was on the defensive now. 'I haven't begun to form any conclusions. I've had too much on my mind,' she qualified with a bitterness she couldn't hide.

'Like Fenton?' he came back immediately, his mouth tightening, and Cleo felt drained and hopeless, her face paper-white. What was the use? What was the use?

'No, not Fenton,' she told him wearily, and felt her head begin to ache. It wasn't the strict truth, of course. Fenton had been on her mind, but not for the reasons Jude persisted in believing.

And her depression deepened when he stated flatly, 'I don't believe you. But you're going to have to root him out of your mind and start concentrating on how to pull Slade Securities out of the mire. After all,' he slammed his empty glass down on the drinks table, making her flinch with the leashed violence of the action, 'I've a sizeable interest in the company now—you signed your shares over to me as a payment for the right to get your hands on enough ready cash to satisfy your lover, remember? So when you've come up with a few ideas, let me know, and we'll discuss them.' He picked up his suit jacket and hooked it over his shoulder. 'I'm going to bed now, and I suggest you do, too.' He paused at the door, his voice cutting, 'I don't need to remind you that those shares were only a down payment for my services as your husband. And I intend to extract what's owing. With interest.'

He closed the door quietly behind him and she stared at its blank surface mutinously. There was no way she was going to climb into the huge bed they had shared since returning from their honeymoon. No way on God's sweet earth! Tight with rage, she paced the room, pouring herself a generous dose of brandy and swallowing it recklessly.

She was seeing a side of him she hadn't known existed. She had always admired his objectivity, his ability to see all sides of a given situation, a given problem, his careful weighing of every angle. But in this situation he was seeing only the side he wanted to see, refusing to admit there could be another. And that wasn't like the man she had come to know, like and respect. He was acting out of character, being deliberately cruel, and his treatment of her was an insult.

Every time he killed her attempts to tell him the truth he insulted her. And if he thought she was going to share his bed then he had to be out of his mind! And if she had any sense at all she would walk out on him now and never come back. And he could whistle for what he thought she owed him!

But walking out would point to her guilt—in his jaundiced eyes, it would! He would believe she had gone to Fenton. And besides, she admitted drearily, she still loved him, believed, crazily, that there was still a chance for them. Somewhere.

But tonight she wouldn't sleep with him.

There was a slip of a dressing-room adjoining the master bedroom and it contained a narrow bed. Jude had used it for the first two nights after their wedding because she had stipulated they wouldn't sleep together for the first two weeks of their marriage.

He had respected her wishes, for some reason choosing to use the tiny room rather than the far more comfortable guest-room. And she had admired him for that, for the way he had obviously wanted to spare her any puzzled looks she might have received from Meg. He had been a different man then, she thought miserably as she made her way reluctantly upstairs. He was a frightening stranger now.

She couldn't use the dressing-room, of course, so Meg would have to draw her own conclusions. Because even if Jude were already asleep, which she doubted, he would hear her and wake no matter how quietly she moved across the bedroom. But she had to sleep somewhere and the guest-room was the only other choice, because she wasn't sleeping with him. She had too much pride to share intimacy with a man who hated and despised her, even if he was her husband.

The bed in the guest-room was always kept made up and aired, and the room itself was only slightly less luxurious than the one she and Jude had shared until now. But she wasn't interested in her surroundings, and a sob built up in her throat, hurting, as she unzipped her dress and reflected that her marriage, which had once seemed to hold so much promise, was dead before it had properly come alive.

Clad only in a pair of midnight-blue satin briefs and tiny matching bra, she pulled back the bedcovers and viewed the cool linen sheets with less than enthusiasm.

'I prefer our bed,' Jude said, from right behind her, and before she knew what was happening he had scooped her up into his arms and her eyes widened with shock, for one still second, before she realised exactly what was happening and began to pummel her fists against his naked chest.

'What the hell do you think you're doing?' she spat, burningly, shamingly aware of his near nakedness, and hers. He was wearing only silky pyjama bottoms, and her scantily covered breasts were pressed against the warm satin of his skin. And, shamingly, a sheet of heated sensation flooded her body at the contact and she grew still, her body painfully rigid as she tried to hold herself away from him.

Her breath caught in her throat, a dry, painful sob, as he carried her out of the room. She would not be manhandled this way, but her renewed struggles had no effect at all on his effortless stride as he carried her along the dimly lit corridor to their own room.

'I'm taking you to my bed, where you belong,' he answered her angry question tersely. 'Scream if you like. The Thornwoods are safely tucked up in their quarters at the rear of the house. I doubt if they'd hear if you blew a trumpet.'

Pushing the bedroom door shut behind him with his foot, he crossed the pale ochre wool of the carpet in three long strides, dropping her to the smooth olive green cover of the bed and was down on top of her, his hips pinning her to the mattress, before she could move.

'This will be rape,' she warned throatily, her eyes glittering feverishly between the tumbled strands of her silkily silver hair, her breath coming quickly, making the rounded peaks of her breasts rise and fall rapidly.

'I don't think so.' He captured her clenched and flailing hands in one of his and shifted slightly, making her aware of his arousal, and she moaned, low in her throat, just once, as his lips descended to take hers.

Desperately, she clamped her mouth shut, trying to ignore the fever of need he was already arousing within her as his tongue forced her lips apart. But, as she had unconsciously known he would, he won that battle and she capitulated weakly to the insistent pressure of his mouth. And then, as if he knew he had her subdued, mindless, he trailed moist kisses down the length of her throat and on and down to circle her breasts, tormenting the aroused peaks until she could have screamed her frustration, her unwilling yet insistent need.

Then, gently, he eased the fabric of her bra aside, revealing first one tautly inviting breast and then the other, and she writhed frantically beneath him, moaning her rejection of the way he made her feel.

He had warned her that he would make love to her until she couldn't think straight, and this was precisely what he was doing.

Before, when they had made love, she had welcomed him eagerly, lovingly, knowing that at least he cared for her, that he found her body and her wanton response to him exciting. But this was something else, and, as he bent his dark head to suckle on the rosy-peaked breasts her traitorous body offered in open invitation, she made one last feeble attempt to stop him.

'Leave me alone!' It was a plea, a muted cry of despair, and she heard a rough echo of that despair in his voice as he derided,

'I would if I damned well could!'

And his mouth closed over one taut nipple, sucking moistly, making blind desire kick to urgent life inside her and she was lost in the devastating sensation of his hands, his mouth, his body, as he kissed and fondled every inch of her silky, sweat-slicked skin until she was ready to beg him to take her.

And then, poised above her accepting body, his face flushed with the dark blood of desire, he held her thrashing head in his hands, held it still so that she had no option but to meet the blaze of triumph in his eyes as his potent maleness tantalisingly nudged her ardent, feminine moistness.

'Who am I?' Vivid blue eyes froze her soul yet seared her senses, and her body grew still, waiting, tormented, uncomprehending.

'Do you know who I am, what I am?' he insisted, and she closed her eyes, her body aching for the relief only he could bring, the relief he was withholding. He was playing games with her, and she shuddered hopelessly as his voice ground out, 'Open your eyes, damn you! Look at me. I'm not Fenton, so don't even try to pretend I am! I'm your husband, the man who is going to make love to you, again and again, until you don't know who you are or what you are, until all you can know, feel, taste, think, is me!'

And then he took her, almost savagely, as if he would never have enough of her, as time and time again he forced her to the delirious heights of shaming ecstasy.

CHAPTER NINE

CLEO tried to make her mind focus on what she was doing as she neared the bottom of the escalator. Stepping off, she took a firmer grip on her briefcase and was swept along with the tide of home-bound commuters. The Underground in the rush-hour was hell. But then, wasn't everything, these days?

This afternoon, spent with Luke in his office, had been grim. He'd made no effort to hide his dislike. And in her heightened emotional state it had been difficult to take. But she'd managed, though heaven only knew how, ignoring his scathing, 'Wonder Woman to the rescue!' as he'd scanned her outlined proposals for the salvaging of Slade Securities.

'Jude's approved this, I take it?' He'd finally laid the papers aside. 'Or is the whole proposal his brainchild?'

His derisive look had told her that, no matter what she said, he'd would never believe a mere female could come up with such precise figures and projections. He couldn't believe it because it would damage his ego. As far as he was concerned, only a masculine mind was capable of a clear-sighted and logical grasp of finance.

She hadn't disabused him; there had seemed no point. No point in anything these days. And she didn't have the emotional resources to endure a ding-dong verbal fight with him. Jude had drained her emotions dry.

Far from consulting Jude, she had said nothing about the conclusions she'd formed after days and days of concentrated work. True, he had asked her to let him know her findings, so that they could discuss them, and that was because he had a vested interest now. But the salvation of Slade Securities while it was still salvageable was her baby. She owed it to Uncle John. The fact that Jude now had thirty per cent of the voting stock was neither here nor there. She wasn't doing it for him. How could she willingly do anything for him when he persisted in treating her like dirt?

'Cleo?' A hand touched her shoulder and she twisted round, her racing heart a testimony to how edgy she had become over the past ten days, quieting down to normal as she encountered Dawn's puzzled eyes.

'I thought it was you,' Jude's secretary explained. 'Though I couldn't be absolutely sure. You look awful. Lost weight, haven't you?' On that unflattering note Dawn prepared for a natter session, oblivious to the grim-faced throngs pushing past in their rush to squeeze on to homebound trains.

'I've been working flat out.' Cleo put on a brightish smile and lifted one shoulder in a gesture she hoped denoted unconcern. 'You know how it is—too busy to eat properly. Anyway,' she turned the subject quickly, 'how's Sheila settling down in my old job?' Dawn was far from a fool and Cleo didn't want anyone to guess that everything had turned sour between Jude and herself.

Dawn pulled a face. 'So-so. I couldn't stand her at first. She's capable enough but hell—those damned airs and graces. She acted as if she expected me to drop a curtsey every time she walked by.' She grinned suddenly, wryly. 'But we started to gel after that husband of yours reduced her to tears yesterday. I knew exactly how she felt! It's a pity you ever left. You were the only one who could handle him, make him remotely human. He's been worse than ever this last week or so. A real s.o.b., if you don't mind my saying so! And if he doesn't change his tune I, for one, am definitely looking for another job.' Then a doubtful look flickered over her middle-aged face, as if she was afraid she'd said too much. 'I still think of you more as being his PA than as his wife. So excuse my big mouth, but you might do some good if you dropped a word in his ear.'

'I'll see what I can do,' Cleo said. Dawn had her sympathy, but she knew Jude would not listen to what she had to say on that, or any other subject. He would be more likely to walk naked through the centre of London in the rush-hour! And that made her recall the time when he would have made a point of listening to anything she had to say because in those days he had respected her viewpoint, her intelligence. There was nothing he respected about her now. She didn't even respect herself. And the knowledge hurt, filled her chest with pain. Quickly, before Dawn could guess her misery, she excused, 'I have to go, Dawn. Sorry to rush off, but I'm late as it is. And keep your chin up—try to remember, his bark's worse than his bite. And stand up to him if you think he's out of line.'

Not very helpful advice, she guessed, as Dawn's shoulders lifted in a helpless shrug beneath her sedate dark green coat. Cleo didn't want Jude's staff deserting him. She cared about him, still loved him, despite the way he'd been treating her, despite knowing, now, that he would never return her love.

Fenton, and Jude's reaction to the situation—as he stubbornly perceived it—had killed whatever chance their marriage might once have had. And as for that louse, Fenton, there hadn't been a peep out of him since Jude had ordered him out of the house in Bow. Maybe Jude's ferocity had made him think twice about carrying out his threats.

*   *   *

Her feet dragged as she emerged from the tube station at Knightsbridge. It was raining now, the heavy drizzle wetting her charcoal silk suit. It hung on her body where once—before her ill-fated marriage to Jude—it had clung lovingly.

Reluctant to return to the cold comfort of the luxurious Regency house in Belgravia, she lingered in the almost deserted streets, growing colder, wetter, until an opulent saloon swept by, spraying her with muddy rainwater before purring on, its tail-lights glittering in the murk, her existence of no more importance than that of a fallen leaf.

Wiping ineffectually at the mud stains that had probably ruined the suit for ever, the first stirrings of rebellion stirred to life. She was sick to death of being made to feel that her existence was of no importance whatever. Her cousin hated her for some warped reason of his own and her husband didn't give a damn so long as she was an available body in his bed. A body he could use and punish.

She wasn't going to stand for it any longer!

She doubled her pace, her high heels beating a determined tattoo on the wet pavements, her shoulders straight. She still loved Jude but she wasn't going to allow him to make her feel defeated, shabby, worthless. Nor would she allow him to use her body to wreak his own savage brand of vengeance. He gave her no quarter. He made love to her with an eroticism that shamed her when, in the clear light of morning, she recalled the depths of response he was so easily able to draw from her. Somehow, she was going to regain her self-respect!

His lovemaking was a bitter travesty of what they had shared earlier on in their marriage. Erotic it might be, but it was also a method of marking her as his possession, murdering her pride, making her hate herself for her uninhibited and ungovernable response.

Not any more, though. If there were to be any hope for the future of their marriage at all then it would have to be in name only until their differences were resolved—if they ever could be. She would use the guest-room, or move out altogether, and to hell with his objections, because the sort of marriage they had at this moment wasn't worth a damn.

Despite the now drenching rain, her neat pointed chin was set at a grimly determined angle as she ran up the four shallow steps that led to the front door and hunted through her handbag for her key. But the door swung open before her chilled fingers had located the key and Jude snapped, 'Where the hell have you been?'

A frisson of distaste snaked through her and her mouth compressed to a tight line as she pushed past him into the hall. Let him rage if he wanted—she was about to show him she had a mind of her own and would not be treated like worthless garbage!

The old Cleo was back, her fighting spirit stronger than ever after its absence during the last ten days.

'To discuss the future of Slade Securities with Luke,' she answered him tartly, then swung past him. 'Excuse me, I have to get out of these wet things.'

But he caught her, pulling her round, and there was nothing gentle about his grip as hard fingers bit into the fragile bones of her shoulders.

'Luke?' he queried nastily, his eyes narrow azure slits. 'Or was it Fenton?'

Cleo drew in a tired breath, striving to hold on to her new determination to hold her own. 'Luke,' she emphasised stonily, shuddering inside as his fingers bit more deeply. 'And if you don't believe me——'

'Why should I believe anything you say——' he interrupted cuttingly, 'when I walked in on a truth that turned everything you'd ever said or done into a living lie! And if, as you say, you were having a meeting with Luke, why didn't you ask Thornwood to fetch you? Why choose to struggle home through the rain?' He released her, as if he couldn't bear to be this close, his mouth twisting with distance as he told her, 'You didn't ask for Thornwood because you didn't want him knowing where you'd spent the afternoon, he might have let something slip. So you thought it more prudent to make your own way home, regardless of what I might think when you tried to sneak in, looking like a drowned rat! Or were you counting on getting home before me?'

'Get lost!' The words were low and furious. 'You've got a sick mind.' She pushed the sodden briefcase at him. 'You'll find all my conclusions here. Luke approved them, but only because he was convinced everything he read was your idea!' she snapped bitterly, stalking away from him and stamping up the stairs.

Her anger was burned out by the time she emerged from the shower and wrapped herself in a giant blue towel. She might have expected his odious suspicions. He was paranoid where she was concerned. Nothing would convince him that she and Fenton weren't lovers. It was like a worm, eating into his soul, changing him into a man she didn't know.

Morosely, she rubbed herself dry and padded to the hanging cupboard to find something to wear. Something restrained, dignified. Because, over dinner, she was going to deliver her ultimatum. He must leave her alone, physically, allow her to use the guest-room—or to move out—until he was ready to listen to her explanation of her relationship with Robert Fenton. And then, if necessary, if he still couldn't trust her word, he could check with Luke. Luke knew Fenton had been trying to blackmail her.

Thus, bleakly and coldly decided, she reached to the back of the cupboard and pulled out a grey wool skirt, slightly flared, with its matching waistcoat. Worn with a crisp apple green shirt the outfit made her look severe and controlled. Which was precisely the effect she was aiming for.

Bolstered by her appearance—a modicum of make-up and her hair clipped back behind her ears with good old-fashioned kirby grips helped—she braced herself to deliver a mouthful of plain speaking. And at least she had her timing right, she thought relievedly as she tucked in behind Meg and the heated trolley. She would not now have to endure a pre-dinner drink with the man who so plainly found her beneath contempt, who thought lying was a way of life for her.

'Something smells good,' Cleo remarked politely. Her mind had never been further from food, but Meg always took trouble and her efforts deserved to be recognised.

The housekeeper gave her a warm, comfortable smile, 'Lamb casserole with chocolate fudge sponge to follow. You won't mind, madam, if I leave you to it?' She trundled the trolley into the drawing-room, to the small table in the alcove where Cleo and Jude often ate when they were alone to save Meg the bother of setting the huge table in the formal dining-room.

The table, Cleo noted drily, was set with two covers, candles, silver and crystal—all the right props for a ro-mantic dinner for two. But there was no romance in this marriage, just mistrust and a whole load of agony, she mourned silently as Jude laid aside the papers he'd been concentrating on and stood up, a whisky-glass in his hand, bleak tension in his eyes.

'I was beginning to think you'd decided to go out again,' he commented bitingly.

Meg, seemingly unaware of the undercurrents that thickened the air, made the atmosphere volatile, carried on with what she'd been saying. 'Only there's a film on television we both want to watch. But I'll be down later to clear away.'

'That's fine, Meg.' Cleo had her mistress-of-the-house act honed to perfection and she smiled encouragingly as she took the hot plates and dishes from the trolley. 'Run along, Meg. I can see to this. You don't want to miss the beginning.'

She heard Jude cross the room as she ladled the herby, aromatic casserole on to plates and tried to relax muscles that had instinctively stiffened. He sat opposite her, his face stony, and as he unfolded his napkin she handed him his plate of meat and then sat in front of hers, knowing she wouldn't be able to eat a thing.

'I've skimmed through your conclusions,' he imparted coldly as he helped himself to new potatoes and courgettes. 'But I distinctly recall having asked you to consult me before putting anything in front of Luke.'

'Perhaps you did.' Those shares were the only thing he seemed interested in nowadays, she thought sourly—the only thing of hers, at least. She pushed a piece of meat around her plate, still clinging to her air of poised control because she was going to need it when she told him she would not be sharing his bed, and perhaps not even his roof, until things were resolved between them.

'You know damned well I did.' His voice was quiet, level, almost soft, and that was more nerve-racking than if he'd shouted. It was the dangerous tone he used when hauling some unfortunate Mescal Slade employee over the coals if the hapless person had had the misfortune to annoy him.

She shuddered slightly, and he must have noticed the involuntary tremor because his eyes met hers, hard and cold. He poured her a glass of burgundy, which she ignored, and she choked back hot words and found a tone to equal his.

'I don't work for you any more. You did the firing and suggested I move to Slade—if you remember.' She pushed her food around some more, just for something to do with her hands. 'I'm under no obligation to consult you at this stage. I prefer to handle this my own way.'

'The idea was,' he laid his cutlery aside, eyeing her frigidly, 'that we should work together to get the company back on its feet. Or had you forgotten?'

The look he gave her made her want to run away and hide, but she resisted the cowardly impulse and draped one arm over the back of her chair, achieving a casual elegance she was proud of, and told him dismissively, 'It was your idea, not mine. In any case, I don't quite see how it could be managed without a certain degree of accord—something which our relationship distinctly lacks. So I do this alone, or not at all. And talking of togetherness——' she ousted yet another cowardly surge of desire to remove herself from the room and studiedly re-applied herself to her cooling food, even managing to get a tiny onion as far as her mouth '—I'm going to have to insist that we sleep separately from now on. I want nothing more to do with you physically until——'

'Why not?' he cut in smoothly, giving her no time to finish what she had intended to say. 'When you enjoy it so much. We both know I only have to touch you to turn you on.'

And that left her floundering, her cheeks flaming. It was precisely because he could so easily make her want him, need him, abandon her scruples, that she had to sleep alone! She could endure the feeling of degradation no longer!

'Or is it because you are seeing Fenton again, getting all the satisfaction you can handle?' he added silkily, his eyes slitted and dangerous.

Blinking back the pain of incipient tears, fighting the racking ache in her chest, she pushed herself out of her chair. She didn't have to take this! She wouldn't take it!

Her mouth set in a furious line as all pretence of control deserted her, and she ground out, 'I want a divorce.'

It was pointless to go on trying, to even pretend to hope that things could come right for them again. As soon as she'd realised he would never listen to what she had to say in her own defence she should have known it was all over. So why put herself through this agony, the agony of loving a man who only wanted to punish her, and go on punishing her—for a crime she hadn't even committed?

'I've been waiting for this.' She could almost see the violent emotion that emanated from him, and his eyes were narrowed, taking in the flush of rage that burned along her cheekbones, the glitter of angry tears in wide grey eyes. 'I've wondered when you'd get around to asking.'

At his icy words the rage left her, just like that, and she clutched at the back of her chair. Did he mean he'd been waiting for the suggestion to come from her because he wanted out of a marriage that had become intolerable? And had she unknowingly hoped, against all common sense, that he would throw every objection in the book at her, say that, despite everything he still wanted her in his life, that he needed her?

And then he did say that much, but the same words can mean different things, and her face turned paper-white as he drawled, 'Divorce you so that you can marry Fenton, with the so-called Slade Millions safely in your control? No way.' He thrust his chair back savagely, his height, his breadth of shoulder diminishing her. And his face was austere, tight-fleshed, but a derisory dent appeared at one side of his hard mouth as he told her, 'You used me to gain control of your inheritance, the money you needed to lavish on your lover in order to keep him. But it stops there. Right there. There's no way I'm going to hand you your freedom on a plate. You're my wife and that's something you're going to have to learn to live with. And I mean live with. While you're my wife you'll share my roof-space, share my bed.'

It was the most demeaning thing he could have said to her, and she didn't know whether she loved him or hated him now. Both, she supposed, the one being almost indistinguishable from the other. And misery and shame goaded her on.

'There's nothing to stop me walking out on you and going to him,' she flashed recklessly, stung by his hateful words, saying anything at all she could think of that might hurt him as much as he had repeatedly hurt her. And strangely, she felt back in control again, almost coldly so, with only a residue of fury left to inject a very slight tremor into her voice as she curled her mouth down in a sneer. 'According to the way you view me, I'm not the type of woman to balk at walking out on my husband and going to live with my lover.'

There was just a moment of complete silence, very still, heavy, just one moment when she felt she had the upper hand, though she knew she didn't want it. And then he warned, his voice like ice, 'Do that, and I will drag you back, kicking and screaming. And that's a promise. Wherever you go, I'll find you, and make you pay, and go on paying.'

CHAPTER TEN

CLEO spent the next ten days at Slade House. She had left a terse note for Jude, telling him where she was going, and had explained to a sympathetic Meg that she needed to spend time with her uncle, who was a sick man.

She could have gone to her former home, but she'd heard that a firm offer had been made for the property in Bow. Besides, Jude would have had no hesitation in dragging her back, but even he would think twice about the wisdom of dragging her from her uncle's home.

Most of her days were spent in the office in Eastcheap with Luke and others of the board, and she managed to ignore his surly attitude, taking what comfort she could from the knowledge that her plans for Slade Securities looked like working—with no help from Jude. And Grace had confided that her husband seemed much better, more relaxed, now Cleo had joined the company. And that information had to be welcome, not only because of the improvement in John Slade's health but because it meant, in some measure, that Grace was almost ready to accept her at last. Her remark must have cost her something, since it hardly flattered her beloved son!

But today she had opted to stay at Slade House, seeking John's approval for her plans for careful expansion in some areas now that her cutbacks had gone through. She couldn't trust Luke's judgement, and she was damned if she'd ask Jude for his opinion. This was something she had to steer along herself.

Gratifyingly, although she'd had no doubts herself, her uncle had approved her projections.

'I don't think you'll ever really know how pleased I am to have you pulling for the old firm,' he said, closing the last file. 'It made no sense for you to join Mescal Slade.'

Since Cleo could hardly tell her uncle that the prospect of working with his son had given her the mental shudders, she said nothing. She was steering Slade Securities on a steadier track and that was something she was proud of. And, as it was all she had, she clung on to it tightly.

There would have to be a board meeting, of course, before some of her schemes got off the ground, and Jude would naturally be invited along in his capacity of a major shareholder, and maybe he would be offered a seat on the board... She didn't know yet.

And there was another thing he would have to be consulted about... Two days ago she had learned she was pregnant. She didn't know how or when she would break the news...

'Shall we indulge in a glass of Manzanilla? I think we deserve a celebration!' John Slade was on his feet and his old eyes were actually twinkling, and Cleo dragged her mind back to him.

'I'd like that.'

'And how much longer can I look forward to having you here?' he asked as he put the heavy, fluted Georgian glass in her hands.

'I'm not sure.' Cleo sipped the pale golden liquid, not knowing what to say. She had been here ten days already and would have to move on soon. But where? Back to Jude?

She felt safe here, protected. Her uncle had made no secret of his delight when she'd arrived, making the excuse that in her early days as Luke's working partner it would be more sensible for her to base herself here, driving into town each day with Luke and, if necessary, working on with him until the small hours.

But already there was a look in Grace's eyes that hinted at an astonishment that a relatively new bride would willingly separate herself from her devoted husband for this length of time. And only this morning, coming across Luke as he'd finished his solitary breakfast, he had sneered, 'Moved in for the duration, have you? So what happened? Did Jude find out about your involvement with Fenton and throw you out? I wouldn't blame him—I wouldn't want a wife who'd learned all there was to learn from a creep like Robert Fenton.'

Yes, she'd been marking time, but soon, very soon, she would have to decide what to do, where to go. The thought of resuming her marriage, as it had been, made her go cold, but the thought of ending the marriage made her feel worse.

And yet, on the positive side, when Jude learned she was expecting his child—and a child had been his main reason for marrying at all, with the shares thrown in as a welcome bonus—then surely he would be at last willing to listen to her side of the story, if only for the sake of the child to come? And, having listened, he would have to admit he'd been wrong...

'Selfishly, I hope you'll stay another few days,' John Slade was saying. 'But I'll understand if you're impatient to get back to Jude. So why don't you ask him to join you here, just for the weekend?'

Blinking, dragged from her reverie, Cleo managed a non-committal smile. She had come here to gain a brief respite from Jude and the problems of their marriage, so she wasn't about to ask him to join her! She needed time to think, and she couldn't think straight when he was around. But so far the thinking hadn't been done, the very idea of him had her emotions churning, too confused to be sorted out.

'I'll see if lunch is ready,' she told her uncle. The conversation was following paths she didn't want to tread. 'You just relax and finish your drink.'

Leaning against the smooth, cool wood of the study door, she forced herself to take deep, calming breaths. Jude would have to put aside his pride and listen to what she had to say—especially after she'd told him about the baby. It would take time for him to come to terms with the news that he was about to become a parent; she was only just beginning to come to terms with it herself. But then, perhaps, they could start again, try to rebuild the relationship his distrust had shattered.

Maybe she would phone him this evening, suggest they meet somewhere, on neutral ground to discuss their future...

Thus decided, she began to walk along the corridor towards the main hall at the front of the house; the luxurious silence was broken by the sound of her aunt's voice, pitched higher than was normal. 'Jude—what a lovely surprise! You're just in time for lunch. We'll go and find Cleo, shall we? She'll be delighted!'

So he had come to fetch her back! There could be no other explanation for his unexpected arrival, and Cleo's insides felt like jelly and her heart was beating too fast. He had her metaphorically cornered, there was no place to hide. Rather than have them come across her skulking in the shadows, she walked rapidly forward and tried to look pleased and surprised when she turned into the wide main hall, because her aunt's eyes would be on her and that lady was no fool—she would be quick to pick up bad vibes.

'Jude! I didn't expect you—how nice!'

Her pasted smile wobbled at that last lie, and disappeared totally when he answered suavely, 'Yes, isn't it? Nice for both of us.' His smile was warm enough but the azure eyes, set between thickly fringing black lashes, were quite cold. He turned to Grace, his poise, his outward charm, masking a taut purposefulness that only Cleo could detect, and she shuddered uncontrollably as he apologised, 'Lunch would have been delightful, Grace. But I promised myself I'd take Cleo for a break—she's been working much too hard lately. So I've planned a second mini-honeymoon.' A smooth movement gathered Cleo into the crook of his arm and she stood rigidly still, knowing this was a deadly game. She was sickeningly afraid of the outcome. 'I would have come for you sooner,' he was telling her silkily, 'but I got bogged down in endless meetings.' He made it sound like an apology, but the pressure of his hard fingers as they bit into the soft flesh just below her ribs told a different story. 'So, if you'll forgive the rush, Grace, I suggest Cleo throws her things together. We've quite a drive ahead of us.'

'But of course!' Grace's eyes, as they flickered between the two of them, were alight with approval. She had really taken to her new nephew-in-law, Cleo thought dully. Grace thought he was the best thing to happen to the Slade family in a long time.

Although she knew she was being manipulated, that a second honeymoon, a break for his hard-working, adored wife, was the last thing Jude had in mind, she tried to smile, to look happy. Her fight with her husband was a private thing, dark, demanding and devious. She would do anything to prevent it becoming public knowledge.

She had little choice but to obey Jude's smoothly worded yet heavily loaded instructions, she thought as a few minutes later she was bundling the things she'd brought with her into her suitcase. To have put up any objection, no matter how slight, would have been useless in the face of his sugar-coated determination. Besides, it would have alerted her uncle and aunt to the dark nuances of their private life. And that she did not want.

Sitting beside him in the Jaguar XJS he used when he drove himself, Cleo was lost for words. She picked a few openers over in her mind and abandoned them with a bleak compression of her lips. Whatever she said would only result in a row. He had fetched her from Slade House because she was his property, a fact he had been known to point out to her before!

Before too long she was going to have to tell him about the baby, and she didn't want to impart such wonderful information on the heels of yet another row. And she would have to choose her moment carefully because she hoped—oh, how she hoped!—that together they could talk things over and try to make the future come right.

He didn't have to love her, she confessed to herself with a deep-seated disgust at her own humility, but if he could only revert to feeling about her the way he had, with respect and liking, then it would be something she could work on.

She closed her eyes, the bright sunlight of late spring mocking her depression. But she willed herself to relax, to find some of the strength she would need when Jude at last thought fit to break his scathing silence. And eventually she sank into an uncomfortable dozing state, the tension that stretched edgily between them unabated as mind images, rather than dreams, tormented her jumpy brain. They were all of Jude—of the way he had been and the way he was—and she snapped back into full consciousness and became immediately aware that they were passing through deep countryside, unfamiliar to her.

'Been enjoying the sleep of the just?' His words were edged with sarcasm, telling her that he had known precisely when she had opened her eyes. 'Have I ever told you that you look innocent, like a child, when you sleep?'

She ignored that opening gambit. It was an invitation to yet another attack and she wasn't going to oblige him. Instead, finding a level tone, she asked, 'Are you making a detour for some reason? We should be back in town by now, surely?'

'When you chose to run away you left me with no option but to bring you back,' he replied obliquely, his profile ungiving.

'I did not run away!' she snapped, unable to prevent the hot words coming. Their future was precariously balanced, not to mention their child's, and this in-fighting wouldn't achieve anything useful, she was well aware of that. But she didn't see why she should always be put in the wrong. 'You knew where I was, and why,' she qualified stonily.

'I knew you'd run out on me. You could have worked with Luke just as easily from home,' he stated unequivocally. And, morosely, she supposed he was right. She had been running away from a situation that was intolerable.

And as if he'd read her thoughts, he told her levelly, 'Things can't go on as they are,' and she wondered, with a wrench of pain, if he'd decided to go for a divorce, after all. He could be extracting no pleasure from the bitter thing their marriage had become. Even his revenge, his need to humiliate her, had to lose its savour eventually.

'So what are you going to do about it?' She heard herself sounding surly, though that hadn't been her intention, and averted her head to stare out of the window, appalled by the ready sting of tears in her eyes, determined he shouldn't see them, because that would be the final humiliation.

'Start talking it out,' he informed her coldly. 'It's more than time.' He changed gear smoothly and gentled the softly growling vehicle through tight bends which had clusters of stone cottages on either side, and the tiny flicker of hope his words had brought to life was doused by the acid of past experience.

'Do you mean you'll actually let me get a word in among those accusations you're so good at?'

She bit the words out snappily then, for some reason, began to tremble as he told her, 'That's why I decided to borrow Fiona's cottage for a day or two. We can have complete privacy—and I've a feeling we're going to need it. I've a few things to say to you, and no doubt you'll have more than a few to say back,' he added drily, halting at a leafy intersection and peering at an ancient finger post.

'It's quite a time since I visted,' he imparted with the coolness of a stranger, and she stared at him, hardly able to believe that he had actually gone to such lengths in order to talk things out. And he was saying, 'Fiona's in Paris at the moment. Part business, part pleasure, so we shall have the place entirely to ourselves.'

A few hours ago that thought would have appalled her. She had gone to Slade House to escape the torment of living with him. But now, he had said he wanted to talk things out, would allow her to have her say, and that was progress. A tingle of real hope rippled through her, and she was looking through rose-tinted glasses when they drew up in front of a squat stone cottage bordering the narrow lane, and Jude introduced, 'Fiona's hideaway. Small but secluded.'

'It's perfect!' It was tiny, like a child's drawing, a straight, peony-bordered path leading from the wicket to the centrally set front door. The rest of the garden was given over to vegetables in tidy rows.

Cleo couldn't imagine Jude's elegant sister barrowing manure, forking and hoeing, and Jude, following her thoughts in the almost uncanny way he had, said, 'An old boy from the village has the use of the garden in return for keeping an eye on the place. It works well. He gets all the fresh fruit and vegetables he needs, and she feels the place is safer from the attention of vandals if it looks as if someone with a spade is about to come out of the garden shed.'

Smiling, he handed her a key. It was the first real smile she'd had from him since he'd walked in and found her with Fenton. It was a smile she could have lost herself in and her heart picked up speed, pattering rapidly, making her feel like a love-sick fool.

'Let yourself in,' he said. 'Look around while I pull the car up into the orchard. It's the only gateway wide enough.'

She walked slowly along the path, enjoying the warmth of the late afternoon sun, the fresh country smells. Life was beginning to wear a happier face. And as for their marriage, well, maybe the symptoms were grim, but the prognosis was good. It would have to be. She would make it so!

The key turned easily in the lock and Cleo stepped straight into a parlour that might have been modelled on an illustration in a Beatrix Potter book. Red and white checked curtains decked the tiny windows, rag rugs were scattered about the floor and squashy, slightly shabby flower-patterned armchairs surrounded an open fireplace, while four ladder-backed chairs were placed around a pine table which sported a vase of dried teasles.

A dresser and a rocking chair completed the décor, and Cleo gave Fiona full marks for not turning the interior of her country cottage into something artfully twee.

The whole cottage, she discovered, was basic, functional, and just right. True, there was only one bedroom, the second having been converted to a bathroom at some time. But if everything went as she prayed it would, she need have no reservations about sharing that big brass bed with Jude.

Going swiftly back down the twisting stairs, she told herself to take it easy. Pointless to hope for too much. Every time she'd tried to talk to him in the past, to put her point of view, they'd ended up further apart than before. But despite her warnings to herself she couldn't help hoping...

She found him in the kitchen; her suitcase was on the floor with a battered canvas tote bag beside it, and there was a carton of groceries on the table.

'I'll get out of this stifling gear.' He indicated his formal grey business suit and picked up her suitcase, the tote bag which must contain his things. 'Like the place?' he asked, turning in the low doorway, and there was a softness in his eyes that warmed her heart. She couldn't help smiling, her pleasure showing through the cool façade.

'I love it!' She would have said the same if he had brought her to stay in a hen house, because she just knew everything was going to be fine.

'Good.' He made a movement as if to go on his way, but something seemed to hold him and she saw, just for a second, a look of puzzlement deep in his eyes. And then it was gone, and it might never have been because the azure depths were as they so often were—slightly on the cold side of bland—before he finally turned away.

As she heard his feet on the stairs she turned to the box he'd left on the table. Unpacking it would give her something to do, calm her. She felt slightly sick, every sense highly tuned because, one way or another, the next day or so would set the pattern for the rest of her life.

The box was crammed with enough food to last them for days and she moved about the kitchen quickly, stowing a fresh chicken, butter and bacon in the fridge, leaving the steak out because they could have that tonight. She was crouching, pushing the cartons of milk into the already full fridge, when he said, from behind her, 'I'm going to split logs. I'll light a fire, the evenings get chilly.'

She turned, looking up at him over her shoulder, and her heart flopped over. He had changed and he looked, as ever, superb. Faded denim jeans clipped long legs and lean hips, and his dark checked shirt had long sleeves, pulled up to the elbows, revealing hard, sinewy forearms liberally sprinkled with dark hair. And she only had to look at him to know she would always love him, no matter what happened.

'Perhaps you could make a start on a meal,' he suggested. 'We both missed lunch.' He was leaning against the table, half sitting, seemingly relaxed, and she was about to tell him, fine, she'd do just that because suddenly she was hungry, too, when the words died in her throat as he said softly, 'You look washed out, despite the sleep you had coming down here. Been pining over the news?'

'What news?' She was reluctant to tell him that her sleepless nights had been caused by her misery over him, and she stood up slowly, closing the fridge door with a nudge of her knee, repeating, 'What news? What are you talking about?'

'Fenton's engagement to Livia Haine, the millionaire brewer's daughter.' His mouth dented derisively. 'You can take it from me, they deserve each other. She's a first-class bitch.'

'I didn't know.' Her heart began to thump, sounding thunderous in her own ears. Fenton engaged? It was the best news she'd heard in years! If he was set to marry money, which had always been his ambition, then he would keep his act clean until he'd secured the lady with a plain gold ring. He must have been working on it, and that would be why she'd heard no more from him. Unsavoury details, involving his debts, wouldn't be what he'd want to see splashed around in some sordid gossip column. She was safe from Robert Fenton at last!

Carefully keeping her face straight, she pushed a strand of silvery hair back from her face with the back of her hand. 'I hadn't heard.'

'No?' Jude said. 'Didn't he at least warn you to expect that sickening photograph in the papers yesterday, alongside the announcement of their engagement? Apparently,' he added drily, 'it was a whirlwind romance.'

She didn't care what kind of romance it had been, and if Jude was right and the lady in question was a bitch then she wasn't about to waste her sympathy on her behalf. And she was about to say just that when he forestalled her again, levering himself away from the table, his face expressionless.

'I thought, with Fenton out of your reach, we could talk things through, lay out the guidelines for our future, our marriage. Because, believe me, he won't want to continue with your relationship if he's got his hooks into another heiress—one who's free to marry him.'

And with that he strode from the room, leaving her gaping. He must have decided to borrow the cottage, to fetch her away from Slade House, when he'd learned of

Fenton's engagement. What he'd said hadn't been
flattering, but at least he was willing to talk things
through, try to make their marriage work. And he would
listen to what she had to tell him, and they could begin
again.

She could understand his initial revulsion when he'd
walked in on what must have appeared to be a torrid
love scene between herself and Fenton. But she hadn't
been able to understand why he had refused to hear her
defence. After all, it wasn't as if his emotions were
involved...

Her hands shook a little as she washed the salad they
would eat with the steak, her insides wriggling around
with what she recognised as nervous excitement. If theirs
had been a normal marriage she wouldn't be feeling this
way. She would have been desperately hurt by his total
lack of trust, her love for him terminally ill by now because the type of mistrust he harboured couldn't co-exist
with love.

But he had never loved her, never pretended to. The
love was all on her side, and she'd known she would
have to be the one to make their marriage a workable
thing. And now, at last, she was going to be able to work
on it again.

Reaching the steaks out of the fridge, she paused, un-
decided. She could still hear the regular sound of the
axe and it looked as though Jude was all set to split
enough wood to last through a month of chilly evenings.
That being so, the meal could wait for the time it would
take her to freshen herself up.

Her mind made up, she was already at the door to the
stairway when Jude came in from outside, a pile of logs
in his arms, and she halted, uncertain of what to do.

'Would you like me to put the steaks on now, or have
I got time to change first?' she asked, her colour rising

as his blue eyes lazily swept her slender jeans and shirt-clad figure. There was a hint, just a hint, of the old warmth in the look he gave her and her heart flipped over with love for him. Everything was going to be all right; she had never been more certain of anything.

'You look good to me as you are.' His gaze lingered on her rumpled hair. 'But if it makes you feel better, go ahead and change. But don't take all night about it, we've a lot of talking to do.'

And that was vastly reassuring. He had said he'd listen to what she had to say, and at last he was talking to her as an equal, his voice softer than she'd heard it for weeks—not bitingly bitter, as it had been, coming out as if he hated her, felt her to be beneath contempt.

She shot him a grateful look, unable to stop herself, to disguise her love. Not that she wanted to, not now, not ever again.

After showering quickly in the tiny bathroom, she rummaged through her suitcase, making a mental note to unpack before going to bed. But, for now, she picked out fresh oyster satin lace underwear and a fine wool sweater dress. Although the day had been bright and warm, the evening, as Jude had prophesied, was turning chilly. The very thought of him made slow colour burn over her skin as she wriggled into the soft wool dress.

The shade of muted peacock green suited her and the garment fitted her perfectly, skimming her slender body without a wrinkle or ruck. The deep V of the neckline created a shadowy cleft between her breasts and, unconsciously, she twisted in front of the mirror, running the palms of her hands over the flat plane of her stomach.

There was no sign of any swelling, but then there wouldn't be yet, and she bit softly on her full lower lip, filled with an unfathomable love for the tiny life she carried, for the man who had fathered her child. Then she turned away quickly, heading out of the room, filled with an emotion so intense it threatened to explode inside her unless something was done about it, and quickly!

She would tell Jude about the baby over dinner—if not before! She couldn't wait a moment longer to share this wonderful secret with him. Explanations about Robert Fenton could wait until later—she had to tell Jude about the baby they had made, because nothing could be as important as that.

Her feet were light as she ran downstairs to the kitchen, her heart even lighter, but her face fell as she realised Jude already had their meal in the final stages of preparation. She felt cheated, she had wanted to make the meal—a labour of love! Then, smiling at her own silliness, she advanced into the room, sniffing at the delicious aroma of grilling steak and Jude looked up from the crusty granary loaf he'd been slicing and caught her smile, returning it, but guardedly.

'You look good enough to eat,' His eyes swept appraisingly over her lovingly encased body. 'But I couldn't wait. I missed breakfast, too.'

'Can I help?' Suddenly, Cleo was unaccountably shy and was almost relieved when he shook his head, a lock of dark, rumpled hair falling over one eye, giving him a rakish look that set her heart tipping wildly.

'Nope. It's all done. We'll eat in the living-room—go through and pour the wine. There's not room for both of us in here—but you can take the bread with you.'

If the words were clipped in a dismissive tone, she didn't really mind. In his mind nothing had changed and there was still a lot of talking to do, his so-called guidelines for their future to be mapped out. He didn't know, as she did, that there was nothing to worry about and never had been.

He had spread a red-checked cloth that matched the curtains over the table, and the glow from the crackling log fire and the single side-lamp darkened the sky outside the windows to amethyst. She put the bread on the table, near the salad in its shallow glass bowl, smiling as she noticed the careful place settings, the wineglasses, the unlit candle in a porcelain holder shaped like a rose.

He had gone to a lot of trouble and, still smiling softly, she lit the candle and poured the wine, taking her own glass to stand near a window, looking out. The first stars were beginning to blink in the darkening sky, the land shadows merging into a dusky pall, and she knew that before the sun rose again she and Jude would be embarking on a marriage that would certainly have real meaning for her and, hopefully, for him, too.

'Come and get it.' His voice, behind her, startled her into turning quickly and she almost spilled her wine. In the softly diffused glow of light that illuminated the little room his features looked more mellow, his mouth gentler. But his eyes were unreadable, deeply shadowed, and she didn't know what he was thinking.

The steaks were perfectly cooked, but Cleo's appetite had deserted her and she toyed with her food as she watched him hungrily eat his. She was going to have to tell him about the baby, she could contain the secret no longer. And his pleasure would be her pleasure. No, more than pleasure—a deep and ecstatic happiness.

He had talked of children before. Getting children had been the only reason he had married at all. But she had seen their children as abstract things, mere shadowy ideas. But now—this was different. Jude's child was within her, real, living, already loved, and as alive to her as her own flesh, her blood.

And she had to share this miracle with him. Now.

'Jude,' she blurted impulsively, nervous excitement making her voice thin, 'we're going to have a baby. I'm pregnant.'

She hadn't known quite what his reaction would be, but she hadn't expected the blank, shuttered expression that met her as he raised his eyes and looked at her levelly, full in the face, across the table. Nor did she understand the brief flash of pain she saw in his eyes before he laid aside his cutlery and remarked distantly, 'Congratulations. But excuse me if I don't share your dewy-eyed enthusiasm. How can I be sure it's mine, and not Fenton's?'

And something died inside her at that moment. It was hope. All hope was dead. It had struggled gallantly against all the odds and now, with those few words, it had finally expired. There was a bitter taste in her mouth, a tight pain around her heart. This was the end.

'Go to hell,' she said flatly, an indescribable pain pulling her to pieces, and he looked at her once, before thrusting his chair back and standing up, his mouth twisted downwards before he turned away.

'I've just been there.'

CHAPTER ELEVEN

JUDE slid the car to a halt outside the house in Belgravia, his features set in the tight mask he'd worn since she'd told him about the baby.

'I'll drop you off here while I garage the car.' It was the first thing he'd said during the drive home, and his words registered heavily on a mind that was still in shock.

'And Cleo——' this as her numb fingers were fumbling to release her safety belt '——have Meg move my things into the guest-room.'

A logical request, since their marriage was dead, she thought drearily, but bitterness still lived on and it surfaced in her tone as, staring straight ahead, she said tartly, 'I thought we were going to talk things out. That was the point of going to the cottage, wasn't it? I thought I was going to be allowed to put my point of view, for once.'

'Everything changed when you told me you were pregnant.' From the corner of her eye she saw his hands tighten on the steering wheel, making the knuckles white, and she thought she could detect a thread of emotion in his voice. But his tone was as before, flat, when he added, 'With Fenton off the scene, about to be married, I'd thought we might pick up the pieces, make something— no matter how superficial—of our marriage. Every time I look at your child I shall wonder if it's mine, or Fenton's, and not even I could live with that.'

'Fenton and I were never lovers!' The words came quickly, spilling out; they just had to be said, even though she knew she and Jude were finished.

He said wearily, 'Don't lie, Cleo. There's no point,' and she felt tired beyond belief, utterly drained.

Automatically, she moved out of the car and into the house, her feet somehow carrying her to the roomy kitchen where Thornwood was cleaning silver and Meg was putting vegetables through the blender for soup.

'Oh, madam! We didn't expect you home today!' Meg put a hand to her plump bosom. 'Walking in like a ghost!' And then, her startled reaction receding, her eyes narrowed in concern. 'Are you all right, madam? You're very pale.'

'I'm fine.' Cleo's smile was automatic, too. She felt numb. 'I thought I ought to let you know we're back.'

She was talking as though she and Jude were still an entity. But it wasn't the case. They had never been further apart. Even during the time when he'd looked at her with contempt, yet possessed her body with nightly, passionate savagery, there had been the unmistakable bonding of deep, racking emotion. Now there was nothing. Nothing at all.

'No, I won't have coffee, thanks,' she replied to Thornwood's offer. 'But Mr Mescal might like a tray.'

She left the room as silently as she had entered it, feeling like the wraith Meg had likened her to. The Thornwoods had been married a long time. They had grown together. Cleo couldn't imagine one without the other. Would they be able to understand the tragedy that her brief marriage to Jude had become? Probably not. For them, love and marriage would only be seen as a comfortable, comforting, easy thing.

She wouldn't ask Meg to move Jude's things, of course. That was something she had to do herself. An exorcism, perhaps. And it was what she had wanted, she reminded herself as she took formal suits and casual wear in methodical armloads from his half of the enormous hanging cupboard. She had tried to tell him she wanted to sleep alone, at least until he was willing to give her a hearing. But then, of course, there had still been the hope that having listened to her, realised his suspicions had been entirely without foundation—then, and only then, would they have been able to try to rebuild their relationship.

Now, of course, there was no hope left, and the action of clearing his things out was so completely final. It was the end, finis, nothing more to be said. The thought made her want to cry, but she didn't have the energy. The empty, defeated feeling had grown, depleting her mental resources, ever since he'd cleared the uneaten food from the table last night and had told her she might as well go and re-pack as they'd be leaving first thing in the morning.

Still shattered by what he had said about the questionable paternity of the child she was carrying, she had dragged herself upstairs, staring at her reflection and thinking how silly she looked in the pretty, clinging dress, her face a white mask punctuated by the deep dark holes of her eyes. She hadn't unpacked, so there had been nothing to do but curl up on the bed, pulling the soft eiderdown over her cold body, saying goodbye to her marriage.

Later, she had heard him leave the cottage and she'd lain awake all night, her eyes burning and dry as she'd stared into the darkness. At dawn, he had come back and she'd gone downstairs, still in the dress she'd slept in, dragging her suitcase. He had given her one hard look from empty eyes, the strain lines around his mouth making him look older. He must have been walking all night, judging by the way he looked, and immediate concern for him came to life in the emptiness of her heart, and she'd said quickly, 'Jude—sit down, let me

make you some breakfast—and let's try, for pity's sake,
to talk this thing out. Things are nothing like you believe
them to be——'

'Forget it.' He was walking away from her. 'I don't
want breakfast, and there's nothing to be said that would
make any difference to the way things are.'

Ever since that he had treated her as though she didn't
exist. She probably didn't, not to him, she thought as
she slid the last of his shirts into the top drawer of the
chest in the guest-room.

He had never pretended to love her, and as far as he
was concerned he had made a bad error of judgement
when he'd decided a marriage between them could work.
And now he was cutting his losses, cutting her out of
his life. The process, she knew, had only just begun.

'Is that the lot?' He had come into the room quietly.
'I'd have given you a hand if you'd said you weren't
asking Meg to do it.' He didn't look as tired as he had
done, although he was still pale beneath his tan. Meg's
coffee must have helped.

Cleo hunched one shoulder, not knowing what to say.
What could one say in such a situation? She wouldn't
go down on her knees and beg him to listen to her. She
had her pride, if nothing else.

He moved further into the room, unbuttoning his shirt,
and she edged back towards the door. 'I'm going to
shower and change,' he told her. He looked at her as he
spoke but his eyes were empty. The light had gone out
of them. 'I won't be back for dinner, so don't wait up.
Let Meg know, would you?' he said dismissively, and
Cleo slipped out of the door and went to her room.
Tomorrow, after she'd slept, she would think of what
was best to do; emulate her husband and try to cut her
losses, or try to go on.

*   *   *

But no amount of sleep or concentrated hard work helped her to reach a decision over her future. Her days fell into a pattern she hadn't the will to break. Always, after a solitary breakfast, Thornwood, drove her to Eastcheap and collected her at six. An evening working, her papers spread out on the table in the drawing-room, followed a lonely dinner which she forced herself to eat for the sake of her child. Sometimes Jude joined her for the meal and then shut himself away in his study for the rest of the evening, but more often than not he stayed away. He didn't say where he went, or what he was doing, and Cleo didn't ask. She didn't think she cared.

There was no communication between them now, not even anger, and one day soon Cleo was going to have to answer the questions she could see building up behind Meg's eyes. The housekeeper was fond of them both, particularly of Jude, and even if she hadn't sensed the frigid atmpsphere—and she would have to be blind and deaf not to—she was well aware that they used separate bedrooms, that Jude left the house before eight each morning and was rarely back before midnight.

So sooner or later the questions would come, Meg wouldn't be able to help herself. And what could she answer? Cleo wondered tiredly. She could hardly tell Meg the truth, tell her that Jude had seen her sprawled out on the floor, semi-naked, with Robert Fenton, that he believed the child she carried was Fenton's!

It was the thought of the child that finally woke senses that had been entombed in a dull, unfeeling limbo. She had hoped to make her marriage a good thing, to teach him, eventually, to love her as she had loved him. But that hope had died and she'd be a fool if she ever thought of trying to bring it to life. And there was her unborn child to consider. No child could be expected to thrive in a house where its parents rarely met, hardly exchanged two words from one week to the next!

There would have to be a separation, or a divorce. Cleo didn't care which. And if Jude wouldn't agree then she would just have to take matters into her own hands. Move out, and soon.

Thus decided, she settled herself to wait for him. He had, apparently, told Meg he wouldn't be in for dinner, and as far as Cleo knew he hadn't yet spent the entire night away from home. But when the clock struck two in the morning she began to think there was a first time for everything, and it was then she heard the sound of the hall door closing, his footsteps, dragging, as if he were bone weary—or drunk.

Twenty-four hours ago she would have been able to face him with a dreary kind of equanimity. But her emergence from the limbo she had inhabited meant that her emotions were alive and kicking again, torturing her. All through the long waiting hours he had prowled through her mind. A silent, mistrustful, austere image. And, she had to face it, a much-loved image. Despite everything, her love for him survived. He couldn't murder that.

Now, her legs shook weakly as she went to intercept him in the hall, and a hand went up to push tiredly at her hair as she told him, 'I must talk to you.'

'Now?' The hall was dimly lit at this hour, but she could see the lines of strain around his eyes, his mouth, the shadow of stubble that darkened his tautly fleshed jaw.

'I'm afraid so. It won't wait.' She turned back into the drawing-room, her heart beating heavily. She half expected him to ignore her request, to carry on upstairs. He looked exhausted enough to fall into bed and sleep for twenty-four hours.

But he wasn't far behind her and she turned, watching him as he hooked a thumb under his tie, loosening it. And as he slopped brandy into a glass she wondered, for the first time, how he spent the evenings he stayed away from home, where he spent them, and with whom.

She wished she hadn't. Her mind conjured images she didn't want to begin to consider. And the surge of jealousy was painful, frightening.

'Well?' The question was put without any real interest, and that hurt. It was as if she were of no importance at all, something not to be considered, unless absolutely necessary.

She saw him empty his glass in one long swallow and snapped shrewishly, 'Do you need to drink like a fish?'

One dark eyebrow came up at that, but only slightly, as if her presence had registered, just a little, but was of no consequence. He turned to refill his glass, his voice cool. 'Need? Do you begin to know what I need?'

'No!' The response was pushed out of her on a gasp. 'I don't know. Not any more! But I do know this——' She dragged in a deep, ragged breath, getting hold of herself again. She couldn't get through to him on any emotional level, not any more. And, having accepted that, the only sane thing to do was to keep cool, not allow him to know how her heart was beginning the painful process of breaking up again. If she could keep her dignity, and her pride, it would at least be something. 'I know we can't go on like this,' she went on, her voice flat. 'The sort of marriage we have doesn't make any sense. The house is full of silence; you rarely speak. You're rarely at home—and your absences are unexplained. It's no atmosphere to bring up a child in.'

She sat down, too weary to stand now, her eyes pools of fatigue in the pale oval of her face, and Jude said slowly, 'Of course. The child.' His eyes drifted over her as if to find evidence of the new life. 'We mustn't forget the child.' He went to stand in front of the empty fireplace and the dry bitterness in his voice made her throat tighten. 'I am willing to accept the child, give it my name—regardless of whether it is mine or Fenton's. But in exchange, I would prefer it if you didn't instigate divorce proceedings in the near future. We can review the situation in a few years' time.'

Cleo became very still, If she moved now, or tried to speak, she knew she would go to pieces. That he wanted her to remain, legally, as his wife for a few more years meant only that he would prefer to keep up appearances. How she felt, trapped in this bitter travesty of a marriage, was neither here nor there. Then he said, as if he had previously given the matter a great deal of thought, 'However, for the sake of sanity, it would be best if we lived largely apart. The absence of the inevitable tension would obviously be better for the child, too. There would be speculation, naturally,' he continued in the same judicial tone. 'But it would seem feasible that we might have decided it to be in the child's best interests to be brought up in the country. If you'll leave it in my hands I'll arrange everything. As it happens,' his eyes flickered to her stony face, 'Fiona mentioned a property for sale a mile or so away from her weekend cottage. I'll look into the possibilities.'

'Do that,' she choked, shocked by the way she was feeling—as if she had just received a death sentence! And she knew that, although she couldn't live with him, she couldn't live without him.

In a moment she might cry. But she wouldn't shed tears in front of him—in front of the remote, cold-eyed stranger he had become. And she pushed herself to her feet, her legs distinctly unsteady as they carried her to the door. The expanse of carpeting had never seemed so wide, the privacy of her room so far away. But he was at the door before her, holding it open, telling her, 'I'll get something settled as quickly as possible. I'll keep you informed, of course, and you can vet any property I find that's suitable.'

Pausing, the words he was saying sounding more like verbal torture than a reasoned solution to a shared and bitter problem, she looked up into the hard, handsome planes of his unforgiving face and suddenly her eyes narrowed as hatred, quick and burning, filled the smoky eyes that had been huge pools of misery.

'After you're settled somewhere I will try to drop by from time to time,' he was remarking levelly as she pulled her shoulders straight, her voice like a spitting cat as she retorted,

'You won't have to waste your time. I wouldn't let you over the doorstep!'

And he could make what he liked of that, she thought as she swept past him, her head high, two spots of hectic colour blazing along her cheekbones.

As far as she was concerned there was no way their separation would resemble anything like a civilised arrangement!

She had finished with him; no more pining, no more regrets. Nothing! And she wouldn't give him the satisfaction of knowing that her violent reaction to a fairly reasonable suggestion had been sparked by the lingering fragrance of the light but definitely exotic perfume she had detected on his clothes!

He would never know that she was blindingly jealous of the woman, whoever, who wore such a distinctive perfume for him, the woman whose arms he had left before coming home to tell his wife he was in the process of finding some suitable hole to bury her in! And no one could tell her—no one!—that he hadn't been

scheming and plotting to discover the best way of being
rid of her long before she had told him things couldn't
go on the way they were. And no wonder he didn't want
a divorce just yet—a wife in the background would be
the perfect let-out for a man whose mistress became too
demanding!

Her fury carried her up the stairs at a pace that might
have astounded her had she been capable of thinking of
it. She was not going to be put where she didn't want
to go! She would not be discreetly hidden away, an unwanted wife, allowing her highly sexed, highly attractive, non-committed husband to conduct amorous
affairs with the beautiful, available women who would
be only too delighted to bring a little warmth and comfort
to his lonely life!

'So there you are! Meg said she thought you were sunning
yourself.'

Cleo opened her heavy eyelids to see Fiona walking
over the immaculately tended lawn at the back of the
house. The small garden was Thornwood's pride, every
plant treated as though it were a precious child, and it
provided a corner of peace and beauty, unexpected in
the heart of the sprawling, mighty city.

'No, don't move,' Fiona commanded softly, settling
herself on the sun-warmed grass as Cleo swung her long
legs from the sun lounger. 'You look so comfy! And
congratulations on your super news! How are you,
anyway?' Long, deep blue eyes—so like Jude's—narrowed as they swept Cleo's drawn features. 'Junior giving
you a bad time?'

'Ah.' The wrinkle of perplexity cleared from Cleo's
brow as the penny dropped. Jude must have told his sister
about the baby. She wondered drily if he'd also said he
believed it to be Fenton's. Cursing the colour that

flooded her face at that horrible thought she lay back, trying to look relaxed. 'A little.'

It was nothing like the truth. Jude's baby wasn't giving her a bad time, and if it ever did she wouldn't complain. Her baby was the only thing she had and already she loved it with a fierce maternalism that amazed her. The coming child meant more to her than her high-powered job, her private fortune, more than Jude. Much more. Unconsciously, her mouth formed a grim, straight line. She had cut Jude out of her life. He was devious, cruel and she was well rid of him.

'How was the Paris trip?' Cleo carefully turned the subject, but Fiona was having none of that.

'Fine,' she dismissed with a throwaway gesture of long-fingered hands. 'But I didn't break into my lazy holiday to talk about that.' She wriggled out of the short-sleeved jacket of her silvery-grey cotton skirt suit and the hot sun caressed the skin of her bare arms, turning it gold. 'Jude tells me you're working too hard. I'm glad to see you taking it easy today.'

That surprised her; she didn't think he noticed what she did, or cared. But she wasn't going to be the one to explain that the marriage was over. 'I didn't feel like going in today. Maybe I'll get something done at home this afternoon.' And that was the truth. Another day cooped up with Luke had been more than she could face this morning. Jealous fury had kept her awake most of the night and she'd surfaced at dawn, determined to do as Jude had obviously done, and cut her losses, decide for herself what to do with her life.

'He also told me you were on the look-out for a country home—somewhere to bring the baby up in,' Fiona said slowly, and Cleo asked, her mouth dry,

'When did you see him?

Had Jude confided in his sister, told her his marriage was over? They were very close...

'Last night.' Fiona plucked at the silky fabric of her scarlet sleeveless top, the heat in the sun-trap of the garden getting to her. 'He came to the cottage where I'm supposed to be treating myself to a spot of relaxation after the madhouse of the Paris fashion world. And the upshot was, I've never felt less relaxed in my life.' The blue eyes were shrewd. 'Look—I've got a lot to say to you, but I'm parched. Why don't I ask Meg if she can find us a long, cool drink?'

'I'm sorry—let me go——'

Cleo was on her feet, annoyed with herself for her lack of hospitality, but Fiona had a mind of her own and was on her feet, too, standing close as she instructed, 'I'll do it. Stay here and rest. And that's an order!'

Cleo frowned, her eyes finding her sister-in-law's, puzzled. 'The perfume you're wearing?' she asked slowly. 'Were you wearing it last night?'

'Sure.' Fiona looked as though she thought Cleo had gone slightly mad. Then she smiled disarmingly, 'I've been drenching myself in the stuff ever since I had it made up for me in Paris. Like it? There's this little place—they blend fragrances for individual customers. Cost the earth—but worth it!'

She swung away, up the short flight of stone steps that led to the terrace, disappearing into the house through the open french windows of Jude's study, and Cleo sank down on the grass, her head resting on her jean-clad knees. The relief was overwhelming, stupidly, gloriously overwhelming.

Jude hadn't been womanising last night. He had been visiting his sister, and it was her perfume that had clung to his clothes! The knowledge shouldn't have made any difference—nothing could alter the fact that their marriage was over—but it did. But it made her feel vulnerable again, consumed with pain, because the reason for her fury was gone, undermining her grim determination to cut him completely out of her life, to make her future empty of even the memory of him.

'Our luck's in!' Fiona appeared with two tall glasses, ice-cubes clinking. 'Freshly made lemon juice——' She handed Cleo a glass and sank down beside her, sipping her drink thirstily. And when the last drop was gone she put the glass aside and said seriously, 'I'm about to interfere—with no apologies whatsoever. There's something badly wrong between you and Jude, and don't explode——' this as Cleo spluttered on her drink '—because it won't do any good. I intend to get at the truth.'

Cleo put her glass aside and stared Fiona straight in the eyes. 'Just what did Jude tell you?' Her stomach was tying itself in knots. Fiona meant well, but she was probing an open wound. No amount of interference on her part could alter a single damn thing!

'Nothing,' Fiona disclaimed. 'But he didn't need to. He arrived at the cottage around nine, looking like death, and he hung around until almost one—despite the heavy hints I dropped about needing my beauty sleep. And towards the end of our rather draggy conversation he let drop that he was looking for a country property for you to retire to—like immediately—in order to give the baby, when it comes, the space and freedom to run around in. And when I mentioned that Dene Place, not far from my cottage, was on the market he said it could well be the answer, if it was remotely suitable, as I'd be on hand most weekends to give you some company. Now I'm not a fool, Cleo,' Fiona stated the obvious, examining her fingernails with absorbed interest. 'Firstly, when he told me about the baby there was nothing coming over from him—no pride, excitement, nothing. He might as well have been telling me you'd ordered a new set of pans for the kitchen. And as for a country house, for you and baby to immure yourselves in—well, that makes no kind of sense. Even I, who scarcely know one end of a baby from the other, know it would be some time after it was born before it could go romping merrily through meadows and climbing trees and fishing in the brook.'

She spread her hands, still regarding them intently, and Cleo felt sick as Fiona went on slowly, deliberately, 'A country place would be fine for weekends and so forth—but as a permanent thing, for a pregnant lady and, later, a mum with a small round bundle under one arm, no way. So I decided that as I was unlikely to get any sense out of that dumb brother of mine I'd come and harass you. And what I see doesn't offer much comfort. So what goes on, Cleo?'

But Cleo couldn't answer; the words simply couldn't get past the painful lump in her chest. She would have given anything at that moment to be hard enough to achieve a brittle smile, to say not to worry because there was nothing to worry about. That she and Jude had decided, quite amicably, to call it a day—no hard feelings on either side. But that was something she could never do. Despite everything, her love for Jude ran too deep for that. It was still real, alive, and hurting. She had received very little affection in her life since her parents had died, and love, when she had finally experienced it, was too precious, even now, to sully with lies.

'Jude means a lot to me,' Fiona said softly, her blue eyes compassionate as they held the grey, dark-ringed ones. 'And when I first saw you two together I knew you were right for each other. I'd always known it would take a special kind of lady to snare the hard man's heart. And I was glad to know he'd found her at last.'

Those words, the very real affection in Fiona's voice, were Cleo's undoing. She had never snared Jude's heart—she'd merely captured his interest with the offer of those shares, the statement of fact when she'd told him he could always be sure she hadn't married him for his money. She'd alerted the logical brain to her possibilities as a wife at a time when he'd been considering marriage for the sake of an heir.

Unstoppable sobs shook her slender frame and Fiona's arm, coming swiftly around her shoulders, opened the floodgates. Between deep, painful sobs, the tears she thought she had cried all out, the whole dreadful, tragic story of their brief stormy marriage was told.

'You mean that louse was trying to blackmail you and that pig-headed, obstinate brother of mine refused to listen to a word you said?' Fiona pushed a slippery strand of pale hair back from Cleo's flushed face. 'You poor baby.'

There was a crusading note in Fiona's voice and Cleo's eyes clouded with panic.

'Please,' she said, her voice thick, 'promise me you won't say anything to Jude?'

'It's time someone made him listen to the truth.' Fiona's mouth firmed. 'You are both fine, beautiful, brainy people, but as far as the emotions are concerned you haven't enough gumption between you to figure your way from A to B!'

'Please!' Even to her own ears, Cleo sounded demented. But Fiona simply didn't understand! How could she, when she hadn't lived through the searing agony of it all? Somehow, though, she had to try to make her understand a little of the way it was. Desperately, she clutched at the other woman's hands.

'Don't you see——' she appealed, her eyes intense. 'Telling Jude the truth now wouldn't mean a thing. We got along fine to begin with, I grant you that, and I had begun to hope he'd learn to love me.' Her voice wobbled at that, at the hurting memory of hopes long dead, but she forced herself to go on because it was important. 'He never did love me, it was a marriage of convenience, simply that. And things started to go wrong before he could begin to develop any deep feelings for me. He began to despise me for what he thought I was. It's understandable, if you stop to think about it. He didn't love me, so he had no real reason to question the evidence of his eyes, and I suppose I had too much pride to stand there and bellow and force him to listen to what I had to say. In a peculiar kind of way I felt he had to ask me for the truth, or at least to show a willingness to listen whenever I tried to bring it up.' She shrugged wearily. 'I thought that if I was beginning to mean anything to him at all he surely must want to hear my side of things. But he didn't, of course, because all the time his dislike of me was hardening. He'd made a bad mistake in marrying me and he wanted me out of his life. And if you think about it you'll realise for him there can be no going back to the days when he thought I was a reasonable proposition as a wife, the mother of his children. So promise me, Fiona,' her grip tightened, 'promise you won't say a word. The truth might make him feel uncomfortable—bad, even—but what's the point of that? There's been too much mistrust, contempt, to make our marriage even begin to look like working again. If there'd been love on his side, too, then it might have stood a chance. But there never was. It's better for both of us to make a clean break. So please promise you'll say nothing?'

Fiona stood up, disentangling her hands, her face strained.

'If it's what you want to hear and it will put your mind at rest, then all right, my dear. I promise.'

CHAPTER TWELVE

'THE estate agents' particulars are in here.' He passed her a large envelope then fastened his seat-belt. 'You might like to glance at them on the journey.'

'Thank you,' she said stiffly, her words almost inaudible, and as the Jag turned out of the quiet, early morning London square her fingers tightened on the envelope. She knew she would make little sense of the contents, even if the particulars of the house they were going to view had been written for an idiot's consumption.

It was going to be another glorious day, the sun already warm as it streamed through the window at her side. Jude was casually dressed in lightweight stone-coloured jeans, a black body-hugging T-shirt that emphasised the whiplash power of his shoulders and chest. But there was nothing casual about his attitude; she could feel the tension in him and it was as tightly coiled as her own. Her edginess was reaching impossible proportions, every one of her senses sharply aware of every move he made, every breath he took.

Until last night she hadn't seen him since he'd told her it would be better if they lived apart. He hadn't been home. If he'd been away on a business trip she hadn't known about it and she'd had too much pride to ask. But last night he'd come to her room, tapping on the door politely, like a stranger. She'd been already in bed, sitting up staring blankly at nothing as she'd tried to bring her mind to the point of making plans for her future, where she would go, and when.

'I picked up the keys to Dene Place,' he'd told her flatly, his eyes a stranger's eyes in the gauntness of his face. 'I'll drive you down to take a look at it tomorrow. We might as well make an early start. Eight o'clock?'

And on that he had gone, closing the door quietly behind him, tangible evidence of the way he had shut her out of his life.

Three days ago she would have told him to get lost, that she could find a place on her own, didn't need his help. But since that traumatic conversation with Fiona she had done some serious thinking. It was pointless to be on the defensive, to fight. Her relationship with Jude was written out, the end of a chapter in her life. It was something she had to accept, no matter how painful, so there was no point in making things even more difficult.

As for Dene Place—well, if it was remotely suitable then she and her child might as well live there as anywhere else. At least Fiona would be around most weekends, and that was a plus. She had taken an instinctive liking to Jude's sister and she knew all there was to know about their disastrous marriage. There would never be any need to pretend with her; Fiona was on her side, and that had to count for something.

A sigh was dragged from her, right up from her toes, and although she'd been scarcely aware of it, absorbed in her thoughts, it had registered with Jude and he said roughly, 'It will soon be over, Cleo.'

Her eyes flicked to him briefly, noting the twist of his mouth, the hard bones of his profile jutting against the taut skin. Was he talking about the journey? Or the sick farce of their marriage? She didn't know and she wasn't asking, and she closed her eyes and didn't open them again until the car drew to a halt and he cut the engine.

They were parked in front of tall wrought-iron gates, set between stone posts, and Jude got out. 'I'll open the gates.' Cleo slid out of her seat, closing the car door behind her.

'I'll walk up,' she told him, passing him as he swung the gates open. The iron creaked as it moved on its rusty hinges and she didn't look at him. It hurt too much.

She would look over the house, and if she liked it she would buy it. And she'd move in as soon as remotely possible, install a computer link-up with Slade head office, go on from there. For the sake of appearances, Jude didn't want a divorce just yet and neither, particularly, did she. She would never re-marry, and as for being free—well, she'd never be free of him, she knew that, because she would always love him. Love him, hate him, there seemed little difference.

Once today was over she probably wouldn't have to see him again, or not very often. He'd continue to make himself scarce until she was settled in a place of her own. She knew he wouldn't want to spend time with her.

Dene Place was a Queen Anne house, not too large, and the gardens were a wilderness, but the fabric of the building seemed sound. The bare, dusty floorboards echoed with the hollow sound common to all empty houses as she explored, leaving him to follow if he felt he had to.

The view from the first-floor windows was benignly rural—meadows, trees, gentle hills—and she could be reasonably content here.

'What do you think?' Jude had walked up behind her and she stiffened, her eyes staring, not seeing anything now. Then she made herself turn, a slight smile pinned to her face, and he was closer than she had expected.

Her bare arm brushed against his and the shock made her stumble. He put a hand out to steady her, the action automatic, and she sucked in her breath, moving away quickly. His slightest touch still set her alight. There was nothing she could do about it.

'I like it,' she took up his question, anxious that he shouldn't guess how he still affected her physically. 'I'll buy, subject to surveyors' reports, and I'll handle the whole thing. There's no need for you to put yourself to any more trouble.' She wanted the thing settled now, and this place would be somewhere to hide, to lick her wounds.

'It's not too isolated for you?'

Her eyes fled to his, hard, bright eyes because she was crying inside. He looked weary, gaunt, as if he'd lost weight and the loss had been rapid, but, her mouth a tight line, she pushed concern out of sight.

'I wouldn't let that bother you.' She wouldn't be lonely—or only for him. She would have her work and, later, her child. She moved rapidly through the empty room but his voice stopped her before she reached the door.

'You hate me, don't you?'

'Yes!' Her reply was instant, savage, her lips pulled back against her teeth. He confused her emotions, made love and hate seem the same thing, and she could no longer stand the bitter tension. She had to get out of here, find some space, some air to breathe that wasn't tainted with the stench of tension.

Almost stumbling in her haste, she sped from the room and across the large, square landing, taking the stairs quickly, hearing his voice behind her. But for all her haste he reached the foot of the stairs at the same time as she, grasping her shoulders roughly.

'You little fool!' His voice was driven hoarsely through white lips. 'You could have fallen, killed yourself, killed the child!'

Shaken, trembling inside, she returned his angry glare, tugging her arm away from his hurting fingers.

'I would have thought that might have suited you admirably,' she said coldly, nastily. 'Two unwanted encumbrances out of the way in one fell swoop! Why should you care?'

'Of course I damn well care!' he bit, his mouth compressed as he faced her, his hands gripping her shoulders again. 'I care like hell what happens to you and my child!'

Cleo's eyes flicked upwards, searching his. One of them wasn't thinking straight. Either she was hearing things she wanted to hear or he'd made a Freudian slip, admitting paternity in the emotional heat because that was the way he'd wanted it.

His strong hands were still gripping her shoulders, she could feel every fingertip burning through the thin fabric of the sleeveless dress she wore. And he was too close, too male, and too much loved.

'Did I hear what I think I heard?' she asked acidly. She felt his hands drop to his side. 'Do you actually admit the child is yours?'

'Yes.' The admission made his face go hard and she stared at him disbelievingly. Had he finally reached the conclusion that she could be trusted? Had he cared about her enough to work it out for himself? The hope she'd thought was dead stirred to reluctant life again. She was a fool to want him still. He had caused her more pain than she could ever have believed she was capable of handling. Yet love couldn't be turned on and off like a tap, however much one wished it could be.

'I don't blame you for hating me, Cleo, and I have a lot to apologise to you for.' His face was bleak, his teeth biting down on his lower lip as he spread his hands hopelessly in a gesture of defeat she wouldn't have believed him capable of. Then he moved away from her, staring out of the open door to the sunlit tangle of the gardens. 'I don't have the right to expect you to accept my apologies, but I hope you'll believe me when I say I'm desperately sorry—for everything.' He turned then, facing her, his eyes shuttered. 'Under the circumstances I'm willing to give you the divorce you want. It's the least I can do.' A muscle worked spasmodically at the side of his jaw and his voice was husky as he swung on his heels, making for the open door. 'If you want to look around outside while we're here I'll wait for you over there.'

Her mind was reeling. None of this made any kind of sense! He had at last decided he'd been wrong about her, that the child she carried was his—he had even apologised! And yet, he was willing to divorce her! A few days ago, still believing the worst of her, he'd stipulated no divorce for several years!

There was a stone seat against the rosy brick of the high garden wall and he was making for that, to wait for her. All notions of exploring the grounds left her head as she ran after him, her feet slithering on the weedy gravel drive, the full skirts of her summery blue dress flying around her long bare legs.

He heard her rapid footsteps, turned, his eyes puzzled and she told him breathily, 'You can't leave it at that.'

'No?' Whether he deliberately misunderstood her, she couldn't tell, but he went on, 'Don't worry. According to the estate agent, the house is solid. But we'll get surveyors' reports in any case. And as the garden itself is immaterial to me, I'll wait here.' He sank down on the stone seat, his eyes closed wearily—or dismissively—and she snapped,

'I wasn't talking about the house, dammit!'

His eyes flicked open, azure slits. 'If you've got something to say, say it.' He sounded bored and she couldn't understand him, not at all.

'It's about the divorce.' She sat beside him, her heart pattering. She knew she shouldn't hope, but she really couldn't help it. Telling herself that he plainly regarded her as a boring encumbrance, to be offloaded as soon as possible, didn't stop her remembering how he'd said he cared what happened to her and her child.

'It will take time, Cleo, but I'll put the wheels in motion tomorrow.' He spoke gently, as if to an impatient child, and she shook her head abruptly, sending her hair flying about her face. He was obviously determined to misconstrue everything she said!

'I meant,' she began with gritty patience, 'that there doesn't need to be one, surely?'

'What are you? A masochist?' He jerked up from the seat, his body tense with an inner violence she couldn't understand. The line of his mouth was savage. 'It's the only course that makes any sense. When Fiona told me how Fenton had been trying to blackmail you—told me what had really happened——' He smacked one fist into the open palm of the other hand. 'My God! If I see him again, I'll kill him!'

'Fiona told you?' Cleo's mouth was dry. She had thought she could trust Fiona, but the broken promise didn't really signify, not now. She had idiotically believed he'd decided to trust her all on his own, because he cared about her.

'Fiona promised——' she began woodenly, her voice trailing away, and he looked at her, almost sympathetically.

'I know. And yes, she told me. But you obviously don't know her well enough. She always makes her own mind up, and would break a promise with about as much compunction as she would break an egg if she believed good would come of it. You told Fiona what had really been going on between you and Fenton—why didn't you tell me?'

'Oh, God!' Cleo buried her head in her hands, almost laughing but nearer to tears at the injustice of his remark. 'Because you damn well wouldn't listen!' She shot him an angry look. 'Fenton was doing his best to rape me when you walked in that day. And all you could do was jump to nasty, insulting conclusions!'

'I'm sorry!' he groaned, dropping to the seat beside her again, and Cleo, flicking him a sideways look, saw that his hands were shaking. But the spasm was over in a second and he was back in control again, leaning forward, his hands dangling between his knees, loosely held and almost relaxed.

'As I said before, any apologies of mine have to be inadequate and the only thing I can do—after making life intolerable for you—is agree to your request for a divorce.'

She stared at him, wanting to shake him. Of course she had asked for a divorce, but that had been in the heat of the moment, in desperation! Didn't the brute know divorce was the last thing she really wanted? She loved him, she carried his child, he was her husband, for pity's sake! But could she tell him all this, would her pride let her? And could they ever be happy together again? Could they make the marriage work?

She didn't know, but she was willing to try because, somehow, pride didn't come into it any more. And she was turning words over in her mind when he said coolly, 'I shall want access to the child, of course, on a regular basis. You won't make any difficulties over that?'

And then she knew, and the knowledge chilled her, and it was her turn to jerk to her feet,

'Of course I won't.' She pulled herself to her full graceful height, her face ashen. 'Now you have everything you wanted, don't you? A child as an heir, the shares—so what would you want with a wife?'

She twisted on the heels of her strappy sandals and marched away, her back rigidly straight, her emotions heaving. 'I'm going to look over the grounds,' she spat over her shoulder. 'While you sit there and count your blessings!'

She could see it all now. Every last thing had become hideously clear. He had already been thinking of children when she had made that reckless proposal. Not because he particularly liked children, but because he needed an heir. And along she had come—presentable, intelligent, and wealthy in her own right, dangling the Slade shares as bait!

Those shares had been the deciding factor, and now he had them, and he would have the heir he'd wanted—so what possible use could he have for a wife?

Tears were streaming down her cheeks, blinding her, and she stumbled through a thicket of shrubs, not knowing or caring what she was doing, and she heard him call her name.

He was close behind and there was nowhere to go, and she hated herself for the weakness of tears because now he would know.

'Cleo.' A hand held her, another pulled at branches as he extricated her, and then both hands cupped her face, tilting it, the pads of his thumbs wiping the shaming tears. 'Does it matter to you so much?'

'What?' Her mouth was mutinous. Two could play the game of deliberate misunderstandings.

'The divorce. It's what you wanted, after all. And I owe that to you, at least.'

Angrily, she jerked her head from his hands, her eyes flickering, looking for escape. But there was nowhere to go; he was blocking the only way out of the tangle of bushes she'd landed herself in.

'It's what you want,' she denied. 'So why not take it? You already have everything else you wanted—an heir on the way, those shares——'

'Those wretched shares again!' He looked puzzled, as if she'd just told him he'd grown a second head. 'Damn the shares! I'm already in the process of handing them back to you, in any case. I've got enough on my plate without having to contend with that doddery old board of so-called directors, and Luke—sweet heaven preserve me from Luke! It's your baby, your problem, and that's what I've always ever intended. All I ever wanted to do was help you sort the mess out. I thought you might need me.'

Uncomprehendingly, she studied his closed face, shuddering as he added bitterly, 'But you never did need me, did you? Or only as a name on your wedding certificate! And I don't blame you for that, at least you were honest about your reasons for wanting to marry me. I was the one at fault, all the way down the line.' His mouth twisted in self-derision. 'Too wary to insist on knowing why you had to get your hands on your money, too blind to see beyond what my eyes were telling me—that you and Fenton were lovers—and, right at the beginning of it all, too damn smug about my wretched plan of campaign.'

'What plan?' Her brow furrowed and she took a tentative step towards him but he turned away, his face dark with an emotion she couldn't identify as he glanced at his watch.

'It's not important now. Believe me, Cleo, there's nothing more to be said, nothing useful. And it's time we left—if you've seen all you want to see.'

He was walking away, across the shaggy, overgrown lawns and she stared after him, not understanding anything. She felt limp and wretched, her mind in turmoil. He'd said he had never wanted the shares. He'd said so many things that hadn't made sense.

She was used to solving tricky financial problems but she didn't come near to understanding the man who was now striding away from her, not looking back. And she knew that if she let it go now, he would never look back again. He would close his mind on the brief episode of their marriage and she would never begin to understand the enigma who had once been her husband—once, and always, loved.

'Jude!' She ran after him, her feet flying over the grass, and she caught up with him before he reached the car.

'Ready?' he asked, only the slight roughness in his voice betraying any emotion at all.

'No.' She caught his hand, almost sobbing as she recognised the sheet of electifying sensation that engulfed her at the physical contact.

He turned slightly surprised eyes on her, and she saw them cloud, then, as they swept her face, darken with what she might have believed to be torment if she hadn't known better.

She knew she must look a heap, her hair mussed, her face hot and crumpled from crying, from the heat—so far removed from her usual cool and impeccable self that she might be a different person.

'I want to talk to you,' she said, her voice betraying her savaged emotions.

He removed his hand from her curling fingers, which didn't augur well, she thought distractedly, but no matter, she was determined enough and could see, at last, that she had been to self-contained, too afraid of admitting her feelings, too unimaginative to question her own ideas concerning *his* feelings, *his* motivations.

'We've got our lines crossed somewhere,' she told him reasonably. She really did have to stay calm now, quite unemotional, otherwise she would never get the opportunity to know him more deeply, understand why he was as he was.

Ignoring the thunderous bar of threatening brows, denoting a rapid loss of patience, she said, 'You've told me you have no interest in the Slade shares—except on my account. And we both know you married because you want children. And yet——' she took a deep breath, trying to find the right words '—and yet, even though you know I never deceived you with Fenton, that our child will be born in about seven months' time, you are insisting on a divorce. Have I become so repugnant to you? Help me to understand.'

'Can't you leave it alone, woman?' His voice was harsh, the words flying at her bitterly. 'Must you twist the knife in the wound?' His height and breadth, the savage line of his mouth, made him menacing and she moved away from him instinctively, wanting to ease his pain but not knowing how because she didn't know the reason for it. 'Do you want my blood, as well as my peace of mind? I married you because I loved you—I'd been falling in love with you since the moment I first saw you.' The words were torn from him, wrenched out with anguish, and Cleo's heart stopped, then slammed on again and she wanted to go to him, to hold him and love him, but knew that if she touched him he would explode into a savage repudiation of all the hurt and anger he was feeling. She had to allow him to spill out the poison, the pain, she had to stand and watch, and listen, and it wasn't easy.

'And so I hatched my plots, my cunning plans. Emotional involvements between boss and employee don't work, and I wanted our involvement to become very emotional indeed. So I started a rumour. The Mescal Slade takeover of Slade Securities. Very neat!' His mouth curved down with self-condemnation. 'As I saw it, you would hear the rumour and come to me about it. And I would suggest your doing precisely what you are doing—move to your family's company and pull them clear. So far, so good. Their decline was real, as you know, and you were the obvious person to do the job— the best, too. But there was a lot more to it than that, because when you no longer worked for me I could date you, try to make you love me, ask you to marry me. I had it all worked out,' he smiled mirthlessly, 'but before the rumour got to your ears you beat me to it—didn't you just?'

He pushed his hands into the pockets of his jeans, his wide shoulders held straight and proud as he turned away from her, and she held her breath, knowing that she had to stand there, and listen, when one word from her would put things straight. But she couldn't say that word, not yet. He was revealing a side of his character she hadn't known existed, giving her glimpses of vulnerability and self-doubt that made him doubly dear to her.

'Your proposal knocked me senseless,' he said quietly. 'I was being offered, just like that, exactly what I'd hoped and dreamed of having. You—as my wife. And I took the chance, not daring to ask myself exactly why you needed that money because I wanted to hold on to the dream of hope. Hope,' he grated bitterly, 'that I would be able to teach you to love me. It didn't matter why you wanted to marry me, only that you did. Can you understand that, Cleo?'

'Of course I can.' Her voice was ragged, her clear eyes bright with tears of happiness. And he was calmer now, the hurt and anger partly expunged by his bitter, tormented words. 'Jude——' She moved towards him but he shrugged away.

'I don't want your pity. The blame's all mine. I took what I wanted most in the world, and then I spoiled it. I loved you so much that the very thought of you made music in my soul and then, when I was beginning to believe you were growing to love me, I killed all hope of that ever happening. I found you with Fenton and the truth, to me, was what I'd seen. I knew you hadn't married me because you loved me, and there you were, with Fenton, with the money, or some of it, that you'd been forced to marry in order to control, lying around. A sweetener for the lover you couldn't marry because your guardians wouldn't have approved.' His voice deepened. 'If only you'd told me, Cleo, as soon as we were married, exactly why you had to have that money, I would have made damn sure he never came within a mile of you. And if you had,' he gave her a tired, hopeless ghost of a smile, 'I wouldn't have treated you the way I did, killed any hope I ever had of teaching you to love me.'

'I should have done.' She swayed towards him, her face pale, regrets eating her. She could have saved them both so much misery. But he did love her, had loved her all the time, and that was the most wonderful, unbelievable thing in the world.

Unhesitatingly, he cradled her in his arms, concern darkening his eyes, and she murmured, 'I wish I'd told you everything, but I was so afraid of what he threatened to do—not for myself, but because of Uncle John. And

I was ashamed of myself for getting into such a situation in the first place. I didn't want anyone to know, least of all you. It was something I had to sort out for myself.'

'I know. Please don't upset yourself, Cleo.' His voice was infinitely kind, heartbreakingly sad. 'How did he get hold of that hotel receipt? Don't tell me if you don't want to—it's certainly none of my business, and if you were lovers—well, that's not my affair, either.'

'We were never lovers,' she denied, happy, at peace at last, within the circle of his arms. 'He'd asked me to marry him secretly, but I'd turned him down. I'd already recognised my feelings for him for what they were—infatuation. And once that was out of the way I knew I didn't even like him. Anyway——' She dredged her memory. It all seemed so long ago, so unimportant. Everything seemed unimportant when set beside the knowledge that the man she loved so desperately had loved her all the time. She pressed her face closer to the wall of his chest, feeling his warmth, the masculine strength of him, the gentleness . . .

'Anyway,' she continued quickly, anxious to get this out of the way, lay the ghost of her supposed affair with Fenton finally and for ever. 'He seemed to take my rejection fairly well, said he'd like to keep in touch, that sort of thing, suggested we went for a day in the country—we'd done that whenever I could spare time from my studies—I'd always found it relaxing. So, we went. He was driving my car. We had a picnic lunch, explored a ruined castle we came across, began to make our leisurely way home. But he appeared to lose the way and the upshot was, we were approaching some village—Goldingstan—in the early evening. And there was a bridge, and I never knew how it happened, but he seemed to lose control of the car. It wasn't a bad accident—the left wing was crumpled and I ended up with bruised ribs.'

She shivered slightly at the memory, knowing, now, that it had all been set up, carefully planned. 'By the time he'd walked into the village and found a garage willing to tow the car in for a check, it was too late to do anything but stay where we were. I was feeling a bit groggy by then, and sat in the lounge of the Red Lion while he booked us in, explained what had happened, and ordered supper. It was only when he'd taken me up to the room that I discovered he'd booked us in as man and wife. He said there weren't any other rooms available, and I don't know whether I believed him but I did know I wasn't up to making a fuss, finding the landlady and so on. But I didn't sleep with him. I spent the night in an armchair, and for some reason—the aftermath of the shock of the accident, I suppose—I slept right through until eleven next morning when he woke me and told me that the landlady had been knocking on the door because it was time we vacated it. And that's all there was to it.'

She felt his arms tighten around her, heard him swear, low in his throat, then he murmured, 'It's done with now. You need never worry about him again, I'll see to that.' He released her gently, pushing her upright. 'Are you all right?'

He looked concerned, and she nodded, her heart full, almost hurting with happiness, with her love for him, as she prompted, 'When you read that Fenton was engaged you decided, with him beyond my reach, as you thought, that you'd try to make our marriage work again—but I told you about the baby and you immediately thought——'

'Don't!' he pleaded hoarsely. 'I think I was insane with jealousy by then. And now you know why I'm willing to give you the divorce you asked for. I treated you despicably, and divorce is the only thing I can do for you now.' He shrugged minimally. 'I think we should go now. I've said more then I ever intended to, bared my soul until it's raw. Soul-searching never suited me!'

His wry attempt at humour, to lighten the anguish he was obviously feeling, made her heart contract with love for him, and there was a shaky smile on her lips as she said, very clearly, so that there could be no mistake, 'I don't want a divorce. I never did. I love you, and I need you, and if you won't believe me,' her voice rose to the kind of wailing quiver that would have appalled her in any other circumstances, 'and if you turn your back on me one more time, I'll——'

Words failed her, no threat too dire to utter, but her throat choked up with tears and laughter and utter, utter relief as she saw incredulity replace blankness, and open joy replace that.

'Do you mean that?' He seemed frozen to the ground, making no move towards her, but she did it for him, going to his arms, clinging, holding him, tears not far away, laughter just below the surface, making coherent speech impossible. But his arms enfolded her and the gentle caress of his hands said more than words. And then, with his broken words of love murmured against her lips, her throat, she told him, with the need of all lovers, exactly how and where and when her love for him had begun, and grown, exactly how it was for her, now, and always. And the sun passed its zenith, the lazy heat of the slow afternoon enfolding them as they clung together, as if neither could bear to release the other. Ever.

It was the Thornwoods' evening off, Cleo remembered as she and Jude entered the empty house later that evening, hand in hand. He turned her, catching her in his arms, and she murmured, 'You know, I think I'm hungry. Just let me shower, then I'll fix us something to eat.'

'You shower.' She felt him smile against her lips. 'I'll bring something up to the bedroom to appease your appetite.'

And so he did; himself, champagne and two glasses, which was perfect, and Cleo, already reclining against the satin-covered pillows, fresh from her shower and languid with love for him, told him, 'Lovely, I'm ravenous!' and saw his eyes darken with desire, soften with something that came near to adoration.

His eyes wandered over the drift of amber silk that was her négligé, and he turned away with every appearance of regret, telling her as he stripped off his T-shirt, 'I'll be two minutes under that shower, no more. By the time you've poured the champagne I'll be back.'

And he said, over the noise of the water, 'We'll buy Dene Place, shall we? I've taken a fancy to it. You could say it's where I found you.'

She didn't answer, he wouldn't have heard her if she had. In any case, she didn't need to. They wanted the same things, always would, and they both knew it, now.

And when he came back, the bronze of his skin glistening with a thousand tiny droplets of water, she felt the familiar yet devastating kick of desire in her loins and closed her eyes. Suddenly, stupidly, she felt shy, like a new bride, as if their loving would be for the first time.

'Fiona said,' she uttered thickly, sensing him close, standing over her as she lay back amongst the pillows, 'that you and I didn't have enough gumption between us to figure our way from A to B in the world of the emotions. I think she could have been right.'

'So do I.' His voice was very near now, his clean breath fanning her cheek, and as the mattress depressed beneath his weight and his knowing hands began to remove the silken barrier, working their indescribable magic, he murmured throatily, 'It's a problem we're both going to apply our minds to, aren't we, my darling love? Not to mention our bodies, of course. We'll learn our way from A to B together—and far, far beyond. You and I, my love,' his voice deepened, 'are going to be an unbeatable combination.'

A PROMISE TO REPAY
Amanda Browning

CHAPTER ONE

IT WAS almost time. Kate Hardie felt her heart start to thud as the adrenalin pumped through her. She glanced down at her hands. They were trembling, but not from fear. For four years she had waited for just such a moment as this, knowing that if she was patient it must surely come. And it had. Yet it had been by sheer chance that she had seen the notice of the engagement in the paper a month ago. To cap it, luck had been on her side too, because it had been quite ridiculously easy to discover the time and place of the wedding. A word in the right ear, and she had known that Aidan Crawford was marrying the Honourable Julia Howell today at three o'clock.

Kate balled her hands into fists. This was her right. An eye for an eye. She owed it to her brother. The memory brought a glitter to her eyes and a tightness to her lips. No man could do what had been done to those she loved and get away with it!

She closed her mind to the sound of cars arriving, of doors opening and closing, and laughing greetings, and didn't try to hold back the memories. It seemed only right that today of all days she should remember exactly why she was here.

She had been twenty-two then, and Philip, her brother, only fourteen. There had been just the two of them since their parents had been killed in a motorway pile-up two years before. Life had not been easy, but they had managed. They had lived in a small flat that her job in an estate agents just allowed her to afford. There hadn't been much money left over for luxuries, but it hadn't mattered because they were together.

Then Philip had become ill. One day he had seemed the happiest, most healthy teenager she knew, and the next he had started to fade away before her eyes. It had felt as if they had visited every hospital, seen every specialist in the country before they finally reached a diagnosis. It was a little-known disease, but a treatment had been found that gave a good chance of recovery. The only problem was that Philip would have to go to America, and the cost of the treatment itself was prohibitive.

She had tried to raise the money, of course, but she had had nothing to sell, and no collateral for the size of loan she required. As her options slowly ran out, so her brother's deterioration seemed to increase its pace. Though she had tried not to show her concern, especially in the face of his stoical cheerfulness, she had been almost frantic with worry by the time she'd remembered Aidan Crawford.

It had seemed like the answer to all her prayers. Her father had once told her—perhaps with some premonition of his early death—that if anything should happen to him and her mother she could go to this man for help. They had been friends for many years and still corresponded. If she had trouble, he would do all he could to help.

And so, filled with a new hope, she had found a London address in the telephone directory and gone to see him.

With a shiver, Kate came back to the present. She glanced outside and saw that the bride had arrived. Soon she would have her revenge for that night, four years ago, when her world had been ripped apart. Philip had been so sick that she had hated to leave him, but there had been no time to waste. So she had gone, and while she had pleaded her cause her brother had been rushed into hospital. Still, there might have been time, if the money had come, to save him, but Aidan Crawford had refused.

She had gone home in an agony of despair, to discover what had happened to Philip, but before she could leave for the hospital she had received a telephone call telling her her brother had gone into a coma. He had died in the small hours of the next day. The double blow had been too much. She had gone into shock, recalling very little of that night beyond Aidan Crawford's refusal which had, to her mind, set the seal on her brother's fate. It had left her with a burning hatred of the man who could have saved Philip, and she had vowed that one day he would pay.

She had remained in shock for days. Not even the sad little funeral had penetrated the ice that had settled inside her. Something vital within her had died. She hadn't been able to feel anything any more, and she hadn't wanted to. Back in the echoing emptiness of her flat, she had known only one thing: that lack of money had given one man the power of life and death over her brother. Wealth could have kept Philip alive, and wealth meant power. A determination was born in her then that, some day, somehow, that wealth and power would be hers.

Barely a week later she had run into an old friend, Rae Purcell. Over coffee they had rekindled that friendship and Kate had discovered that Rae was now a talent scout for a modelling agency. She had rhapsodised over Kate's looks. Anxiety and lack of appetite had worn her always slim, leggy figure into perfect model lines. Grief had fined her face, showing up the good bones and the haughty remoteness in her eyes.

When Rae had suggested that the agency would love that look of icy hauteur, and that she could make a fortune, Kate had been sceptical, but Rae had been right.

Having gone along with the idea simply because it was easier than arguing, almost overnight, it seemed, she had found herself the new sensation. The agency and the advertisers had loved her. In no time at all she had been commanding the sort of money that made the head spin.

Suddenly, the goal she had set herself had come within her grasp and she reached for it with the single-minded energy of one obsessed. She had worked every available hour of the day, going wherever she was asked, knowing that every job successfully completed was money in the bank. Even when she'd become financially secure, she hadn't stopped. Work filled her life. Men were something that made forays into the periphery, but never came close. She worked with them, dined and dated them, but never did they break into her 'real' life.

Besides, she felt nothing. Their kisses and caresses left her cold and unresponsive. Naturally her aloofness, far from being off-putting, was like a red rag to a bull. Someone coined the nickname 'Ice Queen', and it stuck, but she didn't care. Nothing was allowed to interfere with her goal. If a man became too possessive, too intrusive, she dropped him, and that was the end of it.

If it made her enemies, she didn't care about that either. Men had no place in her scheme of things. She was fully aware that each wanted to be the one to 'thaw' her, but only she knew the impossibility of it. So she watched their antics from her lofty position, not amused, but simply indifferent.

But she had never forgotten the vow she had made. With the patience of a cat she had waited—until at last the waiting was over.

Another glance through the tinted rear window of the car revealed a now empty churchyard. The bride and her father had passed inside. Faintly, the opening chords of the bridal march reached her. It was time to go.

Automatically she checked her appearance in the mirror set in the side panel. Reflected back was a face whose beauty fully deserved the epithet 'Ice Queen' that had been bestowed on her. Though she had never met her, Kate had inherited her Nordic blonde looks from her maternal grandmother as well as her name. In repose, hers was a cool and haughty beauty that stated clearly 'look but don't touch'. Yet determination glittered in her cool blue eyes in contrast to the fullness of her lips, which hinted at a sensuality as yet unrealised.

All Kate saw was a control which satisfied her that all was well. Her nimble fingers lowered the veiling of the elegant hat perched atop her head and which hid her long silver-blonde hair. The cerulean blue exactly matched the suit she wore and the high-heeled shoes on her feet. As she edged to the door, she paused to press the intercom button. On the other side of the partition, a uniformed chauffeur lifted his head.

'Turn the car, John, and wait for me here. I shan't be long,' she declared in her cool, slightly husky voice, and climbed out.

Her feet made a satisfyingly determined crunch on the gravel path as she made her way through the lych-gate and up to the entrance. As she had hoped, all eyes were on the four figures grouped before the minister, not on the latecomer. Her own eyes lingered briefly on the tall, dark-haired figure in grey morning dress, but scarcely appreciated the way the material sat upon his broad shoulders and slim hips. For one vital instant her nerves jolted at the sight of him, then in another second she had slipped into the shadows of a back pew on the groom's side, and was opening the hymn book.

It was strange how the mind could work on two separate levels. Her lips formed the words of the hymns and made the necessary responses as the service proceeded, while her thoughts dwelt solely on the moment to come.

They said revenge was a dish best taken cold, and never had she needed to keep a cool head more. When she had made her plans, she had had no doubts that she could do what she intended, and she had none now. Although the flames of hatred burnt inside her as strongly as ever, she knew better than to let the emotion overwhelm her. It had been a long wait, but it was almost over.

'If any man can shew any just cause, why they may not lawfully be joined together, let him now speak, or else hereafter for ever hold his peace,' the minister intoned, and the familiar tension hung on the air as everyone waited, willing the seconds to pass so that they might breathe again.

The silence lengthened. Relief replaced the tension, and it was at that precise instant that Kate's voice rang out clearly around the stone walls and vaulted ceiling. 'I do.'

There was a moment when the silence deepened with shock, and everyone turned towards the rear of the church. Kate rose and stepped into the aisle. With her back to the door, she knew she was little more than a dark shadow against the sunlight. But the congregation were clear to her, and she almost laughed at the varying degrees of stunned stupefaction the faces revealed. Then her gaze fixed on one man.

'He can't marry her. He already has a wife—me,' she declared, and pandemonium broke out.

The noise rose to a crescendo of outrage and disbelief. Then there were people everywhere, blocking out her view of Aidan Crawford's handsome face contorted in fury. Kate used the diversion to walk away. It wasn't part of her plan to wait around to answer questions. Yet in the doorway something compelled her to pause and look back, drawn by a pair of eyes that bored into her. Through a gap she met those grey eyes. For a second it was as if they were the only two people present. Even the noise seemed to fade. A shiver of pure, unadulterated fear ran down her spine, and she stiffened, glad that he could not see who she was, for she knew she had just made a very bad enemy.

It took a surprising amount of effort to turn her back on those mesmerising eyes, but she did, and walked away on legs that felt strangely weak. Nobody attempted to stop her retreat, and she went quickly back to her car and climbed in. She shut the door on an uncomfortable sensation of having been hounded, telling herself that it was ridiculous to feel that way after only one look.

'You can take me home now, John,' she ordered, glad to hear that her voice at least sounded calm, and sank back against the seat as the car moved smoothly forward.

Closing her eyes, Kate heaved a deep sigh. Finally, it was over. She had kept faith with herself. She had ruined Aidan Crawford's life—just as once he had destroyed hers. Not as devastatingly, perhaps, but it was enough. She wished him joy of what was left. Let the desolation that she had lived through be his now.

Deftly, Kate rolled the veiling up from her face. It had served its purpose. Though her face was well known in some circles, she doubted if anyone there had recognised her—especially him. She didn't want him to know. She wanted him to wonder—and learn to hate her the way she hated him. Nothing less would do.

For a moment she saw his eyes again—grey spears of ice, promising retribution. But he was helpless. Her moment was complete. Revenge, she discovered, had a sweet taste after all. Reaching forward, Kate opened the small bar set into the console facing her, and poured herself a small measure of brandy.

'To you, Aidan Crawford.' She raised her glass in salute. 'May you continue to burn in hell!' she cursed him, and with a laugh swallowed the contents at a go.

CHAPTER TWO

LATER that evening Kate stood before the cheval-glass in her dressing-room and smoothed the soft jersey fabric of her dress over her hips. The style was simplicity itself, and something of a trademark of hers. A black shift that clung to every curve, with long tight sleeves and a slit neck that had virtually no shoulders. It emphasised her willowy figure, the skirt ending above the knees of her long, slender legs.

She was dressing for a very special occasion and she was using infinite care, down to the last finishing touches. Her hair she had swept up into a pleat that revealed the swan-like grace of her neck. In her ears, platinum and diamond studs gleamed, and about each wrist she now fastened narrow diamond bracelets. Enough to relieve the plainness of the dress and no more. Make-up she had applied cleverly to give the effect of wearing very little—a technique garnered from her years as a top model, and one she now passed on through the modelling school and agency she had started this year. All in all, she was pleased with what she saw as she slipped her feet into black stilettos.

There was a suppressed gleam in her eyes as she looked forward to the next few hours. Tonight she was crowning her success with a party. A spontaneous idea she had acted on during the drive home, using the car phone to issue her invitations. Down below everything was in readiness. She was about to celebrate the end of a chapter in her life. What had at times seemed an impossible dream had come true. She had bested Aidan Crawford and felt euphoric with triumph.

The distant sound of the doorbell interrupted her silent appraisal, and with a final look she quickly left the room, flicking off the light as she went. Descending the stairs, she heard voices in the drawing-room and her step lightened as she recognised them. Maggie, her housekeeper, turned as she came in, the low-voiced conversation ending abruptly, so that Kate knew she had been the topic under discussion. She frowned. That had been happening all too frequently lately and she wasn't sure she liked it. Yet it was impossible to get angry. Maggie had been with her for four years now, and the older woman had often been part minder, part mother, rather than full-time housekeeper.

Her eyes flickered to the other occupant of the room. The short, dark, slightly plump figure belonged to her friend Rae. Her confidante and, more recently, her assistant. In fact, Rae was the only one who knew what the celebration was about, although Kate sometimes wondered how much Maggie knew and how much she simply guessed about the devil that had driven her young mistress. But the housekeeper could be very close-mouthed when she wanted. Like now, as she took Rae's coat with a significant look before facing Kate.

'I was just telling Miss Purcell that everything's ready. I've left more food in the kitchen and there's plenty of ice in the freezer. Just ring down and let me know if the food starts to run out.'

Kate expelled her breath in an irritated sigh. 'Maggie, you're a dreadful liar. You two are making me paranoid. Just what is it you're conniving behind my back?' She waited a second or two and received no answer. Maggie merely looked solemnly back at her, and Rae's face was expressionless. 'OK, don't tell me, but I promise you this. When I've more time I fully intend to find out exactly what's going on. Meanwhile, thank you, Maggie. It looks as if there's enough here to feed an army,' she declared, eying the groaning table. The housekeeper grinned and went out. Left alone with her friend, Kate turned to find herself being looked at critically. Her brows rose in a haughtily dismissive gesture that had been known to quell strong men. Rae merely ignored it.

'You look like the cat who's got the cream,' she said tartly.

Looking away, a self-satisfied smile curving her lips, Kate adjusted a salt cellar by a thousandth of an inch. 'Do I?'

'So you really went and did it?'

Detecting criticism, Kate turned around. 'I said I would,' she replied shortly. They had had this argument before and she hadn't liked it then. Rae, of all people, should have been on her side.

Which she clearly wasn't as she retorted, 'There's no need to look so pleased with yourself. Think of the poor woman he was going to marry.'

Kate looked away, lips pursed mutinously. 'I have. Though she doesn't know it, I've probably saved her from a lifetime of misery!'

'It pleases you to think so, but two wrongs don't make a right,' Rae pointed out acidly.

'You've always been against it, right from the start!' Kate accused bitterly, feeling uncomfortable and—well, betrayed. 'Why?'

'Because I've seen, first-hand, just what this thirst for power has done to you, Kate,' her friend replied bluntly. 'It's made you a cold, bitter woman. I know what Aidan Crawford did to your brother, but in my opinion it's nothing compared to what you're doing to yourself. You've treated every man as if they were him, turning the screw and enjoying it. You like to see men squirm, don't you? You're proud of it.'

'That's not true!' Kate denied swiftly, hurt by this unexpected attack. How could Rae think that? 'I let them know where they stand. It's not deliberate. What they do then is up to them. Why should I care if they make fools of themselves? Its not my responsibility, for heaven's sake!'

'Isn't it?' Rae queried cynically. 'What about Jonathan?'

Kate stiffened. 'What about him?' she demanded, voice tight and defensive.

'The way you treat him is downright shameful! The man's in love with you!'

'Which is his misfortune, not mine!' Kate shot back.

'Oh, can you hear yourself?' Rae exploded angrily. 'I'd slap you if I thought for one moment it would do any good!'

Genuinely shocked, Kate stared at her. 'If I'm such a terrible person, why do you bother to stay around?'

Rae threw up her hands. 'Because I'm worried about you. This isn't you. I've known you a long time, right from school. You aren't a hard or vindictive woman, Kate, but if you don't change soon then you will be. I know you've been through a lot, but you can't keep treating people the way you do. So far they've all been gentlemen, but one day one of them isn't going to take kindly to the brush-off. You could get badly hurt,' she finished in genuine concern, and Kate lost her own anger as she found herself on more familiar ground.

'You worry too much. I can look after myself,' she reassured her friend, smiling.

'Famous last words,' Rae commented wryly. 'Oh, well, I've done my best. I should remember good advice usually goes ignored.'

Kate laughed and bent down impulsively to kiss her friend's cheek. 'I'm glad you care, but really, there's no need.' The doorbell went again as she straightened.

'There are the others. Remember, this is supposed to be a party. Forget to be disapproving and enjoy yourself. It's what I intend to do.'

And she did, flitting from one laughing group to another, on a high that had little to do with the glass of champagne she held. Revenge had acted on her like a powerful drug and she glowed like a neon sign. Never still, she was everywhere making sure everyone had enough to eat and drink, so that it was almost eleven before Rae caught up with her again when she came to rest at the now much depleted food table.

'I see Jack Lancing's here,' she referred to the TV celebrity who had caused quite a stir when he arrived half an hour ago. 'You know he's a wolf in wolf's clothing, don't you?'

Kate swung round in exasperation. 'Oh, Rae, not again, please! Besides, what's so special about his being here? He attends lots of parties.'

'The grapevine's been linking your names for the past two weeks, that's what's special. The man is trouble with a capital "T".'

Kate topped up her glass of champagne and sipped at it appreciatively before answering. 'So am I. Didn't I prove that today? I know very well what Jack wants, and you know he isn't going to get it. In the meantime, it can't hurt me to be seen with him. We're good publicity for each other.'

Rae snapped her teeth on a harsh comment and took a breath. 'And what about Jonathan? You've ignored him ever since he arrived. Do you think that's fair?'

Kate followed Rae's glance to where a sandy-haired man stood brooding over a drink in a corner. 'I can't stand a man who sulks. Good heavens, he knows almost everyone here! It wouldn't hurt him to mingle!'

'He told me you invited him to dinner, and he turns up to find a party!'

'The invitation was made over a week ago. I hadn't planned the party then,' Kate shrugged, ignoring a tweak of conscience that reminded her that she'd forgotten all about Jonathan, her mind taken up with Aidan Crawford.

'That's no excuse and you know it! You can't use people like this.'

Kate scowled. Why did Rae constantly rehash this old complaint? Tonight she could have done without it. 'I treat people the way they treat me.'

'No, you don't,' Rae contradicted swiftly, 'you treat them the way Aidan Crawford treated you, callously. But you fail to realise that they aren't all like him.'

'I'm not going to give them the chance to be. I don't ask for anything, and I don't give anything!' Kate declared fiercely.

'Honestly, Kate——!' Rae began, but was interrupted by the strident ringing of the doorbell.

Kate was relieved. She hated arguing with her friend. Rae just couldn't accept that she was quite happy with the way she lived her life. 'Saved by the bell!' she quipped, then frowned, for whoever was outside had their finger set firmly on the button. Wondering who on earth it could be, Kate swiftly excused herself and made her way into the dimly lit hall.

The irritating clamour went on and on. 'All right, all right, I'm coming!' she muttered fiercely, flinging the door wide and preparing to give the impatient caller a piece of her mind. In the event, she only managed to utter one word, and that a croak, as she saw exactly who stood on her doorstep. 'You!' she gasped, in mingled shock and horror.

'Celebrating?' Aidan Crawford queried contemptuously, his icy eyes dropping to the glass in her hand, then passing beyond to where the noise of the party spilled out.

At the sound of his voice, Kate rediscovered the ability to move and speak. She lifted her chin. 'As a matter of fact, yes, and you weren't invited,' she informed him coldly and slammed the door closed.

At least, she would have done if he hadn't thrust his foot into the gap to stop her. All her strength was nothing compared to the force that flung the door wide again. Kate was compelled to take a hasty step backwards to avoid injury.

'Oh, no, you don't, you little bitch!' Aidan Crawford snarled as he stepped inside, and she couldn't help but fall back before his determined advance.

Only a step or two, though, before her pride brought her to a halt, her eyes flashing fire. 'How dare you? Get out, before I have you thrown out!'

He closed the door with an ominous thud. 'Thrown out? I don't think so, lady. You and I have some talking to do.'

A red rage seemed to burst before her eyes, and she lifted her hand as she stepped forward, wanting to strike out at that hated face. But the blow never landed. He foiled her easily, catching her wrist in a grip that burnt and choked off the blood, making her wince in pain.

'Kate? Are you all right?' Unnoticed, Rae had come out into the hall, brought by the noise, along with several of the others. Her eyes became saucers when she saw who it was, obviously recognising him from his many appearances in the newspapers. 'Oh, my goodness!'

Before Kate could utter a word, Aidan Crawford was speaking. 'This is a private argument. I'm sure *Kate* doesn't want it made public, do you?' He appealed to her, but his look was a threat.

Even so she might well have ignored it if she hadn't glanced at their audience and seen the gleam of delight at her predicament in more than one pair of male eyes. It told her clearly that a call for help would go unanswered. They were all on Aidan Crawford's side, silently willing him on to deliver the come-uppance they considered was long overdue. Even Rae looked uncertain, and that made Kate lift her chin.

'No,' she concurred stiffly.

His smile was grim, and she knew he hadn't missed the atmosphere. Looking about, he spied the door on the opposite side of the hall. 'We'll go in here.' He opened the door and literally propelled her into the dark room ahead of him. 'Excuse us,' he added in mock politeness before shutting the door pointedly. 'Where's the light?' he demanded as Kate struggled to free herself from his grasp. 'Damn it, keep still, or you'll only get hurt. Now where's the damned switch?'

'Behind you,' Kate gritted through her teeth. A second later she blinked as light flooded the room, revealing a comfortable sitting-room before he adjusted the dimmer to a low glow that threw shadows everywhere. Kate had eyes only for the man who still held her fast, and they glittered with all the loathing that was in her. With his back to the light, his menace was even more pronounced. 'Take your hands off me!'

She was released with an alacrity that would have been insulting if she hadn't been so angry. Kate was trembling with the force of it. She could feel it as she rubbed life back into her wrist. 'Don't ever touch me again.'

This time the flashing eyes were his. 'Why should I ever want to? Believe me, once is enough,' he declared with deliberate offensiveness.

Colour flooded her cheeks, and just as quickly faded again, leaving her white-faced. 'My God!' She turned quickly on her heel and crossed to where the telephone sat on a small table. Her hand came to rest on the receiver. 'If you don't leave my home this instant, I shall call the police.'

Far from being alarmed by the threat, he started across the floor towards her. Or so Kate thought, until, too late, she realised what he was actually doing. With a cry of dismay, she watched helplessly as he bent to the small wall fitment and brutally disconnected the telephone.

'You're calling no one until you've answered some questions, sweetheart.' There was nothing endearing about that endearment, and to punctuate his point he placed himself pointedly between her and the door.

Kate refused to be quelled although her nerves jolted. To have Aidan Crawford here, in her house, was something she had never dreamed of. It had thrown her completely. Rather belatedly she realised how incriminating her reaction must have been, and tried to bluff her way out. 'I'm afraid macho tactics don't impress me, Mr... Perhaps you could start by telling me just who you are and what exactly you mean by barging into my house!'

He looked her up and down, his disgust at the tactic apparent. 'It's a little late in the day to start playing ignorant. You knew who I was the instant you opened the door. You also know why I'm here. So let's quit playing around shall we?' he advised cuttingly, a dangerous edge to his voice.

Kate stared at his grim face for a moment or two before moving over to an armchair. Sitting down, she crossed one shapely leg over the other, and relaxed. Or rather pretended to. There was altogether too much tension in the air for that. It registered in the way her fingers tightened on the plush arms before she made them relax.

Her blue eyes were mockingly defiant as she looked at him. From what he said, he clearly recognised her, but if he imagined she was still the gullible fool he remembered he was in for a rude awakening. 'How did you find me?'

A reluctantly appreciative laugh came from him and he shook his head. 'My God, you're cool! You could be talking about the weather! Is wrecking lives a hobby with you? Does it give you a buzz, playing God?' The anger in him was awesome.

Kate's heart raced, but she had long ago learned the art of hiding her emotions. It was part of her stock-in-trade. 'This time it did, certainly—and you haven't answered my question.'

His teeth came together in an audible snap. 'I, too, have friends. One of them took the number of your car. Another pulled strings to find out who it belonged to.' He closed the distance between them in what Kate could only describe as a menacing prowl. 'Surely you knew I'd have a burning desire to see you? To have a cosy little chat about this and that.'

She certainly wasn't about to tell him she hadn't contemplated the possibility. 'I have absolutely nothing to say to you.'

Aidan Crawford's hands clenched, and he thrust them angrily into the pockets of his trousers. She realised two things then: that he would rather his hands were about her throat, and that he still wore morning dress. A detached part of her mind registered that the clothes suited him, and that he must have lost some weight. Her memory conjured up a more heavily set man. But that didn't stop him being far too tall and overwhelming. His very presence dominated her room as he wanted to dominate her.

'Well, I've got plenty to say to you. Just who the hell are you, Ms K. Hardie, and who gave you the right to do what you did today?'

Who was she? What kind of game was he playing now? Immediately her anger resurged. 'You know damn well who I am! I swore you'd be sorry, and I hope you are!'

Grey eyes narrowed to slits in a face that seemed carved from granite. 'Lady, you're crazy. I've never seen you

in my life—before today. But I don't think I'm ever likely
to forget you!'

'And that's exactly the sort of answer I'd expect from
someone like you!' Giving up all pretence of relaxation,
Kate jumped to her feet and paced angrily away. 'You
make me sick! It's all a game to you, isn't it—destroying
people's lives? Well, today you had a taste of your own
medicine, and I hope it chokes you!' she spat out
contemptuously.

'Why, you little——' he bit off the rest with an iron
control. 'It wasn't just my life, was it? What about
Julia?' he demanded coldly.

Kate laughed triumphantly. 'She may not know it, but
I did her a favour. At least I saved her from discovering
what a swine you are the hard way!'

He stared at her incredulously. 'My God, you're
insane!'

'It's no thanks to you that I'm not!'

Once more his eyes narrowed. 'Meaning?' he growled.

Kate crossed her arms. 'Oh, come on, Mr Crawford,'
she sneered. 'This is Kate Taylor-Hardie you're talking
to.' She saw the flicker of recognition in his eyes and her
lips thinned. 'So, you do remember me after all. I
thought you might.'

That he was holding on to a violent temper by the
merest thread was patently obvious as he spoke in clipped
tones. 'I vaguely recall a Christopher Taylor-Hardie, but
he died some years ago. Are you telling me you're a
relative?'

As if he didn't know! 'All right, if you insist on playing
this ridiculous game, I have no option but to go along
with it. Christopher was my father.'

'Your father?' It was clear from his tone that she had
surprised him. 'I had no idea he had children, but
then——'

Kate interrupted him with an angry gasp. This was intolerable! 'That's a lie!'

Grey eyes flashed a warning she couldn't ignore. 'I'm getting sick and tired of being called a liar by you, *Ms* Hardie. My acquaintance with your father was brief. I doubt he ever discussed his children. So how could I possibly know of your existence?' he ground out harshly.

Now, now she had caught him out in a blatant lie! 'How? I'll tell you how! Because four years ago I came to you for help, Aidan Crawford. I'm hardly likely to forget that you turned me down!' Nothing could ever wipe out *that* memory.

Whatever reaction she expected, it wasn't the one she got. Aidan Crawford went absolutely still, then very slowly he took his hands from his pockets. Kate could almost see the cogs turning in his mind, and the wariness that came into the eyes that never left her face.

'You came to *me* for help?' There was a curious quality in the question that she couldn't pinpoint.

'For Philip,' she corrected shortly, watching the play of emotions on his face as he searched for a memory.

'Philip?'

'My brother,' she ground out painfully. 'Before he died, my father told me that if ever we were in trouble we could come to you. And I believed him!' She uttered a harsh bark of laughter. 'More fool I! You could have helped, but you didn't, and Philip died. He was fourteen years old! He may have been desperately ill, but there was the chance of a cure. A chance you refused to give him!'

A change came over him. He was still angry, but for the moment, other emotions had surfaced. Ones whose source she couldn't guess at. 'I see. I had no idea, but I begin to understand. The man your father knew, the one he advised you to contact, was *my* father. I was named for him. Surely the age difference would have told you that?'

Momentarily diverted, Kate frowned. 'My father was a professor; it was quite possible for him to befriend a younger man. He was only forty-two when he died.'

Aidan Crawford nodded. 'That's true, whereas, in fact, my father was older than him. But that doesn't change the facts. At the time of your brother's death, I wasn't even in this country. I never saw you.'

The conviction, the absolute certainty in his tone stunned her for a moment. She wondered if she was indeed going mad. But she knew. Damn it, she knew! 'Oh, how could you say that? I saw you as clearly as I'm seeing you now, on the very day Philip...died,' she challenged angrily.

A nerve began to tick away in his jaw. Kate saw it quite clearly as he came to stand before her, though the subdued lighting threw shadows over half his face.

'You saw me? We were this close?' he asked quietly.

Her stomach lurched. 'Yes, we were this close,' she choked out thickly.

'Then you must have seen this,' he stated softly, and turned his face to the light.

Kate gasped. 'This' was a silvery scar that stretched from the left side of his mouth, over his cheekbone, to the corner of his eye. Her hand flew to her throat. 'How did that happen?' The question issued in a whisper, her eyes reluctantly lifting to lock with his.

'In a cricket match, when I was ten,' he informed her, still in that same soft tone. His lips twisted. 'Someone took exception to being bowled out.'

Her eyes rounded in horror. Not so much at the thought of the vicious attack, but at the other implication. 'No! It's impossible! You can't have...you didn't have a scar!' she cried, head reeling.

'Andrew doesn't have a scar.'

The statement slammed her heart against her chest. 'W-who?'

'Andrew—my twin brother.'

There was something in his eyes which said he was telling the truth, but Kate couldn't believe him. To do so would mean... 'You're lying. It's just another trick. I don't believe you!'

Her denial didn't anger him, instead he looked resigned. 'I shouldn't imagine you would.' His hand went inside his coat and drew out a wallet. 'Fortunately I have my passport on me, expecting, as I was, to be using it for my honeymoon.' The observation was dry, but Kate scarcely registered it. She was too caught up in studying the photograph he was showing her. The face was his, complete with scar, and so was the name: Aidan Crawford. Yet it proved nothing, and she said so. He smiled grimly and pulled a photograph from the wallet. 'This was taken some years ago now, but it should prove, beyond doubt, that I'm telling you the truth.'

There were four people in the picture, taken on a sunny day on the lawn of a large house. A family scene of husband and wife, and two sons—identical save for the still recent scar one bore on his left cheek. Kate closed her eyes.

'They never could tell us apart, until he gave me this,' he observed, and she opened her eyes again to see him fingering the silver scar broodingly. He retrieved passport and photo and returned them, with his wallet, to his coat.

Kate felt all the fight drain out of her. She could scarcely take it in, and yet it was all too horribly true. A pain shot through her temple, and she lifted trembling fingers to massage the spot. She had to think! Inevitably her eyes were drawn to where Aidan Crawford stood watching her, face devoid of all expression.

'Are you saying that I...that...?'

'Asked Andrew for help, not me,' he confirmed. 'I'm afraid my brother has a warped sense of humour. If he could do me an ill turn, he would. Up to and including pretending to be me.' He supplied the rest in a flat tone that she suspected hid a great deal.

Kate was appalled. 'Oh, God!' she gave a moan of disgust. 'What have I done?'

'Precisely. What have you done, *Ms* Hardie?' The icy sarcasm stung, as it was meant to.

She paled and glanced away, mind dazed by what she had learnt. 'How could I know? I thought he was you. I've hated you with every breath I took,' she confessed in an anguished whisper.

'Because you believed I was the one who refused to help Philip?'

Her head jerked up, she'd almost forgotten he was there. 'Yes, because of Philip. I wanted revenge.'

Aidan Crawford breathed in deeply. 'And so you took it today—against the wrong man.'

Kate knew that, however softened his tone, the anger had not lessened. She gathered together the tatters of her lost composure and drew it on. 'Against the right man, as I thought. I was ignorant of there being two of you.' If she had only known, perhaps... but it was too late for 'if's.

'Do you think that excuses your actions today?'

Of course it didn't, but she had been thrown to the wolves once by a Crawford, and it wasn't going to happen again. She drew herself up proudly. 'I don't ask to be excused. I did what I had to do, and I can't be sorry for that.'

'So you have no remorse about destroying two sets of hopes at a blow?' he demanded with a cutting edge she felt keenly.

'Would your brother have felt remorse?' she challenged back.

'No,' he stated baldly.

'And what of the real Aidan Crawford? Would he have turned Philip down?'

A grim smile curved his lips. 'We'll never know, will we?'

'That's tantamount to saying yes. You Crawfords stick together! Remorse? I'm only sorry it was the wrong man!'

'Somebody has to take responsibility for what happened today, and that somebody is you, *Ms* Hardie. What do you intend to do about it?'

Perhaps she had done wrong, but she would never admit it to this man. Who, by his own admission, was as bad as his brother! Schooling her features, Kate returned to her seat. 'Do? I don't intend to *do* anything. And I certainly don't intend to let you make me feel guilty.'

He looked at her as if she was a species he hadn't encountered before and had only contempt for, now that he had. 'But you are guilty. As guilty as hell, and we both know it. You owe me, Kate Hardie.'

She lifted her chin at the coldness in his eyes. 'I owe you nothing. As far as I'm concerned, the Crawford family deserves all that it gets.'

Aidan Crawford drew himself upright. 'Don't make the mistake of underestimating me, Ms Hardie. You owe me, and that's a debt I intend to collect, with interest.'

He meant it, and at that male threat her stomach knotted despite her will. To combat it, she raised her brows disdainfully. 'You can try, but you won't succeed. It wouldn't be wise for you to underestimate me, either.'

He smiled thinly. 'Oh, I won't. I've seen what you can do, but you're out of your depth. I hope you know how to swim, because you're going to need to.'

Kate rose gracefully, lips curved into the faintest of smiles. 'I'm impervious to threats. I'm not the gullible fool I was four years ago. I've learned a lot since then. I've learned to hate, and that's strengthened me against men like you and your brother. So, if you've said all you had to say, you'd better go. You're interrupting my party.'

Aidan Crawford looked her up and down. 'Vengeful and unrelenting. Remorseless and cold. The perfect Ice Queen, *Ms* Hardie.' He used her nickname contemptuously.

'Precisely,' Kate returned, refusing to rise to the bait. 'So I very much doubt that you'll be collecting your debt,' she finished sweetly.

To her chagrin, he laughed. 'Did you think I referred to payment in kind? Oh, no, Kate, there's nothing about you that would tempt me to risk frostbite. There are other ways of paying a debt, and in your case undoubtedly more pleasurable.'

Just why that taunt should have stung so, she couldn't imagine, but it did, and her cheeks flushed. 'I'm relieved to hear it. And now, Mr Crawford, would you kindly get out of my house?' she snapped.

Having shot a bow at a venture and seen it strike home, Aidan Crawford smiled and walked over to the door. 'I'm going, but I'll be back. You can count on it.' With that parting shot, he left. A few seconds later, Kate heard the front door open and close.

As it did, all the strength seemed to drain from her legs and she had to reach hurriedly for the mantelpiece to keep herself upright. Suddenly she was shaking so violently that her teeth chattered. All the hard-won cool composure fled, as round and round her head went the same words—he was the wrong man.

With a groan she rested her forehead on her hand. Triumph had become disaster. How Andrew Crawford must be laughing! Her conscience, subdued by her need for revenge, rose to smite her. She had sown the seeds of destruction on two innocent people instead of reaping the looked-for harvest. No matter what she had said to Aidan Crawford, the guilt *was* hers. But accepting that didn't mean she would give in to threats! The thought of it stiffened her spine a little. In the wrong she may be, but she didn't believe there was anything he could do to her, threaten all he might. Besides, there was nothing she *could* do now. The milk had been spilt.

Kate raised her head and met her own eyes in the mirror. Rae's words came back to her. Was she really a vengeful and bitter woman? Steeling herself, she took a long, hard, honest look at herself—the person she had become in these last four years. Rae *was* right. She was on a path that would turn her life into a wasteland. Unless she altered course, she'd have to watch as that person in the mirror grew into a sour, embittered, lonely old woman!

The thought was too awful to contemplate, as was the memory of the two lives she had just ruined. It was too late to help them, but was it really too late for herself? Couldn't she prove Rae wrong? Did she want to? The answer was an unequivocal yes. She had been cold-blooded and vindictive because she hadn't cared about anybody or anything. Indifferent to whom she hurt or how. Brutally honest now, she acknowledged sickly that she had walked over people's feelings and enjoyed it. Had enjoyed her power over men particularly. It was a savage indictment but she didn't spare herself. She had been wrong, and she had driven herself at such a pace that she had lost touch with how to be a human being.

She shivered. What if she was too late? But no, it couldn't be, otherwise she wouldn't have been given this chance to change direction. Yet what did she do now? Philip was dead, her victory turned to tragedy. She had more money than she could ever spend, so there was no need to work all the hours God sent. All of a sudden, she felt aimless, a little lost and very much alone.

What on earth did she do with the rest of her life?

The soft tap on the door made Kate jump, so deep in thought had she been. She looked up, disorientated, the party only a vague memory.

'Who is it?' She was glad to hear her voice sounded normal.

'Only me,' Rae announced as she came in. 'I heard him go. When you didn't immediately come out, I thought I'd better come and see if you were all right.' Hazel eyes registered her concern.

Kate sighed deeply, feeling exhausted. 'Surprisingly enough, I'm fine.'

'I can see you are. Personally, I thought you'd come to blows. I've never seen a man so angry.'

Heat scorched her cheeks. 'Yes, well,' Kate muttered diffidently, 'he had a right to be.'

'Had a right...!' Rae exclaimed, then frowned darkly. 'Run that by me again. I could have sworn you said——'

'I did,' Kate interrupted before her friend could get into her stride. 'He was the wrong man, Rae. The Aidan Crawford I knew had no scar, whereas this one, the real one, has had one since he was ten. Given to him by his twin brother, Andrew.'

'Twin brother?' Rae sat down heavily on the couch. 'Then it was Andrew who... Oh, Kate, you'd better tell me everything.'

Sitting beside her, Kate outlined their conversation as briefly as possible, reliving her own shock in the telling. Rae was alternately shocked and angry.

'Of course you couldn't have known,' she said, when Kate fell silent. 'Not only the wrong Aidan, but the wrong twin too! Who would have thought his brother could be like that? The thing is, what *are* you going to do?'

'There's nothing I can do to undo what I did,' Kate replied softly, voice laden with guilt.

'I suppose not,' Rae admitted. 'He can't take you to court, can he? I mean, is there a law about claiming to be someone's wife when you're not?'

Kate pulled a face. 'If there is, I'm sure I'll find out,' she said drily.

'Don't joke, Kate, this is serious!'

'I assure you, I don't find it funny,' Kate confessed as she stood up again. 'Come on, we'd better see what the others are up to. Its very quiet.'

'That's because they've all gone,' Rae explained, following her out. 'Jack Lancing began the exodus. He suddenly remembered somewhere he just had to be. I don't think he wanted to be here if the police were called in. Wouldn't suit his image.'

Kate stopped and looked over her shoulder, one eyebrow raised. 'Naturally I assume you threw yourself bodily in his way to stop him?'

Rae grinned, unrepentant. 'I'll be bruised for weeks to come.'

A reluctant laugh escaped from Kate's lips. 'You're incorrigible! But I'm glad you're my friend. I've a feeling I may be needing you.' She hesitated and then said somewhat diffidently, 'I've decided you're right. It's time I sorted myself out.'

'Oh, Kate! I think I'm going to cry!' Rae declared, moisture flooding her eyes.

Kate shifted a lump in her throat. 'Don't you dare, or you'll start me off!' she ordered huskily. 'I . . . don't feel very proud of the way I've behaved. If only I'd realised before it was too late,' she murmured remorsefully.

With ready sympathy, Rae reached out to squeeze her arm. 'It was like a fever, Kate. It had to run its course.

Just to hear you speak this way... Well, you don't know how long I've waited to say "welcome back". I'll be here if you need me, all you have to do is ask.'

Choked, Kate wondered how close she had come to losing a friendship she really valued. 'Thanks,' she said gruffly, and it came from the heart. Fighting emotional tears, she pulled a face. 'Oh, well, let's go and survey the damage.'

Much later, she wearily climbed the stairs to her bedroom, feeling much as the Ancient Mariner must have done when he'd shot the albatross. Events were set upon a course she couldn't change no matter what she wished. The real Aidan Crawford had exploded into her life and turned it upside-down. Nothing would ever be the same again.

She didn't know just how prophetic those words were to be.

CHAPTER THREE

SUNDAY mornings were generally the only days of the week that Kate got to lie in, and usually she looked forward to it. This particular Sunday morning, however, she awoke early, her body bathed in perspiration, her mind haunted by the lingering fragments of a nameless fear. She sat up, feeling the fine tremors that still shook her limbs, breaths shallow and heart still racing. She could remember nothing, only echoes of unnamed things that had turned her dreams into a nightmare.

She must have had them before, everyone did at some time or other, but she could never recall feeling quite this degree of terror. Brushing her hair from her eyes, she climbed from the bed and went into her bathroom, drawing a glass of water and drinking it thirstily. Her eyes met their reflection. Why now? Was it her conscience talking or an isolated incident brought on by stress?

Yes, surely that was what it was. To say yesterday had been stressful was putting it mildly. It was stress, so there was no need to get worked up because the remnants lingered in her mind like curling fingers of mist. She could dispel it. Work was the answer, some furious activity that would thrust the residue from her and allow her to relax. Fortunately there was plenty of that.

Showering swiftly, she dressed in jeans and sweater, and went downstairs to tackle the mountain of washing-up she and Rae had stacked in the kitchen the night before. It worked, but only to a degree. For with the nightmare dismissed, although her hands were busy, her brain wasn't, and her mind had a disturbing tendency to wander. Things she had said and done these past four years rose up like ghosts to haunt her. Each new flashback brought a shudder as her resurrected conscience pricked her. It was like seeing a picture of someone intensely familiar, and yet a total stranger. Her behaviour had been so outrageous that it was a wonder Rae's prediction hadn't already come true.

That didn't bear thinking about, and she shook her head, reaching out to switch on the radio, drowning her thoughts in music. She didn't hear Maggie come in half an hour later, and stand silently watching as she vigorously wielded the dishcloth. Consequently she jumped violently when a hand reached by her to switch the radio off.

'Goodness, Maggie, you gave me a scare!' she exclaimed weakly, hanging on to the sink.

'So I see,' Maggie observed, looking her over critically, and not missing one of the signs of her troubled night. 'Something must be bothering you, to get you down here at the crack of dawn washing-up. Especially when there's a perfectly good dishwasher in the corner.'

Kate turned back to the sink and fished around for another glass, uncomfortable with the other woman's perception. 'I thought the activity would help.'

'And did it?'

'Yes and no,' Kate admitted with a sigh. Pausing, she glanced over her shoulder. 'You may as well know, I did something pretty awful yesterday.'

Maggie's brows rose. 'And now you're feeling bad about it?'

Kate nodded. 'That and a lot of other things.'

The older woman rolled her eyes heavenwards. 'The saints be praised! I was beginning to think the day would never come. Here, let me look at you.' Careless of the dripping cloth, she took Kate by the shoulders and brought her face to face. 'Yes, there she is. A little ragged around the edges, maybe, but the Kate I heard so much about.'

Kate's colour fluctuated and a lump rose in her throat. 'Not you, too, Maggie?' she protested in a croak. 'You've been talking to Rae.'

'Didn't need to. I've got eyes in my head. All she did say was to look after you, because you were hurting. Don't blame her. She loves you and she's been worried about you,' Maggie declared, releasing her with a suspicion of moisture in her eyes. 'She said you never cried for your brother, and I could see there was such an anger in you. But it's gone. Whatever happened yesterday, it's gone, and I for one am not sorry.'

Kate felt humbled. Now she realised what all those hastily broken-off conversations were about. There had been so much she had been unaware of. 'Neither am I, Maggie, neither am I,' she confessed, and they exchanged a smile of understanding.

Clearing her throat, Maggie reverted to her usual briskness. 'Ah well, this won't buy the baby a bonnet! I'll get started on the lounge and leave you to it.' Collecting the dustpan, brush and duster from a cupboard, she went out again.

Leaving Kate a prey to more thoughts she found uncomfortable. From the reaction of the two people closest to her, her behaviour had been pretty obnoxious since Philip died, but it was a measure of true friendship that they hadn't given up on her. She probably deserved that they had, but she was inordinately grateful that they hadn't.

With another shake of her head, she returned to the dishes, washing and drying them, and had just begun to stack them away when Maggie reappeared.

'Must have been a wild party,' she observed, checking the water in the kettle before switching it on and reaching

for the teapot. 'Somebody ripped out the telephone in
the sitting-room.'

For the second time that morning Kate jumped, colour
darkening her cheeks. She wondered how on earth she
could have forgotten the incident—but then, so many
things had happened last night. As the unwelcome
reminder of Aidan Crawford recalled. She was glad she
had a legitimate reason to turn her back as she stacked
plates in the cupboard. 'Oh, yes, the telephone.
Um...things did get a little out of hand for a while.'
What an understatement that was!

Maggie paused in the act of spooning tea into the pot.
'You should have rung down. John would have come
up to help.' Her husband was Kate's chauffeur-cum-
gardener, and they lived in a cottage in the grounds of
Kate's house.

'Oh, it wasn't that bad,' Kate reassured hurriedly. 'I
soon sorted it out.' She crossed her fingers to negate the
blatant lie. 'You'd better arrange for someone to come
and repair it tomorrow.'

The tea made, Maggie carried two steaming mugs to
the table and sat down. 'John will fix it. More to the
point, you'd better make sure you don't invite that
particular party here again.'

That made Kate laugh with genuine humour as she
joined the other woman. 'It's OK, Maggie. I've no
intention of doing so.' However, the amusement faded
as she drank her tea. Not inviting Aidan Crawford was
one thing to decide and another in reality. She doubted
very much if the lack of invitation would keep him out
if he was determined to get in.

She dislodged the unsettling thought by reminding
herself she had already decided his threat was an empty
one. Nevertheless, she was glad of the work involved in
tidying up that kept her busy until lunchtime. The most
she could face to eat was a salad, much to Maggie's

clucking disapproval, then, still feeling far from settled, she collected her quilted coat from the hall closet and took herself off for a long walk.

She couldn't remember the last time she had had such exercise. Another reminder of how her life had changed. It was a brisk late winter day, the sunshine cheering but without warmth. Yet it was a clean sort of day that made looking to the future hopeful rather than resigned. By the time she had made her way home again, Kate felt invigorated, almost a new person, ready to make drastic changes in her life.

She was making mental plans for a holiday, the first in four hectic years, when her attention was diverted by the sight of a minibus, clearly broken down, not far from the house. Emblazoned on the side was the name of a school, and pressed against the windows were half a dozen curious faces.

With a *frisson* of shock, Kate realised that only days ago she would have walked straight past. For no other reason than that she was too caught up in her own ambitions and she had no time for others. Her footsteps slowed, and she felt a sickening wave of self-disgust. What sort of values were those? The picture she was seeing of herself was appalling. And it was so unlike her—the real Kate—who had somehow got lost when Philip died.

She loved children, had always dreamed of having a large family of her own. Yet she knew she would never have any, and that was a private grief. Something she had accepted years ago. To have children she would have to have a husband, and past experience had shown her that her own inadequacies made that impossible. The hurt was as clear now as if it was only yesterday. She had been so certain of the way her life would go, but fate had had other ideas.

She had dated like any other teenager, but she had experienced none of the excitement her friends talked about. At first she had fought against the knowledge, trying to feel something, even going so far, in a short-lived engagement, to pretend that she did. It had been a fiasco that had finally shown her the truth—that, as a woman, she had something vital lacking.

So she had vowed never to marry. She had accepted, because she had no other choice, that she would never have a husband and family of her own, yet it hadn't stopped her liking children. So to realise she had cut them from her life these last years was a kind of betrayal. Somehow she had to find herself again, and here was the way to start.

With only the briefest hesitation, she walked up to the young woman who appeared to be in charge and who had her head under the raised bonnet.

'Do you need any help?'

The woman straightened, brushing back a riot of auburn curls with a hand that left a greasy streak across her cheek. She looked cheerfully harassed. 'Oh, thank heavens! Do you know anything about engines?'

'I'm afraid not,' Kate admitted ruefully, 'but my house is just over there. You're welcome to use the telephone to get help.' She pointed to where the roof was just visible over the trees, and received a wide smile.

'That's very good of you. The principal will be having kittens by now. I would have walked to the nearest callbox but I couldn't leave the little ones, and they're too tired to walk.'

Kate looked to the window where six faces were peering at her hopefully. The youngest, a little girl with blonde plaits, gave her a gap-toothed grin and Kate felt something tug inside her. She found herself saying, 'If they can manage to walk up to the house, I'm sure we can find some milk and biscuits for them while you make your call.'

The woman looked doubtful. 'I don't want to be any trouble.'

'You won't be,' Kate assured her. 'I'll help you with the children.'

She didn't need more encouragement than that, and quickly organised her charges into pairs on the pavement. Kate felt a tug on her coat and looked down into a pair of large blue eyes. They belonged to the little girl with the plaits.

'I'm tired,' she lisped.

Kate hunkered down, a warm smile softening her features. 'Are you, poppet? I suppose I'd better carry you, then. Come on.' She held out her arms and the little girl went into them, curling her own arms confidingly about Kate's neck. Kate's heart twisted painfully as she stood up, and she realised how much she still wanted a child of her own. The impossibility of it meant there would always be this aching void in her life.

There was a sadness in her eyes as she led the way with that warm bundle in her arms. A half-remembered prayer slipped into her mind: oh, Lord, give me the strength to change what I can, and the grace to accept what I can't. Never had the words been so heartfelt than now, when her life was poised at the crossroads.

If Maggie was surprised by the small invasion party, she said nothing, merely shepherding the small flock into the kitchen where she dispensed milk and biscuits while Kate showed Amy, as the woman had introduced herself, to the telephone. There followed one of the liveliest couple of hours she could remember as they waited for the mechanic to arrive. The children, all orphans, were a lively bunch who soon lost their reserve and embarked on a rowdy game of football on the lawn with a ball Maggie had conjured up from somewhere.

Kate was truly sorry when news came that the minibus was repaired and Amy declared they must go, having imposed themselves on her long enough. Life had come into the house and she was reluctant to abandon it. She helped the younger ones into their coats, knowing her home would seem empty when they were gone, and the one she would miss the most was little Megan. The infant had stayed close to her all the time, chatting away nineteen to the dozen, until she had fallen asleep, and Kate had settled her carefully in an armchair in the sitting-room.

While Amy shepherded the others out to the minibus which had been brought up to the door, Kate went to fetch Megan. It was astounding how quickly she had wormed her way into her heart, she thought, as she picked up the warm armful. Pure instinct had her head lowering, lips brushing a flushed cheek. She straightened with a fond smile, easing damp curls away from the smooth forehead. Then the sensation of being watched made her tense and turn her head swiftly to the door.

Kate's heart thudded at the shock of finding Aidan Crawford's tall figure filling the doorway. A vastly different-looking man from the one she had seen last night. In jeans, Argyll sweater and black leather jacket, he looked no less powerful and threatening, yet more ruggedly handsome, and with an animal magnetism that even she couldn't be unaware of. A trickle of sensation traced its way up and down her spine.

She stiffened automatically, at once made uncomfortably aware of her make-up-free face, mussed hair, and the child in her arms. She paled, skin tightening, and then hot colour rose in her cheeks as she saw on his face an expression somewhat akin to shock. It was replaced in quick succession by disbelief and anger before, spine stiffening, he wiped his face clean. Yet there was a peculiar tension in the air that made her swallow to moisten a suddenly dry mouth. For a moment, silence reigned as they simply stared at each other.

'A young woman outside told me to come in,' he broke the silence in a voice that sounded gravelly and tight.

Amy, Kate thought with a groan, knowing the other woman could have no idea how unwelcome this visitor was, especially if he had made it sound as if he was expected. How she hated to be caught at a disadvantage like this. More so when she had not expected to see him again. Consequently her tone was at once defensive and peremptory.

'What do you want?'

His only reaction was a slight narrowing of the eyes. 'To talk to you. I said I'd be back,' he reminded her.

There was no sense in telling him she hadn't taken him seriously. She had fallen into the oldest trap of under-estimating her opponent, and now here he was, and she was in no shape to cope with him. She had hardly come to terms with the new person inside her; certainly it was no time to put it to the test with Aidan Crawford.

She was about to send him on his way in short order when the bundle in her arms stirred.

'That hurts, Auntie Kate,' Megan protested, and Kate realised she had been squeezing the child unconsciously.

Contrite, she forced herself to relax and dropped a quick kiss on the little girl's cheek. 'Sorry, sweetheart. Come along, I'm going to take you out to Amy now.' She looked up at Aidan Crawford and discovered him watching her with an intensity that was disconcerting. 'You'd better wait here,' she suggested ungraciously, and he nodded and stepped aside.

Kate went past him, expelling a breath she hadn't realised she was holding. She had the crazy feeling she'd just escaped—but from what, she couldn't say. She didn't like the way he set her nerves on edge, and the sooner he left again, the better.

It was the work of a moment to carry Megan outside and pass her on to Amy, who was voluble in her thanks, and once again apologising for the trouble they had caused. There followed a noisy departure with much calling and waving that she returned until a turn in the drive took the minibus from her view behind the shrubbery. Her hand dropped to her side, and the smile died on her lips as the quiet descended once more, leaving only echoes in the mind.

To take her thoughts from the path they wanted to tread, she turned them to Aidan Crawford as she reluctantly faced the house. Why had he had to turn up now, of all times? Shivering, she tried to rub warmth into her arms. His presence made her feel vulnerable all at once. So much so, that, when she did make her way slowly back into the sitting-room, she was even more stiffly defensive.

He was standing with his back to the window, but she didn't doubt for a moment that he had watched the scene outside. She was aware of a surge of anger. She didn't want him invading her privacy like this. She wasn't ready, caught as she was in the middle of a painful rebirth. And because the fledgeling Kate couldn't hope to cope, she summoned up remnants of the old Kate to face him.

'The children seem to like you,' he observed, making no effort to hide his surprise.

She bridled instantly. 'I happen to like them, too,' she informed him tartly.

That raised an eyebrow indicative of scepticism. 'Do you keep it hidden because it doesn't go with your image?' There was just enough mockery in his tone to set her teeth on edge.

'I keep it private because it is just that.' Or would have been until *he* burst in on it uninvited.

'If you value your privacy so much, why allow children in?' he asked curiously.

It would have been simple to say she needed them, but an imp of perversity made her tilt her chin at him instead. 'Perhaps I enjoy playing Lady Bountiful,' she rejoined sweetly.

To her surprise he thought about that for some seconds, then shook his head. What he said next took the ground from under her feet. 'I might have believed it if I hadn't seen your reaction to the little girl. No one can fake affection, and children pick it up more quickly than adults. Which makes me wonder why you don't have children of your own.'

The casual question speared her heart with a pain so keen that she couldn't hide a small gasp. His perception was frightening. No one else had seen so much in so short a time. She tried to smile, knew she had failed, and turned away, masking her discomposure by crossing quickly to the small selection of drinks set up on a tray on the sideboard. She felt queer and shaky inside, and wondered what was the matter with her. Whatever it was, she was determined he shouldn't see it. Still with her back turned, she produced a falsely bright laugh and shrugged.

'I've been too busy, I suppose. But maybe one day I will do just that,' she lied, dropping her lids over smarting eyes. She sought for control and finally found it. 'Can I get you a drink?' Good old Kate, she thought, slipping into her role gratefully, and turned to face him enquiringly.

'Not for me, thanks. It's a little early,' Aidan Crawford declined smoothly, but his gaze was narrowed and watchful.

Fearing he had seen too much, Kate hurried on. 'What did you want to see me about?' She was proud of the coolness of her tone, especially when she thought she could guess. She hadn't forgotten his threat.

'I went to see Julia today.'

She raised her brows even as a pang of guilt smote her. She had been trying not to think of his bride-to-be. The effects of her actions yesterday were spreading like ripples on a pond. 'Naturally I assumed you would. However I don't see what that has to do with me.'

'I know you don't, but you will.' The promise was edged. Her offhand tone had annoyed him. 'Julia, my dear Kate, was still bloody furious,' he informed her succinctly.

He didn't need to try and make her feel guilty, she'd already accepted her culpability. 'But surely you told her the truth?'

'But surely,' he mimicked right back, 'you didn't expect her to believe me?'

That gave her pause, because initially the possibility must have been in the back of her mind. Since learning of her mistake she had assumed...clearly too much. Another rush of guilt made her frown, and conversely her tone became light, almost frivolous. 'She's upset. I'm sure if she loves you she'll——'

Aidan Crawford broke in abruptly. 'I see that amuses you. Perhaps this will, too. Julia doesn't love me; she never did.'

Kate actually found herself shocked into silence. Everything she had planned was happening, only now, of course, she didn't want it to. A rather reluctant sympathy for him was roused. The only platitude that came to mind was that, better he should find out now about the fickleness of his fiancée than later. She began to say as much.

'I'm sorry——'

'Don't be. Neither did I love her. What we had was a mutual understanding.'

The sheer cold-bloodedness of the way he spoke of an institution she had always held sacred rapidly dispelled her sympathy. Her lip curled in a way that many a man would have recognised with dismay. 'In that case, there's no reason why you can't still be married,' she returned witheringly. They sounded as if they deserved each other.

Aidan Crawford laughed, but not with humour. 'Ah, but then you don't know Julia. There's every reason. Julia abhors scandal. She especially dislikes being made a laughing stock.' He spoke as if he were repeating her word for word. 'Her pride wouldn't let her contemplate marrying me now.'

Dear heaven, and these were the people who had caused her to change her life! She was disgusted. 'I'm sure you can find a replacement, given time. Love being surplus to requirements!' she mocked.

He turned away then, to stare out of the window, hands sliding into his pockets. 'As you say, love being unnecessary, I'm sure I could, but time is something I don't have.' Once again his brief laugh was mirthless, almost as if the joke, if there was one, was on him.

Kate shrugged, ignoring a tweak of intrigue. 'That's your problem. I don't know what you expect me to do.'

He turned round again, grey eyes glinting. 'What I expect you to do, *Ms* Hardie, is quite simple . . . and is something only you can do.'

There was something in his tone that had the fine hairs rising all over her body. She found herself staring at him as if mesmerised. His voice was perfectly level as he went on, and he never once took his eyes off her.

'I need a wife. But for you I would have had one. I don't have time to look for another, and I don't believe I need to. You elected yourself my wife yesterday, and I'm holding you to that. You owe me, Kate Hardie, and I'm collecting on the debt.'

They faced each other across the cosy room which had suddenly become an arena.

'You can't be serious!' From somewhere Kate managed to find her voice.

'I've never been more so,' he promised shortly.

'Then you're mad. Totally and utterly mad!' She tried to laugh, but the look on his face, the determination, was quelling. Her heart began to thud. He meant it!

'No, not mad. Just playing the game with the cards I've been dealt,' he declared forcefully.

Yet underneath the anger, the new Kate detected a note of...surely it couldn't be desperation? Except there was a certain tension in him that went beyond anger, finding an outlet in the frustrated way he dragged a hand through his hair. It stopped her on the verge of an outright no.

Curiosity got the better of her. 'Why?'

His mouth drew into a thin line. 'The why comes later, after you've agreed to marry me,' he told her grimly.

A laugh was forced out of her at his sheer arrogance. 'You're crazy if you expect any woman to make that sort of leap in the dark!' She threw up a hand in disbelief. 'And just why should I agree to marry the man who...who...?' She faltered to a halt as she realised what she was saying.

His thoughts were there ahead of her, and there was a tight smile on his lips. 'Who did nothing to you. Who would have helped your brother if he had known in time. The man whom, by your own admission, you set out to destroy yesterday. If you need a why, there's a simple one. Moral obligation.'

Kate paled. Every word he shot at her was true. She was ready to admit that, but not that he had come to the wrong person. How could she say that she couldn't help even if she wanted to? He was asking the impossible—the one thing she couldn't do. It set her at odds with herself and made her feel uncomfortably vulnerable. She didn't like that, and quickly summoned up the old image to protect herself.

'I'll admit I was in the wrong, Mr Crawford, but marriage isn't part of my plans. You'll have to look elsewhere,' she told him shortly.

He made a move towards her, controlled it, and crossed his arms. 'I've already told you there's no time. I'm not asking for a lifetime commitment. All I need is a wife for a limited time.'

Kate hesitated. She was the last person he'd choose unless he had no option. So whatever it was must be important. She was to blame and certainly owed him. But could she live with this man in a temporary marriage that was more like a business deal? She looked at him, and knew she couldn't. But for the scar, he was Andrew Crawford—a constant reminder of Philip. No! It was impossible. Even a day would be too long!

'No. I'm sorry. Long or short, it's out of the question,' she refused huskily. 'If I wanted a husband at all, believe me, I would never pick you.'

Something flashed in his eyes. 'Damn it! Do you think that given a choice I would ever pick you? A woman who's cold and vindictive? Who treats men with such icy contempt? Oh, no. I'd choose a woman who's that in every sense of the word. One who's warm and responsive, loving and giving—none of which qualities you possess the smallest fraction of. A man wants a real woman in his bed, Kate, not an Ice Queen with nothing to give!'

Pale as a ghost, she stared at him as each word struck home in her heart with carelessly brutal accuracy. There wasn't a part of her that didn't tremble. Not even the old Kate, fully in control, could have withstood that bombardment. Tears she had thought she was long past shedding glittered in her eyes. When he had finished, she swallowed painfully.

'You don't understand!' she protested, the words breaking from her unbidden. The minute she watched his lips curl she wished them unsaid.

'On the contrary, I understand you only too well. You've no heart, and for that I pity you.'

To have him pity her was too much. 'What a lucky escape for you, then, that I said no!' she jeered, but her voice broke on the last and she turned her back on him abruptly.

The silence that fell was thick with seething emotions. Into it Aidan Crawford's surprised voice said questioningly, 'Kate?'

It fired her to face him once more, chin lifted proudly. Only the brilliance of her eyes gave anything away. 'I think we've both said more than enough, don't you? I won't change my mind, so you'd only be wasting your time. In which case, I think you should leave.'

For one tense moment, she thought he was about to argue, that he was going to follow up the curiosity her reaction had aroused. But her mask was back in place now, giving the lie to that instant of vulnerability, and she saw the moment when he shrugged mentally and decided he must have imagined it.

Without another word he crossed to the door, but instead of going through it he paused to look back at her. The contempt in his eyes was chilling, and Kate braced herself.

'Damn you, Kate Hardie. I hope you can live with yourself,' he flung at her bitterly, and then he did go, crashing the front door behind him, making her flinch.

Shivering in reaction, Kate hugged her arms around herself. He had gone, and this time she knew he wasn't coming back. Her lips twisted. Who would want to return to someone who wasn't a real woman? Immediately she was disgusted with the lapse into self-pity. Damn him. He had got through her defences like a hot knife through butter. With accusations that had been levelled at her before, but never with such success.

They hurt. All the more because they weren't true. For four years she might have behaved as if a softer side didn't exist, but .it did, and now she was reaping the result of the image she had created. It was too painful. She didn't want to feel like this. For a moment she wanted the old Kate back, but knew that that person could never be complete again. The mirage might defend her, but it could never stop the hurt. In one night she had changed too much, gone too far down a new and untravelled road. There was no going back.

It wasn't going to be easy facing the world without her shell, but at least she wouldn't have to see Aidan Crawford again. That cold-blooded marriage he had planned was horrible, putting him on a par with his brother. Anger stirred her, and she whipped it up. They used people. Used them for their own ends. She was glad she'd said no, her guilty conscience subdued by his mercenary behaviour. She hadn't destroyed anything of value. He had as good as told her that. So she had no reason at all to feel guilty!

Furthermore, the Crawfords were out of her life for good, and that was exactly the way she wanted it.

CHAPTER FOUR

UNFORTUNATELY, the past had a way of rearing its head, but Kate wasn't thinking of that as she prepared the following Sunday evening for a charity gala. She had been committed to going months ago, so there was no getting out of it, which was what she felt like. However, she was used to putting on a bright face, and at least the cause was a worthy one.

A greater part of her reluctance was due to the fact that Jonathan Carteret was to be her escort. As she took a leisurely bath, her thoughts turned to him. Jonathan presented a new dilemma. She had treated him shabbily because he was becoming too persistent, much too intense. He would still have to go, but the trouble was the new Kate couldn't reconcile herself to treating him as cavalierly as the old Kate would have done. She didn't want to hurt him any more than she already had.

She sighed as she reached for the sponge and soap. This past week had been an experience she wouldn't want to undergo again. Her attempts to soften her ways had been met with deep suspicion which had stung. But she hadn't given up, and had reached Friday with the knowledge that her colleagues had stopped laughing and were prepared to give her the benefit of the doubt.

But that still left the problem of Jonathan. Rediscovering her conscience was painful, bringing ghosts to haunt her. Climbing out of the cooling water and wrapping herself in a large fluffy bathsheet, Kate pulled a wry face. If Aidan Crawford could see her mental agonies, how he would enjoy it! Damn! She must stop thinking about him. His parting words had taunted her all week, much to her discomfort.

Once again she determinedly pushed him to the back of her mind, hoping that this time he would stay there, and got on with the business of dressing. As a rule, she enjoyed deciding what to wear for maximum effect, but tonight it wasn't surprising that her mind wasn't really on it. Even so, surveying the end result critically, she knew she looked her best with her hair swept up, and the strapless blue taffeta evening dress rustling enticingly as she walked. The diamonds at her ears and throat were real, but the fur cape Jonathan slipped about her shoulders before they left the house was not. She believed passionately that fur looked best where it belonged—on the animal.

The Opera House was ablaze with lights and buzzing with excited voices. Everyone who was anyone was present, the ladies' jewels and dresses adding to the glittering occasion. Their progress to their box was slow. Every few yards there was a friend to exchange greetings with. Only the severest control and the full recourse of her training stopped Kate from doing what she wanted to do, which was escape from the throng and get a moment's peace. By the time they did reach their seats, her nerves were distinctly brittle, the muscles of her face aching from smiling constantly.

Kate took her seat with a sigh. She hadn't been looking forward to the evening, but at that stage she didn't know it was to turn into one she would never forget.

The selections from opera and ballet failed to completely hold her attention, though many were her favourites. She had too much on her mind. Jonathan's constant attentions to her every need, which once she would have accepted disdainfully, made her feel uncomfortable, and not a little embarrassed. His dog-like devotion was demeaning, and knowing she was entirely responsible made her despise herself.

Consequently, she felt snappy and irritable when the interval came, and when Jonathan asked her if she was quite comfortable for the nth time, she exploded nervously.

'Oh, for goodness' sake, Jonathan, do shut up!'

For the first time she saw a mutinous look on his amiable face. 'I don't suppose you'd talk to him like that,' he said curtly.

Surprised, Kate blinked. 'Him—who?'

Jonathan's laugh was bitter. 'Who, she says! Macho man with the strong arm tactics, that's who. I didn't see you putting up much of a fight the other night. I've always respected you, Kate. You should have told me that wasn't what you wanted.'

Kate could only stare at him, stunned at the swiftness with which the worm had turned. Of course, she knew who he meant, but his interpretation of what he had witnessed shocked her. 'If you think I enjoyed that, you were mistaken. I didn't protest because I didn't want to cause a scene.'

'I'll bet!' he sneered, all sign of mild manners gone. 'Just what went on in there, Kate? He didn't look the type to ask permission. He's the sort who takes what he wants. And what about you, Kate, did you enjoy it?'

She was too stunned to make any sort of denial, and could only exclaim helplessly, 'Jonathan, this isn't like you!'

He stood up jerkily. 'How would you know? You've never looked at me long enough to find out!'

Which was true. She'd only seen a docile lap-dog, not the human being she'd used. 'I'm sorry,' she apologised softly, attempting to mollify, an art she was out of practice with. 'You're right. I've behaved badly. We

should talk, but this isn't the time or place. Later.
I... have something important to say to you.'

Jonathan laughed harshly. 'Let me guess what it is!
And to think I thought you were special! I'm going to
the bar. Do you want anything?'

Kate winced. It wasn't the most gracious of offers,
but she knew better now than to try and laugh it off.
'Thank you, I'd love a glass of water.'

'With ice, naturally,' he added pithily, the perfect
parting shot. The door closed behind him with a decided
click.

Kate subsided with a shaken breath. She'd never seen
Jonathan in such a mood, and she had to admit it made
her uneasy. She had hoped to break with him in a
dignified way; now she wasn't so certain that would be
possible.

A soft tap on the door interrupted her thoughts, and
she looked around quickly, aware that it was too soon
for Jonathan to have returned. She was right. The man
who came in bore no resemblance to her escort. Kate
felt fatalistic. It didn't surprise her at all that Aidan
Crawford should turn up to haunt her. It was turning
out to be that sort of week. She refused to look away
from him, for she had nothing to fear. But as he came
closer to her, her eyes registered a disturbing fact. His
face bore no scar!

Kate paled with the shock of it. For this wasn't Aidan
Crawford but Andrew who stood before her. He was
exactly as she remembered him. She wondered how she
could ever have mistaken Aidan for him. They were alike,
yet so unlike. Grey eyes looked out at her from the
handsome face, assessing and coveting. How could she
have forgotten them? Or the overly sensual lips that
spoke of a corrupt life of indulgence. His crocodile smile
very nearly made her shudder.

Her reaction was alarming and totally unexpected. A cold, sick dread settled in her stomach. The hairs on the back of her neck rose atavistically, and suddenly she was finding it difficult to breathe. A corner of her mind registered the signs of anxiety, and though she couldn't say why she knew she was afraid of this man. Every instinct she possessed was urging her to run, yet, of all the things she had learnt over the years, to show nothing of what she was feeling was by far the most important now.

He took Jonathan's seat and relaxed back, crossing his legs. The grey gaze he ran over her was possessive, noting the agitated rise and fall of her breasts. 'Kate,' he greeted her, her name slipping off his tongue reminiscently.

Until it happened she had never thought it could, but her flesh actually crawled. She could sense that inexplicable fear growing, trying to take over, and she fought it down. He was trying to unsettle her, but he was going to fail. It took all her will-power to slow her pulse rate down to near normal. 'Andrew,' she returned smoothly, hiding her revulsion. Never had the Ice Queen persona been more necessary.

In reply he threw back his head and laughed. 'So, you've met my estimable brother at last. Darling, you were perfect. I don't think I'll ever forget that marvellous scene in the church.'

At the endearment Kate's nerves jolted badly and her stomach turned over. 'You were there?' She saved her composure by a whisker, but the effort tensed every nerve and muscle.

'Of course. I am family, you know,' he laughed again. 'You should have stayed longer. Aidan was almost beside himself, and Julia was throwing a fit. I couldn't have planned anything better if I'd tried.'

Oh, God! She experienced a savage impulse to claw that satisfied smirk from his face and reveal him for the vermin he was! She felt contaminated just at being near him. Yet she allowed nothing to show on her face. 'I didn't see you.' If she had, how different things might have been.

'I know. You had eyes for one man only. But I saw you, Kate. You've come a long way since we first met. You've grown more beautiful.'

The compliment made her want to be sick, and deep inside an insidious trembling began. 'I've certainly grown older... and wiser,' she admitted.

Andrew Crawford smiled. 'But no less impulsive. How well I remember that impulsiveness! Of course, as soon as I saw you, I knew what you were doing. It's a pity you didn't get your revenge. I appreciated your initiative, though I doubt anyone else did.'

'I'm *so* glad it amused you,' Kate rejoined sarcastically, while her mind assimilated his words. What did he mean—her impulsiveness?

'Now, now, don't be bitter. You should have known you couldn't beat me.'

'I couldn't beat you if I didn't know you existed. But I do now,' Kate observed coolly, wishing him gone. Feeling oppressed by the thickening atmosphere.

Andrew Crawford shook his head. 'Ah, Kate, that's no way to talk. Besides, you can't annoy me when I'm celebrating Aidan's downfall.'

The antipathy he obviously felt for his brother was incomprehensible to Kate. 'What did he ever do to you?'

Not for an instant did the smiling mask slip. 'He exists, isn't that enough?' he answered simply. 'But he wishes he didn't—and all because of you, Kate. I guessed you'd be here tonight, so I came to commiserate with you. A nice try, but I'm too clever for you. Still, that shouldn't stop you from joining in my little celebration.'

His vanity was breathtaking! 'Oughtn't I to know exactly what it is you're celebrating?' Somehow, an intensely feminine instinct overrode her disgust, telling her that this was important. Andrew Crawford had come to gloat, and not just about his victory over herself. Whatever it was, his vanity made an audience a necessary part of his enjoyment.

'I was only waiting for you to ask. My dear brother Aidan is about to lose a fortune. You've no doubt heard of Cranston Electronics? It was started by our maternal grandfather after the last war, but it was Aidan who built it up into a worldwide concern. He was tipped to succeed old Cranston as chairman when he retired, and that happened about six years ago. Now Aidan was always his blue-eyed boy, but there was one thing they never could agree on. The old man wanted him to marry and my brother always refused. They had some monumental rows about it, the last of which I was privy to. Grandfather told Aidan that unless he married before his thirty-eighth birthday he would be written out of his will. That didn't mean just money, but company shares too, the controlling interest would go elsewhere.

'To cut a long story short, Grandfather died just under two months ago, and not two weeks later Aidan announced his engagement. A month later and the wedding almost took place. Now that almost seems like indecent haste to me. It didn't take a genius to realise the old man had done what he said he would and poor Aidan had been brought to heel after all. He would have won it, too, if it hadn't been for you.'

Kate was left absolutely speechless with disgust. This man wasn't human! His sheer vindictiveness and spite sickened her.

'The beauty of it,' Andrew Crawford continued, 'is that I didn't have to do a thing.'

No, Kate thought, I did it for you. What else have you done to him without ever getting your slimy hands dirty? You're sick and evil, and I can't even pity you. She had had enough. She had to get away—right away to where she could breathe clean, fresh air. Even as the wish came, the means of achieving it arrived. Jonathan walked in, halting abruptly when he saw she was not alone. Recognition of her companion sent him rigid as he held out the glass he brought with him.

'Your drink, Kate.' His voice was clipped and angry.

She knew what he was thinking, but didn't bother to disabuse him. There was an angry sparkle in her eye as she smiled her thanks and claimed the glass.

'Lovely, Jonathan, I've been waiting for this,' she declared, and in the next instant had thrown the contents full in Andrew Crawford's face.

The smile was extinguished like a flame, leaving behind a dripping glare as he shot to his feet. 'Bitch! I'll make you sorry for that.'

Perhaps he would, but Kate didn't care. She was too angry and disgusted and only wanted to get out of there. She ignored him and turned to the astonished man at her side.

'Take me home, Jonathan,' she commanded, rising quickly, leaving the box as fast as her legs would allow.

'What was that all about?' Jonathan asked as he caught up with her in the corridor with her cape.

Shuddering, Kate pulled the folds around her. She was trembling so badly that only her anger kept one foot in front of the other. 'You don't want to know. Believe me, you don't want to know.'

'It's that man,' he persisted belligerently. 'What is he to you, Kate?'

Kate turned on him impatiently. Couldn't he see this was the wrong time and place? 'He's nothing to me. *No* man is anything to me, Jonathan,' she finished, far more pointedly than she had intended, and caught her lip between her teeth in dismay as he stiffened.

'I see. Well, that certainly puts *me* in my place, doesn't it. They were right, weren't they, all those others? You just use men.'

She winced. This was not the way she had wanted it to be. Instinctively she placed her hand on his arm. 'Jonathan——' she began falteringly, only to have him shrug her off distastefully.

'I got the message already. You'll have to find someone else to lead around by the nose. I'll see you home, but there's no point in our seeing each other again.'

Kate couldn't blame him for taking out his anger on her—she deserved it. She had handled the situation very badly from start to finish. 'I'll get a taxi,' she said quickly, wanting only a speedy end to another disastrous evening.

'I was brought up with the good manners to make sure my partner arrived safely home after a date whatever the circumstances,' he contradicted her, and stood aside stiffly for a quelled Kate to lead the way out.

The journey home was silent. Neither of them had anything to say. Jonathan escorted her right to the door like the perfect gentleman he was, bade her a curt goodnight and walked out of her life with his dignity intact.

Quashed, Kate let herself into the house and made straight for the lounge, switching on lights as she went. She wasn't much of a drinker, but she needed the brandy she poured for herself just then. The tremble in her hand was proof enough, and she drank it down quickly. It started a warmth in her stomach that gradually steadied her limbs. No man had ever made her feel afraid simply by his presence the way Andrew Crawford had. It was inexplicable, but it had been very real, and she was still unnerved. She knew she should hate him, but not why she should react the way she had. And why, if she felt that with him, wasn't it the same with his brother? It made no sense—it simply was, and she was angry with herself for being upset by it.

She couldn't get out of her mind the picture of Andrew Crawford's gloating face as he told her of his brother. It was all a game to him, and he didn't care who got hurt in the process, so long as he won.

With a cry of disgust, Kate flung the empty glass into the grate where it shattered into a thousand pieces.

'Damn you, Andrew Crawford! Damn your loathsome soul for winning again!'

He had used her to beat his brother even as he beat her, and now he was beating them both. Her impotent anger soared, then dived into despair. But only for a moment.

'No!' The fiercely defiant word echoed around the room as her pride surged anew. 'No,' she said again. She was too angry to despair, too sickened with disgust. She *would* not let him win.

Tonight Andrew Crawford had made a mistake. He had crowed too soon, and to the wrong woman. He had overreached himself, for he knew nothing of her meetings with his brother. He had gloated, wanting to make her suffer even as his brother was, but all he had succeeded in doing was making her angry. So angry it was like a volcano inside her, looking for a way out.

Now she understood Aidan Crawford's anger and frustration. Why hadn't he told her about the will? Stupid, she already knew the answer. Why should he reveal his most private problems to a woman who had helped to destroy him? He couldn't be expected to know that he would be appealing to her own sense of morality. He didn't believe she had one!

But he was going to find out differently, because to-night his brother had made her angry enough to cast

aside all caution and do the one thing she had never
thought to do—marry Aidan Crawford.

It was no longer a matter of owing him, or of seeking
revenge. It was simply doing the right thing. She knew
she would never forgive herself if she did nothing, for
it was a matter of principle. She had it in her power to
do right where wrong was intended. Personal feelings
no longer came into it. They could be put aside.

With her mind made up, Kate wasted no time. Going
through to her study, she reached for the telephone
directory, found the number she wanted, and punched
it out firmly. At the other end, the phone rang and rang.
Kate wondered if he was asleep, but shrugged off any
feelings of dismay. For this call, Aidan Crawford
wouldn't mind being roused from his bed. Finally, just
as she was about to give up, the receiver was lifted.

'Crawford here,' a well-remembered voice snapped
irritably.

The sound of it made Kate shiver. She took a deep
breath. 'Mr Crawford, this is Kate Hardie. I've changed
my mind. If you still need a wife, I'll marry you,' she
declared coolly, even as her heart gave a wild panicky
leap.

There was silence for perhaps ten seconds, and when
he spoke his tone had altered dramatically. 'I'll be right
over,' he stated equally coolly, and the receiver went back
down, cutting them off.

Kate stared at the lifeless instrument in her hand and
slowly lowered it to the rest. She had an overwhelming
sense of having burnt her boats. She had just agreed to
marry the brother of the man who had ruined her life—
and it felt as though the limb she had climbed out on
could barely support her weight. More, he was on his
way over right now. She hadn't bargained on that.

She glanced down at her evening dress. She would have
to change. She couldn't meet him dressed so—Ice

Queenishly. God, how she was coming to loathe that name. The anger that had carried her this far began to evaporate. She prayed she was doing the right thing, but she had given her word, and that had always been her bond.

Swallowing down a sense of panic, she went up to change.

The doorbell rang as Kate was making her way downstairs, and she went to answer it with a distinct feeling of trepidation. This meeting was going to be a test of character. While changing she had debated what line to take. They were hardly on the best of terms, but she would rather they were a little friendlier to make the task ahead of them easier. So she had decided to abandon the persona he hated so much and meet him on new ground, showing him that she did have a softer side.

Aidan Crawford stepped inside without waiting to be invited, making the well-proportioned hall shrink in size by the sheer vibrancy of his presence. She was very much aware of his narrow-eyed regard as she closed the door, and was glad she had changed into the peacock-blue mohair sweater and cream trousers. She could imagine his remarks if she had met him in all her finery! Especially as he was dressed very much as she had seen him that other afternoon.

She turned to him at last and tried to find a faint smile, but her face was far too tight with stress. 'There was no need to rush over, you know.'

He looked at her levelly. 'I disagree. You probably have a habit of changing your mind as often as you do your men. I wanted to get here while the mood was still on you.'

Kate paled, her heart sinking at his attitude. Naïvely, she realised, she had expected gratitude. Clearly a mistake. 'Mood?' She clamped her hands together because they showed a distinct tendency to tremble, and she was loath to let him see she wasn't in total control.

'Of regal beneficence. I'd be interested to know what happened to make you decide to repay your debt to this lesser mortal,' he drawled sarcastically.

In a flash the old Kate had resurrected herself. 'I might tell you if you stop insulting me long enough!'

Far from being rebuked, he only smiled. 'They do say, if you can't take it, don't dish it out.'

That brought swift colour to her cheeks. 'Perhaps they do, but *they* don't need a wife in a hurry,' she told him pointedly. 'Are you deliberately trying to make me change my mind?' she demanded to know. If he was, he was doing a grand job of it!

Aidan Crawford inclined his head. 'My apologies. I had no idea you were so... sensitive.'

It took an effort, but Kate ignored that goad. It wasn't a very auspicious start, but she wasn't giving up yet. She must stop letting him get to her. 'Let's go into the sitting-room,' she suggested, and led the way. She took the seat she had occupied last night and watched as he settled himself in the chair opposite. 'Would you like coffee? I can soon make some,' she offered politely, but he shook his head.

'Not right now, thanks,' he declined, and fixed his grey glance on her pale face. 'So, you'll marry me. Why the sudden change of heart?'

She had known he would ask that question, and had decided, as she changed, that the truth was probably the best answer.

'I met your brother tonight. He was... celebrating.' There was no way she could hide her revulsion at the memory. She glanced at her companion and found he had gone quite still. Yet to her mind he seemed to be bracing himself, waiting for something he knew he wouldn't like.

'Celebrating?'

It was as if the softer Kate was tuned in to a new level of awareness. Ultra-sensitive to invisible undercurrents, she sensed that, although he didn't show it, he was in pain from an old wound, and that what she had to say would tear it open again. She knew, as surely as if he had told her, that he loved his brother despite everything, and the wounds of receiving only hatred in return were bitter. The thought of inflicting more pain was contrary to a nature she had thought buried long ago. But it, too, was still there, dormant but not dead. She wished she could avoid the next few seconds for his sake, but he had to know.

'Actually, he came to gloat,' she explained, feeling her way.

'Go on,' he encouraged hardily.

Kate licked her lips nervously. 'At first I thought it was just over my mistaking you for him, but that wasn't all. He...thanked me for ruining the wedding, because it meant you would lose control of Cranston's.' She stopped because it was hard to go on when he had paled so much that the scar stood out vividly on his cheek.

She felt helpless, stirred by an inexplicable urge to offer him some comfort, and not knowing how to handle the startling revelation of the feeling. It brought a bubble of hysteria to her chest. Not only did he not look the sort of man you would give comfort to, but even if he was, she wasn't the woman he would accept it from. The very thought was crazy—she was crazy!

She cleared her throat abruptly. 'You should have told me about the will.'

'The will!' he declared harshly, then left his chair to stalk to the window, staring out into the darkness. 'Just what the hell has Andrew been saying?' He threw the question at her over his shoulder.

'That your grandfather had cut you out of his will unless you married, and that you'd lose control of the business,' she told his rigid back, seeing the way he squared his shoulders as he listened.

'I see. So that's it,' he said flatly.

'You should have told me,' Kate repeated.

'The company is my business,' he stated firmly.

Kate stared at his uncompromising back. 'You tried to make it mine,' she reminded him.

He turned round at that. 'Are you saying that if I had told you this last week, you would have agreed then?'

The grey eyes seemed to bore into her, and she was forced to drop hers. 'I'm...not sure,' she answered huskily, and that was the truth. Without the extra goad of Andrew Crawford's delight, would she have had the nerve to do this?

His brother seemed to have no such doubts. 'Don't try to kid yourself, Kate. You aren't doing this for the company or me, but for yourself. You still want your revenge,' he told her bluntly, and Kate came to her feet, stirred by the small grain of truth in what he said. She was human, and the old Kate couldn't be wiped out that quickly.

She dragged a hand through her hair. 'Perhaps I do, but so much has happened, I'm not sure of anything any more. All I do know is that I won't let your brother win again. You want your company, and I'm prepared to do my best to help you get it. Why I'm doing it really doesn't matter in the long run, does it?' she challenged.

A curious expression crossed his face for a moment before it closed up. 'That's the question, isn't it? I happen to think it does. I love my brother, Kate. I'm not about to stand by while you try to hurt him.'

Kate gave a broken laugh. 'That's crazy. He's the one who's hurting you. He hates you.'

He came back to her then. 'And because of that, do you think I should hate him in return? I'm afraid it doesn't work that way.'

'My brother, right or wrong?' she jeered.

His eyes narrowed angrily. 'I can't—won't—change the way I feel.'

'And he knows it, and hates you all the more for it,' Kate exclaimed in disbelief.

Aidan Crawford's expression remained stony. 'I meant what I said, Kate. I won't have him hurt. I won't have you playing your tricks on him.'

She withdrew into herself at once, remembering that inexplicable fear. 'There's no danger of that,' she returned frigidly. 'Believe it or not, I don't want to hurt your brother—even should such a thing be possible, which I doubt. All I intend to do is stop him from using me to hurt you,' she protested strongly, willing him to accept what she knew to be the truth.

'And so you nobly agreed to marry me,' he drawled cynically.

'Yes,' Kate concurred shortly, 'but there are conditions.'

A mocking smile twisted his lips. 'Naturally. I wouldn't expect you to do this for nothing.'

Kate's teeth came together in a snap. 'I don't want your money. I have more than enough of my own. I meant that I will only marry you on the strict understanding that the marriage is one of convenience.' There was a sound basis why she needed his agreement. She saw no good reason for holding her own inadequacies up to his ridicule for what was to be only a temporary marriage. He had enough weapons already without stripping her pride away, too. If he objected, then the deal was off. She didn't wait long for his answer.

'That, my dear Kate, is the only type of marriage I'd be prepared to undergo with you,' he whipped back smartly.

There was absolutely no reason why his words should strike home so sharply, but, like so much else he had said, they found her vulnerable spot with an accuracy that was frightening. And because she didn't know how to handle it she hid her reaction behind a surge of anger that was pure Ice Queen.

'There's no need to be so insulting. After all, I'm doing *you* the favour, remember.'

His look was every bit as chilling as hers. 'So you are, but let's get something straight right now. The Ice Queen image doesn't impress me one jot. I'm not about to start grovelling to you. If that's what you expect, then thanks, but no, thanks,' he concluded cuttingly.

Kate blanched. Nobody spoke to her like that! Not with such searing contempt. 'How dare you?' she choked. 'What sort of woman do you take me for?'

Aidan Crawford lifted his hand and caught hold of her chin in a relentless grip that she immediately fought against but in vain. Inside her chest, her heart started a frantic beating as he gave her a long searching look before replying. 'I take you to be what I now know you to be. I haven't been idle. I've been learning *all* about you. Kate Hardie, the eternal virgin. Reeling men in with the promise of your sensuality. Making them your slaves so that they'd do anything for the chance of breaking into the citadel you guard so jealously. And when their antics cease to amuse, when they bore you, you drop them, don't you, Kate? No man will ever break down the wall because you won't let them. No man could love you more than you love yourself. No man could do you justice. So you remain inviolate and scorn the fools who break themselves against your walls.'

Horrified by the picture he painted, Kate couldn't unlock her gaze from his. It was a scathing indictment that made her shrivel up inside, because it had been ninety-nine per cent true less than forty-eight hours ago.

'That's . . . horrible,' she gasped, her heart beating achingly fast.

'The truth often is,' he agreed chillingly. 'But be warned, Kate. I'm not like any man you've ever met before. I don't ask, or plead, or grovel. I don't play by your rules, only my own.' His voice dropped to a husky growl. 'I take what I want. Like this . . .'

Before she had a chance to do more than register the shock of his intent, his head had swooped and his lips claimed hers. Automatically Kate froze. Then every nerve in her body shattered like glass as something resembling an electric shock went through her. All concept of what a kiss could be was exploded by that searing touch. The heat from his lips sent her blood rushing crazily along her veins and she couldn't move as his kiss forced her head back, ravishing her mouth. Her body became an alien thing she didn't recognise as for the first time it responded to a call as old as time itself. Dizzily, she felt her bones dissolve, her flesh quickening, as tiny flames of pleasure burst like fireworks inside her. Nothing had prepared her for this intense excitement as the kiss went on and on. Overwhelmed, she trembled and a moan forced its way from her throat as she unconsciously swayed towards him.

As if that was the sign he had been waiting for, he lifted his head at last and looked down into blue eyes darkened by conflicting emotions, his own hooded and watchful. From somewhere Kate found the strength to pull herself free of his touch, vitally aware that her body was telling her it didn't want to move. It wanted to press closer, experience again that strange new excitement. With a shudder of pure shock, she raised a visibly trembling hand to cover lips that even now craved the touch of his. Seeing it, his own mouth curved into a tight line and a muscle started to tick in his jaw.

'Don't worry, Kate, you'll remain inviolate. That was only a sample of what I would do if you break the rules. You see, I have my conditions too. I'll agree to your terms so long as you obey mine. There will be none of your usual tricks while you remain married to me. Other men are out, as of now. Play the part of my devoted wife, and you'll remain as virginal as the day you were born. But try to play with me, or anyone else, and the contract is void. Is that understood?'

Kate had difficulty concentrating. Her eyes followed the movement of his lips like a magnet, though her ears scarcely heard the words. They seemed to come from a long way away. When at last they penetrated her consciousness, she flinched. Swallowing hard, she had never been so thankful to have her reaction misinterpreted. What had seemed like aeons to her had been no time at all. He had no idea of her startling reaction to his touch. And he never would. She wasn't fool enough to place in his hands any weapon that he could use against her. Right now, he thought that, wanting no man's touch on the purity of her body, she feared him. She was only too happy to let him carry on thinking that way, for the truth was much more potentially devastating.

'Yes, I understand,' she croaked. Her throat dry and aching, she went on in a strained voice, 'Now you understand this. Don't you ever, *ever* touch me again!'

The implied threat bounced off him. 'Don't give me cause to,' he returned smoothly. 'So, we have a deal?'

Every protective instinct screamed at her to say no, but she had given her word. 'Yes.' That one word rang with the slamming of any escape route.

His smile failed to reach his eyes. 'Good. I'm glad we understand each other.' With a carelessly graceful movement, he shot back his cuff and glanced at his watch. 'It's late. I'll leave now, but we still have a great deal to discuss. I'll pick you up at one tomorrow, and we'll talk over lunch.' He was already moving towards the door as he spoke.

Kate walked with him like an automaton. He left with a mocking rejoinder to sleep well. Severely provoked, she only just managed to stop herself from slamming the door behind him.

Sleep well! She doubted that she would ever sleep soundly again after tonight. Sagging back against the closed door, Kate raised her fingers to her lips wonderingly. She could still feel the touch of his, burning her hotly, and she moaned faintly. How had it happened? One moment he had been an angry antagonist, the next he had turned her world upside-down. She, Kate, who hadn't thought she could feel anything, had been aroused to her very core by Aidan Crawford of all people!

Why him? The question taunted her. He despised her. He certainly hadn't forgiven her, and felt no respect for her at all. To come alive at one kiss from him wasn't a fairy-tale, it was madness. Sheer lunacy that must not happen again. She had got away with it because he hadn't expected her to respond, but she couldn't always count on being that fortunate.

In future, her defences must be rock-solid, until she had this unfortunate attraction under control. It surely wouldn't be long. Good heavens, she didn't even like the man! No, it was just one of those crazy things that would pass, and until it did she would just have to be on her mettle. In that he was on her side.

He thought she was a virgin who was determined to remain one because no man was good enough to touch her. It was a lie she was going to have to uphold because she certainly wouldn't tell him that until he'd kissed her she had believed herself to be frigid, unable to respond physically to a man. Yet, in perpetuating the lie, she would have to perpetuate the character she had just come to realise she didn't want to be. It was a cruel irony that she wasn't going to be allowed to change on the outside, when on the inside she was already a different person. She knew she could play the Ice Queen standing on her head, but the trouble was that it would no longer be any real protection. She was vulnerable inside to hurts that the old Kate hadn't been aware of.

She knew now she had agreed to walk a path fraught with danger. Just how she was going to survive the journey lay in the lap of the gods.

CHAPTER FIVE

As soon as Kate reached her office the next morning she sent for Rae. Her assistant arrived full of her usual good humour, making Kate, who had hardly slept a wink, feel even more hung over. There had been an added refinement to her bad dream last night. Far from being an isolated incident, it had intensified. It had begun to take shape and form. No longer shadows, yet not quite substance. She had never felt so threatened before, and it had showed in the pale face and haunted eyes that confronted her in her mirror. Only excellent make-up had helped to hide the worst of the ravages.

She was tired and overwrought, and not up to what she had to do today. Removing the slim jacket that matched her black pencil skirt, which today she had teamed with a violet silk blouse, she sat down at her desk and took a deep breath.

'How would you feel about holding the fort for me for the next few weeks, Rae?' she asked without preamble.

Her friend's eyes widened. 'Why? Where will you be?'

Kate's nails tapped out a nervy tattoo on the desk-top. 'I'll be on honeymoon. I'm getting married.'

'Married!' Rae sat down with a thump on the nearest chair. 'Did you say married?' she queried faintly, as if doubting her sanity—or Kate's—or both.

'I did,' Kate nodded, watching Rae's disbelief turn to concern. 'Do you think you'll cope?' she added quickly, hoping to avert the uncomfortable questions she saw forming.

71

Rae waved a hand irritably. 'Of course, once I get over the shock. But this is all very sudden. If it isn't a secret, would you care to tell me who the prospective bridegroom is? Not Jonathan?' she queried in some alarm.

Kate pulled a face, but was glad of the momentary reprieve. 'No, not Jonathan. In fact, we won't be seeing each other again. His decision, not mine.'

Rae gave a silent whistle. 'Chucked you, did he? I didn't think he had it in him.'

'Neither did I.' Kate recalled her own astonishment wryly.

'So, who is it, then?' Rae persisted.

This was the moment Kate had been dreading, but there was no avoiding it. 'Aidan Crawford,' she supplied levelly.

The way Rae's chin dropped would have been funny if Kate had been in the mood for laughing. 'Oh, my God, Kate! What on earth are you doing?'

'It's a long and complicated story——'

'Just the sort I like,' Rae interrupted swiftly. 'I'm sitting comfortably, so you'd better begin.'

With a helpless sigh, Kate bowed to the inevitable. As concisely as possible she related the essence of her meetings with the Crawfords. Rae listened silently, a deep frown creasing her forehead as Kate came to the end.

'It's all very well to be noble, Kate, but marriage?'

'There's no other way,' Kate said quietly. 'Besides, I gave my word.'

Rae sighed helplessly, knowing only too well the significance of that. 'I hope you know what you're doing. OK, I know it's supposed to be a business arrangement, but what do you know of him, really? Did you know he's thought to be the sexiest man this side of the Pond? They say he's got what it takes by the bushel.'

Recalling her own reaction to him, Kate's colour rose as she was unable to deny it.

Rae hadn't finished yet. 'Someone at the party recognised him. They were only too keen to pass on that information. The betting as to whether he would succeed where others had failed was quite brisk,' she concluded bluntly.

Kate flinched. 'Oh.'

Rae instantly reached out a hand. 'Me and my big mouth! But you hurt a lot of people, Kate, and the business you're in isn't the kindest. The best thing you can do is forget it. That's all in the past now, anyway. The point is, I have a bad feeling about this.'

This was no time for Kate to admit that she felt the same. She had to be confident. 'I'll be all right. I'm not his type. And as you well know, I'm not about to put myself into a dangerous situation. I *have* to do this, Rae. I really don't think I have any choice.' She fell silent, feeling that sense of fatalism quite distinctly. A dull headache had started up, and she rubbed at it, trying to ease it.

Rae watched her thoughtfully. 'Headache?'

Kate sighed. 'I didn't sleep too well.'

'It's more than that. I know the signs, Kate. You look drawn. What's wrong?'

Unable to repress a shiver, Kate looked up. 'It's nothing, really, just some bad dreams. A reaction to stress. Everyone has them,' she insisted, as if trying to convince herself rather than her friend.

'Does everyone look like you do after them? Do you want to talk about it?' Rae offered. 'Doesn't it seem a bit odd to you that you should get them now? Perhaps something triggered it off? The only thing that's happened lately is Aidan Crawford's eruption on to the scene. Could there be a connection?'

Kate's nerves rioted. 'Of course, but it would only be due to stress. A guilty conscience at work. So please can we forget it?' she begged, wanting the distressing conversation to end. It was bad enough having the dreams without dissecting them too. 'What I really wanted to know was if you'd be a witness.'

Rae seemed about to protest the change of subject, then let it pass with a defeated shrug of her shoulders. 'I'd never speak to you again if you hadn't asked me. We've been through a lot together, and I won't desert you now. Even if I think you are crazy,' she added drily.

Later, when Rae had gone, Kate sagged with relief. That was one hurdle over. The most difficult was yet to come. With a sigh she reached for a folder of letters and buried herself in work. There was a great deal to be done, loose ends tidied up, before she could leave the running of the agency in Rae's capable hands. It would mean that for a while, at least, she wouldn't have to think.

At five to one, Rae popped her head around the door, her expression bland. 'There's a Mr Crawford to see you.'

Over at the filing cabinet, the nerves in Kate's stomach lurched and twisted themselves into a knot. 'Thank you, Rae,' she returned levelly, and would have asked for a few minutes to compose herself, only her assistant stepped neatly aside to allow Aidan Crawford into the room.

She had thought she was prepared to meet him, had regained her control after last night's startling revelation. But the second he walked into the room, she knew she was wrong. Even as her heart started a crazy beat, she was telling herself he was just a man, and she knew how to handle them. Stay cool and distant, that was all it would take. But it didn't work out that way.

Hands closing on the cold metal of the drawer, her knowledgeable eye took in the fact that the grey suit he wore today was by Armani, no less. It fitted his long-legged, leanly muscular physique to perfection, and she was suddenly tossed into the stormy seas of her newly awakened senses.

She had never experienced anything like it. The impact was electric, as if someone had plugged the room into the mains. Her skin prickled. It seemed as if every inch of her was aware of every inch of him. Such intense physical attraction was uncharted territory for Kate. It frightened even as it exhilarated. She knew that, even if the room had been crowded, her sensitised radar would have picked up his presence. It was uncanny, as if she had been programmed to respond to just this one man. She recalled that kiss vividly, and her lips tingled. Deep inside her, something throbbed into life.

Unable to move, she couldn't take her eyes off him. In thrall, she knew how it felt to be a rabbit caught by the headlights of a car.

A sardonic smile hovered about his mouth as he crossed the room towards her, purpose in every stride. Dulled as her reactions were, she realised what he intended to do and weakly put out a hand to ward him off. It proved to be a fatal mistake, for he captured her hand neatly and used it to pull her towards him so that he could press on her lips the kiss she had wanted to avoid.

Her reaction was instantaneous. She went up like dry tinder. She seemed to have no bones, and her blood turned thick and hot in her veins. Heavy eyelids closed over dazed eyes. Helplessly her lips parted at the touch of his, their sensitive skin aching to respond, only there was no time. The merest brush of his lips over hers, and then he was lifting his head again, leaving her blinking bewilderedly up at him.

'Darling,' he greeted smoothly. Kate's colour fluctuated wildly. She heard Rae's sharp intake of breath before she shut the door on them.

She was set free immediately. He moved away from her, back rigid with rejection, leaving her in no doubt, should she have wondered, that his actions were purely for show. While she had been overwhelmed by the sensations going through her. Dear God, he only had to touch her and she was like putty in his hands! It had been last night all over again, only much more intense. She could hardly credit her own complete loss of self.

But at least he hadn't guessed. Though she had done nothing to help herself, her secret was still safe. Hating herself for feeling an attraction that was so one-sided, she slammed the file drawer closed with a clatter.

'Why did you do that?' she demanded angrily, not a little of that anger directed at herself. How close she had come to betraying herself!

Resting on a corner of her desk, he studied her curiously. A strange light glittered in his eyes. 'Just setting the scene,' he murmured drily.

A shiver ran down her spine as she saw that light. He couldn't have guessed. There hadn't been time. She looked at him, swallowing hard, but whatever she had thought she had seen was gone. She crossed her arms. 'Well, you don't have to bother for Rae's benefit. She knows exactly why I'm marrying you. So I'd rather you kept your hands to yourself. I don't want to be touched, and I certainly don't want to be kissed!' Liar! her senses accused. Her body was so vitally aware of him that her breasts actually ached. Like a schoolgirl with a crush, she wanted more, not less. It was like a fever! Kate stiffened her spine. Everyone knew how hotly a fever burned, but, if you starved it, it would die down. That was what she had to do. She was crazy to feel anything for this man, and it would be insanity to allow him to find out that she did!

He looked grimly amused. 'I know that well enough without your telling me,' he declared harshly. 'The way you freeze off a man speaks for itself. But brace yourself, my sweet Kate. Perhaps your friend didn't expect me to kiss you, but plenty of other people will. *We* know this marriage is a business deal, but everyone else has to believe it's real. To do that we'll have to hide our mutual aversion and pretend we love each other. For that, I'll kiss you when and where I have to, and I'll expect you to respond.'

Kate was glad her hands were hidden because the way they started to tremble would have been telling. The pictures he conjured up sent flames licking her skin. She felt like a punch-drunk boxer. After years of celibacy, suddenly one man had kissed her twice and she was experiencing the heady sweet tug of desire. So far she had been able to hide it from him, but if he carried out his threat she didn't know how long she could keep on doing so.

She called herself all sorts of a fool for not considering all their agreement would entail. He'd expect them to kiss and touch as normal lovers would. And because she was bound by her word, there was no way out of it. A shudder ran through her at the idea. But once again it wasn't quite fear.

He saw the betraying movement and misread it. Anger sparkled in his grey eyes. 'Come down off that pedestal you're so proud of, Kate, or I'll force you down. My touch won't contaminate you. Remember, a shower will quickly restore you to that state of unsullied virtue you admire in yourself,' he reminded her contemptuously. 'Tell me, doesn't it ever get lonely up there in that rarefied atmosphere?'

Kate drew in a very painful breath. Never had she had to face such withering scorn, and with little or no armour to fight it. At all costs she had to bolster his misconception. 'You're enjoying this, aren't you?' she challenged huskily.

He stood abruptly and moved to the window, his back to her. 'It has a novelty value I hadn't looked for. I don't think I'm going to be bored,' he agreed mockingly, and turned, hands braced behind him on the sill. 'You don't like male men, do you, Kate? You like to be the dominant one. Unfortunately for you, this marriage will have only one master—me. It should prove quite instructive for you—and entertaining for me.'

'I won't be used as any man's entertainment, Mr Crawford!' she declared thickly, welcoming the anger she felt at his statement. 'I'm a human being, not an object you can pick up and put down as you please!'

Grey eyes glittered triumphantly as he said softly, 'Neither am I, Kate. Nor were any of the men you discarded so blithely.'

Trumped, Kate could only stare back at him impotently, knowing it was true. Her heart took up a sickening thud.

'Look on it as poetic justice,' he went on when she remained silent, 'and take your medicine like a good little girl. To start with, my name is Aidan. You'd better get used to saying it, because nobody is going to believe in a marriage where you go around calling your husband Mr Crawford.'

He had her backed into a corner, and the only way to hide her inner turmoil was to come out fighting.

'It would serve you right if I called the whole thing off. Then what would you do—with no wife?' The jeer was pure Ice Queen.

Aidan's nostrils flared as he took an angry breath. 'I'd do the best I could on my own.'

'And lose!'

His eyes narrowed. 'Probably. But you won't call it off, will you, Kate? Not if you want me to believe you possess a heart after all. You're doing this for me, aren't you? Or was I right when I said it was still revenge you wanted?'

Once again he held the trump card, and Kate had to swallow her anger with an effort. 'Damn you!'

He laughed at her chagrin. 'You'd better get your act together, my love. Now, if you're ready, we'll go. I've a table booked for one-thirty.'

Without another word she turned her back on him, reaching for her jacket. But before she could put it on he had taken it from her and was holding it out for her to slip her arms in. He met her startled blue gaze with a raised eyebrow, and there was nothing for Kate to do but accept his assistance. The possessive weight of his hands on her shoulders was a silent reminder of his dominance. She stood still because her pride wouldn't let her run, but she had to close her eyes, and suddenly she felt as if she were in a long dark tunnel, aware only of possessive hands on her shoulders—but not the same hands at all. She gasped, and instantly the feeling was gone, leaving behind only the shuddering reaction of a nightmare.

Shaken to the core, she felt herself pale as the tremor ran through her. Dear lord, what was happening to her? Was she going mad? The thought tumbled round and round her brain, so it was some seconds before she became aware that Aidan's hands still held her.

He had to have felt her shock, and she knew he had when he turned her round. She refused to look at him, but he countered that by tipping her chin with a firm hand. She saw the shock in his face as for a brief moment he saw what she had striven to keep hidden—the fear and distress in her eyes. It caused his grip to slacken and she pulled away then, dipping her head and compressing her lips.

'Kate?' Her name was an appalled question she ignored and she grabbed up her purse from the desk.

She had never experienced anything like that before, and why had he had to be there to witness it? Whatever it was, she didn't want to talk about it. Didn't even want to think of it! When she turned to face him, she was in control once more.

'Let's go, shall we?' she said in clipped tones, and didn't wait for an answer but swept out of the door. With a muffled imprecation, she heard him follow her.

He didn't attempt to stop her until they were outside in the street, but once there, he caught her by the arm and swung her round.

'What happened in there?'

Kate widened her eyes. 'Happened?'

A nerve ticked in his jaw. 'You know damn well what I mean, Kate. For a moment you looked—afraid, and it's not the first time it's happened either.'

'Don't be ridiculous,' she scoffed with a tight little laugh, alarmed at his perception. 'How could *I* possibly be afraid?'

'Exactly what I thought, and yet I know what I saw.'

From the determination in his eyes, she knew he wasn't about to drop the subject, and it occurred to her that the best form of defence was attack. With a practised ease, she cast a provocative look up at him through her lashes.

'Did you feel sorry for me, Aidan?' At her question, she had the doubtful felicity of seeing his expression wiped clean.

'I see.' The two words chased chills up her spine. 'I thought I'd warned you against playing off your tricks on me, Kate.'

She had never realised quite how threatening a soft voice could be. But, having set her course, she wasn't about to change tack. What had happened was private. Almost a waking nightmare. Perhaps it *was* part of her nightmares, and they were things she could never discuss with anyone, let alone him. So, she brazened it out. 'You did, but I had to see if you really meant it.'

'Now you know I did. And now I know what you're capable of, I won't be falling for that line again. Now let's get the hell away from here before I'm tempted to throttle the lying breath out of you!' he gritted through his teeth, and set off down the street at a pace she had to trot to keep up with.

Aidan had booked a table in one of those French restaurants so often found tucked away in side-streets. They were shown to a secluded corner where they could talk without fear of being overheard. He ordered for both of them without consulting her, and Kate, her appetite completely vanished, would have argued if she hadn't seen the challenging glint in his eye and decided not to rise to the bait. It was galling, though, to see his lips curve in amusement at her caution.

Sipping at a glass of white wine while they waited for their meal to arrive, Kate broke the silence that was making her feel distinctly edgy, even though she had sworn not to speak first. 'So, what happens now?'

Across the table, Aidan casually crossed his legs. A movement that drew her eyes and dried her mouth at the way the material stretched over his muscular thighs. He was as graceful as a big cat, and just as dangerous, as he relaxed back in his seat, clearly enjoying having her at a disadvantage. 'I'll arrange a special licence. We can be married by the end of the week.'

Though she had been expecting something like this, her stomach still knotted anxiously. 'So soon?' Good lord, did her voice have to sound so croaky!

Aidan regarded her steadily. 'We have no time to lose. My birthday is only days away. There's no time for a formal wedding, and the fewer people who know about this, the better,' he finished grimly.

'You mean . . . your brother?'

'I mean that the Press would have a field day if they got wind of the fact that, days after I should have married one woman, I marry the woman who stopped that marriage by claiming she was my wife. That kind of publicity I can do without. So far I've managed to keep last Saturday's fiasco out of the papers.'

Kate chewed on her lip. 'Would it prejudice your case?' That particular angle hadn't occurred to her, and now that it did it brought with it another wave of guilt.

'Frankly, I doubt it. A marriage is all the will requires. But I'd rather not have to put it to the test. My grandfather's eccentricities could have further codicils as yet undisclosed. I presume I *can* trust you not to talk?'

That brought a spark to her eye. 'Would you accept my word if I gave it?'

For answer he rested both arms on the table and leant forward. 'There's an old Arab proverb which says, "Trust in Allah, but tie up your camel." On your recent behaviour, can you give me one good reason why I should trust you?'

That was one goad too many. 'Because you don't have a choice?' She smiled at him sweetly.

It was probably fortunate that the waiter arrived with their meal at that point, because Aidan's face had darkened dramatically. He was forced to hold his tongue, however, and Kate jumped in quickly as the waiter departed, deflecting what he might have said.

'If your grandfather entrusted the company to you, why did he make that will?' she asked curiously.

Aidan's laugh was soft. 'Because he didn't approve of my lifestyle. Like any other young man, I played the field. That was acceptable so far as it went, but the old man expected me to settle down one day. Unfortunately, marriage never appealed to me after I'd seen the results of my own parents' marriage, and divorce. We didn't see eye to eye, and I could be as stubborn as he. But the old goat won in the end, didn't he? If I wanted control of the company, I had to find a good woman to marry and, more importantly, become the mother of my sons.'

To Kate he didn't sound bitter at all, more wryly affectionate. Whatever their differences, they had respected each other. She wished she could have been privy to some of their battles. They would have been very illuminating!

'And now that's me,' she said softly, feeling a strange curling warmth inside her.

'God forbid!'

Hurt seemed to explode inside her, touching every nerve at the same moment, so that no part of her was free of it. 'You don't think I have what it takes to be a good mother?' By some miracle the words came out coolly.

He eyed her soberly for so long that she felt ready to squirm in her seat before he replied. 'For us the question is irrelevant, but as a matter of fact I do. I've seen you with children. You can't hide that sort of affection.'

Crazily, Kate felt again that warm glow of pleasure at his words, and it left her feeling confused. 'Thanks,' she said gruffly. A thought occurred to her. 'Would you have remained married to Julia?'

'That was the general idea. However, you can rest assured, Kate, that our marriage will be strictly temporary.'

Instead of being reassured, Kate experienced a stab of pure jealousy. It left her confused and irritated, and that was reflected in her sharp tone as she said, 'Won't it look strange if you turn up with a completely different woman as your wife?'

Aidan shook his head. 'Fortunately no. Stateside, only my father and Netta, my stepmother, knew I was getting married.'

Kate frowned heavily. 'But surely they'll find it odd?'

Again he shook his head, and there was a curve of grim amusement about his mouth. 'They were at the wedding so they know I'm not marrying Julia. They flew home yesterday before I heard from you, but I rang them later. They know all about you.'

The room seemed to tilt alarmingly. 'All? You can't mean...?'

'Oh, but I do. They know you were the mystery woman, and they know you've agreed to help me out. They're willing to accept you on those terms.'

She stared at him, appalled. 'How could you? My God, they must despise me!'

'For that you've only yourself to blame. If you want respect, you have to earn it,' he shot back with both barrels.

Kate reeled as blow followed blow. 'I think I hate you!' she said through gritted teeth.

Aidan uttered a harsh laugh and leant across the table towards her. 'Do you, Kate? Well, to mangle a quote, I don't give a damn. All that matters is that we give a convincing performance while we're in the States.'

'The States?' Kate gasped, 'But I thought...'

He smiled tightly. 'We'd have a honeymoon?' he finished for her.

'Well...yes.' He'd said he was having one with Julia, so naturally she'd assumed...

He followed her thoughts. 'Julia and I would have had two weeks. It was all I could afford due to business commitments. So I'm afraid you'll just have to do without a honeymoon, Kate. My father lives in Washington; we'll be flying over to stay with him after the wedding. So that means no more Ice Queen, Kate. Winter's over, it's time to thaw. Make up your mind to it. As soon as we touch down in America, the curtain goes up on our little play, and I'm expecting nothing less than rave reviews on your performance.'

CHAPTER SIX

KATE stared out into the darkness, oblivious of her slim figure reflected in the window of the hotel room. In the light she could see the snow falling. Winter in New York. How romantic it sounded. Perhaps for others it was, but not for her. Sighing, she let the heavy brocade curtain drop back into place, blocking out the cold, and glanced at her watch. It was nearly six o'clock. Very soon now, Aidan was going to return. The thought simply made her feel colder.

The past week had been hectic, punctuated by the recurring bad dreams. The effect was noticeable. She had lost weight she could ill afford, her appetite dwindling to nothing. Thankfully there had been no repeat of that incident in her office, and she had managed to rationalise it away as just a freakish isolated occurrence.

It hadn't been so easy to come to terms with her unwanted attraction for her husband. She had seen him only briefly before the wedding, and on those occasions she had been too keenly aware of him, though he hadn't as much as touched her. Mostly he had kept in contact by telephone, but even his voice had the ability to raise the fine hairs all over her body. It had become an act of total concentration not to give away the smallest sign of what she was undergoing, and it was exhausting.

Aidan's mood had been difficult to calculate. Their meetings had been businesslike to the point of abruptness. He would arrive, give her his instructions and then leave as soon as possible, which had hardly been a boost to her confidence.

They had been married only that morning in the presence of Rae and a man whose name she couldn't call to mind—Tim somebody or other. To prove it she wore the rings Aidan had given her on her marriage finger. She had protested about the engagement ring, but he had bought it for her anyway, and now it sat, a round sapphire surrounded by diamonds, next to the chased gold band. An uncompromising symbol of the fact that she was now his wife.

The die had been well and truly cast.

There had been no celebration; there hadn't been time. They had gone straight to the airport to catch their flight to New York. Not Washington, as she had expected. She had found out why when they'd arrived here at their hotel. No sooner had the porter left than Aidan had gathered up his briefcase, informed her he had a business meeting, and disappeared. She had been alone ever since.

Alone she had discovered that their suite consisted of two rooms, a sitting-room and a twin-bedded bedroom with en-suite bathroom. Foolishly, it had never occurred to her that they would have to share the same bedroom. As far as she could see, there was absolutely no reason why they should, and every reason why they shouldn't. Sharing a room, there were a hundred ways she could give herself away. Besides, the chances were high that she would have those dreams again. They were getting worse, scarcely missing a night. She absolutely didn't want him to witness that. It would be the final humiliation. When he came back, she was going to demand that he find them alternative accommodation.

Almost as if she had magicked him, Aidan walked through the door. Tossing his briefcase on to a chair, he tugged at the knot of his tie. Kate thought he looked tired, but right now that wasn't as important as her own problem. Already tense at the idea of this confrontation as she was, her tingling reaction to his appearance only added to the strain.

'Have you any idea what time it is? Where have you been?' she demanded crossly.

He looked at her, eyebrows mockingly raised. 'How very wifely you sound, Kate. Does that mean you missed me?'

'Do I look as though I've suddenly gone mad?' she shot back scornfully.

To her surprise, he laughed, a deep, warm sound that chased shivers up her spine. 'Admittedly not. But you do look as though someone's ruffled your feathers. Are you going to tell me what's wrong, or do I have to guess?' he enquired sardonically, moving across to the drinks cabinet and pouring himself a straight Scotch.

Kate held her temper by a whisker, having learned by now when he was being deliberately provocative. It had been this way all week. Almost as if he was testing her to see how far he could push her before she exploded. Well, she hadn't, and wouldn't, give him that satisfaction.

'I want to change this suite,' she told him shortly.

That irritating eyebrow rose again. 'Demands so soon? Don't tell me, the colour doesn't match your beautiful blue eyes.'

He very nearly knocked her off balance with that. Beautiful eyes! She hadn't thought he would find anything about her beautiful. Startled by her own thoughts, she stared at him, and only belatedly saw his watchful amusement and realised she had been neatly diverted.

'Don't patronise me, Aidan. You know what I mean. I want a bedroom of my own.'

He took a sip from his glass before saying simply, 'No.'

Her lips parted on a tiny gasp. 'What do you mean, no?'

Aidan settled himself on the couch and stretched out his legs. 'Are you having difficulty with the language? No means no. Or let me put it another way. Short though this marriage might be, I intend to start as I mean to go on. I'm not putting its credibility in doubt by having separate bedrooms.'

Kate crossed her arms to hide the sudden tremor of her hands. 'And my feelings don't count, I suppose?' she demanded huskily.

'They're a luxury I can't afford. Count your blessings that you have a bed to yourself. As for bedrooms, one is all we need,' Aidan informed her bluntly and tossed off the remains of his Scotch.

'Then I'll sleep in here. I take it you have no objections if I sleep on the couch?' Kate snapped sarcastically, wishing for the hundredth time that she had thought of this before agreeing to marry him.

His grey eyes narrowed on her thoughtfully. 'What's the matter, Kate?' he asked softly. 'Afraid you'll reveal more secrets?'

Every nerve in her body seemed to jolt violently. Her legs felt suddenly too weak to hold her, and she sank down rather hurriedly on the arm of the couch. 'Secrets? I don't know what you mean.' Oh, lord, what now?

Aidan looked at her keenly, then, setting his glass aside, he put his hands behind his head. 'Don't you know you talk in your sleep?' he asked curiously.

For a moment, she really thought she was going to faint. Her heart started to race, and yet it felt as if it was being squeezed in a vice. She paled. 'What?'

'I said, don't you know you talk in your sleep?' he obligingly repeated. 'You were quite eloquent on the flight over.'

Talk in her sleep? She couldn't have—could she? She had been tired enough to sleep. Could she have spoken aloud? If so, what had she said? Panic was only a step away, and she fought it down with anger. 'Is this some perverted sort of joke? I assure you I don't find it funny.'

'No, I can see that,' he mused. 'I wonder why. What are you afraid of?'

Oh, God! Her chin came up. 'Nothing! And I *don't* talk in my sleep,' Kate insisted firmly.

Aidan's smile was bland. 'How would you know? You were asleep at the time.'

If he wanted her rattled, then she was, seriously. But he was the last person who would know it. She rallied, forcing herself to remain calm. Her shrug was a masterpiece of acting. 'Interesting, was it? I'd *hate* to think I was boring you.' She sounded bored, whereas she was desperate to know what she had said—even as she dreaded that knowledge.

'Interesting? It probably was. I couldn't say,' Aidan parried aggravatingly.

God, how he was enjoying watching her squirm, the rat! 'Why not?' she demanded angrily, watching the smile cross his face. 'Oh, I get it! You intend to hold it over my head, is that it?'

His teeth flashed whitely. 'What a suspicious mind you have, Kate Crawford. Could you really reveal anything dreadful enough for blackmail?'

This time she didn't attempt to shrug it off. 'I don't know. You tell me,' she gritted out between her teeth.

A laugh rumbled up from way down in his chest. 'Now that sounds like a very guilty conscience talking. My, my, Kate, what have you been up to?'

She knew then, knew she hadn't said anything at all. He had just wound her up and she, fool that she was, had walked straight into it. 'Damn you! It was just a big try on, wasn't it?'

'And you fell for it. Never mind, Kate. Call it one for the boys. Besides, it wasn't a total lie, although mumble would be a better description than talk.'

Kate stared at him for a moment, then took a deep breath. 'This is the way it's going to be, is it? I have to pretend to be happily married, while you take cheap shots? I don't think that's going to fool anybody.'

Aidan sobered and slowly sat up to rub a hand around his neck. 'You're right, it won't,' he admitted, then he grinned reminiscently. 'But you rose so beautifully that I couldn't resist it.'

Kate stared at him, a slow anger coming to the boil like a pot on a stove. While she had been worried to death, he had been teasing!

'Why, you . . . !' She looked around for something to throw, found only the cushion, and launched herself at him, using it like a weapon.

After his first stunned reaction, Aidan sprang into action, fielding the swings neatly until he could make a grab for the cushion. All the while a slow rumble of laughter came from him.

'My, my, Kate, this isn't very regal of you!' he gasped, dodging as she flailed away.

Liking the sound of his laughter, but hating him, Kate growled and swung harder—only to miss him completely. With a yelp she spun round, losing her balance. But she didn't fall, for an arm snaked round her hips, fielding her neatly, and in the next instant she was lying on the couch, breathing heavily, with Aidan's long body stretched over hers, his arms about her—a gleam in his eye that twisted her heart.

Their eyes locked, and everything seemed to go still. In breathless fascination she watched the colour in his eyes deepen. Saw the way his gaze dropped to her lips. They tingled as if he had already touched them, and a tiny moan escaped her. His head rose, cheeks flushed, and she saw the moment when he thought of drawing back overthrown by a compulsion that was too strong.

'Kate.' His voice was a husky groan as he lowered his head to hers.

If he had kept silent, she might have kept her head, but the passion in his voice was her undoing. His lips moved hungrily on hers, tasting, biting, seeking a response that, with a whimper of need, she gave willingly. Her lips parted, welcoming his invasion, and the world burst into flames around her. It was as if the battle went on, yet now their arms clung, hands offering fevered caresses that raised body heat to scorching point.

What Kate had felt when she alone responded was as nothing to this. She ached to be touched, to touch. Gloried in the arousal of his body grinding against hers. Every kiss sought to quench this dizzying spiral of need, but only added fuel to a fire that rapidly threatened to blaze out of all control.

His mouth left hers, searing a path down her neck that brought tiny gasps of pleasure to her lips. Nimbly his hands dealt with the buttons of her jacket, pushing it aside to reveal the swollen perfection of her breasts in their thin lace covering. Slowly one hand glided up to possess one peak, and it felt to Kate as if he had claimed her very soul. She cried out and Aidan went still, raising eyes gleaming hot with passion.

'Sweet heaven, Kate, but I want you,' he growled huskily, voice tinged with shock.

It was that which brought sanity back with a vengeance, crashing her down to earth, to shiver in the aftermath. What was she doing? He wanted her, but he hadn't expected to, probably didn't even really want to. Yet he'd take her because she had just shown she was willing—very, very willing. But afterwards, what then? He didn't love her or need her. She was a convenience, no more. While he was used to a casual fling, she wasn't, and never would be. But even more importantly she had been criminally careless, forgetting how serious a risk she would have been taking.

Thanking whatever gods prevailed for bringing her to her senses in time, she pushed him away and clambered hastily to her feet. Still shaking, she kept her back to him.

'That wasn't part of the deal, remember?' she declared icily, fastening buttons haphazardly.

She heard the brush of cloth as he stood up, then he was swinging her round to face him, anger stamped all over him. 'What the hell does that mean?'

Kate lifted her chin. 'Just a reminder to keep your hands to yourself in future.'

'You wanted me,' he ground out thickly.

'And then I didn't,' she returned, acid-sweet, hating herself for the way his face closed over.

His eyes flashed a warning. 'Why, you little...!' he bit off harshly. 'I see, still playing your tricks, are you, Your Highness? There's a word for women like you—but I guess you've heard that already,' he added scornfully. 'Just so far and no further, eh, Kate? That's a dangerous tactic. You can push a man too far by heating him up and then freezing him off. But don't worry, I'll keep my lustful hands to myself in future!'

Feeling flayed to the bone, she forced herself not to look away. 'Good!' she snapped back.

Aidan shook his head. 'Lady, you are something else! It's a good thing we're going out, otherwise I might be tempted to throttle the life out of you.'

Nerves jolting, she ignored the threat. 'Going out?' she queried, mouth drying as she watched him refasten shirt buttons she must have undone only minutes ago.

'The man I saw today has invited us to join him and his wife for dinner. When he heard we hadn't had a celebration, he booked a table at one of the top nightspots.'

'Why didn't you stop him?' she exclaimed at once.

He ran a tired hand through his hair. 'Because we have to start somewhere. If we have any rough spots, I want them ironed out.'

Loath as she was to admit it, he had a point. She had never had much confidence about fooling people. At least this way they would have a trial run. Even so, there could be problems.

'Do they know about Julia?' she asked anxiously.

'No. Mitch is a business colleague. I dine with him and his wife Sarah when I'm in New York. So you won't be expected to know things from my past. Any ignorance we do show will have a good excuse. It was a whirlwind romance, remember. We have the rest of our lives to get to know each other.' There was more than a hint of mockery in his tone as he finished, and his eyes gleamed at her.

This time she didn't rise. 'Thank heavens for small mercies! A little knowledge of you goes a long way. Like paraffin. You spill a small drop, and everything for miles around smells, tastes and oozes it!'

His eyes followed her as she gracefully crossed the room to the bedroom door. 'Do I detect a note of criticism?'

'I wouldn't have the nerve,' she rejoined shortly.

'Sweetheart, you've got nerve enough for anything— I know.'

It seemed a good note to leave on, and Kate went through the door. In the bedroom, she leant back against the door and eyed the two large beds. That had been a very narrow escape, but the Ice Queen had saved her once again. She winced at the memory of his scorn. She hadn't meant to tease, but it would have been madness to give in to an attraction that had no future. She closed her eyes. How her body ached with the promise of fulfilment denied. She'd have to be more careful. If he should ever guess how vulnerable she really was, how false the Ice Queen was, what would he do? If he really tried to seduce her she knew she'd have no weapons to fight him. She'd surrender before the first shot was even fired! She couldn't afford that.

She looked at the beds again. It wasn't going to be easy, sharing this room. Though she had stated her intention of sleeping on the couch, she knew realistically that she couldn't. That option wouldn't be open to her at his parents' home. She would have to get used to sharing, and tonight was all she had. The thought knotted her stomach. Aidan might believe she had the nerve to do anything, but this was something else entirely.

She hadn't bothered to unpack just for one night. Now she retrieved an uncrushable violet jersey dress from her case, together with fresh underwear, and took them into the bathroom. There was a lock on the door and she used it, knowing that Aidan would have no qualms about walking in if she didn't.

Wrapping a towel around her hair to keep it dry, she showered swiftly, dried herself on a luxuriously thick bath sheet, then stepped into the chocolate silk and lace teddy. Make-up came next, and her years as a model had got its application down to a fine art, so that it hardly looked as if she was wearing any at all. Lastly came the dress. It was soft and clingy, with long sleeves and a cowl neckline. It was a particular favourite, and she generally wore it when her confidence needed a boost. Tonight seemed to fit the bill perfectly.

Satisfied at last with her appearance, Kate gathered up her discarded clothes. The white suit that she had been married in looked tired and forlorn draped over her arm. Reflecting some of her own feelings. Banishing the maudlin thought, she unlocked the door and re-entered the bedroom, only to be brought up short by the sight of her husband standing mere yards away, clad only in his trousers.

During her career, Kate had become inured to the sight of near-naked males. She had classed them in her mind as models, and therefore sexless. The same couldn't be said about Aidan. His chest was broad and tanned, well-developed and with a fine mat of silky dark hair.

Staring, transfixed, she went hot and cold. Memory of those heated moments in his arms stirred her body into vibrant life. Dear God, he was so tall, so broad and strong. Fully clad, he was a force to be reckoned with. Now, barely clothed, he looked like some lethal, proud jungle animal. Intensely male. Her throat closed over and her mouth went dry. The pull to go across and run her hands over his taut skin was so strong, she had taken a step before she even knew it. Appalled at her wanton thoughts, she took her anger out on him.

'Must you do that here?' Even to her own ears her voice was high-pitched and tense, and she couldn't look him in the eye. She flung the clothes down and rummaged in her case for her black shoes and black leather belt with hands that shook.

Aidan, meanwhile, had looked up in surprise from unfastening the buttons of a clean shirt. 'Do what?'

Her fingers trembled so badly, it took two attempts to fasten the belt in the right hole. 'Change,' she snapped.

Aidan dropped the shirt into the case. 'Oh? And just where would you have me do it? In the corridor?'

Her feet went into her shoes in two jerky movements. 'There is a bathroom.'

'Which you were using until thirty seconds ago,' he pointed out. 'Even so, I'm not standing here naked, Kate, so I'm at a loss to understand this show of outraged modesty.'

Kate looked up, ready to shoot back an answer, but lost the ability to utter even a squeak as she watched him crossing the space between them. He stopped mere inches away so that she could feel the heat coming off him, and every frantic breath she took held the scent of him.

'Or am I getting my signals crossed here? Is it outrage, Kate, or something else? Wasn't I supposed to take no for an answer just now? Were you disappointed because I turned out like all the others? Did you expect me to follow you in here and take what we both wanted? Is that it, Kate? No surrender, but to the victor go the spoils?' Aidan's voice had become low and husky, with a hint of intimacy that chased shivers along her spine.

She was at once aghast at his misinterpretation and dismayed at her own inability to move away. Her brain said move, but her feet seemed rooted. 'I...'

'Yes, Kate? You...what? Want me to kiss you? Is that it? You want me to storm the citadel and claim it for my own?'

Dry-mouthed, she took a step away, voice uttering a husky denial. 'No!'

'I wonder why I don't believe you.' Laughing, he caught her back with strong hands on her arms. 'I can feel you trembling, Kate, so I think you're going to have to prove you mean that.'

Seeing his head lowering, she began to struggle. But he was too strong and her efforts only half-hearted. A helpless moan of capitulation broke from her throat. Then his lips were claiming hers, his arms going about her to pull her close to the hardness of his body—and Kate was lost, as she had known she would be. A shudder of pure pleasure racked her as her breasts came into contact with the wall of his chest. Her eyes closed and her head fell back, lips parting to the gliding invasion of his tongue. Dizzily she met that silken thrust, joining in an erotic dance that sent spears of flame down through her to start up a delicious throbbing.

With a sigh, her arms reached up around his neck, one hand combing into the thick dark hair, fingers tightening convulsively as the kiss went deeper and deeper. The glide of his hands along her spine brought a shiver of delight, and mindlessly she pressed closer still to his blatantly aroused body.

It was Aidan who broke away first, chest heaving as he dragged in air. Bereft, she moaned, and opened her eyes to look up into his face, uncaring that she was revealing all her pent-up longing.

Smouldering eyes locked with hers. 'Where are your claws now, little cat?' he murmured with a husky laugh, and took her parted lips once more.

It wasn't the kiss that triggered off the violent trembling of her body, but the name he called her. Without warning she was catapulted back into that long dark tunnel, nauseated by an overwhelming feeling of disgust and loathing. She was trapped. Oppressed. A force uncaring of her pain, blind to her fear and dread was killing her—killing the woman in her.

She wanted to fight, but she was shaking so badly there was little she could do. With a despairing sob, she kicked out, and the next instant she was falling, finding herself pinned beneath a stifling weight. Her mind went into shock, long shudders of revulsion shaking her slender frame. Turning her head, she stared blindly at the wall, hating the knowledge that she was helpless.

Above her, Aidan went quite still. His body, still pressed so close to hers where they had landed on the bed, couldn't fail to register the tremors that shook her. Shifting on to his elbows, he stared down at her averted face, his own white with shock.

'Kate?' He used a hand to turn her to him. 'What the hell?' His shock was evident as he saw the blank eyes in her pale face. 'My God! Kate! *Kate!*'

From far away she heard her name and she looked up into a face very nearly as white as her own. A serious, concerned face in which a scar stood out sharply. With a choking gasp, time and place returned. This was Aidan, and they were in the hotel. What had she done? But she already knew. It had happened again, just like that day in her office, only much, much worse. Dear God, was she going crazy?

'Let me up!' The frantic command had none of her usual control, and she thought for a panicky moment it was going to be ignored. But then Aidan rolled away to the side and she was free. Without looking at him, she scrambled to her feet with scant dignity. Trembling hands smoothed her dress down, then lifted to check her hair. It hung raggedly about her face, loosened by the struggle, and her nerves jolted.

Biting down hard on her lip, with jerky movements she tried to pin it back, but the pins had vanished and suddenly it was all too much. Tears stung her eyes as she searched the floor. 'Where are the damn pins?' Her voice was a thread away from hysteria and that terrified her into gulping it back.

The bed creaked as Aidan stood up, then he was before her, hand holding out the lost pins. 'Don't panic, they're here.'

'I'm not panicking!' Her eyes shot to his, saw the concern there, and darted away again. 'Thanks.' She took the pins from him, trying to avoid contact.

Unseen by her, Aidan frowned. His hand went to stop her turning away. 'Kate, what——?'

'Don't touch me!' She stepped backwards hastily, terrified that if he did, it would all happen again. Then, realising that she was only making a bad situation worse, she forced herself to be calm. 'Please, don't touch me. I—I couldn't bear it right now.' Going to the nearest mirror, she swiftly put her hair to rights, trying to ignore the other figure reflected behind her that didn't take his eyes off her.

'Kate, we have to talk about this. It's pretty clear something frightened you, but I wasn't about to rape you, whatever you thought. I think I have the right to know what's going on.'

'Rights!' Kate spun round. 'You have no rights over me! No man does! If it comes to rights, then I have the right not to be pawed by you...!' She faltered to a halt. She was over-reacting, his frowning expression told her so. 'Excuse me.' Abruptly she moved across to the bathroom, locking herself in.

Resting her hands on the sink, she took several deep breaths, shudders racking her as, very slowly, she forced herself to calm down. What was happening to her? First the nightmares, and now this. What did it all mean? She covered her face with her hands. They had to be connected, but how? Dear heaven, it was frightening to have this going on inside her and not know what it was all about!

And there was Aidan, demanding explanations. Which she couldn't give because she didn't know herself! How could she explain the inexplicable? She'd have to brazen it out somehow, find a lie he would accept. But what? She bit her lip. If only Rae were here, they could talk it through. Rae cared. Aidan didn't. She couldn't have just anyone poking and prying into her private agonies! She'd just have to survive on her own. But she didn't mind admitting she was scared—scared of what she might uncover.

For now, though, she had to shake it off. There was Aidan to face and the evening to get through. With that in mind she made minor repairs to her make-up, took a steadying breath, and let herself back into the bedroom. A quick glance showed her Aidan was by the window. She had to take control of the situation, bring normality back.

'You'll have to hurry, or we'll be late. I'll be in the other room,' she said calmly.

'Don't for a minute think I've given up, Kate,' he told her as he turned, letting the curtain drop. 'I mean to know.'

Kate paused, summoning up a cool smile. 'Know? I'm sorry, I have no idea what you mean,' she murmured, crossing to the door into the sitting-room.

'I see. Nothing happened. I imagined it all? We weren't making love and you didn't freak out?'

Summoning up her reserves, she faced him fully. 'I didn't "freak out", as you so quaintly put it. I merely put an end to something I found distasteful.' She managed to instil ice into her voice, and was quite pleased with the result. Until Aidan countered after a short silence.

'How distasteful?'

Damn him, why couldn't he just accept it? Now what did she say? 'Frankly, I couldn't stand you touching me,' she invented desperately.

His brows rose and he crossed his arms. 'Is that so?' he asked, silky-smooth.

Alarm shot through her. 'Would I lie to you?' she countered.

He rubbed his chin thoughtfully. 'Now that's an interesting question, isn't it? I'm something of a mean poker player myself. Should I call the bluff? I'll have to think about that one. While I do, you think on this. I can keep running as long as you can. Whatever scared the life out of you isn't going away, and neither am I.' That last statement was punctuated by the bathroom door closing after him, followed by the gush of water.

Kate went into the other room and sank into an armchair, knowing that, far from being over, the real battle was only just starting. He wasn't kidding, and he already knew far too much. Far from being daunted, he had retrieved her mythical gauntlet and taken up the challenge. Now she was locked in a war she had to win and it made her more than ever determined that his curiosity—and that was all it surely could be—wouldn't be satisfied. She was no mean fighter herself, as he was about to find out.

When Aidan walked quietly into the room half an hour later, he found her sitting composedly on the couch flicking through a magazine. Though he hadn't made a noise, Kate's inner radar was ultra-sensitive to his presence, and the nerves in her stomach flip-flopped crazily as she looked up. Their eyes locked in silent battle.

'Ready for the fray?' His tone was cool. Only his eyes gave away the fact that he didn't mean their dinner engagement.

'I just have to collect my coat and bag,' Kate supplied equally coolly, rising gracefully. In the bedroom she quickly glanced in the mirror. Thank God she didn't look as tense as she felt. Gathering up her things, she went to join him.

Mitch and Sarah Norman, a friendly couple in their fifties, were waiting for them in the hotel lounge. Their congratulations were as warm and genuine as they were themselves, and Kate felt a twinge of guilt at deceiving them. A feeling that grew when Sarah handed her a gift-wrapped package as they sat over drinks.

'It's not much,' she excused, 'but when Mitch told me Aidan had just got married, I had to get you something.'

The something turned out to be a crystal goblet, beautifully engraved with their names. Kate felt a lump of emotion grow in her chest. It reminded her of just what a sham this marriage was.

'Come back, Kate,' Aidan's humorous prompt brought her back to the present.

Blinking, she realised they were waiting for her to say something. She produced a smile. 'You really shouldn't have, but thank you. It's quite beautiful. Oh...!' The soft exclamation left her lips as she studied the engraving. 'They've put Katrine.'

'Oh, dear, don't tell me that's wrong! I was sure it was what Aidan told me,' Sarah looked positively crestfallen, and Kate hastened to reassure her.

'It is. It's just that hardly anybody calls me that. I'm just plain old Kate,' she laughed self-consciously.

'But it's such a lovely name!' Sarah exclaimed. 'So feminine. It suits you. Don't you agree, Aidan?' she appealed to the younger man.

Kate just had to look at him, one eyebrow raised tauntingly. He met the challenge by sliding his arm round her waist and bringing a riot of colour to her cheeks in the process. She went rigid, muscles tensing to pull away, when the bite of his fingers on her waist warned her to sit still.

His lips brushed her cheek. 'Act One, Scene One, remember!' he warned her in a sibilant whisper.

She subsided at once, excruciatingly aware of his hand resting so possessively on the curve of her hip. A prickly heat broke out all over her. For all the good it did, the material of her dress might not have been there.

Sensing her acquiescence, Aidan raised his voice. 'I do, as a matter of fact,' he said, eyes locking on the frantic pulse that beat in her neck. 'A graceful name for a graceful lady.'

He sounded so sincere, so convincing, that Kate was startled. Smiling, his eyes held hers. The message was clear and it irritated her. She had to play up, it was all an act. She swayed towards him, smile as warm as a snake. 'Is this good enough for you, darling?' she whispered acidly.

His eyes glittered, and with barely a pause he closed the gap and took a kiss that stole her breath away.

'However,' he went on smoothly as he eased reluctantly away and surveyed the flush on her cheeks with approval, 'There are times when she's most definitely a Kate. I had the devil's own job persuading her to marry me. Didn't I?'

Angry at the triumph she saw in his eyes, she rose swiftly to the bait. 'Are you implying I'm a shrew?' she demanded dulcetly, only her eyes flashing daggers. He responded with a grin.

'I'd be careful how I answered that, Aidan,' Mitch advised with a chuckle. 'People have been known to head for Reno on less provocation.'

'I'm not afraid of Kate,' Aidan replied, returning her stare for stare, and there was something in his tone which said, But I'd love to know what she's afraid of, that put her on her mettle.

'No,' Sarah interjected teasingly. 'We know what you're afraid of, don't we, big baby?'

'Sarah, I swear, if you utter one word, your days are numbered,' Aidan threatened, but the older woman didn't turn a hair.

'Phooey! You're all talk, you men. If I feel like telling Kate, I will. A woman needs all the edge she can get.' She gave Kate a broad wink and turned to her husband. 'When are we going to eat? I'm starving.'

They made a move then. While Mitch paid the bill, Aidan took the goblet to be locked in the safe overnight. That left the two women together. Sarah took Kate's arm as they wandered into the lobby.

'Spiders,' Sarah revealed confidentially. 'Aidan can't stand them. If you don't believe me, just wait until he finds one in the bath! Oh-oh, here they come! Now, remember, don't say a word. Just keep it in mind. You'll know when to use it.'

Kate smiled and forbore to tell her there wouldn't be time because the marriage was only temporary. All the same, it was nice to know he had a weakness.

Dinner, considering the company, should have been a sparkling affair, but Kate found it difficult to relax. It had been an exhausting day, one way or another, and it was draining to have to watch her behaviour. It took all her skill to keep her answers cheerful and her smile in place. It was left up to Aidan to keep the conversational ball rolling, which he did with considerable panache. He revealed an unexpected sense of humour, not unlike her own, and was at times so downright wicked that she had to laugh. But her appetite was small, and she only picked at the meal.

By the time they went on to the nightclub, Kate was definitely feeling the strain, but the other couple had gone to such trouble to give them a good time that she didn't have the heart to say she'd had enough. They drank a champagne toast while the cabaret was on, and then the band struck up and couples took to the floor.

'Kate?' Aidan's hand came to rest on her shoulder. 'Shall we?'

There was no good reason for refusing to dance, and, giving him her hand, she allowed him to help her to her feet and lead her out among the dancing couples.

On the dance-floor, Aidan turned her into his arms. She tried to keep her distance but somehow it just wasn't possible. Nothing seemed important when she was this close to him. Bowing to the inevitable, she closed her eyes, forgetting everything but the pleasure of having his arms close around her. They fitted together perfectly, as if they were made for each other. Within seconds, her body had relaxed, moulding itself to his, feeling every movement as he steered them around the floor, one muscular thigh brushing tantalisingly between hers with every step. The crowd faded away. There were just the two of them.

'Enjoying yourself?' Aidan asked, voice husky, his breath warm on her cheek.

Kate looked up, eyes dreamy, and beyond his head she could see the sky. Blinking, she realised he had steered her out on to the balcony. They were quite alone in the darkness. She didn't answer his question. She couldn't.

A snowflake came to rest on her cheek and melted. He reached up to brush the moisture away gently. 'Oh-oh, Kate, I think the Ice Queen is melting.'

Before she could reply, his mouth brushed hers, and she forgot all she might have said. All she could do was respond mindlessly as he wrought havoc of the most delicious kind with lips and tongue; stroking the sensitive inner skin, teeth nipping at pulsing lips until she moaned and he deepened the kiss, arms drawing her close into the prison of his arms.

When he let her go, she was dazed, and could only stare up at him, seeing the stars glittering in his eyes.

'So,' he murmured huskily, 'you can't bear to have me touch you, eh, Kate?'

Blue eyes rounded as shock tore through her. She tried to break free, but he wouldn't let her. She was obliged to stay where she was, but she refused to look at him as pleasure died inside her.

'Very clever!' she declared huskily.

'I thought so. Hell, Kate, don't be bitter because I called your bluff,' he chided gently.

'Whatever you're trying to do, it won't work,' she shot back, near to tears.

He gave her a small shake. 'Little fool, can't you see I'm only trying to help?'

Stormy-eyed, she stared up at him. 'All I see is curiosity, and I won't pander to that.'

He swore viciously under his breath. 'Why can't I be genuine in my willingness to help?' he demanded.

'Because there's no reason why you should!' she retorted fiercely. 'I'm nothing to you but a convenience. I'm useful and you want me. That's all.'

Anger got the better of him. 'And you want me, don't forget. I could take you to bed and make you tell me,' he threatened in frustration.

She gasped. 'Try it and I'll tell you just one thing. Go to hell!'

'And join you? I don't think I'd like it there!' Aidan said succinctly, and Kate winced at the accuracy of his thrust. 'Kate, you can trust me.'

She shuddered, crazily aware that she wanted to and knowing she couldn't risk it. It added an edge to her voice. 'Trust a Crawford? That'll be the day!'

'You will in the end,' he promised.

She shook him off—or tried to. 'I don't need help, from you or anyone—but especially from you!'

His face tightened with anger. 'OK, if that's the way you want to play it. Remember this, though, there are no rules. The gloves are off. If it gets rough, you've only yourself to blame. Now smile, darling, we're being watched. You love me, remember.'

God, he was hateful! Angrily she plastered a smile on her face as they went inside, and, though it felt stiff and unnatural to her, the Normans didn't see anything wrong. A short time later the party broke up.

Silence reigned in the cab that bore them back to their hotel for their first night together. Turning her head slightly, Kate found she could study his profile. Occasionally his scar caught the light, but funnily enough she generally barely noticed it. There was a strength in his face, and a gentle humour too. He could be angry and mocking, but she had never seen his grey eyes glitter with malice as his brother's did.

Everything pointed to his being a strong man, one you could trust. Had she been wrong to throw that offer back in his face? But she had become used to relying only on herself, of hiding the terrors that stalked her. And she was afraid of pity. She couldn't bear that. So she had to have done the right thing, hadn't she?

A sudden intrusion of light glittered off his eyes, and she realised he was watching her. How long for, and what was he thinking?

'Change your mind, Kate,' he urged softly.

She looked away and hurried into speech. 'I liked Sarah and Mitch.'

He sighed. 'They're nice people.' His voice was pitched low and slightly husky. 'They liked you too, Katrine. Katrine,' he repeated, the word rolling about his tongue. 'Do you know what your name sounds like? The brush of silk on soft scented skin. Katrine.'

Kate smothered a gasp. She had never thought that the mere saying of her name could have so many nuances, and all of them raising the fine hairs on her skin. To combat a sudden breathlessness, she declared, 'I prefer Kate.'

Aidan's bark of laughter was oddly harsh. 'Of course you do.'

'Don't try to seduce me, Aidan,' she warned tautly.

'Could I?' His voice mocked her, and she gritted her teeth.

'I won't fall for that line a second time!'

'Won't you?'

She gasped. 'I hate you!'

'Really? But then, you hate all men, don't you, my little Ice Queen?'

It was a statement, not a question, and one she was grateful not to be obliged to answer, for they drew up outside their hotel. But she was aware of a sharp thrust of pain at his scorn. Because it wasn't true. She didn't hate him—not all the time. There was just no percentage in liking him, and falling in love was out of the question. Not that she was likely to fall in love with him. She wasn't that stupid!

CHAPTER SEVEN

As SHE had feared, the nightmare came. It crept into her sleep in the darkest, loneliest hours of the night, when her defences were at their lowest ebb. Now the shadows were gaining substance, and the terror intensified. She was in a room, a strange room dominated by a bed. A room so large she couldn't see the corners, but she knew that something evil lurked in the darkness beyond her vision. And though she knew, she couldn't move to run or fight it off as it came inexorably closer.

Beneath the sheets of the hotel bed, Kate's moans grew increasingly louder, her head thrashing from side to side as she witnessed her dream-self remain still, even though she willed it to move, to run. But there was no escape, and she wept and cried out—a sound to chill the heart. Then, as the oppressive darkness crowded in, she heard her name, faint and far off, but getting stronger, nearer.

'Kate!'

The voice was sharp, the hand on her shoulder imperative. With a gasp she obeyed, opening eyes still dark and haunted by terror. The transition to waking was instant, but the fear remained with her. She saw Aidan sitting on her bed in the low glow of a lamp, his hand still on her shoulder, and her heart jerked.

'What?' The sound was thready and fearful.

Aidan frowned, grey eyes reflecting concern. 'You called out in your sleep. You were crying.'

Her hand went to her cheek, feeling the moisture there. 'Oh, God!' The thing she had feared most had happened. She drew in a shaky breath. 'I'm sorry I woke you.'

He let that pass, eyes watchful. 'That was some nightmare you were having. I take it you've had it before?'

'Yes.' She ran a hand through her hair. It was damp with sweat, and the silk pyjamas she had put on earlier were clinging uncomfortably to her skin. It had been a bad one tonight, and the awful thing was that it was becoming clearer. Each night there was more revealed, and the fear grew apace with it. Shivering in reaction, Kate sat up against the pillows and closed her eyes. How much more could she take? These dreams were heading her somewhere, and she was scared, really scared of what she might discover.

She flicked a glance at Aidan, caught the glow of the lamp on his naked chest and hastily looked away. Tonight they had shared a room, and she had seen so much more in her dreams. Could there be a connection? Those other incidents—once he had touched her, the other he had used that name. Perhaps it was only coincidence, but something was happening. Yet, undeniably, twice he had called her back from the edge of something too terrible. Lord, how she wished she understood!

Licking her lips, she looked at him once more. 'I'll be all right now,' she lied, knowing it was doubtful if she'd sleep again tonight.

'Sure you will,' he agreed sceptically. 'I'll get you some water.' He disappeared into the bathroom and was back again in seconds with a tumbler. Handing it to her, he resumed his seat, watching as she drained it. 'Feeling better?' He relieved her of the glass and set it aside. 'Care to talk about it? Something must have triggered it off.'

Still strung out, she very nearly laughed. Her husband was the last person with whom she could ever discuss her bad dreams. How could she say, 'I think it's you,' when she still couldn't explain it herself? So instead she lied. 'There wouldn't be much point. Once I wake up, it's gone.'

'You were struggling as if your life depended on it when I tried to wake you. What were you protecting so fiercely?'

Drawing up her knees, she propped her head on them. 'I told you, I don't remember,' she gritted through her teeth. A sudden welling of hot tears stung the back of her eyes. 'I don't remember,' she added despairingly.

Watching her downbent head, Aidan chose his next words carefully. 'Do you want to?' he asked gently.

She looked up, eyes wild. 'Have you been sent to torment me?'

His eyes narrowed. 'Is that what you think?'

'I don't know! I don't know anything any more. I don't...' she dropped her head '...think you'd better take any notice of me. I'm so tired. So very, very tired. This isn't me talking. You know it isn't.' Her voice fell to a whisper he had to strain to hear. 'Don't nightmares ever end?'

'The night-time ones, almost always.'

'But they don't. They don't,' she contradicted brokenly.

Sighing, he brushed the hair from where it clung to her cheek. 'This one has, for now. Go to sleep, Kate, you're burned out. There's nothing to fear. I'm here. You're not alone now.'

Not alone. It sounded so good. She'd been alone for such a long time now. Her eyes probed his for long seconds before finally she lay down again, hugging the covers to her chin. She looked at him in confusion. 'Why are you being kind to me?'

Standing up, he switched off the light. 'Everyone deserves a little kindness sometimes, Kate.' His voice reached her through the darkness. 'Go to sleep.'

Kate closed her eyes, not expecting to sleep, but it rolled over her in waves, and this time there were no dreams to disturb her. It was Aidan who lay awake in the darkness thinking.

The next time Kate stirred, pale winter sunlight was filtering through a crack in the heavy curtains. Brushing the hair from her eyes, she focused on the clock. It showed a little after nine. Her first thought was that she was late for work, then memory returned, and she quickly glanced over her shoulder at the other bed. It was empty, and she subsided with a sigh of relief.

She was glad of these moments alone to get her thoughts together. The nightmare was as vivid as always, but so were other, more disturbing things. She remembered Aidan and his unexpected kindness—and, more uncomfortably, she recalled the things she had said. How could she have been so stupid? Now he was no longer guessing, he knew something was wrong. What sort of feeble idiot did he think she was now, unable to cope with a bad dream?

It was with a crawling sense of embarrassment that Kate showered and dressed in tailored black trousers and a burgundy sweater. Every time she thought of what had passed, she cringed, and that made her furious with herself. She was just zipping on a pair of high-heeled ankle-boots when Aidan appeared in the doorway. She glanced up and in silence they stared at each other while the heat rose in her cheeks.

'Good morning,' he greeted gently.

In her sensitive state, she fancied she saw pity in his eyes, and, immediately defensive, she snapped back, 'Is it?' and glanced away.

Unseen, his brows rose. 'I've seen worse for the time of year.'

She refused to look at him. 'Really?'

Now his lips did curve. 'What's the matter, Kate?' That question, too, was gentle.

A lump rose in her throat. 'Nothing. I overslept, and I don't like it. You should have woken me.' With nowhere else to go, her anger was channelled towards him.

Aidan merely shrugged. 'There's no rush. The snow stopped during the night, so, providing we don't leave it too late, we should make Washington without any trouble. I ordered breakfast. Ten minutes, OK?'

'Fine,' she said shortly. Did he have to be so cheerful? Why couldn't he be distant or angry? Angry was much better. 'I'll be there. I've almost finished, but I'll get on faster with you out of the way!'

Unperturbed, he laughed. 'That sounds like my marching orders. Oh, and by the way, I like your hair like that. It's softer. It suits you.' With another brief smile he disappeared again.

Bemused, she stared after him, then, irritated out of all proportion by her reaction, she tugged at the zipper, caught her finger in the teeth, and swore, pungently. Stomping over to the mirror, she glared at her reflection. Her hair hung about her face in a silver cloud. She had brushed it till it shone, but hadn't pinned it up. Yes, it looked softer, but it made her face look vulnerable. So he liked it, did he? Why? Because he thought she was a soft touch after last night? Ready to reveal everything? Well, he was damn well wrong! With angry movements she pinned every last wisp of it back into its pleat.

Keeping her make-up to a minimum, Kate walked into the sitting-room just as the breakfast trolley was being wheeled in. As she seated herself at the table by the window, she was aware of Aidan's quizzical glance at her hair, but he said nothing until they were alone.

'I suppose if I'd said I liked it pinned up, you'd have let your hair hang free, you perverse little madam!' he mocked derisively.

Because it was all too true, her reply was short and snappy. 'Not at all. Nothing you said would influence me one way or another. I happen to like my hair up. It keeps it out of the way while I'm working.'

'Ah, I see,' Aidan murmured as he poured coffee for them both. 'But you're not working now,' he pointed out reasonably. 'So why don't you let it down?'

'Because...' she began, only to falter at the challenging look in his eye. For no accountable reason, her heart kicked.

A slow smile curved his lips. 'Because then you wouldn't look like the woman you want me to believe you are?' he supplied for her.

Now she knew she was right to be worried. How he had arrived at that deduction, she had no idea, but that he had was alarming enough. This had to stop now. She forced a laugh from her tight throat. 'You're being ridiculous,' she informed him, reaching for her coffee. 'A hairstyle is a hairstyle.'

'And a fraud is a fraud.'

The cup she had been raising to her lips almost fell from her nerveless fingers, and she set it down hastily. 'Fraud?' She strove to be casual, but somehow it came out on a quaver. She would have got up and walked out if there had been any strength in her legs, but as it was she had to remain and face this startling turn of events.

Aidan helped himself to ham and eggs before carrying on. 'I did some serious thinking last night, after your nightmare,' he revealed, bringing colour to her pale cheeks.

Kate saw a means of diverting him and jumped at it. 'Actually, I was meaning to talk to you about that,' she interrupted swiftly.

He looked up. 'Really? You're not eating. Aren't you hungry?'

She automatically reached for a slice of toast, feeling she was being reeled in by an expert. Abandoning the food to her plate, she took a deep breath and tried again. 'I wanted to apologise for disturbing you. I think I made rather a fool of myself.'

'Do you?'

It wasn't a statement she'd expected to be questioned, even as mildly as he did, and it put her right off balance. 'Don't you?' she snapped.

Aidan shook his head. 'No.'

Feeling hounded, Kate threw up her hands. 'I don't understand you!' she cried.

If it was possible for a broad smile to broaden, his did then. 'That's a pity, because I think I'm beginning to understand you.'

Icy fingers of warning chased their way along her spine. 'I don't want you to understand me,' she declared through her teeth, and then could have bitten her tongue out at the impulsively revealing words.

'I know you don't, but I told you yesterday you couldn't stop me,' he told her while munching on some toast. Kate, appetite vanishing, watched him, feeling vaguely nauseous. 'Want to know what I came up with?'

'No,' she rejoined pointedly, hands clenching into fists. 'But somehow I don't think that's going to stop you telling me.'

His laugh was appreciative. 'You see, you do understand me after all. But we were talking about you, Kate. Not only are you a fraud, but you're an illusionist too. The swiftness of the tongue deceives the eye.'

Expecting more along lines that already set her nerves jangling, Kate was surprised when he stopped. 'Is that it?' she demanded in disbelief.

'There is one other thing,' he informed her ominously.

'And that is?'

'I think you ought to know that I don't believe the Ice Queen exists.'

Shocked, her mouth went dry. 'You know she does. You've seen her yourself,' she insisted, fighting a desperate rearguard battle for her defences—her only defences.

Aidan shook his head. 'Perhaps she did, but not any more. Oh, she tries to. Every now and again when you're under threat, there she is, but you can't maintain it. So why don't you let her go, Kate? You don't need her any more,' he urged gently.

'I do——'

'No you don't,' he interrupted. 'She's lost her street credibility, at least with me. You may have needed her once. I don't believe you need her now, unless you think I'm a real threat, and I'm not, Kate. Hopefully, you'll soon come to believe me.'

'And then what?' she croaked, helplessly.

'Then, my dear Kate, we can begin to help you.'

Her hands balled into fists. 'I've told you——'

'And I've heard you. Think about it. Don't make any quick decisions. Forget the past. Start here and now.'

Kate stared at him, unsure just what was going on behind that charming face. Overnight he had changed tack, leaving her floundering helplessly in his wake. She was a good swimmer, but suddenly she seriously doubted that that would be enough. Yet she had to try, for pride, if nothing else. How bitterly she regretted that lapse last night, for she was paying for it now.

'I don't understand why you're doing this,' she observed shakily, striving for normality by sipping at her coffee and grimacing at its cold bitterness.

Obligingly, Aidan poured her a fresh cup. 'I know, but you will in time.'

Hot coffee went a long way to restoring her equilibrium. 'On the whole, I think I prefer you ranting and raving at me.'

'Of course you do,' he agreed easily, 'but that's because people in a temper very rarely see further than the end of their own anger.'

'I think you're a very devious, dangerous man,' Kate declared with a sense of being caught tighter and tighter in a trap.

Aidan merely smiled that enigmatic smile that was beginning to grate on her nerves. 'Remind me to tell you about Abraham Lincoln some time.' Draining the dregs from a second cup of coffee, he pushed himself to his feet. 'I'm going to pack while you finish your breakfast. I've ordered a hire car for ten-thirty.' He stopped behind her as he passed. 'On second thoughts, keep your hair up, Kate. I've just discovered you've got a deliciously inviting nape.'

Before she had any idea of what he intended to do, he had done it. Warm lips brushed the tender cord. Kate gasped as tiny electric shocks tingled down her spine, creating havoc with her breathing. She jerked away, and Aidan uttered a husky laugh.

'Just checking,' he excused himself, and went on his way.

At the table, Kate sagged in her seat, feeling drained. She couldn't believe what she had just been through. She had a panicky sense of having walked into the wrong play, where, though everything looked familiar, she had no idea what was going on. Which wasn't strictly true. She had created a mystery and he wanted to solve it. This was just another try from a different angle. Like his seduction number last night. Well, she was forewarned now, and wasn't about to fall for it. She wasn't a source of free entertainment!

And yet ... He had sounded so sincere. She groaned aloud. What on earth was she going to do?

It had snowed quite heavily overnight, but the snow-ploughs had been out on the highways and they had no trouble leaving the city and heading for the capital. The car was a Mercedes and very luxurious, and Kate was content to simply sit back in comfort and watch the world go by. Aidan was a good driver, taking account of the conditions, and she felt perfectly safe with him.

It was a novel sensation, and her mind dwelt on it as she looked out at the snowy landscape. It gave her other things to consider. If she felt safe with him, could she also trust him? More importantly perhaps, would she respond as she did to someone who was basically untrustworthy? She didn't think so. But emotions were fickle; they didn't need only good ground in which to grow. So how on earth was she to decide who to trust—and did she really want to? If only she knew why he was really doing this. What did he want of her? What did *she* want of him? Why were there only questions and no answers?

She tried to think of something else, but that merely replaced one anxiety with another. The meeting with his father and stepmother was not one she was looking forward to. There was just no way she could imagine them welcoming her, knowing who she was and what she had done. All right, she was making amends, but that would hardly endear her to them.

Feeling the tension starting to mount as the miles ticked past, she sought for another diversion, and said the first thing that came into her head. 'You were going to tell me about the President.'

So abruptly did she break the silence that had settled about them that it had Aidan's head snapping round, and very nearly deposited them in the ditch.

Muttering curses under his breath, he straightened the car. 'For God's sake! What were you trying to do? Kill us both?'

Alarm at how close they had come to a real accident made her snappy. 'Perish the thought!'

'Perish is right!' he growled back instantly, then sighed. 'Now what's this about Bush?'

'Not Bush. President Lincoln.'

'Lincoln?' She could see him frown, then the moment light dawned. 'Abraham Lincoln! Ah!' A smile curved his lips. 'Abraham Lincoln, Kate, was a wiry little terrier. He stood so high, but he had a bark like a wolfhound. We got him from the SPCA. He'd been badly mistreated by his owner, but instead of cowering, as you might expect, he'd come out snapping and snarling. You see, he didn't trust anybody, so he attacked everyone. But his eyes... You could see in his eyes that he wanted to be loved. He wanted someone to say, Hey, I don't care how much you bite, I'm going to love you anyway. That's why I took him home. We had some royal battles, but in the end he accepted me and trusted me.'

Kate listened in stricken silence, a huge lump of emotion filling her chest. There was a warmth in his voice that curled fingers about her heart—choking her so that she couldn't breathe.

'Stop the car!' she ordered hoarsely.

Aidan shot her an alarmed glance. 'What's wrong?'

Wrong? 'Just stop the damn car!' she ordered again, and when he pulled over to the side of the road her fumbling fingers found the catch, and she stumbled out into the cold, biting air. Huddling her coat about her, she took a couple of slithery steps away from the car and drew in air in a gulp.

Snow crunched underfoot, but she didn't need that to tell her Aidan had joined her. The hairs on her neck were already at attention. 'What are you trying to do to me?' The words were broken, painful.

Hands stuffed into the pockets of his fleecy-lined denim jacket, Aidan eyed her back watchfully. His breath froze in the air as he said slowly, 'I'm trying to get you to trust me, so that I can help you. I told you about Abe because you're so like him. You strike out, snapping and snarling, making everyone think you're wild and vicious. When all you're really doing is protecting yourself behind a mask.'

Kate paled. It was as if he could really see inside her, see things that nobody else did. He was stripping her layer by layer, leaving her with the frightening feeling that nothing was safe from him. There was no secret he wouldn't find. No truth he wouldn't unveil.

With a heavy sigh, Aidan reached out his hands and turned her round. His face was pale and full of gentle concern. 'Kate, you've got to trust somebody some time.'

She shrugged him off. 'Why can't you just let me be?'

'Because I've never been the sort to pass by on the other side.'

'Try it once, you could get to like it!' she riposted like a ricochet, knowing she was losing ground to his gentleness.

Aidan half smiled. 'Snap away. I've got thick skin.'

He was telling her!

She looked helplessly up at his grimly determined face. He wasn't going to give up! He'd work on her like that dog until he'd won her over!

Gentle fingers reached up to brush a tendril of hair from her eyes. 'Whatever it is, Kate, you don't have to face it on your own any more.'

Her throat closed over. Oh, God, why had he had to say that? Lord knew she had had enough. It was so tempting to give in to the sound of his voice and the look in his eyes. She was so tired of fighting this fear on her own. Why fight it? Why not, just once, lean on someone who was stronger than her? She dropped her lids over gritty eyes. 'All right,' she said in a small, defeated voice.

For a brief moment Aidan closed his eyes and breathed in deeply. When he looked at her again, his expression was cautious. 'Do you want to sit in the car?'

Kate shook her head, knowing she would have to speak now or she would lose her nerve. 'No.' She turned away, pulling her collar up about her ears. Her eyes travelled over the frozen beauty of the winter landscape. 'There's not much to tell, not really. I have these . . . nightmares. You know that. At first I couldn't remember what happened in them, I only knew the fear I felt.' She swallowed hard. It was painful to reveal it all. 'They started from nowhere.'

'Not nowhere. Wasn't it when you met me?'

The soft question drew her round, her eyes large in her pale face. 'Yes. How . . . ?'

'I'm not blind, Kate. I've seen the changes this past week,' Aidan supplied. 'But that's not all, is it?'

'No,' she agreed huskily and cleared her throat. 'They've started to become much clearer. Each time there's more.' She shuddered, and at once he closed the distance between them and enclosed her in the strength of his arms.

She didn't even think of fighting him.

'Tell me.'

She closed her eyes, hand clutching the cloth of his jacket. 'I feel fear. I can't see it, but it's there, oppressing me. I want to run, but I can't. I'm trapped in a large room and all I can see is me and a bed. Oh, God! I want to run so badly, but I can't. It's . . . horrible!' She shuddered violently.

'Ssh.' His hand came up to stroke her hair. 'Poor Kate, no wonder you're scared. You shouldn't have kept this to yourself for so long.'

'I thought it was only the dreams, but...I'm seeing things in the daytime too. Oh, God, Aidan, it frightens me so.' She looked up at him in undisguised anguish. 'Am I going crazy?'

'No!' he denied forcefully. 'Don't ever think that. I'm no psychiatrist, Kate, but it seems to me that the dreams are your subconscious mind's way of revealing something you've blocked out. If I'm right, it must have been something pretty bad for you to blank it out. I know you're frightened, but it's something you're going to have to face in order to heal. I'd like you to see...a friend of mine. You'll like her. I've never known her to be anything but kind and understanding. I think she'll confirm what I've said, but, whatever the outcome, you won't be facing it alone, Kate. I'll be with you every step of the way.'

Her eyes probed his. 'How can you say that when this marriage is only temporary?' The thought brought a dart of pain to the region of her heart.

His arms tightened. 'I have no intention of abandoning you, Kate.'

She looked away, resting her head on his shoulder, enjoying the sheer male smell of him as she breathed in. It felt so right, so good. Yet she feared to trust it. 'I don't know why you're doing this.'

'Does there have to be a motive? Do you always suspect everyone? People do do things purely out of a sincere wish to help.'

'Not in my experience,' she said painfully.

'That was unfortunate.' He sighed. 'This is different.'

'How can I be sure of that?'

'Because your instincts tell you to trust me.'

He was right, they did. Why else did it feel so comfortable and safe in his arms? She couldn't ever remember feeling so protected. After years of fighting in the wilderness, it felt so good to surrender her arms. She had found that magical peace she hadn't even known she was searching for.

'Kate, do you think you were raped?'

The soft question brought her head up, breaking the spell. 'Raped? I...don't know.' Could she have been? But surely if she had, she wouldn't respond to Aidan as she did, would she?

'Never mind, it just seemed to fit what you've told me. Forget it for now. Just remember, you don't have to be afraid alone. I'll help you, Kate. You have my solemn promise.' He smiled down at her.

The warmth she saw made her feel strange inside. Uncertain, and suddenly embarrassed at the way she was still clinging to him, Kate stepped back. 'Don't make promises you can't keep,' she advised stiffly.

He turned her round, the arm he placed about her shoulder pointing her towards the car. 'When you know me better, you'll know I never do,' he said calmly.

Vitally aware of the solid strength of him, Kate chewed her lip. Did she want to know him better? Right this second she didn't feel she knew anything—except that she felt strangely bereft when he removed his arm to allow her to get into the car again.

Seconds later they were on their way again. Kate sat in silence, her mind going over all that had happened. Trust him, he said. There were no strings. Yet there had to be a motive. Nobody made the kind of commitment he just had without reason. Or did they? Were her suspicions a hangover from the old Kate? What did she know of him? Only his anger. Perhaps this wasn't out of character for him. Perhaps she ought to revise her opinion of him. After all, that was based on her own misconceptions. So wouldn't it be wise to suspend judgement and wait and see what happened next?

Yes, that was what she would do. Besides, she needed the breathing-space. So much had happened so quickly that she sometimes felt in a permanent daze. With any luck she might also find out what it was about him that made her react to him the way she did. She needed to know that, desperately.

They stopped for a late lunch at a restaurant that seemed straight out of Washington Irving. Kate could feel the atmosphere in the genuine oak beams and latticed windows, and for no accountable reason felt all the tension ease away.

'I thought you'd appreciate it,' Aidan declared watching her take it all in.

She smiled back at him. 'Oh, I do. It's lovely. Do you come here often?'

'I try to when I visit Dad. If you like, I can show you some of the sights of Washington while we're here.'

'I thought you'd have work to do.' Surprise mingled with a wave of pleasure.

Aidan shrugged. 'Nothing that can't wait. So, what do you say?'

'I say yes, thank you. I'd love that,' she responded without hesitation, but the warmth in his eyes made her suddenly self-conscious, and she looked down at her drink, confused by new and conflicting emotions.

The meal was as good as the atmosphere suggested and Kate found herself relaxing more and more as she listened to Aidan talking. Her eyes were drawn to him constantly, eating up every expression. She found herself laughing at the tales he told her of holidays in the Adirondacks, even joining in with one or two stories of her own. She enjoyed his amusement. Aidan had a deep warm laugh that set his eyes alight and took years off him. Kate was fascinated by the swiftly changing moods that crossed his face as he spoke.

She knew he was talking to put her at her ease, and she was grateful, but as time passed she forgot even that. He was weaving a spell about her that made the cold outside disappear, shrinking the world to the golden circle of light thrown by the lamp above them. She could have stayed there forever, watching his hands as they moved to illustrate his point. The intrusion of the real world, via the latest weather forecast, made her feel she was losing something special.

Sitting in the car on the final leg of the journey, she found her eyes still drawn to him as he concentrated on his driving. A stray lock of hair had fallen over his brow and she automatically reached out and brushed it back. He flicked her a glance then, and smiled, and her heart turned over.

She returned her glance to the world outside, heart beating erratically. Dear heaven, it would be so easy to fall in love with him. It was a statement that set her on a seesaw of emotions. She couldn't have already done so, could she? Was that what all this was about? All the swings of mood, the uncertainty and confusion? She'd never been in love, so she didn't know. Wouldn't it be the height of insanity to love Aidan Crawford?

Her eyes sought their reflection in the glass. Was it already too late?

By mid-afternoon they had reached Washington. His father and stepmother lived in the suburbs, in a large, rambling house set in its own grounds. They must have been listening out for the car, for no sooner had Aidan parked in the driveway than the front door opened and three dogs rushed out, closely followed by two humans.

While Aidan dealt with a more vociferous welcome, it was left up to his father to help Kate from the car. Which he did with a smile in which she could detect no hint of reserve. He was a tall man, like his son. In fact, the likeness was striking. Except that Aidan Crawford Senior's hair was pure white. This, Kate thought, is what Aidan will look like in years to come, and the thought was oddly comforting.

'So, you're Kate,' his father declared with a curious glint in his eye, not unreminiscent of his son. 'You stirred up a fine hornets' nest, young lady.'

Kate flushed to the roots of her hair. 'I know. I'm sorry. I ought to explain——'

'No need,' he cut her off. 'You had your reasons. If Aidan knows and understands, that's good enough for us. Welcome to the family.' He proceeded to kiss her on both cheeks.

'Yes indeed, you're very welcome, Kate,' his wife Netta added, but Kate knew instantly that the woman wasn't as sure as the man that her presence was a good thing. She was reserving judgement. Something Kate could fully understand and accept. Nevertheless, she received a swift hug from the woman who, though neat as a pin and with salt and pepper hair, barely reached Kate's shoulder.

'It's freezing out here,' Netta hurried on, taking Kate's arm. 'I'll take Kate inside and make some tea while you deal with the luggage.' She gave her new daughter-in-law a conspiratorial wink. 'They'll turn up in half an hour or so, knowing them, but I don't propose to freeze to death. We'll leave them to it. Aidan tells me you run your own modelling agency. That must be fascinating.'

Thirty minutes later, when indeed the men did finally come in, Kate and Netta were on their second cup of tea before a blazing fire in the sitting-room. Conversation had been easy, for Netta had the knack of putting people at their ease. However, Kate knew she hadn't imagined that hint of reserve, though she hadn't met it again. She realised that Netta's protective instinct was strong, but, as Aidan had said, she was prepared to give the younger woman the benefit of the doubt.

'Any chance of some of that for us?' Aidan Senior asked as he came to toast his hands over the flames.

Netta stood up. 'I'll make some fresh. What did you do with the dogs?'

'Shut up in the den. Aidan didn't know if Kate liked them,' he called after his wife, then turned to his daughter-in-law. 'How are you with dogs, Kate? I hope to God you're as daft about them as my son is. All three are his.'

Kate moved up as Aidan came to sit beside her on the couch. 'We always had dogs when Philip was alive.'

Aidan Senior nodded. 'Ah, yes, your brother. That was a sorry business, Kate. I liked your father very much. You have my assurance that, had I known, I would most certainly have helped. Cold comfort, I know. I can only apologise for Andrew. I'm afraid there's a devil in him that *I* could never control, and *he* was never willing to try to. His mother and I divorced when the boys were quite young. It seemed the ideal arrangement to take one each. Andrew was her favourite, and that was his undoing. She never could curb his excesses, and now, of course, it's much too late. You could say I got the better bargain. Aidan was easy to raise, never giving me a day's worry more than a growing boy should. But it's the weak who really need our help, not the strong. I'll always wonder if Andrew might have turned out differently if he had come to me.'

'He would only have pretended to change,' his son put in wryly. 'And that would have been worse, Dad. You can't blame yourself for anything. He was just born wild.'

Aidan Senior came and laid a hand on his son's shoulder, squeezing firmly. 'I know, son. We all love him, and make excuses. But one day, mark my words, he'll go too far, and do something that we can't forgive him for. I'll tell you now, it's not a day I look forward to.' He sighed heavily, looked at Kate and smiled. 'But we were talking about the dogs. You'll like these. All of them are daft as a brush. Get Aidan to introduce you to them later, then we'll let them loose.'

Netta returned then, carrying a fresh tray of tea, and overheard the last part of the conversation. 'The only thing you need worry about is that they'll lick you to death!' she declared drily. 'By the way, Aidan, we've put you in the main guest room. It will be yours and Kate's room now. We've moved most of your things across, but we've left you to arrange it how you like.'

Kate felt the tension in Aidan immediately, but when she glanced at him he was smiling. 'Thanks, Netta. I'll have that tea first, then we'll go up and unpack.'

A quarter of an hour later, he led the way upstairs, carrying their cases. Outside one door, he stopped and set down a case, reaching for the handle. He paused then, giving her a long sideways look before shrugging mentally and swinging the door open.

'This is our room,' he said in a curiously flat tone, and stood back to allow her to precede him.

Already tense from picking up the vibrations from him, Kate stepped inside, and knew immediately why he had been acting so strangely. It was a beautiful room, decorated in cheery spring tones, but there was only one bed.

Behind her, Aidan set the cases down and closed the door. 'I'm afraid I hadn't given much thought to the sleeping arrangements once we got here. But I'm sure you know you have nothing to fear from me. As you can see, it's a big bed. We won't even have to touch.'

'No, we won't,' she agreed as she crossed to the window, pretending to take an interest in the snow-covered grounds. It wasn't fear that dried her mouth at the thought of sharing the bed with him, but something that set her heart beating erratically in her chest. In the glass, she saw Aidan come up behind her. Saw his hands lift, then hesitate a second before he rested them lightly on her shoulders. Their warmth seeped into her, relaxing the tension in her muscles. Their eyes locked in the glass. He smiled and she gave in to the temptation to lean back against him. Only his fingers tightened abruptly, halting the movement before they could touch.

'You know, in days gone by, a knight would lay his sword down the middle of the bed as his pledge of honour,' he told her in a low voice.

There was something in his tone that made her stiffen. 'What are you trying to say?'

Aidan released her, hands thrusting into his pockets as she turned round. 'I guess I'm trying, not very clearly, to say that you needn't fear I'll try to make love to you.'

A hot tide of embarrassment stained her cheeks. 'Oh, I see.' Ducking her head, she brushed past him, going to their cases. What a fool! What an idiot! How obtuse could she be? He was trying to tell her he wasn't interested. As kindly as he could, considering she had virtually issued a silent invitation. Kindness, she knew now, was one of his strong points. It wasn't his fault she had embarrassed herself. Nor could he know how that gentle rejection hurt.

She rallied quickly, but her laugh had a brittle quality. 'Well, that's a load off my mind. Now I'd better unpack. I'll do yours for you too, if you like,' she gabbled to hide the fact that something inside her had suffered a deep wound.

Behind her, Aidan gave her an odd look as he lifted his case on to the bed. 'Thanks, I'll take you up on that. I hate unpacking.' With a smile he left her to it.

Kate slumped down on to the bed as the door closed behind him. Aidan was treating her like a big brother, and instead of being relieved she felt cheated. She didn't want a brother, she wanted . . . A moan escaped her. Oh, lord, she *had* fallen in love with him. Friendship wasn't enough—not nearly enough! She wanted everything from him, no half measures. The depth of her feeling was shocking. How had it happened so quickly?

She didn't know, she only knew it was so, and that in the face of his brotherliness it was hopeless. He didn't want her and the wisest thing she could do was follow his lead and salvage a little of her pride. She might have done a foolish thing, but she needn't compound it by letting him know.

They took the dogs for a walk after dinner, and returned to mugs of hot chocolate and marshmallow. It had been an exhausting day, and in no time Kate was almost nodding over her drink. She didn't protest when Aidan drew her to her feet, but wished his parents goodnight and followed him from the room.

In their bedroom, Aidan gathered up his robe. 'You take the bathroom, I'll use the one down the hall.'

Kate watched him go out again with mixed emotions. He was being thoughtful, and she knew she should be grateful, but the fact was she wasn't. It was a hopeless situation. So funny, she'd end up crying in a minute! Biting down hard on her lip, she gathered up her nightdress and headed for the bathroom.

She hoped to have been in bed before Aidan returned, but he was already there when she stepped out of the bathroom. Her stomach clenched on a scalding wave of desire as she saw him relaxed against the pillows, naked to the waist.

She must have paled because Aidan's tone was sharp as he said her name. She stared into her husband's concerned grey eyes.

'Are you OK?' he asked, making to get out of the bed.

'Of course,' she said swiftly, stalling the movement.

'I thought you'd had one of those flashes,' he went on.

Flustered, she made a business of hanging up her clothes. 'No. My head thumped, that was all. It's probably just a headache,' she lied.

It took all of her nerve to cross to the bed and climb beneath the covers as if she hadn't a care in the world. Stiff with tension, she lay as far away from him as she could, lest she betrayed herself by touching him as she longed to do. She held her breath when the bed rocked as Aidan turned the light out. Ears straining in the darkness, she waited for the change in his breathing as he fell asleep. Only then did she begin to relax, despairing that she would ever be able to sleep herself. But her exhausted body took charge at last, drawing her over the edge into an uneasy sleep.

Her own scream woke her hours later, and she found herself sitting up in the darkness, shaking as with an ague, tears streaming down her face.

Everything seemed to happen at once. Beside her, Aidan was shaken into immediate wakefulness, hand shooting out to switch on the light as he too sat up. As he did so, the door burst open, showing his father and Netta framed in the doorway, their faces wearing identical expressions of shock and alarm.

Still shaking, Kate dropped her head in her hands and turned to him. Aidan's arms enclosed her at once. Over her shoulder he glanced at his father and stepmother.

'Good lord, Aidan, what happened? Is Kate all right?' Netta's voice was shaken.

'It's a nightmare. She's had them before,' Aidan explained shortly.

'Is there anything we can do, son?' his father asked, frowning in concern.

'Thanks, Dad, but I don't think so. We can cope. You go back to bed.'

'Well, all right, but you know where I am if you need me,' Netta offered.

They left reluctantly, leaving the couple on the bed alone.

At once Kate groaned. 'Oh, God!' she choked out huskily.

'You screamed. Can you remember why?'

She shuddered. 'He was laughing,' she admitted sickly, recalling it all.

'He?' Aidan prompted. 'Kate, you've got to tell me who,' he urged.

'I don't know who...I couldn't see. It's all...bits. I remember stairs...and laughter. Gloating, horrible...a man's laugh. Oh, God!' she sobbed into his shoulder.

'It's OK. It's OK. It's over now,' he soothed her like a child.

Swallowing hard, she found some control. 'I'm scared. What does it mean?'

'I don't know, Kate. I only wish I did, so I could spare you this.' His voice was a groan muffled by her hair.

Kate slipped her arms around his waist. 'Hold me. Don't let me go,' she pleaded raggedly.

'I won't, sweetheart. Hush now, don't cry any more.' He lay down with her in his arms, pulling the covers up over them, then finally switching off the light.

For Kate the minutes seemed to go by like hours, but slowly the tremors began to die away, until finally they stopped altogether. She was aware of the warmth that came from him seeping into her rigid muscles, easing their awful tension. Occasionally a shudder would rack her, but they, too, became less frequent. She became aware of his heart beating solidly under her ear, a steady, comforting sound. She wanted it never to end. She wanted to stay in his arms forever. If only he could love her as she loved him. If only... A tiny sighing breath escaped her lips, and her fingers slowly uncurled. Her eyelids dropped.

She slipped into sleep with a soft whimper that reminded the man who held her of a lost child. Heaving a deep sigh, he closed his own eyes at last.

CHAPTER EIGHT

KATE stirred with a wonderful feeling of warmth and
security. The reason for it eluded her until she sighed
and stretched, and became aware of the warm body
pressed close to hers. She remembered then the
nightmare, and how Aidan had comforted her until she
had fallen asleep in his arms.

A slow smile spread across her lips, she felt comfortable, protected—safe in a way she had never experienced before. Some time during the night they had
moved, and now they lay spoon-fashion, his arm a
pleasurable weight about her waist. She knew she ought
to move, but she wanted to savour this moment for as
long as possible. Fantasise a little that he held her like
this because he loved her. She felt ready to purr, and
like a cat, had an instinctive desire to curl up and go to
sleep again.

Only it wasn't to be. Behind her Aidan stirred. His
arm tightened fractionally about her and her heart
skipped a beat as she heard him give a satisfied sigh.

'Mmm, this is nice,' he murmured, voice still husky
from sleep.

It brought goose-pimples out on her flesh, and a re-
surgence of that flash-flood wave of desire. It also
brought a swift dart of pain, because clearly he didn't
recall who he was holding so tightly. The danger was
that she wanted to stay there, pretend he did know. But
it was a destructive temptation that could only embarrass
them both. So she swallowed hard and did the only thing
she could.

'I think I'd better get up,' she suggested, sounding just as husky as he did.

Expecting him to let her go immediately, having recognised her voice, it was a shock when he merely groaned, moving closer. 'Do you want to? Myself, I could stay like this for ever.'

Her eyes rounded like saucers. It wasn't fair that he should tempt her so. Gritting her teeth, she made herself go rigid. 'Aidan! This is me, Kate, remember!' she pointed out tautly.

Sighing, he came up on one elbow to look down at her. 'I remember,' he murmured, sleepy eyes roving warmly over her, starting up flash-fires that pinkened her cheeks. 'Good morning.'

Oh, lord, why did he have to have eyes you could drown in? She couldn't think of one sensible thing to say.

'Lost your tongue?' he teased, smiling easily.

Bewildered, she lay transfixed, quite forgetting all the reasons why she should move. 'This is silly.'

His eyes grew warmer. 'That's not the adjective I'd use. Do you know, you're a very cosy armful, Kate Crawford?'

Her heart started a reckless beat. 'No, but you hum it and I'll join in,' she quipped breathlessly.

He laughed, a sound that warmed her to the core. 'Ah, Kate, you're a woman after my own heart. I knew I couldn't be wrong. Where have you been all my life?'

Perhaps it was reckless to allow this to go on, but she didn't care, even if she had to pay for it afterwards in heartache. Just this once she wanted to throw caution to the wind. She peeked at him from under her lashes. 'Part of it, I wasn't even born.'

'I'm not that old!' he protested, then sobered a little. 'How do you feel today?'

'Much better, thanks to you,' she answered truthfully. But for him, she wouldn't have slept at all.

'No hangover?'

Surprised, she hadn't thought about it, but there was none of the usual dread. 'No,' she said, smiling with relief.

'That's good,' Aidan murmured, moving so that she shifted on to her back. 'Because I have a confession to make. I would very much like to make love to you, Kate Crawford.'

She gasped. 'W-what? But I thought...'

His finger came up to press against her lips. 'I know you did, but you got the wrong end of the stick.' His voice thickened. 'I want you very much, but yesterday was the wrong time.'

She wasn't stupid. She knew he wasn't saying he loved her. Knew, too, that he would accept her refusal if that was what she wanted. He was leaving it entirely up to her. But she didn't want to refuse. She loved him. For a little while he could be hers. If that was foolish, only she would know. She wasn't going to look further than that.

'Is today the right time?' she whispered huskily.

His fingers lowered to where her pulse throbbed rapidly in her neck. 'I hope so.'

'So do I. Kiss me, Aidan,' she urged with a breathy passion.

A husky laugh broke from him. 'Oh, Kate, that should be——'

He got no further, for her arms went up around his neck and drew his mouth down to hers in a kiss that wiped out any doubts. It was like before, only more piercingly sweet. The fire inside them swiftly broke the bounds of their control. Each kiss was deeper than the last, more sensually arousing. She shivered with pleasure as his hand stroked down to her breast, kneading it until it swelled to fill his palm, and then his lips followed, teasing her nipple through the silky nightdress, driving her wild until with a moan he took her into his mouth, making her cry out with pleasure.

Kate felt molten with desire, her body restless with an ache that demanded appeasement. Her hands glided over the silken skin of his shoulders and back, loving the feel of him, delighting as he shuddered beneath her touch. She longed to feel his flesh against hers without any barrier.

So it was doubly shocking that when Aidan's hand lowered to begin a slow glide up her thigh, she went absolutely rigid, and in a voice filled with loathing, she cried out 'No!'

Aidan's face was as white as hers as he raised his head to look at her. 'Kate?'

Gulping down a wave of panic, she stared at him. 'I can't. I'm sorry, I can't,' she answered in a voice that was thin and tight.

He didn't move, simply took a deep, steadying breath. 'What happened? What did I do?'

She lifted a hand to her forehead. 'I don't know. It just... Your hand... I couldn't go on. I'm sorry,' she whispered, eyes wide with alarm.

Very carefully he moved away from her and sat up. 'Did I hurt you?'

She shook her head. 'No. That's just it. I don't know what happened. Everything was fine—and then it wasn't. I'm sorry,' she said again, feeling absolutely awful.

Aidan let out a puff of breath. 'It's all right. No harm done.'

How must he be feeling? Her own body still ached with frustration. 'I wasn't teasing you. I wouldn't do that,' she apologised, sitting up and drawing her knees up under her chin. 'I don't know why I froze like that. I didn't want to.' If he thought she had been playing tricks, she didn't know what she would do. Damn, why did everything seem to be against them?

Aidan's arm snaked around her shoulders and drew her stiff, huddled figure into his side. 'Stop apologising, Kate.'

'Why is this happening to me?' she questioned in a small voice.

'I don't know,' Aidan replied seriously. 'I'm not qualified to make a judgement. You need to talk. I don't think you can put it off any longer. I want you to see a...friend of mine.'

Kate went still. A friend? He'd said something like that before but she hadn't paid much attention. Now a prickle of alarm ran down her spine. 'What sort of friend?'

Hearing her caution, he hesitated a moment before responding. 'A psychologist. You'll——'

Kate didn't wait to hear more but flung herself away from him in a furious burst of defensive anger. 'Oh, no. No way am I going to see one of those!' she cried, standing up quickly.

Startled by her violent reaction, he stood up too. 'Kate——'

'Don't "Kate" me, Aidan,' she cut in tautly. 'I'm not going and that's final!' Dear lord, that was all she needed! A psychiatrist! Someone to tell her she was finally going off her trolley—or worse!

Aidan's lips tightened. 'You little fool, it's for your own good!'

'Why? Because you think I'm crazy, don't you?' she exploded, nerves as tense as bowstrings.

His hands came to rest on his hips. 'I do not think you're crazy. That much I do know. What I can't tell you is what's happening. You want to know, don't you?' he demanded forcefully.

Her chin went up. 'No, I don't!'

'Is that so?' he challenged belligerently, as angry as she was now, eyes narrowing on the pulse that beat rapidly in her throat. 'What are you afraid of? That you'll discover the truth—or I will?'

Her gaze faltered at that. 'I don't know what you mean.'

'No? Then I'll explain. Perhaps you don't want me to discover that what happened just now was only a tease after all,' Aidan expanded softly.

'That's a lie. I told you what happened!'

His brow rose. 'Then there's no reason to be afraid, is there?'

Kate's heart lurched. 'That's blackmail. I might have known a Crawford would resort to those sort of tactics!' she sneered.

Aidan's nostrils flared as he took an angry breath, then visibly she saw the tension drain out of him. 'All right, Kate, you win,' he said tiredly. 'I won't force you to see one.'

She eyed him doubtfully, even as relief made her legs feel wobbly. 'Good.'

A short silence followed as they faced each other across the bed. Finally Aidan grinned.

'You don't seem overjoyed by your victory.'

'I am,' she rejoined swiftly. 'It's just…I am, all right!' she finished as if daring him to make something of her less than enthusiastic reaction.

Aidan inclined his head, then went to the wardrobe to retrieve clean clothes. 'I'm hungry. I'll see you downstairs in ten minutes for breakfast, OK?' Without waiting for her answer, he was gone.

Leaving Kate feeling as if somehow, in winning, she had lost. She knew it had been pure cowardice that had made her react so strongly to his suggestion. She had been scared at the thought of what she might be told. The last thing she wanted was some bespectacled trick-cyclist poking about in her mind.

She shivered, and realised she was still in her skimpy nightdress, and, despite the central heating, the temperature outside was making itself felt. Gathering fresh clothes, she hastened into the bathroom to shower and change.

Twenty minutes later, warmly clad in brushed cotton jeans and a creamy lambswool sweater, she descended the stairs and made her way to the dining-room. The door was slightly ajar, and as she approached it she heard Netta's voice.

'I appreciate how you feel, Aidan, but I think you're making a mistake.'

'But you'll do it for me anyway,' Aidan's voice cajoled confidently.

Netta groaned. 'I need my head examining!' she exclaimed drily.

Kate pushed the door open at that point and found them smiling fondly at each other over the remains of breakfast. They both turned at her entrance.

'Good morning, Kate. How do you feel?' Netta greeted warmly.

Kate returned her friendly smile. 'Much better, thank you. Whatever it is Aidan wants you to do, don't,' she advised, taking an empty seat and glancing across at him with a glint in her eye.

'Oh, I generally make up my own mind about things,' Netta returned with a laugh.

'He's not above blackmail,' Kate added direly.

'I know,' Netta agreed. 'His father's the same. I only give in to it when it's to my own advantage. Now, what can I get you for breakfast? How does fresh coffee and croissants sound?' she offered, rising and collecting the dirty dishes.

'It sounds delicious,' Kate concurred. 'Let me help you with those.' She went round to collect Aidan's plate. As she reached for it, he caught her wrist, making her glance down quickly.

'Are you sure you won't change your mind?' he queried.

Her mouth set. 'Quite sure, thank you. Now, if you wouldn't mind letting me go?'

'Stop pestering the girl, Aidan. Go and take the dogs for a walk or something. Kate's quite safe with me,' Netta ordered as she would a five-year-old.

Although his brows lifted, he didn't argue. 'I know when I'm not wanted,' was all he said before he obediently left the room.

Kate followed Netta into the kitchen with the crockery and helped her stack it in the dishwasher.

'He's a good boy really,' his stepmother declared as she retrieved the croissants from where they had been keeping warm and put them on the table. 'His heart's in the right place. Sit down, Kate, and help yourself, unless you'd rather go in the other room.'

'No, this is fine,' Kate insisted, pulling out a chair. The kitchen was warm and cosy and smelt of fresh bread and coffee. She broke a croissant apart and spooned on some jam.

'You gave us all a scare last night, you know,' Netta observed, setting a cup of coffee at Kate's elbow and sitting down with her own. 'Nightmares can be terrible things. Have you had many?'

'Too many,' Kate responded wryly.

'You poor thing,' the older woman sympathised. 'Are they always the same? I can remember having ones about water when I was young. But that was because my father thought the best way to learn to swim was simply to chuck you in the deep end,' she explained with a laugh.

Kate smiled half-heartedly. 'I only wish mine were like that. They're all different. In the beginning I saw nothing, but felt fear. Now there's more and more detail, and the fear is worse.' She shivered and reached for her coffee, sipping its warmth gratefully.

Netta's expression was concerned. 'No wonder you're frightened. You've no idea what it means?'

'No,' Kate admitted, combing her fingers through her hair, loosening the pins so that soft tendrils escaped. 'Aidan thinks I may have been raped, and I've blocked it out.'

Netta considered that for a moment. 'I suppose it's possible. I wouldn't blame anyone for wanting to forget that! But how do you feel about it?'

'I know it's ridiculous, but I don't *feel* as if that happened to me,' Kate sighed.

Netta stirred her coffee thoughtfully, watching the liquid circling round. 'Then it probably didn't. Yet you've clearly blocked out something pretty traumatic. The mind blanks out something we can't cope with, so that the conscious mind knows nothing. However, the subconscious relives the trauma in dreams.'

Kate listened to the older woman in numb disbelief. From friendly interest and concern, Netta had become all clinically technical. A slow anger started to burn inside her.

'I don't believe it!' she exclaimed, breaking into the flow of words.

Netta's head shot up at once, and met accusing blue eyes. 'Oh, dear,' she said softly.

Kate ground her teeth. 'You're the "friend", aren't you, Netta?' she demanded to know angrily.

The other woman sighed. 'I told him it wouldn't work.'

'O-oh!' Kate fumed, jumping to her feet and pacing away to the window. At the end of the snowy garden she could see Aidan playing with the dogs. 'The rat!'

'A rat, certainly, but a concerned one,' Netta said from behind her. 'He wants to help. He knows you're frightened, but he knows, too, that we can help to overcome that fear. You know, Kate, very often the fear of knowing is worse than the thing itself. You've told me so much, and I think I can help you. Now that you're here, why don't you tell me the rest? I promise that anything you say will go no further. Aidan will know nothing unless you tell him. What do you say?'

Anger warred with a need for understanding as Kate kept her eyes on that distant figure. A sigh left her, and she turned. 'All right.'

Netta gave her an approving smile. 'Good girl. Now, you sit down again and I'll get the coffee-pot. I think we're going to need it.'

An hour later, Kate let herself out of the back door and huddled her coat closer about her. She felt drained after that talk with Netta, but more confident, too. Aidan, damn him, had been right! But that didn't stop her from being furious over the way he had gone about it.

As her feet crunched through the icy snow, the dogs bounded up to meet her and she fended them off with a laugh, their warm breath tickling her rosy cheeks. Over them, she saw Aidan straighten up, hands going into his pockets as he waited for her to approach him. Toe to toe she faced him, finding it incredibly hard to hold on to her anger in the face of his shame-faced grin.

'That was a rotten trick to pull, Crawford,' she snapped, eyes flashing shafts of blue fire.

'If Muhammad wouldn't go to the mountain...' he returned watchfully.

'Rotten, low and underhand!' she added wrathfully.

His lips twitched. 'It worked.'

'That's no excuse. The end doesn't always justify the means, you know!'

'I wanted to help.'

'You were interfering! Damn you, I could hit you for what you did! You had no right!' She stamped her foot and caught one of the dogs who had slumped down beside her. The yelp had her biting her lip in consternation. 'Now look what you've made me do!' she cried, hunkering down to inspect the damage. There wasn't any, but all around there was plenty of snow. A light of devilment entered her eyes.

In a flash she had swept up a double handful, swinging round and up to send it flying into his face. Aidan had no time to move, and the flakes caught him squarely, melting and dripping down his neck.

'Why you little...! OK, you asked for this.' He bent down, and, with a swiftness born of long practice, fashioned a snowball that winged her way in seconds flat, catching her on her chest.

Within minutes a furious battle had been engaged, but it was no contest. Aidan was too good. He caught her twice to her once, and with formidable accuracy. Her anger fled as she gave way to helpless laughter, slipping and sliding, trying to avoid snowballs and dogs who got underfoot and leapt about barking in wild excitement. Finally one caught her in the face and she staggered back, tripped over a darting dog and stretched her length in the snow.

Laughing, Kate brushed the snow from her eyes and looked up into Aidan's face as he came down beside her.

'Still angry with me?' he asked breathlessly, brushing snow from her face and the hair that had escaped and now lay like a halo about her head.

Her heart kicked in her chest. How on earth, she thought helplessly, did anybody stay angry with him when he looked like that? 'No,' she admitted huskily.

'Then I apologise, humbly. I was only thinking of you. Forgive me?'

She had to firm her resolve to say snappily, 'Don't push your luck!'

He responded with a grin. 'What did Netta say?'

Kate raised her brows. 'Haven't you ever heard of the confidentiality of the medical profession?'

'I have, but I'm not asking her, I'm asking you.'

She sighed and held up her hand. 'Help me up.'

Aidan stood at once and pulled her to her feet, and began to brush the snow off her back. There was a garden seat nearby and they sat on that. One of the dogs came and rested its head on her knee and she stroked it idly.

'Well?' Aidan prompted.

'She said the nightmares were my subconscious reliving something I had deliberately blanked out. That somehow you had triggered it off by reminding me of that trauma I could remember—Philip's death.'

'And?'

Kate flickered a glance at him then away again. 'Clearly a man is involved, and the bed. She thinks there's a chance you could be right. Whatever I've blocked out, it's traumatic, and there's nothing more so than rape,' she told him quietly. What she didn't say was that Netta had put forth another possibility. That she had blocked out something *she* had done, and not something that had been done *to* her. The implications of that were even worse than the other, and she would rather keep it to herself.

'She also said I have to be patient, because the memory won't be rushed. She advised me not to fight it, just let it come, and try not to worry.'

'In other words, forget about it as much as you can,' Aidan said thoughtfully.

Kate pulled a face. 'You make it sound easy.' She didn't for a minute think it would be.

'At least we can make it easier. I promised you a sightseeing trip, and that's what we'll do. Keep you too busy to think. What do you say?' he put forward.

'We can try,' she agreed sceptically.

'O, ye of little faith,' Aidan laughed, standing and pulling her up with him. 'Come on, let's get out of these wet clothes before we catch pneumonia, then I'll prove to you how wrong you are.'

Kate allowed herself to be ushered towards the house, not believing for a minute that it would work, but happy to go along with it for the chance to spend time with him in harmony.

As it turned out, Aidan was right. She had very little time to think. They spent that day and those following touring the nation's capital. Aidan was completely relaxed as he gave her a mini history lesson at the Jefferson and Lincoln Memorials. Hand in hand they strolled through the museums and art galleries. With his arm around her shoulder, she stood in driving snow outside the White House, listening to him, uncaring that her feet were freezing and that her nose was bright red.

It was a magical time, and Kate fell more and more deeply in love with him. They went skating by the light of the moon, or took the dogs for long walks, and even went tobogganing on a sled Aidan unearthed from the cellar. Her memories were all of laughter, for by some quirk of fate the nightmares seemed to have stopped.

Everything would have been wonderful, except for one thing. The unexpected realisation that she was in love with Aidan, and the new emotions this awakened in her, had made her forget something vitally important. Never having expected to fall in love, she had never expected to want a man the way she did Aidan. Had never imagined how compelling was the need to have that love consummated. Now, rather late in the day, reality returned.

But for fate, she could even now have been pregnant, for it had never occurred to her to take precautions. It had never seemed necessary. Now the possibility forced her to face facts. To have Aidan's child would have been wonderful, if the marriage had been founded on love and commitment. To bring a child into a marriage pre-destined to fail would be irresponsible. Aidan would make a good father, and he would probably insist on the marriage's continuing if there were a child, but that would only lead to destruction. It was tempting, but the risks were too great, because although she loved him all she knew was that he wanted her. However painful, she had to be sensible, and that left her with only one course to take: to draw back from the brink.

It was hard, but in this she found she had Aidan's help, and it brought her near to tears. For his under-standing was based on a misconception. He thought her physical withdrawal in bed was due to the same reason as before. With a sensitivity that left her humbled, he shrugged off his own frustration, insisting on holding her in his arms, giving her the comfort of untroubled nights, that she knew were a strain for him by the fact that he got very little sleep at all.

When she tried to protest, he told her not to be silly and wouldn't listen to any argument until she was forced to give up. But the guilt gnawed at her. She couldn't understand why he would put himself through that for her. When she found the courage to ask him, he pretended not to hear, leaving her in a state of helpless confusion.

Yet they were, on the whole, happy days, so far removed from the anger of their first meeting that that time seemed like a million years ago.

On Thursday evening Netta and Aidan Senior took them out to dinner in belated celebration of the wedding. Since that long talk with Netta, all hint of reserve had gone, and she and Kate had formed a bond that Kate knew she would sorely miss when this marriage ended, as it was doomed to do. Meanwhile, she had taken to living each day as it came and was storing up memories for the future, while trying hard not to think that the future would not include Aidan.

For tonight she had chosen to wear a simple cocktail dress of lavender jersey with long sleeves and a V-neckline. Netta had decided on a russet-coloured two-piece, while both men looked extremely elegant in white silk shirts and black dinner suits.

A table had been booked at the country club, and consequently there were a lot of introductions to be made and congratulations to receive. Dinner itself was a lively meal, for Aidan's father took it upon himself to acquaint Kate with some of the wilder stories of his son's youth. Aidan took it all in good part, laughing at himself easily, before adding one or two tales that made his father blush.

It had been a long time since Kate had felt part of a family, and it gave her a warm feeling inside to have been accepted so readily by these two genuinely nice people. She was totally unaware of how much she had blossomed in their company, or that more than one significant look was exchanged over her head that night.

Halfway through the evening, when father and son had been called away to help settle an argument, the two women found themselves temporarily abandoned. Netta chose that moment to raise her glass to the younger woman.

'I drink to you, Kate. I'll admit I had reservations about you in the beginning, but I take them all back. You've worked wonders. Aidan isn't the same man these days. It's all due to you. You make him very happy. Life hasn't always been good to him, you know. But I can see you love him, and that's what he needs,' she declared with a smile.

Kate felt choked. 'Thank you, Netta.' Her eyes were drawn to where Aidan and his father stood talking to friends. 'I do love him, very much,' she admitted aloud for the first time.

Netta covered her hand. 'And he loves you.'

Kate smiled and didn't contradict her. 'You've been very generous to me, considering Aidan and I met under very... difficult circumstances. I was so mixed up then, but I'm glad now that I changed my mind and decided to help him. When Andrew told me about the will...' She let the sentence tail off.

'What will was that?' Netta asked, her attention partially caught by a friend at another table.

Kate blinked, frowning at her mother-in-law's distracted smile. 'You know. The one Aidan's grandfather made, cutting him out if he didn't marry,' she explained slowly.

Netta frowned. 'His grandfather? But... Oh!' Slow colour rose in her cheeks. 'Oh, yes, of course, that will.' She laughed nervously. 'You must forgive me, my mind was wandering. Naturally we were all very pleased.'

Kate felt a ball of anger grow in her stomach as she watched Netta gulp at her drink. Her eyes flew to Aidan and narrowed as she saw him laugh. Of all the underhand... 'There was no will, was there?' she demanded to know in a wrathful voice that had quelled many a strong man in its time.

'Well, naturally there was a will, Kate,' Netta argued tensely.

'But no time limit. No threat of losing control of Cranston's!' Her teeth ground together. 'Aidan made it all up, didn't he? He even had you go along with it. Why?'

'Whatever he did or didn't do, he had good reasons for. But I'm afraid if you want to know you'll have to ask him, Kate,' Netta regained her poise.

Kate flashed her a look. 'Don't think I won't! He tricked me. Everything he said was a lie! He didn't need to marry me or anyone! So why pretend he did?'

To Kate's surprise, Netta chuckled. 'An intelligent girl like you ought to be able to work out the answer to that, my dear.'

'What do you mean?' Kate frowned round at her.

'Oh, Kate, it isn't only a female prerogative to feel vulnerable, you know. Think about it. Now smile, they're coming back.'

Kate looked up to find the two men bearing down on them. With an effort she wiped her face clean of anger as Aidan came to her side.

'Dance, Kate?'

Her smile didn't reach her eyes as she gave him her hand and allowed him to lead her on to the dance-floor. This time, when his arms enfolded her, she refused to melt. She was far too angry, and Aidan was far too astute not to pick it up.

'What's the matter, Kate?'

'Nothing. Why should anything be wrong?' she queried, acid-sweet.

She felt his wariness in the stiffening of his body. 'I don't know, but I'd bet a fortune there is.'

Kate's fingers curled into fists on his shoulders. 'The same fortune your grandfather left you in his will? The one you married me for?' she went on dulcetly.

For a moment he didn't speak, and then when he did, there was an odd note in his voice. 'Ah,' he murmured.

This time she looked up, her eyes flashing angrily. 'I'll give you, "ah", you liar!' she breathed furiously.

'Kate, you look magnificent when you're angry,' he told her on a distinctly unsteady note.

She ignored the provocation with an effort. At least he wasn't pretending ignorance. 'Why? Just tell me that. Why?'

'The why ought to be simple, Kate, if you think about it,' he said softly.

'Meaning you aren't going to tell me?'

'I told you once that angry people don't see further than their own anger,' he pointed out, aggravatingly calm.

'I don't need any more potted psychology, thank you very much! If I was as intelligent as both you and Netta seem to imagine, I'd never have married you in the first place!' she declared, aggrieved, and turned her head away, refusing to look at him for the remainder of the dance.

Whether it was the music or some other influence, she didn't know, but gradually her first anger began to die away. At the same time other thoughts started to seep in. The main one was that he hadn't needed to marry her at all, and yet he had tricked her into doing so. It made no sense. Unless... Her heart gave a wild lurch. No. It couldn't be. He couldn't...love her, could he?

It was a notion that sent her thoughts winging in all sorts of crazy directions. Yet the more she probed his motives, the more it seemed to be the only one that made sense. And yet she couldn't accept it. Didn't dare to, lest she be wrong. To have an impossible dream suddenly brought within your grasp was unnerving.

In an agony of uncertainty, she heard the music finish. She looked up at him then, hot colour invading her cheeks as she met his intent grey eyes.

'Aidan?' Her voice was barely more than a whisper.

He smiled. 'That was the last waltz. We'd better join Netta and Dad. With luck we can leave before the crush starts.'

That was all she got out of him until they arrived home nearly three quarters of an hour later, the traffic on the roads being unseasonally heavy. Netta offered to make them all a nightcap when they got in, but Aidan refused, declaring he was tired. So they both said goodnight and made their way upstairs.

They had both been using the en-suite bathroom since that first night. Now Kate watched as Aidan swiftly divested himself of shoes and suit and bagged the shower first, with a grin that made half of her want to hit him, and the other kiss him.

Kate sank on to the bed, kicked off her shoes and scowled after him. He could afford to sound cheery. His world wasn't in utter turmoil. His—— The glum thoughts were cut off abruptly by a startled yelp from the bathroom. Straightening in alarm, Kate stared at the door. What on earth? She was just about to get up and investigate when the door shot open and Aidan reappeared like a bullet.

He stopped when he saw her watching him, half pointed into the room he had left so precipitately, then changed the move into raking a hand through his hair.

The other one was holding on to his only covering—a towel sat at a very rakish, not to say dangerous, angle.

Kate bit her lip on a sudden urge to giggle. She'd never seen him so discomposed. 'Whatever is it?'

Aidan looked from her to the bathroom, then uttered a defeated sigh. 'Oh, hell, what's the use! How are you with spiders, Kate?'

'Spiders? I... Oh!' Now she understood, and her hand came up to hide her smile. 'What would you do if I hated them too?' she asked mockingly.

'Kate!' Her name was ground out in heavy warning.

She rose gracefully. 'All right, where is it, this monster?' she asked wearily, arming herself with a handkerchief he had left on the dresser.

'God, women! It's in the shower. So if you wouldn't mind hustling your butt. We don't have all night,' he gritted out.

She found it where he said—a giant of its kind, less than quarter of an inch from leg, to leg, to leg... She caught it up in the hankie and shook it out of the window. Turning to go back to the bedroom, she was in time to see Aidan's head pop round the door.

'Has it gone?' he demanded.

Kate had to bite down hard on her lip to stop from grinning. She looked him up and down. 'My hero!' she said unsteadily, watching his face darken.

'You're enjoying this, aren't you?'

'How old did you say you were?' she murmured, walking past him.

Aidan took a deep breath. 'Kate Crawford, you're a wretch!'

She couldn't help it, she just couldn't hold the laughter back any longer. 'You should have s-seen your f-face!' she gasped, collapsing on to the bed in gales of laughter. Tears were streaming from her eyes, so she didn't see the way his face changed, eyes dancing with retribution—and something else.

'Funny, was it?' he queried mildly, advancing.

Kate barely noticed as she nodded and wiped her eyes. 'I'm sorry, I'm sorry! I know I shouldn't laugh, but...oh, Aidan, you looked so...so...' Her voice trailed off as he dragged her to her feet.

'That,' he said, dropping a kiss on her startled lips, 'was for laughing. And that——' he did it again, lingering a shade longer '—was because I enjoyed it the first time. And this——' his arms closed about her, lips fastening on hers, demanding a response she couldn't withhold '—this,' he repeated huskily, 'is because I love you, Kate Crawford.'

With a swift peck on her nose, he let her go. Stunned, Kate plopped down on to the bed, and with a grin that flipped her heart over Aidan disappeared into the bathroom.

It took a full minute for the realisation of what he had said to penetrate her brain, but when it did she was galvanised into action. Jumping from the bed, she rushed into the bathroom to yank open the glass door of the shower.

'What did you say?' she demanded breathlessly as the steam slowly evaporated.

Like a snake his arm shot out, encircling her waist, drawing her in under the spray and into his arms. She was soaked in seconds, but she didn't care, blinking up at him as his hands framed her head.

'I said I love you,' he repeated solemnly. One eyebrow rose at her silence. 'Nothing to say?'

Her head shook helplessly. 'Oh, Aidan! I love you too. So much. I thought...'

'You think too much, and all the wrong things. Just shut up and kiss me,' he growled, and brought her head up to his.

It seemed to Kate that as their lips met they exchanged souls, so piercingly sweet was it. An affirmation of something that transcended the purely physical. But then, as always, chemistry took over, and each kiss became deeper as the flames took hold. Gasping, she threw her head back as he rained kisses along her jaw and down the cord of her neck. Eagerly she pressed her body against his, made vitally aware that he was naked and that her sodden dress and tights were scant barrier.

Then they were no barrier at all as Aidan slid down the zip and peeled them away from her, and she moaned her pleasure as flesh met flesh. Delicious thrills chased each other along her spine as the hairs on his chest teased her aching breasts, and she arched herself closer, trying to ease their need. The feel of his hands caressing and moulding her was electrifying and with a groan she pressed her lips to his shoulder, tasting him with her tongue. His hands dropped to her buttocks, bringing her dizzily up against him and unconsciously her nails dug into the flesh of his back.

Aidan gasped, head raising from its plundering of her nape. 'Hey, little cat, that smarts!' he growled with a laugh.

But Kate wasn't laughing. Her body froze, jack-knifing away from him. She backed away, arms crossing protectively over her breasts. 'Don't call me that!' she cried, the words tearing from a painfully tight throat.

Aidan had taken a step towards her, but now he stopped, hands clenching into fists at his sides as he strove for control. Slowly he reached out and turned off the water. The silence that fell throbbed with their seething emotions. Kate turned away, unable to bear the grim tautness of his face. She heard the door click open, then the fluffy folds of a towel were draped about her shoulders. Slowly she turned, tucking in the ends. Aidan had draped a towel about his hips, and her eyes rose upwards, over a chest that heaved as he steadied his breathing, then sought his face.

She ran a hand over her brow. 'I'm sorry. It was that name. He called me that. I can't bear it!'

Aidan's hand came out to run caressingly up and down her arms. 'What am I going to do with you?' he sighed.

Tears sprung to her eyes. 'Oh, God, Aidan! How can you love me when I do this to you?'

He drew her in to his chest, chin resting on her hair. 'I'm just crazy, I guess. Crazy in love with you.'

She closed her eyes. 'It isn't fair!'

'It won't always be like this, you know.'

'How can you be so sure?' she whispered.

'Because we love each other. We'll work it out. When you hear me complaining, that's the time to worry. Come on, let's get to bed. It's late and we're both tired.' He disappeared into the other room.

Kate dried herself, then rubbed her hair until it was only barely damp before returning to the bedroom to slip into a clean nightdress. Aidan was already in bed. He watched as she went to the dressing-table and picked up her brush, beginning to run it through her hair.

'Come over here and let me do that,' he commanded gently, and, with only the slightest hesitation, she did, sitting down on the edge of the bed, while Aidan rose on to his knees behind her and started to brush her hair.

Kate closed her eyes as the rhythmic strokes drained the last of the tension out of her. The silence was punctuated only by the sound of their breathing. They could have been alone on a desert island. A sigh escaped her.

'How could you love me? I was so awful when we met,' she said huskily.

There was a smile in his voice as he answered. 'I asked myself the same question. I came there to make you feel guilty and, to my surprise, I found myself saying and doing something completely different. The simple fact was that I saw you holding that little girl, and from that moment on I was lost.'

She was surprised. That long? He'd loved her that long? 'Truly?'

'Truly,' he repeated wryly. 'When I realised, I thought I'd been as foolish as all those other men, and I was determined not to let you know. Demanding that you marry me was an inspired moment—a moment of lunacy, I sometimes thought. Yet I wanted to have you. To be the only man in your life. Andrew's mix-up over the will gave me just the excuse I needed.'

'Then why were you marrying what's-her-name?' she wanted to know.

'Julia? The truth is I never expected to fall in love, yet I wanted a family. The time seemed right, and Julia was someone I'd known for a long time and liked and respected. But then I met you, and there was nobody else for me. When you turned me down, I went away thinking what an idiot I was, and that your refusal was probably the best thing all round. Yet I couldn't get you out of my mind all that week. I don't know if I'd have tried to contact you again or not, but then your call came. I was intrigued, and if I'm honest, I was relieved that you'd given me the excuse I needed.'

Kate grimaced. 'Andrew's lie.'

'Andrew didn't lie. He believed it. To him it was the truth. He never could see beyond his own hatred. He wanted me to lose everything, so what he overheard was never doubted. And if anyone had tried to convince him otherwise, he would only have believed it more. There's no reasoning with him.

'For once his blindness worked in my favour. You called me, and I was well and truly caught,' he told her simply.

Kate sighed. 'But I was so horrid to you!' she exclaimed remorsefully.

'No more than I was to you. I said things I regret, simply because I was vulnerable. To my mind I'd fallen for you despite all I knew of you and against my own better judgement. I had no plan other than to survive from day to day, but almost from the day we met I realised you weren't at all the way you seemed. That gave me hope that one day I could make you love me.'

A large lump formed in her throat and she had to swallow twice to remove it. 'I didn't know. I thought I hated you, but I was never indifferent. No man had got to me the way you did. You scared me. Perhaps I loved you long before I realised. When I knew, I didn't think you could feel anything for me. I was sure you must hate me, because I'd been every bit as bad as you thought I was,' she confessed.

'I soon discovered it wasn't wise to take you at face value. I found you were quite a different person. Vulnerable in ways I wouldn't have believed from your reputation. I could see you needed help, but you fought me. You fought everything. I just held on to the fact that a woman who loves children couldn't be all bad. I'm glad you like them, for I do too.'

Kate caught her breath. Reaching up, she took the brush from him, holding it before her like some kind of shield. 'You want a family?'

His gentle hands kneaded her shoulders. 'A large one. Four at least. How about you?'

She closed her eyes. Their dreams were the same. It would have made everything perfect, except for one thing. She licked dry lips. 'I always wanted a family, too. But what if we can never have them? What if——?'

He drew her into his arms, cutting off her hesitant words. 'Sweetheart, I refuse to think in terms of never. If I did that, I'd never have married you and never discovered you love me.'

Kate twisted round, her face pressing into his neck as she fought back tears. 'Oh, Aidan, I love you. So very, very much,' she breathed against his skin.

His lips brushed her hair. 'That's all I want to know. Let the future take care of itself. Believe me, we're going to be very, very happy. This is where you belong, Kate. This is where you stay.'

'Well?' Netta asked, when Kate joined her in the kitchen for breakfast next day. 'Did you work it out?'

To Kate's dismay a fiery blush worked its way up her neck and into her cheeks. Still she joined in when Netta laughed. 'Yes, I did. I must have been blind.'

Netta shook her head. 'That makes two of you. You won't believe the conversations I've had with Aidan over you. Still, all's well that ends well. It's the perfect birthday present for him.'

Kate's jaw dropped; she'd completely forgotten. 'Birthday? It can't be!'

Netta pointed to the big red cross marked on the calendar. 'It is. Tomorrow. He'll be thirty-eight.'

'But I don't have anything!' Kate exclaimed feeling absolutely dreadful.

'Don't panic,' Netta advised. 'I'm going into town today. You can come with me and pick something up. You're bound to find something.'

Netta was right. She found just the thing in a tiny antique shop. It was a small jade carving of a sleeping tiger, and she knew instinctively that he would appreciate it.

She gave it to him over a candlelit dinner the following evening. Netta had suggested the restaurant, and the setting was as romantic as Kate could have wished. He unwrapped the gift carefully, and when he finally held it in his hand, his eyes told her what words couldn't. He raised his glass of champagne to her in a toast.

'You are the most incredibly beautiful woman. Remind me to thank you properly for my present later,' he declared softly, reaching out for her hand.

'I will,' she smiled back, all her love in the dazzling blue of her eyes.

'Then here's to you, my own sleeping tigress. To you and the future.'

In the low lighting, he didn't see the way her colour faded. 'I'll drink to that.' She raised her glass to her lips briefly, then added fervently, 'I'm going to make sure you never have to regret marrying me.'

'That I could never do,' he assured her, eyes holding hers.

Kate smiled, but a shiver ran through her, as if someone had just walked over her grave. Though she tried to shake it off, for the rest of the evening she had a dreadful presentiment of looming disaster.

It was late when they drove home, but the lights were still on, and there was the sound of voices coming from the lounge. Curiosity drew them to the open doorway. It was Netta who saw them first, and she came to her feet in a movement devoid of her usual grace.

'Well, here you are at last. You'll never guess who's turned up, Aidan,' she declared edgily, eyes shooting to the end of the room.

Automatically they followed her gaze. Both froze as a lazy figure rose from his chair.

'I've come to wish you a happy birthday, brother,' Andrew Crawford drawled into the silence that fell.

CHAPTER NINE

INSTINCTIVELY Kate moved closer to Aidan, feeling again that flood of anxiety she had experienced when last she had faced his brother. Aidan's arm fastened about her waist, and she could feel the tension in him. Though he looked relaxed, his whole body was braced for this unexpected meeting.

'Well? Aren't you going to say anything? Or do you intend to stand in the doorway forever?' Andrew taunted mockingly.

'What do you want, Andrew?' Aidan asked warily, refusing to rise to the bait. Kate could sense his reluctance for this exchange as he urged her into the room ahead of him.

Andrew laughed, 'I've already told you. I've no excuse for forgetting your birthday, have I?'

Aidan's free hand was extended. 'And I've no reason to believe anything is ever that simple with you. But I'll call your bluff. Happy birthday.'

They shook hands, Andrew's smile the epitome of brotherly affection, his twin's ruefully watchful.

'You've met my wife, Kate,' Aidan said by way of introduction, and for the first time she felt the impact of Andrew's gaze.

His lips curved reminiscently, but his eyes were cold. 'Ah, yes, Kate. Netta did happen to mention you'd acquired a lovely young bride. I hadn't expected it to be Kate, but the world is full of surprises. As I recall, our last meeting had rather a dampening effect.' Though light, his voice carried an edge nobody missed.

Kate met Aidan's querying glance and explained. 'I threw a glass of water over him,' she said, not bothering to hide her satisfaction.

'She always was impulsive,' Andrew drawled smoothly.

Netta, who had remained silently watching up till now, spoke up. 'If you three intend to talk over old times, I'll leave you to it. Your father went up ages ago, and I need my beauty sleep these days. Andrew, you'll have your usual room, of course. I'll see you all in the morning. Goodnight.'

With her departure, there was a subtle change in the atmosphere. That sense of impending disaster returned to Kate, tensing her muscles as she watched the two brothers confronting each other.

'So,' Andrew said conversationally. 'You kept control of the company. How noble of Kate to step into the breach.'

'The company was never in doubt, Andrew. You should have made sure of your facts before you started spreading rumours. Whatever our personal differences, Grandfather would never have left the controlling interest anywhere but in the family,' Aidan told him softly.

Chagrin darkened his twin's face. 'You always did have the devil's own luck, brother!'

'I was certainly lucky to marry Kate.'

'And how well the marriage has turned out. Netta tells me she's never seen two people more in love than you.'

Kate felt Aidan's arm tighten, and she glanced up, smiling. 'We're very happy,' she confirmed huskily. Looking back at Andrew, her eyes dared him to deny it.

He held up his hands. 'I'm pleased for you. I really am.' A slow smile crossed his handsome face. 'It's strange how things work out. One moment you can be in the depths of gloom, and the next a whole world of possibilities open up. Not having realised you were married, I had nothing to give you, and that upset me. But now I know just the present. I think a toast is in order. You do the honours, Aidan. I'll have Scotch on the rocks.'

'I don't suppose this can wait until tomorrow?' Aidan suggested pointedly.

'Certainly not. It wouldn't be your birthday,' Andrew insisted.

Releasing her, Aidan gave Kate a bracing smile and crossed over to the cocktail cabinet. Andrew watched him for a second, then turned to smile at Kate. She stiffened her spine automatically, chin lifting defiantly.

'I hope Kate's been treating you well.' He spoke to his brother without taking his eyes off her. 'I'd hate to think that all my efforts have been wasted, and that you're disappointed. To look at her, you wouldn't imagine how wild she can be,' he mused.

Kate gasped, her eyes flying from Andrew to Aidan, who had stopped what he was doing and had turned, his body set rigid.

'Just what are you trying to say, Andrew?' he demanded tightly.

His brother ignored him, moving instead to stand before Kate, his hand reaching up to caress her cheek, smiling as she flinched away. 'Well, little cat, are you still using your claws?'

At the sound of that hated name, the world seemed to tilt beneath Kate's feet. Something struck her in the chest like a thunderbolt, stealing her breath and all the blood drained from her face, leaving her white and shaken.

Her, 'No!' clashed with Aidan's,

'My God!'

Malice glittered in his grey eyes as Andrew surveyed the tableau of stricken figures. 'Oh, dear, didn't Kate tell you I'd already had her?' he mocked.

With a groan, Kate's hands flew to her cheeks. She flinched at the sound of crashing glass as Aidan slammed a bottle down and closed the space between himself and his brother in two angry strides. There was murder in his eyes as he roughly spun Andrew round.

'You? It was *you* who raped her?' The words were forced out through a barrier of murderous rage.

Andrew's brows rose. 'Rape?' he queried with a laugh. 'Is that what she told you? Oh, no, I didn't use force, I didn't need to. She went to bed with me for money, my dear brother, and believe me, she was worth every penny!'

Aidan's head went back as if from a blow. He, too, was pale now. 'I don't believe you.'

'Then ask her, dear boy, and see if she dares deny it,' his brother riposted and they both turned towards her.

Shaking like an aspen, Kate felt the accusation of their eyes like a blow. Nausea rose to choke her. She couldn't speak, didn't even see them, only the pictures, no longer blocked, that flashed before her mind's eye. At last everything was revealed to her, and with a strangled moan of self-disgust she turned and fled from the room.

Hall, stairs and landing were just stages in her flight. Her goal was their room, and, once there, she sank down on the side of the bed, body rocking as she bore the pain, arms clamped around her waist.

She knew now, knew it all, and she could no longer hide from the truth. Now she knew why she had feared Andrew, for he alone had known the truth. She had done exactly what he had said, and all the loathing and self-disgust swelled the ball of sickness in her stomach.

She jumped violently as the door clicked open, head shooting round. Aidan stood there watching her, his face so coldly set that he was like a stranger, not the man she had grown to love at all. Dumbly she watched as he shut the door and prowled towards her. He stopped only inches away and she winced as his hand tipped her head up until her neck ached and she couldn't avoid his gaze.

'Tell me it isn't true,' he demanded through his teeth. 'Tell me you didn't sleep with my own brother for money.'

Pain darkened her eyes, and she tried to look away, but he jerked her back roughly.

'Tell me, damn you!'

She swallowed, eyes pleading for understanding. 'I . . . can't,' she croaked, and gasped as he thrust her backwards so that she sprawled on the bed. The angry force of his body followed her down, pinning her beneath him.

There was a wildness in his eyes she had never seen before as he stared down at her. 'Money? Is that where I've gone wrong, Kate? Should I have offered you money to sleep with me?' he bit out in an emotion-filled voice.

Her eyes burned. He was so hurt! She could feel his pain as if it were her own. 'Aidan, don't,' she begged brokenly, trying to escape.

He pushed her back. 'How much, Kate?'

She saw him through a veil of tears. 'You don't understand!'

'Don't I? Don't I? All I understand right now is that you've been driving me crazy, walking on eggshells round you because I believed, God help me, you'd been raped. Now I find it's all a lie and that my own brother . . . God damn you, Kate! Just name your price, but now I'm taking something on account!'

His mouth ground down on hers with the full force of his anger. Sobbing wildly, she tried to avoid him, but he was too strong, too angry and betrayed. She felt the tearing of the soft skin of her lips and tasted blood, and the nausea rose to her throat. With a strength she didn't know she had, she threw out a hand and caught him a blow on the side of the head. It weakened his hold just enough for her to roll from beneath him. Tumbling from the bed, she staggered to the bathroom.

She was only just in time, sinking to her knees to be violently sick. How long it lasted, she didn't know, but finally there was nothing left, and she dropped her head on her hands, shivering with cold. She only realised Aidan was beside her when the toilet flushed, then gentle hands that shook ever so slightly, raised her to sit on the edge of the bath and a cold flannel was wiped over her face.

Only when it stopped did she look up at him. The wildness was gone from his eyes, replaced now by a mixture of remorse and concern.

'Kate, I'm sorry,' he apologised huskily. 'I don't know what came over me.'

She looked away, swallowing painfully. 'Don't you?' she demanded tautly, forcing herself to meet his eyes again. 'What else did he say to you, Aidan? That I enjoyed it too? That I couldn't get enough?' The set of his face told her she was right. 'Don't you know that my flesh crawls at the thought that I could ever have let him touch me? You don't know what it cost me to do that!' Tears flooded her eyes, but she held them back somehow. 'I sank my pride and abandoned my self-respect because I was desperate! Oh, God!' she shuddered with revulsion. 'I feel so dirty. So ashamed.'

White-faced, Aidan's throat worked madly to clear a constriction. 'Andrew did this to you . . . in my name?' he questioned thickly.

Kate shivered. 'I don't want to talk about it.'

'You have to. For your own sake it must come out in the open,' he declared firmly. 'And I have to know everything,' he finished on a grim note.

She knew he was right, however reluctant she was to relive that time in her life. 'Very well,' she agreed in a dull voice, 'but not here.'

She led the way back into the bedroom. The sight of the rumpled bed made her wince, and she avoided it, going instead to the small couch set under the window. She curled up in one corner, arms hugging her knees, lids lowered to shield her eyes. Following her, Aidan perched on a corner of the bed, elbows on knees, hands loosely clasped, belying the tension in him.

Kate drew in a shaky breath, marshalling her thoughts. 'You remember I told you I came to ask you for help for Philip? You never did ask me why. Philip had been ill for some time. The disease was a rare one. Little was known about it, but there was a treatment available that offered a good chance of recovery. But it would mean going to America, and, worse, the cost of the treatment itself was enormous. I didn't earn the sort of money I needed. I was at the end of my tether when I remembered my father had once told me to go to Aidan Crawford if ever I was in trouble. Of course, I'd never met him, but I had no qualms about going to see him. Besides, I was desperate—Philip was getting worse by the hour, it seemed to me. I allowed myself to hope because that was all I had left. And so I went to see him . . .'

Aidan Crawford's house was in one of those quiet, elegant little squares that had the unmistakable atmosphere of understated affluence. A dark-suited manservant opened the door to her summons and enquired her business.

'I would like to see Mr Crawford,' she said as authoritatively as she could. Accurately guessing that his function was to shield his employer from unwanted visitors, she quickly added, 'It's a private matter, and extremely urgent.'

The man looked sympathetically regretful. 'I'm afraid——' he began but got no further.

'Show her in, Bates, there's a good fellow,' a voice commanded from somewhere inside.

A flicker of annoyance passed over the man Bates's face, but he stepped back none the less. 'Very good, sir. If you would care to step inside, miss,' he invited smoothly.

Kate found herself shown into what was clearly the study. Aidan Crawford was standing by the fireplace. He was a big, handsome man, a little younger than she'd expected, and when he smiled at her she quickly noticed that it didn't reach his eyes. They were calculatingly assessing as they roved over her from head to toe. She wasn't used to being stared at this way, and she shivered, the hairs on the back of her neck rising atavistically.

If her mission hadn't been so imperative, she would have turned and walked away as quickly as her legs could carry her, but, whatever her feelings, this man had been her father's friend and she needed his help. So she went forward and shook the hand he held out to her, disliking the possessive way he held on to hers just a fraction too long.

'You wanted to speak to me? In what way can I help you, Miss...?' he paused significantly.

'Taylor-Hardie,' Kate supplied, using her full name to jog his memory, though she rarely used it herself. 'Kate Taylor-Hardie. Yes, I did want to speak to you. We've never met, but you did know my father, Christopher Taylor-Hardie.'

Aidan Crawford rubbed his chin thoughtfully. 'Ah, yes, Christopher.' He moved round behind her as he spoke and his hands came to rest on her shoulders. 'Naturally I'm delighted to meet any relative of his. Let me take your coat.' He relieved her of it before she could protest. 'Now, do sit down, and tell me how I may help you.'

Kate seated herself on a chair facing the desk as he took his seat behind it. 'Actually, I'm here on my brother's behalf. Philip is... Philip...' She hesitated at the brink, not quite knowing how to phrase her request now the moment had arrived. She was saved the trouble.

'Kate... I may call you that, I hope, as a friend of the family? Kate, Philip's in trouble, isn't he? Why don't you tell me all about it?' he invited confidentially.

Mightily relieved, she did just that. At the end of the tale, he sat back in his chair, eyes assessing her once more.

'How much do you need?' he asked finally, and she stated a figure that caught her breath but didn't so much as make him blink. He was so calm, she began to hope her plea hadn't been made in vain. 'That's a lot of money.'

She bit her lip. 'I know, but I can assure you that every penny will be paid back,' she hastened to add.

After a long pause, Aidan Crawford rose to his feet and took a pensive turn about the room. Kate followed him with her eyes as far as she could, until he disappeared behind her. It came as an unwelcome shock when his hands came to rest on her shoulders again, pressing down in a sort of massaging action.

'You know, Kate,' he murmured, 'you're asking a lot from friendship. I'm not running a benevolent society, you know. However, I can't help thinking there's a way for a young woman like you—a very beautiful woman, I might add—to make the risk worth my while.'

Kate very nearly choked, scarcely able to credit what she was hearing. She wasn't green. She knew what he was suggesting, and it was unbelievable. It was like something out of a Victorian melodrama.

'What?' The incredulous question was forced from her. How could this man, her father's friend, be saying such a thing?

Aidan Crawford laughed way down deep in his throat. 'Come now, you're not unintelligent.' His hands began to caress up and down her arms.

She repressed a shudder of intense disgust, her attempt to stand foiled by remarkably strong hands. 'I thought you were a friend!' she exclaimed angrily.

'Oh, I am, but you can't expect me to do this for nothing. If I'm to be generous, surely you can be generous too.'

The idea was sickening. 'You must be mad if you think I'd agree to anything so disgusting!' she uttered in violent refusal.

He bent down so that his mouth was close to her ear. 'It seems a reasonable bargain. One you are, of course, entirely free to refuse. But don't I remember you telling me you'd come here as a last resort? So it seems to me that your answer depends on just how much you love your brother.'

And there he had her. She had nowhere else to go. It was either do as he suggested, or see her brother deteriorate before her eyes. She loved him too much to do that, so she had no choice.

'You're despicable! How can you call yourself a friend?' she choked.

'Is that a yes or a no, Kate?'

'You know it's yes,' she muttered thickly. 'If you give me the money, I promise to . . . meet you whenever you say.'

The hands on her arms urged her upwards and turned her to face him. 'Oh, no. The money comes afterwards, Kate. Of course I trust you, but people can be forgetful. So, we have a deal,' he declared with satisfaction. 'All the best bargains are sealed with a kiss,' he added, and brought his head down.

If she hadn't given her word, she would have run like mad. Honour kept her there although the lips that claimed hers so greedily made her flesh crawl, especially when his tongue insinuated its way between her teeth. Revolted, she only prayed she could bear it as long as necessary.

Although she hadn't responded, he seemed satisfied when he released her. 'I think we'll be more comfortable upstairs, don't you?' he suggested throatily.

There was nothing else for her to do except allow him to lead her back to the hall, and the stairway that led upwards into darkness. Coldness invaded her as she mounted them by his side, feeling as if she was going to her own execution. But she didn't falter, just kept on going, blanking her mind of all thought except that she was doing this for Philip.

What took place behind the closed door of his bedroom was a nightmare. She refused to relax or respond, giving him no encouragement, but she was unable to detach her mind from what happened to her body. He wasn't brutal, just uncaring of her unresponsiveness or her innocence. Calling her his 'little cat', he was not satisfied until long into the night, and by then she was no longer innocent in mind or body. She felt degraded—sullied by a lust that sought pleasure and didn't care if it gave none in return.

Worse, though, followed.

He watched her as she slid from the bed to dress, and when she turned to him and asked for the money, he laughed in her face. 'Did you seriously think I would hand over that sort of money for the pleasure of your body, delectable though it was?' He lay there against the pillows, sheet pulled negligently across his hips, and informed her just how ridiculously naïve he found her. 'I wouldn't give it to you, even if I could, little cat.'

If she had had a knife in that moment, she would have driven it into his lying heart. 'You're beneath contempt! If it's the last thing I do, I'll make you sorry for this, Aidan Crawford!' she swore in bitterness and hatred...

Kate came back to the present to find her cheeks wet with tears. She wiped them away with fingers that shook. 'He just lay there and laughed at me,' she added in a painful whisper. 'He just laughed.'

In the silence that fell, she waited for Aidan's response, but none came. She looked at him anxiously. Did he believe her? She couldn't tell. His head was lowered, but his hands were curled into fists on his knees. As if feeling her eyes on him, his head came up, and she breathed in sharply at the pain and anger in his face.

'Oh, Kate, what can I say? Sorry is too bloody inadequate! When I think...' He halted abruptly, swallowing, then jumped to his feet and paced away to the dresser. The tension in him was awesome as he crashed his fist against the top. 'This time, by God, he's gone too far!' he declared through gritted teeth, then suddenly he headed for the door.

Eyes wide, Kate swung her legs to the floor. 'Where are you going?'

He didn't miss his step. 'To find my brother and do something I should have done a long time ago!' he flung over his shoulder, and disappeared out into the passage.

Kate's heart thumped wildly as she followed him. At the door she heard his descent of the stairs, and by the time she reached them she could hear angry voices coming from below. She froze then, one foot hovering on the top step. Then there was a startled yell and the sound of furniture breaking followed by a sudden silence. Her hand flew to her lips as she watched Aidan appear in the hall, one hand massaging the other.

She must have made some noise, for he looked up sharply. The look on his face was one of grim satisfaction. Slowly he mounted the stairs towards her, stopping when they were level.

'Andrew has decided not to stay after all,' he said drily.

Reeling a little, Kate's eyes dropped to his hand. She took it between hers, thumb rubbing softly over bruised knuckles. 'Then you did believe me?'

His free hand came out to draw her close. 'Oh, yes. Can you ever forgive us for what you went through?'

'Can you forgive me?' she countered, voice muffled by his shoulder. Beneath her cheek his chest heaved.

'You have nothing to reproach yourself for, Kate. There's nothing to forgive.' He eased away a little to gaze down at her. 'I wish there were something I could do to wipe away the past completely,' he sighed.

Kate shivered. 'I just want to forget. To put it behind me once and for all.'

He stared at her, a strange expression in his eyes. 'Can you, Kate?' he asked gently.

A little shaken, she thought she understood. 'I...don't know,' she said honestly.

With a wry smile Aidan turned her about and, still with his arm around her, urged her back to their room. Kate's eye fell on the bed immediately and she went across to smooth it out and turn the covers back. Aidan watched her in silence for a moment then with a sigh he went to collect his robe from the chair.

'I think we both need some sleep before we make any decisions,' he offered evenly.

It was the lack of tone that made Kate look up with a frown. 'Do we have any decisions to make?' she questioned, surprised.

'I think so. That's why I intend to sleep in the spare room tonight.'

The statement fell into the pool of silence and sent ripples through the room, and Kate. She tensed.

'You don't have to.'

Aidan half smiled. 'Oh, but I do. Don't worry, I won't be far away if you need me. But I very much doubt you'll be having the nightmares any more. So, sleep well, Kate, and I'll see you in the morning.'

Before she could even start to find the words to argue, he was gone, shutting the door softly behind him. Slowly she sank down on the bed, eyes still on the door. Why had he done that? Why had he gone? A horrible idea came to her. He had said she need not blame herself, but perhaps he couldn't stomach the thought of her with his brother. Had his kindness hidden a disgust of her now?

Painful fingers tightened about her heart. That had to be it. What other explanation could there be? She felt crushed, for how could she fight that? Yet she must, because she loved him too much to allow Andrew to come between them any more. But what to do? What to do?

The question battered her mind long after she had changed and climbed into bed. But it was hard to think when the bed felt cold and empty without Aidan beside her. Finally, in desperation, she reached for his pillow, dragging it into her arms and holding it tight. His scent lingered there, and she squeezed her eyes to hold back foolish tears and buried her face in it.

Eventually she fell asleep like that, heart aching and no nearer a solution than before.

CHAPTER TEN

KATE stood at the kitchen window, a steaming mug of coffee clasped in her hands. She felt chilled, although the room was warm. Nor was it the snow gently falling beyond the glass that made her shiver. It was the man slowly making his way up to the house. There was a set to his shoulders that made her heart contract.

It was early still. They were the only two abroad this early on Sunday morning. She had been awake when Aidan had crept into their room an hour ago to retrieve fresh clothes. But he had made no attempt to approach the bed, so she had remained silent. He hadn't wanted to talk, that was obvious, but his silence after the events last night had driven her to the bedroom window when she'd heard him leave the house, then to dress in jeans and sweater and come down here to wait for him to return.

As he approached the door, she moved back to the table, somehow needing its solid support. Aidan came in, stamping his feet on the mat and shaking the snow from his hair. He was oblivious to her presence until he turned and saw her standing silently watching, the mug still held defensively before her. For an instant a flame burned in his eyes, but then was swiftly dampened. Turning away, he unzipped his coat and shrugged out of it, hanging it on a hook behind the door.

'Boy, it's cold out there!' he declared, rubbing his hands and blowing on them.

'There's fresh coffee in the pot,' Kate offered, putting her mug down, intending to pour him some.

'Thanks, I'll get it,' he countered smoothly, crossing to collect a mug and fill it. 'You're up early,' he observed over his shoulder.

'So are you,' she pointed out, hating the way they were sounding like strangers talking to fill an uncomfortable silence.

'I guess neither of us could sleep.' Aidan shrugged, and leant his weight against the counter, sipping appreciatively.

She wished she could just cross the floor and go into his arms, but something held her back. Licking her lips in a purely nervous gesture, she sat down. 'Did you enjoy your walk?'

Aidan looked up from a brooding contemplation of his mug and met her eyes squarely. 'It wasn't that sort of walk.'

She'd known that. It was the reason a ball of ice seemed to be forming in her stomach. Last night she had sensed something was wrong. Daylight had only served to intensify the feeling. He seemed so far away, on the other side of a wall that was shutting her out. She thought she knew why, but she had to know for certain.

'You said we shouldn't make any hasty decisions, but I think you've already made up your mind, haven't you?'

With a sigh, Aidan set his mug aside. 'You're right, of course. There's no easy way to say this, so I'll just have to be blunt. I think we should get a divorce, Kate,' he said evenly.

Kate's heart jerked as painful fingers seemed to tighten about it. Oh, God, she was right! 'You're disgusted, aren't you? Whatever you said, what I did disgusts you, doesn't it?' she demanded in a voice that echoed her pain.

He paled and pushed himself upright, taking a half-step towards her before halting abruptly. 'No!' he said forcefully. 'That's not the reason.'

She dragged her fingers through the cloud of silver hair she had left free about her shoulders. 'I don't believe you! What other reason could there be for you to do this? God knows, I disgust myself, so why shouldn't you feel the same?' she muttered thickly.

Aidan was by her side in an instant, hands reaching out to jerk her to her feet. 'Because I don't! I'm telling you the truth, damn it!'

Kate's eyes were molten sapphire. 'Then why?' she questioned in a voice that broke.

He let her go, hands spreading out in a gesture of helplessness. 'Because I think it's for the best,' he declared hoarsely.

'And if I think it's for the worst?'

His face closed down. 'It makes no difference. Our marriage is doomed to fail, Kate. I can see that, and so should you. The best thing for both of us is to end it now.' He looked at her stricken face and swallowed hard. 'Believe me, it's for the best,' he repeated tersely, and walked swiftly from the room.

Sinking down on to the chair again, she stared after him. She felt numb at the way he had so cold-bloodedly killed off everything that was between them. He had said he loved her, he had been so patient and kind, so why this, now? He had said it wasn't because he was disgusted, and yet he knew their marriage was doomed. What did he mean?

Everything had seemed so perfect. Even when she had intimated her fears that they might never have a normal marriage and children of their own.

With a faint gasp, Kate sat up straighter. Was that it? He had told her that that aspect of their life wasn't a problem, but had he come to realise that he couldn't live with it? Had he found that he couldn't take the knowledge that he might never have the children he longed for?

It was the only possible explanation for his change of heart, and one she couldn't argue with. She loved him, and to wish on him a life that would never feel complete was unfair. Under those circumstances, wasn't the kindest thing to break the knot that tied them? He was right. Better this pain now than that which would surely come.

But it hurt so. A future without him seemed bleak and hopeless. Yet she had to face it with as much self-possession as she could. The sooner she left, the better it would be for both of them. She had the perfect excuse. No one would be surprised that she had to return to England, for her business was there. It would be simple enough then to make whatever excuses necessary for the breakdown of their marriage. A clean break was the only way for them now.

The swish of the door made her look up swiftly, heart thudding in her chest in case it should be Aidan, but it wasn't. It was a house-coated Netta who bustled in, eyebrows lifting in surprise when she saw the younger woman.

'Good morning, Kate, you're up early. What brought this on? I met Aidan fully dressed on the stairs, and when I looked in on Andrew a minute or two ago he wasn't anywhere to be seen either!'

Kate hastily composed her face, not wanting Netta to witness her distress and question it. 'Andrew decided not to stay after all,' she explained.

'Good heavens, that's not like him. Andrew loves his creature comforts. To go out in sub-zero temperatures just isn't his style.'

'Aidan persuaded him,' Kate added drily and gained Netta's complete attention.

'Aidan did? Well, well, well. I take it that accounts for the sudden disappearance of my aspidistra?' Netta declared as she came and sat down opposite Kate. 'Not that I mind. I never liked it, but it was a gift from my aunt, and as she still visits I had to keep it on show. So, tell me what happened?' she urged, all agog.

It was impossible to say nothing, so Kate simply said, 'They had an argument.'

'And Aidan hit him? Well, Andrew's had that coming a long time. I'm glad Aidan finally lost his temper with him. It did neither of them any good for him to act as if his brother could do nothing wrong. Oh, it's too late to save Andrew, but at least he should understand that certain behaviour is unacceptable, even at his age.

'The problem is that Andrew was terribly spoiled by his mother. Everything he wanted, he got, and yet he has this jealous belief that Aidan was the one who had everything. Whereas Aidan never asked for much and would have willingly shared what he had. Sometimes it's hard to think of them as twins,' Netta finished with a shake of her head.

'I know what you mean,' Kate agreed. 'They look alike, and yet their personalities are so different.'

'But though we know their differences, other people don't,' Netta pointed out, warming to what was obviously a pet theme. 'From the outside, if it weren't for Aidan's scar, they could be the same. What do other people see? When they look at one, do they see the other? Do they see differences, or are the boys inter-changeable? Do things you attribute to one automatically transfer to the other? And what of the boys? They know they're different, but everyone looks at them as if they were the same. How galling is it never to be seen as an individual, to always know you're a reminder of the other one?'

Kate's nerves gave an almighty jolt. Netta's last words seemed to echo in her mind, gaining strength. 'To always know you're a reminder of the other one.' Incredible as it might seem, Kate knew she had finally seen the light. The candle of hope that had guttered suddenly flared back into brilliance. All her assumptions had been wrong, and she was going to prove it.

Her sudden jump to her feet startled Netta who had still been talking. The words tailed off as Kate rounded the table to bend and give her an affectionate hug.

'Netta, you're a lifesaver,' she declared huskily.

'I am? I mean, am I?' the older woman queried in bemusement.

Kate laughed, a cheerful, happy sound, full of confidence. 'Yes, and don't ever change.'

'Well, naturally, dear, I won't if you say so.' Netta smiled, still floundering. 'I hope you're going to explain.'

'I will, later,' Kate promised, straightening.

'After church. Aidan and I always go to the early service. You two are quite welcome to join us,' she invited.

Kate paused at the door. 'Not this morning, Netta, but, if everything works out the way I think it will, we'll go this evening. That's a promise,' she gave Netta a glowing smile and went out.

Of course, some of the glow dimmed with nervousness as she made her way upstairs and along to their room. Aidan was inside, a stiff-backed silhouette over by the window. He must have heard her come in but he didn't turn. Kate shut the door quietly and relaxed back against it.

'Aidan, do you love me?' she asked him in a low, husky voice.

His start was visible, and he turned abruptly, face a dark shadow against the light outside. 'What kind of question is that?'

'A simple one, I would have thought. I just wanted to make sure, because you know I love you, don't you?' she went on in the same low tone, while her heart was skittering away inside her.

Aidan raked both hands through his hair. 'Kate, this is pointless. Loving you has nothing to do with it.'

She knew a moment of relief. He did love her. Though she hadn't seriously doubted it, still it was nice to know. It made it easier to continue.

'And I don't disgust you because of what I did?'

'Nothing about you disgusts me, Kate,' he told her huskily. 'You have to believe that.'

Her heart swelled. 'I do.'

He spread his hands. 'Then what is this all about?'

Kate clasped her hands in front of her and stared down at them. 'I thought it was about the fact that you'd decided you couldn't accept a marriage that might never be complete. That might never include children,' she said levelly.

'And I told you days ago that that wasn't so,' Aidan shot back swiftly.

Kate looked up with a smile, wondering if he realised that he was shooting down in flames all the obvious excuses he could have claimed. 'I know you did. I said I *thought* it, but then I changed my mind.'

Aidan took an audible breath, hands going to his hips. 'Kate, there had better be some point to this. I'm not made of stone!'

Pushing away from the door, she walked over to him, stopping inches away to raise her hand to his cheek, fingers gently caressing. He flinched, and she heard his swift intake of breath as he closed his eyes.

'I know you're not, Aidan, and I also know you're not Andrew,' she said softly.

His eyes shot open and locked with hers. 'Kate.' Her name was a groan.

She swallowed a lump of emotion. 'Darling, when I look at you, I see you, only you. You don't remind me of Andrew, because you're *not* him.' She had to make him believe that, as she did.

'Because I have the scar,' he agreed tautly, moving away so that her hand dropped to his chest.

Kate shook her head in vigorous denial. 'Without the scar, it would be the same. Don't you understand? My heart knows you. Every part of me responds to you as it never did to Andrew. You're two different people, and looking at you reminds me only of you. Please believe me,' she pleaded in a passionate whisper.

His handsome face broke into lines of anguish. 'I want to, and yet how can I? Kate, every time I made love to you, *he* stopped us. Last night I knew that if I slept with you, I'd make love to you, because, God knows, I want you so desperately. But I also knew it was impossible because you'd already told me you didn't know if you could forget, and in bed I only remind you of what Andrew did. I love you too much to put you through that ever again.'

Tears welled to mist her eyes. 'Aidan, listen. I didn't enjoy what happened with Andrew. I felt degraded, yes, but it's never been like that with you. You make me feel so much joy. I wanted so much to experience everything with you that I was just as shocked as you when I couldn't go on. I couldn't understand it. But now I know. I stopped us, not him. My own self-disgust that I could do what I did stopped me because I didn't want to remember it, and, if I'd gone on, then I believe I would have remembered sooner. But I know everything now, and I'll learn to accept it, so that reason for backing out has gone. I truly believe it won't happen again.'

'But you don't know for sure,' Aidan pointed out roughly.

Kate licked her lips, because she wasn't one hundred per cent sure. She dreaded being proved wrong, because she knew he'd use that to enforce his decision. And yet... 'There's only one way to find out. Surely we owe it to ourselves to give it one last try? I don't want to give you up, Aidan, not now I've found you. Please, darling.'

'Ah, Kate! God knows I want you enough,' Aidan groaned, reaching out to pull her into his arms. 'I just don't want to see you hurt any more. There's been enough pain in your life.'

'And in yours,' she insisted. 'The only thing Andrew's done right is to bring us together. That has to mean something.' She looked up at him, eyes pleading silently for him to take one last chance.

His hand cupped her cheek and he sighed. 'How can I fight you and myself? I need you as I've never needed anyone before. You've given my life purpose. I don't want to lose you, either. Giving you up was the hardest decision I'd ever made. I couldn't go through that again.'

Kate's smile hid her own doubts. 'You won't have to. Trust me. Make love with me.' Her plea was husky with emotion.

For a moment longer he hesitated, then, with a groan of defeat, he lifted her into his arms and carried her to the bed. Gently he laid her down then knelt beside her, hands smoothing her hair into a halo on the pillow about her head. Slowly, with infinite care, he removed her clothes until she lay before him, her creamy skin flushed by the warmth of his gaze. She felt no fear, only an intense pleasure as his eyes told her he found her beautiful.

He stood up to shrug out of his own clothes, and then he came down beside her, one hand reaching out to caress her pinkened cheek. It was trembling slightly, and Kate turned her head to press a kiss to his palm, before looking at him with eyes that reflected her love and need.

Aidan swallowed. 'If anything frightens you, tell me,' he commanded thickly, head lowering to her throat, finding the pulse that beat rapidly there.

'Love me,' she murmured huskily in reply, and with a soft moan he brought his mouth up to hers.

It was like before and yet unlike anything she had ever known. With infinite patience, that drew her inexorably towards the very brink of fulfilment, his lips and hands caressed every inch of her willing, responsive flesh. Drugged by his exquisite sensuality, she couldn't think, could only feel. When his fingertips brushed across the sensitised peaks of her breasts, she moaned, arching in to him, and when he took her into his mouth, she thought she would die of the pleasure.

She had no thought of turning back, not even when his marvellous hands smoothed over her hips and traced a breathtaking path up the soft skin of her inner thigh, seeking the heart of her. When he touched her there, discovering how much she ached for him, she cried out, as waves of pleasure exploded through her at each gentle stroke.

Gasping, she gazed at him in wonderment as he raised his head to witness the havoc he had created. 'I didn't know it could feel like that,' she whispered.

Aidan smiled though his eyes smouldered with a barely leashed passion. 'That's only the beginning,' he told her thickly.

He was right, she discovered, as he began to arouse her again with a feverish passion. Limbs entangled and skin scorched skin as they scaled new heights, discovering untold plateaux of pleasure, where each delight tumbled into the next. Until, shuddering and gasping, he eased his body over hers, taking her with him as they reached the summit and toppled headlong into a dizzying explosion of mutual satisfaction.

They must have fallen asleep, for Kate came awake minutes later with the pleasurable weight of Aidan's body on her. Almost at the same instant he stirred, lifting himself up on his elbows to look at her with a warmth that melted her bones and made her heart turn over.

A slow smile spread over her face, lighting it up. 'It's just as well I'm not the sort to say I told you so,' she murmured, and caught her breath as he moved suddenly, rolling over to take her with him so that she rested comfortably on his chest.

'You can if you want. You were right, thank God. Incredibly and wonderfully right.' He sighed, catching her hand and raising it to his lips.

Kate snuggled closer, loving the warmth of him. Happiness and contentment were a cocoon about them. She sighed. 'What will happen to Andrew now?' The mention of his name had no power to destroy their happiness now, and the question had to be raised.

Beside her, Aidan tensed as scarce forgotten anger returned. 'He won't get away with it, Kate, that you can be sure of. I spoke to Dad earlier. He's going to be pulling some fairly hefty strings. I'm afraid Andrew isn't going to find life such a sinecure any more. My brother has debts. If he wants them paid he's going to have to toe the line. He's going to have to work for his money, and damned hard too. Dad's sending him to Africa. We have mining concerns out there. I think he'll be too damn busy for a long time to cause anyone any trouble.'

There was grim satisfaction in his voice, and Kate couldn't blame him. He had been hurt enough—they both had. Now was the time for healing. Her hair brushed his chin as she pressed a tender kiss to his warm flesh. She felt his immediate response as he gave a deep sigh.

'Have you any idea how much I love you, Kate Crawford? My sweet Katrine?'

Her name on his lips was a loving caress. 'Mm-hmm. Almost as much as I love you,' she declared provocatively.

'Oh, no, you've got that the wrong way round,' Aidan argued.

Kate raised her head, eyes agleam. 'I beg to differ.'

There was a light in his eyes to match hers. 'You're being argumentative, Kate. In fact, you could be called shrewish. So I only have one thing to say to that.'

Kate groaned, and freeing her hand clamped it over his mouth. 'No, you don't! Don't you dare say it! I've heard it all my adult life.'

He pulled her hand away easily. 'But never from me,' he reminded her gently, his own hand cupping her cheeks and easing her up to meet him. 'This will be different. Trust me.'

With deep reluctance, she nodded and he smiled, running his thumb tantalisingly over her lips, leaving them tingling.

His voice when he spoke was barely a whisper. 'Kiss me, Kate,' he said, and Kate smiled and did so willingly because he was right, it was different. She could have sworn he said 'I love you'.

JASMINE CRESSWELL

Internationally-acclaimed Bestselling Author

SECRET SINS

The rich are different—they're deadly!

Judge Victor Rodier is a powerful and dangerous man. At the age of twenty-seven, Jessica Marie Pazmany is confronted with terrifying evidence that her real name is Liliana Rodier. A threat on her life prompts Jessica to seek an appointment with her father—a meeting she may live to regret.

MIRA®   AVAILABLE NOW IN PAPERBACK

LINDA HOWARD

ALMOST FOREVER

THEY PLAYED BY THEIR OWN RULES...

She didn't let any man close enough.

He didn't lrt anything get in the way of his job. But Max Conroy needed information, so he set out to seduce Claire Westbrook.

BUT RULES WERE MEANT TO BE BROKEN...

Now it was a more than a game of winners and losers. Now they were playing for the highest stakes of all.

AVAILABLE IN PAPERBACK FROM AUGUST 1997

MARGOT DALTON

first Impression

Be *very* careful who you trust.

A child is missing and the only witness tells a chilling story of what he's 'seen'. Jackie Kaminsky has three choices. Dismiss the man as a handsome nutcase. Arrest him as the only suspect. Or believe him.

"Detective Jackie Kaminsky leads a cast of finely drawn characters... An engrossing read."
—*Publishers Weekly*

"Jackie Kaminsky is a great addition to the growing list of fictional detectives."
—*Romantic Times*

AVAILABLE IN PAPERBACK
FROM AUGUST 1997

DISCOVER

THE SECRETS WITHIN

Riveting and unforgettable -
the Australian saga of the decade!

For Tamara Vandelier, the final reckoning with
her mother is long overdue. Now she has
returned to the family's vineyard estate and
embarked on a destructive course that, in a
final, fatal clash, will reveal the secrets within....

Valid only in the UK & Eire against purchases made in retail outlets
and not in conjunction with any Reader Service or other offer.

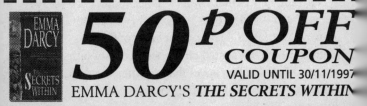

50ᵖ OFF COUPON

VALID UNTIL 30/11/1997

EMMA DARCY'S *THE SECRETS WITHIN*

9 904170 180504

0472 00166